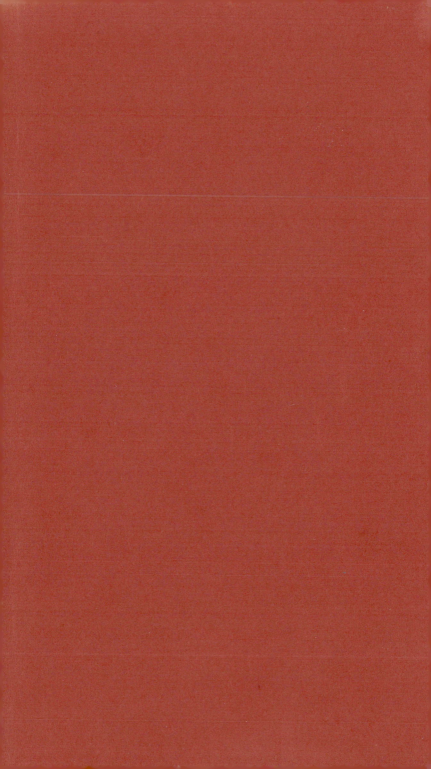

# How to Steal a Dog

Also by Barbara O'Connor

*Beethoven in Paradise*
*Me and Rupert Goody*
*Moonpie and Ivy*
*Fame and Glory in Freedom, Georgia*
*Taking Care of Moses*

# How to Steal a Dog

A NOVEL BY

# BARBARA O'CONNOR

## FRANCES FOSTER BOOKS

Farrar, Straus and Giroux

New York

Distributed in Canada by Douglas & McIntyre Ltd.
Printed in the United States of America
Designed by Barbara Grzeslo
First edition, 2007
10  9  8  7  6  5  4  3  2

www.fsgkidsbooks.com

Library of Congress Cataloging-in-Publication Data
O'Connor, Barbara.
      How to steal a dog / Barbara O'Connor.— 1st ed.
         p.   cm.
      Summary: Living in the family car in their small North Carolina town after
their father leaves them virtually penniless, Georgina, desperate to improve
their situation and unwilling to accept her overworked mother's calls for
patience, persuades her younger brother to help her in an elaborate scheme
to get money by stealing a dog and then claiming the reward that the
owners are bound to offer.
      ISBN-13: 978-0-374-33497-0
      ISBN-10: 0-374-33497-8
      [1. Homeless persons—Fiction.   2. Family problems—Fiction.
3. Conduct of life—Fiction.   4. Interpersonal relations—Fiction.
5. Brothers and sisters—Fiction.   6. Dogs—Fiction.   7. North
Carolina—Fiction.]   I. Title.

PZ7.O217 How 2007
[Fic]—dc22

                                                        2005040166

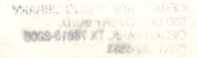

*To the dogs in my life:*

*Phoebe, the sweet one*
*Matty, the angry one*
*And Murphy, the one who stole my heart*

# How to Steal a Dog

# 1

**T**he day I decided to steal a dog was the same day my best friend, Luanne Godfrey, found out I lived in a car.

I had told Mama she would find out sooner or later, seeing as how she's so nosy and all. But Mama had rolled her eyes and said, "Just get on up there to the bus stop, Georgina, and quit your whining."

So that's what I did. I stood up there at the bus stop pretending like I still lived in Apartment 3B. I pretended like I didn't have mustard on my shirt from the day before. I pretended like I hadn't washed my hair in the bathroom of the Texaco gas station that very morning. And I pretended like my daddy hadn't just waltzed off and left us with nothing but three rolls of quarters and a mayonnaise jar full of wadded-up dollar bills.

I guess I'm pretty good at pretending.

My brother, Toby, however, is not so good at pretending. When Mama told him to get on up to the bus stop and quit his whining, he cried and carried on like the baby that he is.

"What's wrong with Toby?" Luanne asked me when we were standing at the bus stop.

"He has an earache," I said, trying as hard as anything to look like my life was just as normal as could be instead of all crazy like it really was.

When I saw Luanne's eyes narrow and her lips squeeze together, I knew her nosiness was about to irritate me.

Sure enough, she said, "Then how come your mama is making him go to school?" She kept looking at me with that squinty-eyed look of hers, but I didn't let on that I was irritated. I just shrugged and hoped she would hush up about Toby.

She did. But then she went and turned her nosy self loose on me.

"No offense, Georgina," she said. "But you're starting to look kind of unkempt."

*Unkempt?* That was her mama talking if I'd ever heard it. Luanne wouldn't never have said that word "unkempt" if she hadn't heard her mama say it first.

And what was I supposed to say to that anyways? Was I supposed to say, "Well, for your information, Luanne Godfrey, it's kinda hard to keep your clothes looking nice when you've been sleeping in the backseat of a Chevrolet for a week"?

Or maybe I was supposed to say, "I know it, Luanne. But my hairbrush got tossed out in that pile of stuff Mr.

Deeter left on the sidewalk when he kicked us out of our apartment."

And then Luanne would say, "Why'd Mr. Deeter do that?"

And I would say, " 'Cause three rolls of quarters and a mayonnaise jar full of wadded-up dollar bills doesn't pay the rent, Luanne."

But I didn't say anything. I acted like I hadn't heard that word "unkempt." I just climbed on the bus and sat in the sixth seat on the left side with Luanne, like I always did.

I knew Luanne wouldn't give up, though. I knew she'd keep on till she found out the truth.

"What if she wants to come over?" I said to Mama. "Or what if she looks in the window or something and finds out we don't live there anymore?"

But Mama just flapped her hand at me and closed her eyes to let me know how tired she was from working two jobs. So every day I imagined Luanne peeking in the kitchen window of Apartment 3B. When she did, of course, she wouldn't see me and Toby and Mama and Daddy eating our dinner and being happy. She'd see some other family. Some happy family that wasn't all broken up like mine.

And then one day, when we got off the school bus,

Luanne went and did the nosiest thing I could imagine. She *followed* me. I was trying to catch up with Toby 'cause he had grabbed the car key and run on ahead of me, so I didn't even notice her sneaking along behind me. She followed me all the way past Apartment 3B, across the street, and clear on around the back of Eckerd Drugstore, where our car was parked with laundry hanging out the windows and Toby sitting on a milk crate waiting for me.

If there was ever a time when I wished the earth would open up and swallow me whole, it was when I turned around and saw Luanne looking at me and Toby and that car and all. I could see her thoughts just plain as day right there on her face.

I wanted to wave my hand and make that dented-up car disappear off the face of the earth. But more than anything, I wanted my daddy to come on home and change everything back to the way it was before.

I set a smile on my face and said, "It's just temporary," like Mama had said to me about a hundred times.

Luanne turned red and said, "Oh."

"When Mama gets paid, we're moving into our new apartment," I said.

"Oh."

And then we both just stood there, looking at our feet. I could feel the distance between us grow and grow until it seemed like Luanne Godfrey, who had been my friend forever, was standing clear on the other side of the universe from me.

Finally, she said, "I better go."

But she didn't. She just stood there and I squeezed my eyes shut and told myself not to look pitiful and, for heaven's sake, don't cry.

And then, of course, Toby had to go and make everything worse by saying, "Mama left a note that she's working late, so we're supposed to eat that macaroni that's in the cooler."

Luanne arched her eyebrows up and then she said, "I haven't seen your daddy in a long time."

That did it. I couldn't stop the tears from spilling out of my squeezed-up eyes. I sat down right there in the drugstore parking lot and told Luanne everything.

I felt her arm around me and I heard her saying something, but I was too lost in my misery to do anything but cry. When I was all cried out, I stood up and brushed the dirt off the seat of my pants, pushed the hair out of my eyes, and said, "Promise you won't tell?"

Luanne nodded. "I promise."

"I mean, not even your mama."

Luanne's eyes flickered for just a second, but then she said, "Okay."

I crooked my pinkie finger in the air and waited for her to give me the pinkie promise, but she hesitated.

I stamped my foot and jabbed my pinkie at her. Finally she crooked her pinkie around mine and we shook.

"I better go," she said.

I watched her hurry across the parking lot, then glance back at me before disappearing around the corner of the drugstore.

"I hate that macaroni," Toby said from his seat on the milk crate. It was just like him to not even give me one little minute to wallow in my misery.

I stomped around to the back of the car and kicked the cooler, sending it toppling over on its side. Ice and water and plastic containers spilled out onto the parking lot.

"Me too," I said.

Then I climbed into the backseat of the car and waited for Mama to come back.

It was way past dark when I heard Mama's shoes click-clacking on the asphalt as she made her way toward the car. I sat up and looked out the window. Even in the dim glow of the streetlights, I could see her tired, sad look. Part of me wanted to stay put and just go on back to sleep and leave her be, but another part of me wanted to get out and have my say, which is what I did.

Mama jumped when I opened the car door.

"What in the world are you doing awake, Georgina?" she said.

"I hate this," I said. "I don't want to do this anymore."

I pushed the car door shut softly so Toby wouldn't wake up; then I turned back to Mama and said, "You got to do something. You got to find us a place to live. A *real* place. Not a car."

Mama reached out like she was gonna touch me, so I jerked away. She dropped her hand to her side like it was heavy as cement. Then she let out a whoosh of breath that blew her hair up off her forehead.

"I'm trying," she said.

"*How* are you trying?"

She tossed her purse through the car window into the front seat. "I just am, okay, Georgina?"

"But how?"

"I'm working two jobs. What else do you want me to do?"

"Find us a place to live." I stomped away from her and then whirled back around. "This is all your fault."

She stormed over and grabbed me by the shoulders.

"It takes *money* to get a place." She gave me a little shake when she said the word "money."

"I'm trying to save up, okay?" she said.

She let go of me and leaned against the car.

"How much money do we need?" I said.

She looked up at the sky like the answer was written up there in the stars. Then she shook her head real slow and said, "I don't know, Georgina. A lot, okay?"

"Like how much?"

"More than we got."

We both just stood there in the dark and listened to the crickets from the vacant lot next door.

Mama draped her arm around my shoulder, and I laid my head against her and wanted to be a baby again—a baby that just cries and then gets taken care of and that's all there is to a day.

Finally I asked her the same question I'd asked her about a million times already.

"Why did Daddy leave?"

I felt her whole body go limp. "I wish I knew." She brushed my hair out of my eyes. "Just got tired of it all, I reckon," she said.

"Tired of what?"

The silence between us felt big and dark, like a wall. Then I asked her the question that had been burning a hole in my heart. "Tired of me?"

Mama took my chin in her hand and looked at me hard. "This is not your fault, okay?"

She peered inside the car at Toby, all curled up in a ball in the backseat.

"We got to go," she said.

"Where?"

"I don't know. Just somewhere else." The car door creaked when she opened it, sending an echo into the still night air. "We've been here two nights now," she said. "The cops are liable to run us off if we don't leave."

She shot me a look when she saw the overturned cooler, so I helped her gather things up before I climbed back in the car. As we drove out of the parking lot, I slouched down and stared glumly out the window. The empty shops we passed made Darby, North Carolina, seem like a ghost town, all locked up and dark.

Mama pulled the car into the alley beside Bill's Auto Parts. When she shut the engine off, we got swallowed up in quiet.

I draped a beach towel over the clothesline that Mama had strung along the middle of the car to make me a bedroom. I could picture Luanne, snuggled in her pink-and-white quilt with her stuffed animals lined up along the wall beside her and her gymnastics ribbons taped on her headboard, and I sure felt sorry for myself.

Then I curled up on the seat, turning every which way trying to get comfortable. Finally I settled on my back with my feet propped against the car door and stared out at the starry sky.

And then I saw it. A sign, tacked up there on a telephone pole right outside the car window. A faded old sign that said: REWARD. $500. And under that was a picture of a bug-eyed little dog with its tongue hanging out.

And then under that it said: HAVE YOU SEEN ME? MY NAME IS MITSY.

*Five hundred dollars!* Who in the world would pay five hundred dollars for that little ole dog?

"Mama?" I whispered through my beach towel wall.

Mama rustled some in the front seat.

"Would five hundred dollars be enough money to get us a place to live?" I said.

Mama sighed. "I suppose so, Georgina. Now go to sleep. You got school tomorrow."

I looked up at Mitsy and my mind started churning.

What if I could find that dog? I could get that money, and we could have a real place to live instead of this stinking old car.

But that dog could be anywhere. I wouldn't even know where to look. Besides, that sign was old. Somebody had probably already found Mitsy and got that five hundred dollars.

I stared out the window at the sign, thinking about Mitsy and wondering if there were other folks out there who would pay money for their lost dogs.

And that's when I got a thought that made me sit up so fast Toby mumbled in his sleep and Mama hissed, "Shhhh."

I folded my legs up and lay back down in my beach towel bedroom. The damp car seat smelled like greasy french fries and bug spray. I closed my eyes and smiled to myself. I had a plan.

I was gonna steal me a dog.

# 2

I thought about my plan for a couple of days before I decided to tell Toby. "You got to keep this a secret," I told him.

I glanced out the back window of the car, then pulled the beach towel over our heads. Mama had left for work, and me and Toby were waiting till it was time to walk up to the bus stop.

Toby nodded in the darkness under the towel. "I will," he said.

I pushed my face up closer to his and said, "You can't tell *anybody*, okay?"

"Okay."

I knew it was risky telling Toby my plan, but I figured I had to. Mama said he had to stay with me after school, so there I was, stuck with him. I couldn't even go to Luanne's or anything. How was I gonna steal a dog without Toby finding out? Then he'd go and tell Mama, for sure. If I made him think he was part of my secret plan, maybe he wouldn't be the tattletale baby that he usually is.

"Here's my plan," I said.

I paused a minute to add some drama 'cause Toby likes drama. He stared at me with wide eyes. His breath smelled like tuna fish, and I was wishing I hadn't covered us up with the towel like that.

"We're gonna steal a dog," I said. "How about *that*?" I grinned and waited for him to say "Hot dang" like he does, but he just stared at me with his mouth hanging open. That tuna fish odor swirled around us inside our beach towel tent. I waved my hand in front of my nose and flipped the towel off of us.

"Jeez, Toby," I said. "Can't you brush your teeth?"

He glared at me. "How?" he hollered. "There ain't no sink in here." He waved his arms around the car.

"Use the water in the cooler," I said.

"No way. It's cruddy."

"Well, anyways," I said. "Don't you want to know *why* we're gonna steal a dog?"

He nodded, sending a clump of greasy hair flopping down over his eyes. He had Mama's straight, copper-colored hair, but I had to go and get Daddy's curly ole black hair that I hate. One more good reason to be mad at my daddy.

I smoothed the crumpled yellowing sign out on the seat between us. "Because of *this*," I said.

Toby looked at it. "What's it say?"

"For crying out loud, Toby, you're in third grade." I jabbed a finger at the sign. "*Reward*, it says. Five hun-

dred dollars reward for this ugly ole dog. Can you believe that?"

"He's not ugly."

"*She*," I said. "Her name is Mitsy. See?" I jabbed at
the sign again.

Toby squeezed his eyebrows together. "Why are we
gonna steal that dog?"

"Not *this* dog, you idiot," I said. "We're gonna steal
a *different* dog."

"What dog?"

"I don't know yet," I said. "That's why I need you to
help me."

I looked out the window again. The alley beside the
auto parts store was empty. I slouched down lower in the
seat and motioned for Toby to come closer.

"Listen," I whispered. "We're gonna find us a dog
that somebody loves so much, they'd pay a reward to get
it back." I poked Toby with my elbow. "Get it?"

"Pay a reward to who?" Toby said.

I sighed and shook my head. "To *us*, you ninny."

"But why would they pay us if we steal their dog?"

I rolled my eyes and flopped back against the seat.

"I swear, Toby, sometimes I wonder about you." I sat
back up and took him by the shoulders, looking him
square in the eyes. "The person who loves the dog won't
*know* it was us that stole it. The person will think we
*found* the dog. *Now* do you get it?"

Toby grinned. "Okay," he said. "Where's the dog?"

"We've got to *find* the dog," I hollered.

I slapped my hand over my mouth and glanced quickly around us. The alley was still empty.

"We've got to *find* the dog," I repeated in a whisper. "Mama said five hundred dollars is enough to get a place to live. If we steal a dog, we can get five hundred dollars, see?"

Toby had a look on his face that made me think I'd made a mistake sharing my plan with him.

"Listen, Toby," I said. "It's the only way we're ever gonna have us a real place to live instead of this car, you hear?"

He nodded.

"Don't you want a real place to live?"

He nodded again.

"Then we got to steal us a dog and get the reward," I said. "And if you tell anyone, and I mean *anyone*, you might as well just say your prayers and kiss this earth goodbye, you hear me?"

"Okay," he said. "But how do we steal a dog?"

"Don't worry," I said. "I'm working on it."

After school that day, me and Toby raced back to the car. When I unlocked it, Toby climbed in the driver's seat and started spreading peanut butter on a saltine cracker with his finger. I climbed in the backseat and locked the doors. Mama had told us to stay put. If anybody asked us what we were doing, we were supposed to say we were waiting for our mama, who was in the bank next door.

I rummaged through my trash bag of stuff. When I found my spiral notebook with the glittery purple cover, I opened it to a fresh page and wrote:

*How to Steal a Dog*
*by*
*Georgina Hayes*

I wrote the date in the margin: *April 5*. Then, next to that, I wrote:

*Step 1: Find a Dog.*

I chewed on the end of my pencil and looked out the window. Someone came out of the side door of the auto parts store and threw a cardboard box in the Dumpster. I slouched down real quick and waited till I heard the shop door slam shut. Then I wrote:

*These are the rules for finding a dog:*
*1. The dog must not bark too much.*
*2. The dog must not bite.*
*3. The dog must be outside by itself sometimes.*
*4. The dog must be loved a lot and not just some old dog that nobody cares about.*
*5. The owner of the dog must look like somebody who will*

*pay a lot of money to get their dog back, like maybe someone who has a big house and rides in a limo or something like that.*

But then I scratched out that part about the limo 'cause who ever saw a limo in Darby, North Carolina?

I chewed my pencil some more and looked up at the top of the car. Dark brown stains formed patterns like clouds up there. Over the driver's side, Mama had used safety pins to put up phone numbers for me and Toby in case we needed somebody. I guess she forgot we didn't have a phone in that stinking car.

As I read my list of rules over again, I felt myself splitting right in two. Half of me was thinking, *Georgina, don't do this. Stealing a dog is just plain wrong.*

The other half of me was thinking, *Georgina, you're in a bad fix and you got to do whatever it takes to get yourself out of it.*

I sat there in that car feeling myself get yanked one way and then the other. So I just made myself stop thinking, and I read those rules one more time.

I was pretty sure I had covered everything. I stuffed my notebook way down in the bottom of my bag and said, "Come on, Toby. Let's go find us a dog."

# 3

"O kay," I said to Toby. "You go that way and I'll go this way."

He squinted in the direction I had pointed.

"I don't see no dogs down there," he said.

I sighed. Maybe I should've asked Luanne to help me. I wanted to, but I just had this feeling she would mess things up worse than Toby was liable to. Not on purpose, but she just would. Mainly because of her mama, who finds out everything we do even if Luanne doesn't tell. And Mrs. Godfrey doesn't like me one little bit. She pinches her face up real hateful-like when I go over there. One time I saw her wiping off Luanne's bedroom door with a sponge right where I had touched it. Like I had left my cooties there to infect her family. And when I used to invite Luanne over to my apartment, her mama would always find a reason to say no. She could pluck a reason out of the air like a magician plucks a rabbit out of his hat. A dentist appointment. A visiting relative. A sudden need to shop for new shoes.

So I knew asking Luanne to help me steal a dog

would probably be a bad idea. But Toby? I could see he was gonna be more trouble than help. But what choice did I have?

"Listen, Toby," I said real slow and calm. "You got to walk down there and *look*. Look in the yards. Look on the porches. Look in the *back*yards, even. Just look, okay?"

He nodded. "Okay." He started off down the street, then stopped. "What do I do if I see one?"

"Come get me."

"Okay."

"And remember the rules for the dogs," I said. "You know, about not barking and all that? Okay?"

"Okay."

We went in opposite directions. The first dog I saw came trotting right up the street toward me. He was brown with tufts of fur that stuck together in clumps. Every few feet, he stopped to sniff the ground.

"Hey, boy," I called to him.

He looked up and wagged his scrawny tail. His face had bald spots on it. One eye was closed up into a slit with gnats swarming all around it. Nope, that dog wouldn't do. Nobody cared about *him*, that was for sure.

I gave him a little pat on the head 'cause I felt sorry for him, then continued on down the street. When I came to a house with a trailer beside it, a dog started barking. A shrill, yipping bark. When I got closer, I saw a dog tied to a clothesline on the side of the house.

A short-legged dog with a smooshed-in nose and a curlicue tail. When he saw me, he raced back and forth along the clothesline, his yippy bark getting shriller and shriller.

From inside the trailer, a man's voice hollered, "Shut up, Sparky!"

Nope. That dog wouldn't do, either. Too noisy.

A few houses farther on, a great big dog with bushy black fur sat by the side of the road watching me. When I tried to pet him, he slinked away with his tail between his legs. Then some woman came out with a rolled-up newspaper. She smacked him on the rear, hauled him off by the collar, and pushed him up under the porch.

"Get under there like I told you," she said.

Then she stomped back up the steps and went inside. She didn't seem like someone who would pay money for her dog.

Finally, at the end of the street, I saw a dog who had *steal me* written all over him. He was clean and fluffy with a red bandanna tied around his neck. He didn't bark when I got closer. He even let me pet him, wagging his tail like he was the happiest dog on earth. I was about to think I'd found the perfect dog to steal, but then I took one look at his house and I changed my mind. The front steps were rotted right off the porch, lying in a heap of lumber in the red-dirt yard. Bricks and boards were stacked to make steps into the tiny house with its peeling paint and torn screens. A plastic window box had come loose on one side, spilling dirt and dried-up brown flowers into the bushes. A rusty old car sat on cinder blocks in the gravel driveway.

Nope. That dog wouldn't do, either. The people in that house weren't rich. I bet they'd never pay five hundred dollars for their dog, no matter how much they loved it.

It looked like it was going to be harder than I thought to find a dog that fit all the rules in my notebook.

I crossed over to the corner and waited for Toby. When I saw him skipping up the road toward me, I called out, "Any luck?"

"I only saw one, and he growled at me."

"Only one? Are you sure?"

"I saw some cats."

"No, cats won't do."

"How come?"

"They just won't," I said. "Let's try one more street. Then we gotta get on back to the car before Mama gets off work."

I hurried over to the next block. Toby kept stopping to pick stuff up along the side of the road. Rocks and acorns and wrappers and things. I had to go back and yank him a couple of times. When we got to the corner, I looked at the street sign. Whitmore Road.

"This one looks good," I said. "Let's go up one side and down the other. You stay with me."

We walked along the street, peering over fences, sneaking into backyards. No luck.

Suddenly Toby pointed. "Look at *that* house," he said.

Just ahead of us was a huge brick house set back off the street a ways. All the other houses on that street were small, one-story, wooden houses with tiny yards and no porches. But that brick house was two stories high. I bet it had a whole bunch of rooms inside.

"Come on," I said to Toby, "let's go check it out."

We ran to the house. It towered over the little houses next to it. The front yard was the biggest one on the whole street, with a chain-link fence all the way around it. Along the fence was a thick hedge taller than me.

I peered over the gate. That house looked like a mansion. It had a front porch with rocking chairs and a swing painted the same color green as the shutters on the windows. In the yard, there were flowers every-where, popping up between the bushes, curling around the lamppost, blooming in pots on the front steps.

And then I couldn't hardly believe my eyes. There in the bushes along the porch was a dog. A little black-and-white dog digging so hard that dirt was flying out be-hind him. His rear end was stuck up in the air and his scraggly tail was wagging away while his front legs worked faster and faster at the dirt.

Then a voice came through the screen door.

"Willy!" A big, fat woman came out onto the porch.

I ducked behind the hedge and pulled Toby down beside me. I put my finger to my lips and said, "Shhhh."

I waited to hear her holler mean things at that dog for digging up the yard. Then I bet she was gonna come storming off the porch and smack him. But she didn't holler. She laughed! Then she said, "What am I gonna do with you, you naughty little thing?"

I crawled on my hands and knees and peeked through the gate.

The woman was sitting on the porch steps, holding the little dog in her lap and letting him lick her all over her face. When she scratched him up and down his back, he stuck his face in the air, closed his eyes, and kicked one leg, leaving streaks of mud all over her shorts. She took his head in both her hands and rubbed her nose back and forth against his nose. Like the Eskimo kisses my daddy used to give me a long time ago when he loved me.

Then she picked the dog up and went inside.

My insides were getting all swirled around with excitement while I went over the dog-stealing rules in my head. I mentally checked them off one by one. That little dog didn't look like he'd bite a flea. He didn't bark one bit. And it was for sure that dog was loved.

I glanced at the house again. That was one big house. That lady *must* be rich. Then, as if I needed one more thing to convince me, something caught my attention. The mailbox next to the gate was kind of rusty and leaning over just a tad, but it had big black letters painted on the side of it that said: THE WHITMORES. Whitmores? That lady was named Whitmore and this was Whitmore Road.

"Toby!" I said. "That lady *owns* this whole street! Can you believe that?"

His eyes grew big and he shook his head.

I grinned and gave him a thumbs-up.

"Toby," I said, "I think we just found us a dog."

# 4

I sat in the car behind the steering wheel and turned the envelope over and over. I read the messy handwriting scrawled across the front. *Mr. and Mrs. Hayes.*

I put it up to my nose and sniffed. I could actually smell my teacher, Mr. White. Sort of like soap and toothpaste and coffee all mixed together. I pressed the envelope against the window and tried to read the letter inside. I turned it every which way, but I couldn't make out a single word.

I was pretty sure I knew what it said, though. Stuff about me. About the homework I hadn't done and the math test I had failed. Probably even about how ugly I looked all the time now, with my wrinkled clothes and my dirty hair. And why was I so sleepy every day? And sometimes I didn't have lunch money. I bet the letter said how Mr. White had tried to call Mama but our phone didn't work. I bet the letter said all that stuff.

I rolled the window down and looked out at the weeds beside the road. It was only April, but it was already beginning to feel like summer. Lucky for us the nights were still cool, though, 'cause Mama made us keep the windows rolled up all night long. She said it was because she hated bugs and flies and things getting in the car, but I think it was because she thought some bad guy might reach his hand in.

I had been glad when Mama said Toby was going to go to work with her that afternoon. But now I was bored. I guess I should've gone on over to Luanne's like I said I was.

I could hear kids over in the school playground. I wished Mama hadn't parked the car so close to school. What if someone I knew saw me sitting there? What would I say? Besides, I didn't see why we had to keep moving around so much. After two nights in the same place, off we went, to some new spot. Now we were parked too close to school and farther away from Whitmore Road. How was I supposed to keep an eye on that dog if we kept parking so far away?

I climbed into the backseat and stuffed the envelope from Mr. White way down inside my trash bag of stuff. Then I pulled out my notebook and turned to the page that said:

*How to Steal a Dog*
*by*
*Georgina Hayes*

I wrote *April 6* in the margin. Then, after *Step 1*, I skipped two lines and wrote:

*Step 2: When you find the dog you want to steal, keep an eye on it for a while. Here are the rules to remember:*
1. *Make sure the dog really doesn't bark or bite.*
2. *If there is a fence, see if the gate is locked.*
3. *Decide whether or not you can pick the dog up or maybe you have to have a leash or a rope.*
4. *Check to see if there are any nosy people living next door or across the street or something.*

I closed my notebook, climbed out of the car, and locked the door with the key I wore around my neck. Then I set off for Whitmore Road.

When I got there, I stopped for a minute to check things out. The street was quiet. There was nobody outside except for some guy working on the engine of his car. Inside one of the houses a baby was crying. A sprinkler sputtered in circles in one of the yards.

I walked up the road toward the house. I hummed a little so my face wouldn't look as nervous as I felt.

When I walked by the man working on his car engine, he didn't even look up. I strolled along beside the hedge that surrounded the big brick house. I quit humming so I could listen. It was quiet in the yard. I glanced back to make sure no one was watching me, then poked my head over the gate to look into the yard.

Birds flew away from a bird feeder that hung from a hickory nut tree. The front door of the house was closed, and I noticed something I hadn't seen the other day—one of those little doggie doors, so the dog could go in and out of the house all by hisself. I figured that was a good sign. It probably meant that the people who lived there were gone a lot, but they still cared about their dog.

Then I remembered my rule about checking to see if the gate was locked. I reached over and lifted the latch. Nope. Not locked.

Suddenly a squirrel came scampering around the corner of the house and scrambled up the hickory nut tree. Not far behind it was the black-and-white dog. He dashed to the tree and peered up into the branches with his tail wagging about a million times a minute.

"Hey there," I called to him.

He sat in the leaves under the tree and cocked his head at me. His face was white with little black spots, like freckles, and black fur around one eye, like a patch. His ears were floppy, but when he looked at me, they perked up. But the best thing about him was that he looked like he was smiling at me. The sides of his mouth curled up and his pink tongue hung out.

"Hey there," I said again.

His doggie smile got bigger and his tail wagged harder, swishing leaves back and forth.

"Come here, fella." I reached over the gate and

snapped my fingers at him. He came trotting right over. I stooped down and stuck my fingers through the chain-link fence. He sniffed and then he licked me a couple of times.

"How you doing, little fella?" I said.

He cocked his head again and looked so cute.

I looked at the house. The front door was still closed and it seemed like nobody was home. I scratched the dog behind his ears, and he leaned his head against my hand with his eyes closed. He was wearing two collars. One was a dirty plastic flea collar. The other one was green with shiny rhinestones and a little silver tag shaped like a dog bone.

"What does this say?" I pulled the dog a little closer and squinted at the words engraved on the tag.

*Willy*, it said.

I turned it over. On the other side it said:

Carmella Whitmore
27 Whitmore Road
Darby, NC

Under that was a phone number.

"Willy," I whispered to the dog.

His floppy ears perked up, and he did that dog smile thing again.

"My name is Georgina," I said to Willy.

Just then that squirrel made its way down the trunk

of the hickory nut tree, and Willy dashed off to chase it again.

I stood up and looked around. Way at the end of the street, two kids were riding bikes. The man who had been working on his car was sitting in a lawn chair smoking a cigarette.

*Uh-oh*, I thought. *What if he saw me?*

I headed back up the street, trying to look like a normal person instead of a person who was thinking about stealing a dog. I kept my head down and concentrated on keeping my feet from running. I didn't look at the man when I passed him, but I caught a whiff of cigarette smoke.

When I got to the corner, I finally let my feet run like they'd been wanting to, all the way back to the car. When I got there, I unlocked the door and climbed in behind the steering wheel.

I put my hand on my racing heart and laid my head against the seat. I was starting to wonder if I really could steal a dog. I'd never stolen anything in my whole life. Luanne did one time. Slipped a pack of M&M's right into her coat pocket. But not me. How in the world was I going to steal that dog?

But then I looked around me at all the stuff inside our car. The Styrofoam cooler full of icy water and plastic containers of tuna salad. The trash bags stuffed with clothes and shoes. The milk crate on the floor with paper towels, shampoo, a flashlight, a can opener.

I looked into the backseat on Toby's side of the car. His blanket all smooshed up in a ball. His pillow. His Scooby-Doo pajamas.

And then there was my side, with all my special things jammed into a plastic bag instead of sitting out on my dresser like they used to. My horse statue. My swimming medals. That little stuffed bear that I got in the Smoky Mountains.

I hated every inch of that car. I put both hands on the steering wheel and pretended like I was driving. I drove and I drove and I drove, the whole time sending bad thoughts to my daddy for getting tired of it all and making us live in a car.

And as I drove along, out of Darby, out of North Carolina, on and on and on, as far as I could go, I felt better about what I had to do. I had to steal that little dog, Willy. No matter what.

# 5

I watched Luanne and Liza Thomas walking to the bus after school, their matching blond ponytails swinging from side to side. They carried their ballet slippers in their Darby Dance School tote bags.

Instead of getting on the bus and taking my usual seat beside Luanne, I had to wait for Toby so we could go to the Laundromat. I watched everybody get on the bus in their perfect clothes so they could go home to their perfect bedrooms. They'd put their school clothes away in real drawers, not trash bags. Then they'd go to soccer practice or ballet class, not to the Laundromat like me.

I blinked hard and stared down at my feet, just in case I looked as miserable as I felt. The toe of my sneaker was wearing out and I could see my blue sock starting to show through. When I heard someone running, I looked up to see Toby racing toward me, his hair flopping down in his eyes.

"Hurry up," I snapped. "I've been waiting for, like, an hour."

"I got on the bus but then I remembered I wasn't supposed to," he said.

*Oh, great,* I thought. I bet Luanne and Liza had themselves a good laugh about that. I bet Liza said, "How come Georgina and Toby aren't riding the bus?" Then what would Luanne say? *Please, please, Luanne.* I closed my eyes and tried to send my thoughts across the parking lot and into the school bus window where Luanne sat. *Please don't tell Liza we live in a car.*

Then I hurried up the sidewalk toward town. Toby trotted along behind me, whining for me to slow down, but I didn't. We headed on over to Montgomery Street where Mama had parked the car near the Laundromat. I unlocked the trunk and tossed my backpack inside. Then I stood on the bumper of the car so I could reach way in the back of the trunk. I pulled a corner of the carpet away and took out the envelope Mama kept hidden there. I thumbed through the money stuffed inside. It sure looked like a lot to me, but I guess it still wasn't enough to get us a place to live.

I took out five dollars and jammed the envelope back under the carpet. Then I gathered up the dirty laundry and locked the car.

"Let's go, Toby."

I stuffed all the clothes into one washing machine.

"If we don't use two machines," I said to Toby, "we'll have enough money to buy a snack."

On the way out, we checked all the coin return slots for money and found two quarters. Then we went on over to the grocery store and bought some saltine crackers and sliced cheese. We went around back to the alley and sat on the warm asphalt to eat.

"Listen, Toby," I said while I peeled the plastic off my cheese. "We need to find some kind of rope or something to tie to that dog's collar."

Toby nodded as he squished a piece of cheese into a little ball and popped it into his mouth.

"Where can we find rope?" I said.

He shrugged.

"Dern it, Toby," I said. "If you want to help me, you've got to come up with some ideas, too, you know. I can't think of everything."

"Okay," he said. "Why don't we buy some rope?"

I rolled my eyes. "We're trying to *save* our money, not spend it. We need to find some rope for free."

Toby looked around him at the piles of cardboard boxes beside the Dumpster. "Maybe there's rope back here somewhere."

I got up and peered into the Dumpster. Just more cardboard boxes.

"Naw," I said. "I think we're going to have to wait till trash pickup day. Then we can look through the stuff that people leave by the road, okay?"

"Okay." Toby squished another piece of cheese and then smashed it between two crackers.

"Let's go put the clothes in the dryer, then check out that dog again."

When we got to Whitmore Road, I motioned for Toby to be quiet.

"We don't want anybody to notice us," I whispered.

We made our way up the road toward the big brick house. When we got to the corner of the yard, I could hear someone out front. I tried to see through the hedge, but it was too thick. I squatted down beside the fence to listen.

"Get the ball, Willy," someone said. I was pretty sure it was the same woman we had seen there the other day.

I could hear Willy making happy little yip noises. Then the woman would laugh and say stuff to him. After a while, I heard the wooden front steps creak and the screen door slam.

I looked at Toby. "I think she went inside," I whispered. "Let's go see."

We tiptoed to the gate and I peeked into the yard. The woman was gone, but Willy was sitting on the front porch. When he saw me, he came bounding down the steps and over to the gate.

"Hey there, Willy," I whispered.

He pushed his nose through the gate and licked my hand.

"Isn't he cute?" I said to Toby.

"Yeah." Toby put his hand out and Willy licked him, too. "When are we gonna steal him?"

"Shhhh." I smacked Toby's knee. "Hush up, you idiot." I looked around us. The street was quiet and empty. I could hear a radio somewhere in the distance, but I didn't see anyone.

"We have to wait till everything is just right," I said. "That lady has to be gone." I nodded toward the house. "And we need some rope, remember?"

"After we get the rope and steal him, where are we going to hide him?" Toby said.

Dang! I hadn't even thought of that! I couldn't hardly believe how stupid I'd been. I'd made all those plans and hadn't even thought about where we were going to *hide* that dog!

I looked at Willy and then back at Toby. "I haven't figured that part out yet," I said, pretending like it was no big deal. "You got any ideas?"

Toby shook his head.

I frowned. "Then we'll have to think of something."


That night, I propped the flashlight up on the seat next to me and tried to do my math homework. Toby's snores drifted through the beach towel wall between us. I used to be good at math, but it seemed like now I wasn't. I gave up and took out my purple notebook. I opened to:

*How to Steal a Dog*
*by*
*Georgina Hayes*

I wrote *April 7*. Then, after *Step 2*, I wrote:

*Step 3: Get ready to steal the dog.*
*1. Keep watching the dog to make sure he is the right one to steal.*
*2. If you need a leash, find some rope or something.*
*3. Figure out where you are going to hide the dog.*

I chewed on the eraser of my pencil and stared out the window into the darkness. Number 3 was a big problem. I wished I could ask Luanne to help me. She always had good ideas about stuff. I looked down at my notebook again. I guessed I was just going to have to figure this out by myself, unless some miracle happened and Toby got an idea.

I closed the notebook and watched the moths fluttering around the streetlight outside the window. Maybe stealing a dog wasn't such a good idea after all. I propped my feet up on the seat in front of me and frowned at my bare toes. My Party Girl Pink nail polish was wearing off and I didn't have any more. I guess it got tossed out with all my other stuff.

"We can't take everything, Georgina," Mama had

hollered at me when Mr. Deeter kicked us out. "One bag," she had said in a mean voice. "That's it."

Just when I was starting to feel a good cry coming on, I heard Mama hurrying toward the car. I sat up and rolled down the window.

"Georgina," she whispered real excited-like. "Guess what?"

"What?"

"I found us a place!"

"Really?" I felt my heavy heart start to lift.

Mama put both hands against the car door and grinned down at me. Her hair was damp and frizzy from working her second job in the steamy back room of the Regal Dry Cleaners. She took her shoes off and climbed into the front seat.

"Yep! We're moving into a house!"

We had only ever lived in apartments before. *Never* in a house. I could already see my bedroom. White furniture with gold on the edges, like Luanne's. Maybe even pink carpet.

"When?" I said.

"Friday." Mama examined herself in the rear-view mirror.

"I look as beat as I feel, don't I?" she said.

"You look all right," I said, but I was lying. She did look beat. Dark circles under her eyes. Her skin all creased and greasy-looking.

I lay back against the seat and felt about a hundred pounds lighter than I had just minutes before. I'd known in my heart that stealing a dog was a bad thing to do, and now I didn't have to. I couldn't believe everything had turned out so good.

# 6

**M**y stomach was flopping around like crazy as we made our way through the neighborhoods of Darby. I couldn't hardly wait to see which house would be ours.

But when Mama turned onto a dirt and gravel road, I started to get a bad feeling. The car squeaked and bounced up the narrow, winding road, deeper and deeper into the woods. When we passed a faded, hand-written sign nailed to a tree, my bad feeling got worse. KEEP OUT. PRIVATE PROPERTY.

"Are you sure this is right?" I said to Mama.

She clutched the steering wheel and sat up straight and tense. "Yes, Georgina," she said. "I know what I'm doing, okay?"

Then, just as I thought my bad feeling couldn't get any worse, we rounded a curve and I saw a house just ahead of us. A ramshackle old house with boarded-up windows and the front door hanging all cockeyed on its rusty hinges.

Mama stopped the car and we all three stared in silence at the wreck of a house. The tar paper roof was caved in and covered with rotting leaves and pine needles. Prickly-looking bushes grew thick and dense across the front, while kudzu vines snaked their way up the chimney and across the roof.

"Well," Mama said, "It ain't Shangri-la, but it's better than nothing."

I couldn't believe my ears.

"*That's* the house we're gonna live in?" I said.

"It's just temporary." Mama turned the engine off and started throwing stuff into a cardboard box on the seat beside her. "Beverly Jenkins over at the Handy Pantry knows the owner, and she said he won't care if we stay here for a while."

Toby started crying. "I don't want to," he whined.

"Hush up, Toby," Mama said. She got out and tried to push through the bushes that grew across the front of the house. "Come on, y'all," she said. "Let's check it out."

I crossed my arms and slumped down in the seat. This just beat all. First I had to go and get a daddy who acted mean all the time and then just up and left us. Now I had a mama who had gone plumb crazy.

"Come on, Georgina," Mama called. "It's not that bad."

She had managed to get to the front door and had pushed it open to peer inside.

"Really, y'all," she said. "We can clean it up and make it nice."

Toby was sniffling, and I knew he was waiting on me to make the first move.

"I bet there's snakes in there," I called out through the car window.

Mama had disappeared inside, but her voice came drifting out to us. "There's no snakes. There's even some furniture. Come on."

I looked at Toby and he looked at me.

"You think there's really snakes in there?" he said.

"Snakes and worse," I said. "Probably rats and spiders and dead stuff."

Toby started wailing. Mama came out and made her way back to the car, pushing the bushes aside to make a path. "Come on," she said, opening the door and gathering up the box and trash bags and stuff.

"No," I said. "I'm staying here."

"No," Toby said. "I'm staying here."

Mama slammed the box down and yanked the back door open.

"Listen here," she hollered. "I'm doing the best I can. At least we'll have a roof over our heads and some room to spread out. It won't be for long."

"How long?" I said.

She sighed. "Not long," she said. "I almost have enough for rent, but most places want a deposit, too.

You two just don't get it." Her voice started getting louder until she was hollering again. "You think all I got to do is snap my fingers and *bingo*!" She pounded on top of the car. "*There's* the rent and *there's* the deposit and *there's* the gas for the car," she yelled. "And *snap*, there's electricity and water and phone. Not to mention food and clothes and doctors and STUFF." She kicked the car when she yelled the word "stuff."

Toby and I jumped.

"Now get out of the dern car and come inside," she said. Then she picked up the box and started back through the bushes toward the house.

I gathered up my pillow and our beach towel wall. "Come on, Toby," I said. "Let's go."

The house smelled damp and moldy. The floor was littered with leaves and acorns. In the front room, a lumpy couch stood underneath the plywood-covered window. Mice or rats or something had chewed through the fabric to the foam stuffing beneath. Stacks of yellowing newspapers were piled in one corner. Two empty cans of pork and beans sat on a rusty wood stove.

I followed Mama into the kitchen. The cracked linoleum floor was sticky and made squeaky noises as we walked across it. I wrinkled my nose and peered into the sink. Twigs and dirt that had fallen through a hole in the ceiling floated in a puddle of dark brown water. I turned the faucet, but no water came out. Not even one little drop. In one corner of the kitchen, a wobbly table was covered with empty soda cans and beer bottles. Cigarette butts were scattered on the floor beneath it.

"Our nasty ole car is better than this place," I said, but Mama acted like she didn't hear me. She set the box on the table and pushed her hair out of her face.

"Y'all bring the rest of our stuff in and let's start cleaning this place up," she said.

That night, I lay on the floor on top of piled-up clothes, covered with my beach towel, and stared at the mildewed ceiling.

In one corner, rain had leaked in and left a dark spot.

I narrowed my eyes, and that dark spot looked just like Willy. His ears and his eyes and even his whiskers. That morning, I had pushed him right out of my mind and now here he was back again, all because of this awful old house.

I could hear Mama tossing and turning on the other side of the room. Toby was curled up next to me. Every now and then his leg jerked. I bet he was dreaming about spiders and snakes.

I wanted more than anything to go to sleep so I wouldn't have to think about stuff, but I couldn't. I just lay there thinking about how everything had gotten so messed up and all. Then I remembered an Aesop's fable that Mr. White had read us in school. The one about the hares and the frogs. I could still hear him reading the moral at the end. "There is always someone worse off than yourself."

*Ha!* I thought. Ole Mr. Aesop must have been stupid 'cause he was just flat-out wrong. There was nobody, nowhere, worse off than me.

# 7

I studied myself in the mirror of the bathroom at McDonald's. My hair hung in greasy clumps on my forehead. Creases from the crumpled-up clothes I had slept on were still etched in the side of my face. I rubbed my hands together under the water and ran my wet fingers through my hair. Then I used paper towels to scrub my face and arms. The rough brown paper left my skin red and scratched.

We'd spent the weekend in that old house and I was beginning to think I'd rather sleep in the car again. Mama had got some stuff at a yard sale to try to make things better. A plastic raft for us to take turns sleeping on. A radio that ran on batteries. An alarm clock. Stuff like that. She even got a great big artificial plant with red and purple flowers. She had wiped the dust off the leaves with her shirttail and set it up on top of the wood stove. I guess she thought that plant would make me glad to be there, but it didn't. If things didn't change soon, I was going to have to go back to my dog-stealing plans. That's all there was to it.

The bathroom door opened and Mama stuck her head inside.

"We got to go, Georgina," she said. "I can't be late for work again."

I followed her out to the car. I couldn't help but notice how her blue jeans hung all baggy, dragging on the asphalt parking lot as she walked. I guess she was getting skinnier.

She had on her green Handy Pantry T-shirt. Her long fingers clutched a cup of coffee that sent trails of steam into the early morning air.

"I'll drop y'all off at the corner," she said, climbing into the car. "Then go on up yonder to the bus stop, okay?"

"Okay." I got into the backseat beside Toby and propped my feet on top of my bag of stuff. Mama had told us not to leave our things in that nasty ole house, "just in case." When I'd asked "Just in case what?" she had flapped her hand at me and told me to stop asking so many questions.

"After school," she said, "you and Toby wait in the car while I work at the cleaners, then we'll go on back to the house after that, okay?"

I stuffed my notebook into my backpack. Today was the day we were supposed to bring in our science projects. I didn't have mine, but I didn't even care. I'd tell Mr. White my project got lost or stolen or something.

"Okay, Georgina?" Mama said, craning her neck to look at me in the rearview mirror.

"I guess." I stared out the window.

"What's the matter?"

I shrugged. "Nothing."

"Come on and tell me, Georgina," she said. "What's the matter?"

I felt a wave of mad sweep over me. *"Everything!"* I hollered. "Okay? *Everything's* the matter."

I kept my head turned toward the window, but I could feel her eyes on me.

"Give me a break, okay?" she yelled into the mirror. "You're just making this harder on everybody, Miss Glum and Angry. What would you like me to do, rob a bank?"

Toby giggled and I shot him a look that wiped the grin right off his face.

"Maybe you could act like a *mother*," I said.

Mama slammed on the brakes and whipped around to glare at me.

"Just what is *that* supposed to mean?" she said.

"Mothers are supposed to take care of their kids," I said. "Not let them sleep in creepy old houses and wash up in the bathroom at McDonald's."

Mama pressed her lips together and I could tell she was thinking hard about what to say. But then she just sighed and turned back around.

We rode in silence the rest of the way. When we got to the corner near the bus stop, I got out and slammed the door. Hard.

"Look after Toby, okay, Georgina," Mama called after me.

"Yeah," I said. "Whatever."

"Was he mad?" Luanne asked me as we headed toward the bus.

"Naw."

"What did he say?"

"Nothing."

"Nothing?"

"Well, I mean, nothing much." I didn't look at Luanne 'cause I knew she would know I was lying. Mr. White had said plenty. He'd said how he couldn't understand my bad attitude lately. And he was so disappointed in my lack of effort recently. And then he had to go and ask me if everything was all right at home.

I had kept my eyes on the Styrofoam planets dangling from a coat hanger behind him. Somebody's stupid science project.

"Yessir," I said. "Everything's fine."

Then he had given me another envelope with *Mr. and Mrs. Hayes* written on it. Would I be sure and have my parents call him, he had said.

And if he didn't hear from them, he was going to have to talk to the principal about the problem. Did I understand, he had said.

"Yessir," I told him. What I didn't tell him was that my daddy was long gone and my mama couldn't even get us a place to live and my things got thrown out with the garbage. I didn't tell him that my best friend didn't even like me anymore and now she had a new friend. All I said to him was "Yessir."

I stuffed the envelope way down inside my backpack and left quick as I could.

On the bus, Luanne and I took our regular seats, and then Liza Thomas got on and stopped beside us.

"Are you going to Girl Scouts today?" she asked Luanne. She had on a red T-shirt with sparkly gold glitter spelling out *Cool Chick*.

"Yeah, are you?" Luanne said.

"Yeah." Liza flicked her ponytail behind her shoulder. "I'll see you there, okay?"

"Okay."

I could feel my jealousy churning around inside. Girl Scouts. I could just see Luanne and Liza there, side by side, working on their outdoor cooking badge or maybe planning a visit to the nursing home. I had to drop out of Girl Scouts so I could take care of Toby after school. Besides, I couldn't pay the dues or go on the trip to Six Flags or anything.

When we got off the bus, Liza waved at us out the window. Luanne waved back, but I didn't. Toby trotted along behind us.

"Wanna come over to my house before Girl Scouts?" Luanne said.

I wanted to say yes more than anything. I wanted to go over to the Godfreys' and lie on Luanne's soft pink carpet, eating graham crackers and working on one of my Girl Scout badges.

"I can't," I said. And that was all.

Me and Toby went on down the hill to where Mama was waiting for us in the car. I hated looking at that beat-up old car with bags of stuff all piled up on the seats. Black smoke puffed out of the tailpipe and the engine made a rattly sound.

"Hey, y'all," Mama called through the open window. "Look what I got." She waved a giant bag of M&M's at us.

"Hot dang!" Toby hollered, racing to the car.

I yanked the door open, tossed my backpack inside, and climbed in. Toby was already ripping the candy bag open.

"I don't want any," I said. Then I took my social studies book out of my backpack and pretended to read Chapter 21 like I was supposed to.

Mama turned around in the front seat. "Georgina," she said. "Please stop making this worse than it already is."

"I'm not."

"Yes you are." She got up on her knees and leaned over the seat to put her face down close to mine. "It won't be much longer now, I promise," she said.

"How much longer?"

Mama sighed. "A few more days maybe," she said.

A few more days? She might as well have said "forever."

I felt the tears running down my face and then Mama's warm hand on my cheek.

"I'm sorry, sweetheart," she said. "I swear, every night I pray for a miracle but I reckon nobody's listening."

"What kind of miracle?" I said. My voice sounded small and pitiful.

"I don't know," she said. "Anything. Money, mostly."

I nodded.

*Okay, that does it,* I said to myself. I was going to have to steal that dog, after all. I had to. It was the only way we were ever going to get ourselves out of this mess and live like normal people again.

So when Mama parked the car and kissed us good-bye, I pulled out my purple notebook and read through all my dog-stealing notes. I put a little checkmark beside the things I had already done. When I got to the part about finding a place to hide the dog, I thumped my pencil against my knee and thought real hard. Where in the world could I hide a dog? In the woods somewhere, maybe? Or over behind the Elks Lodge? Maybe in that old chicken coop out there by Hiram Foley's place?

I closed my notebook and stared out the window at the folks sitting in front of the Dairy Queen across the street.

Stealing a dog had seemed so easy when I'd first thought of it. Now it seemed like the hardest thing I'd ever done.

"Georgina?"

Toby's voice interrupted my thoughts.

"What?"

"Are we still gonna steal that dog?" he said.

"Yes," I said. "We are."

"When?"

"Soon." I pushed my notebook down under the clothes in my trash bag.


That night it was my turn to sleep on the plastic raft. Strips of moonlight poured through the cracks in the plywood that covered the windows, and danced across the dusty wooden floor. I tried to make myself stop thinking so I could go to sleep, but my mind just wouldn't turn off. I went through my plan over and over, imagining myself with that little dog, Willy. Picturing myself running with him in my arms. Seeing myself hiding him someplace. But where?

I threw the beach towel off of me and tiptoed over to

the corner of the room where my stuff was. I took out my notebook and sat down in a beam of moonlight so I could see. I turned to *Step 3* of *How to Steal a Dog*. I wrote *April 12*. Then, under the part that said: *3. Figure out where you are going to hide the dog*, I wrote:

*a. The place where you hide the dog has to be close enough so you can go visit him.*

*b. The place has to be somewhere that nobody goes to or else they will see the dog and maybe turn him loose or call the dog pound or something.*

*c. Try to find a place that is a nice place for a dog to be.*

*d. Try to find a place that has a roof because what if it rains?*

I tried to think of some more stuff, but I guess I was too tired. My mind was finally starting to slow down and stop thinking. So I wrote: *Now you are almost ready to steal a dog*, and put my notebook away.

I tiptoed back over to my raft bed. I pulled the beach towel up under my chin, closed my eyes, and slept a deep, dreamless sleep like I used to when I had a bed.

But I bet if I'd known what was going to happen the next day, I never would have slept that good.

# 8

I stared down at my desk, and in my head I begged Mr. White not to call on me.

"Georgina?" he said. "How about reading us your report on volcanoes?"

I looked at the paper in my hand. I had made my writing real big so I could fill up a whole page like we were supposed to. Everybody else had used their computers or gone to the library, but not me. All I could do was sit in that nasty house making stuff up.

With my face burning, I read my report about how volcanoes are like mountains with a hole in the middle and then fire comes out and hot lava runs down the side. My whole report lasted about two seconds and then it was over and everybody laughed. I was sure I could hear Luanne and Liza laughing louder than anybody else.

Mr. White said, "Shhhh," and put his hand on my shoulder.

"Thank you, Georgina," he said, and my heart swelled up with love for him. My report was nothing but great big made-up words, but he was still being nice to me. He wasn't going to holler at me like he had hollered at Luke Ketchum.

I hadn't been doing too good in school lately, but I still looked forward to being there. At least at school, I knew how my day was going to go. I knew we'd say the Pledge of Allegiance and then we'd raise our hands if we wanted grilled cheese instead of chicken fingers for lunch. Then we'd look up there on the chalkboard and our whole day would be written out. Math and then reading. A spelling test and then gym. No surprises.

Not like after school, when I never knew what was going to happen next. It seemed like something new was always coming my way, and most times it wasn't good. Like that very day of my volcano report, when me and Toby got back to the car and Mama was sitting there all red-faced and crying.

Toby lunged right through the open window and hugged her so hard I thought she was gonna choke. She peeled his arms from around her neck and said, "Y'all get in the car."

I got in my usual spot in the back, but Toby jumped in the front, pushing all the boxes and bags and things aside. He kept on saying, "What's the matter, Mama?" but she wouldn't answer.

Nobody said anything as we sped along the streets of Darby. Mama gripped the steering wheel with both hands, her knuckles white and her elbows locked stiff. When we stopped at a red light, she put her head down on the steering wheel. The light turned green and a big truck behind us honked but Mama didn't even look up.

"Mama?" I said.

Nothing. The truck horn honked again and somebody yelled.

"Mama?" I said again.

The truck roared around us and the man driving it hollered and shook his fist at us.

I had a feeling something bad was about to happen.

"The light's green," I said.

Mama lifted her head up off the steering wheel and stared out at the road. Another horn honked behind us.

"I got fired at the cleaners," she said. "Can you believe that?"

"How come?" I said.

Mama breathed out a big whoosh. "Who knows," she said, " 'Cause I was late once or twice, I reckon. Or 'cause I don't use that pressing machine fast enough. Or maybe just 'cause I'm alive."

She didn't even turn her head when another car whipped around us, honking like crazy.

"Maybe you better get out of the road," I said.

"Maybe I better get out of the whole dern world," she said, and sounded so mean. She swiped at tears and wiped her nose with her hand. "Maybe I better just disappear off the face of the earth. Poof! Like that." She snapped her fingers. "Wouldn't that be nice?"

I felt words bubbling up inside me till they came busting out.

"Yeah!" I hollered. "That *would* be nice."

I kicked the back of the seat and made Mama's head jerk but she kept staring straight ahead.

"Why *don't* you disappear, and then me and Toby can do what we want to. Right, Toby?" I poked the back of Toby's head, but he just rocked back and forth, sniffling.

Another car horn honked, and Mama sat up straight like she had just woke up. She brushed the hair out of her eyes and started driving again.

Nobody said anything as we turned down the dirt and gravel road that led to the house. The car squeaked and bounced and rattled. When we stopped, Mama turned off the engine and the car gave one last little shudder.

We gathered our things and made our way through the prickly bushes to the front porch. And then we all three stopped dead in our tracks and stared at that old house. Boards had been nailed in a giant X over the front door. Someone had written on the boards in great big letters, "This is private property! Keep out!" They had added about a million exclamation points, so it looked like this:

*THIS IS PRIVATE PROPERTY! KEEP OUT!!!!!!!!!!!!!!*

Mama dropped her stuff right off the porch and into the bushes. Blankets and pillows and everything. Then she sat down on the rickety steps and hollered out a bunch of cuss words that echoed through the woods.

Toby got all blubbery, but I just stood there looking at that boarded-up door. I was surprised how bad I felt, seeing as how I hated that house. But I guess it had been better than the car, after all.

I watched the back of Mama's head and I could almost see her sadness swirling around her.

"It's a good thing you made us take our stuff out of there every day," I said.

She just stared out at the woods. Toby was whimpering and pulling the blankets up out of the bushes.

"That would have been awful if our stuff was locked up in there," I said.

Mama kept staring out into the woods.

"I guess Beverly Jenkins was wrong about this house," I said. "I guess the owner doesn't want us here, after all."

Mama turned her head slowly and looked at me and her face didn't show anything. Not mad. Not sad. Not anything. Then she stood up and gathered the rest of the blankets and stuff.

"Come on, y'all," she said.

Me and Toby followed her out to the car and climbed in.

As we made our way back up the gravel road toward

the highway, I hummed a little bit, trying to clear the heavy air in the car.

"Georgina, *please*," Mama said. So I hushed up.

I stared out at the world passing by my window and I made up my mind. I was definitely gonna steal that dog.

# 9

That night, I dreamed Toby was a dog. He sat on the backseat beside me with his head stuck out the window, his ears flapping in the wind. We drove and drove and drove and then we pulled into a long, winding road that led to a castle. Mama stopped the car in front of the giant front door of the castle and said, "Here's our new house!"

Toby the dog started crying and saying how he wanted to go back home where he belonged.

And then I woke up. I peered down at Toby, curled up on the floor of the car sucking his thumb. It was so hot the windows were all steamed up. I rolled my window partway down. Then I leaned back and stared out at the lit-up sign of the Brushy Creek Lutheran Church.

I had gone to that church one time when I was little. With my friend Racene Wickham. We had made May baskets, weaving strips of pink and yellow construction paper, in and out, in and out. I had glued a pink pipe cleaner handle on mine and filled it with clover flowers for Mama.

I remember how on the way home, I'd been all squished in the backseat beside Racene's brothers and I'd clutched that May basket in my lap. I couldn't wait to give it to Mama, even though the clover flowers had wilted and were lying all droopy in the bottom of the basket. But when I got home, Mama and Daddy were yelling at each other and wouldn't even look at me when I tried to show them my May basket.

Racene had moved away to Florida, and now here I was, back here at that very same church, sleeping in my car.

When the sun came up, we headed over to the Pancake House to wash up and get some toast. The bread we had in the milk crate in the trunk of the car had turned green with mold, and Mama had tossed it out the window, right into the church parking lot.

"I want pancakes," Toby said, frowning down at his toast.

Mama sipped her coffee, squinting through the steam, and said, "No."

"Why not?" Toby whined.

Mama slammed the cup down, sloshing coffee onto the table. "Because you can't have everything you want," she said.

I ate my toast and watched Mama scoop all the little plastic tubs of jelly into her purse.

"Y'all go over to the Y after school and wait till I get there, okay?" she said.

"The Y?"

"Yes, Georgina, the Y."

The Darby YMCA was nothing but a room in the basement of the Town Hall. Some kids went there after school to play games and stuff while their parents were at work.

"We can't go *there*," I said.

Mama sighed. "Just do like I say, Georgina."

"But you have to sign up and stuff," I said. "You can't just *go* there. And I bet you have to pay."

But Mama wouldn't even answer me. She counted out some coins, slapped them on the table, and headed out to the car, leaving me and Toby to scramble after her.

That day in school, all I could think about was how I was going to steal that little dog, Willy. While Mr. White read stuff about the Revolutionary War, I pulled my purple notebook out of my backpack and flipped to the *How to Steal a Dog* page. I read through what I had so far. Everything seemed pretty good except for that problem about where to keep the dog after you steal him.

I thought and thought about it, and then, just like a lightbulb going on, I got an idea. I could keep Willy at that boarded-up old house! There was a tiny little porch around back off the kitchen. It was kind of rotten and all, but a dog wouldn't care about that. And that house wasn't too far from Whitmore Road. I could walk that far, no problem. At last, I thought, things were finally starting to look better.

At lunch, I asked Luanne if me and Toby could go to her house after school. I didn't tell her we were supposed to go to the Y.

"Um, I don't think so," Luanne said.

"How come?"

Luanne fiddled with the buttons on her shirt. "I got some stuff to do," she said.

"Like what?"

She shrugged. "Just some stuff with Mama."

I twirled my spaghetti around and around on my fork and listened to the girls at our table going on and on about some movie they'd all seen. Then Luanne piped in and said how she had just loved that movie, too. I kept on twirling my spaghetti and feeling more and more like I didn't want to be there at that lunch table. I wanted to float right up through the ceiling and out into the blue sky. I didn't belong there with those girls. I hadn't seen that movie. I couldn't buy those bracelets they all wore. They had been over at the mall while I'd been washing my underwear in the bathroom sink at Walgreens.

So I just sat there twirling and thinking about Willy.

After school, me and Toby walked over to the Town Hall.

"I'm not going down there," I told him, nodding toward the basement window. "You can if you want to, but I'm not." The sound of kids playing and balls bouncing drifted out of the open window.

Toby shook his head. "Then I'm not going neither," he said.

I tossed my backpack on a nearby bench. "We've got to find some string or something," I said to Toby.

"What for?"

"For Willy. Remember?"

"Oh."

So we walked up and down the street, looking in gutters and Dumpsters and trash cans. I was just about to give up when Toby hollered, "Here's some, Georgina!"

I ran over to the curb where Toby was holding a stack of newspapers tied with heavy string.

"Yes!" I pumped my fist and high-fived Toby. "Good job!" Toby looked just pleased as punch. I untied the string and stuffed it into my pocket. "Let's go back and wait for Mama," I said.


It was nearly dark by the time we saw our car come sputtering up the street toward the Town Hall, leaving a trail of black smoke behind it.

"Sorry, y'all," Mama said when we climbed in the backseat.

"We're starving," Toby said.

"I know, sweetheart," Mama said. "I brought y'all some chicken."

Toby dug through the bag in the front seat and pulled out a piece of greasy fried chicken.

"I got a job," Mama said.

I took a piece of chicken and pulled the soggy skin off. "Where?" I said, dropping the chicken skin back into the bag.

"The coffee shop over by the hardware store." She glanced at herself in the rearview mirror. I wondered if she saw the same tired and worried face that I did.

"Well, that's good," I said.

She took a swig out of a soda can. "I guess so," she said, then pulled the car to the side of the road and stopped.

"What's the matter?" I said.

She shook her head. "I'm just so dern tired of all this," she said.

My stomach clumped up in a knot, and I wished I hadn't eaten that chicken. Why was Mama acting so sad? I needed her to act like everything was okay.

Nobody said anything after that. We just sat there in that car that was our home. Crammed in with all of our stuff. The smell of the greasy fried chicken hovered in the still air around us.

Mama broke the silence when she slapped her hands on the steering wheel and said, "Anyway, so now I'll be at work when y'all get out of school. So come on over to the coffee shop and wait in the car, okay?"

I ran my dog-stealing plans around inside my head. This would be perfect. The coffee shop wasn't far from Whitmore Road. I could grab Willy, hide him on the porch of the old house, and then get on back to the car, no problem. Mama wouldn't even know if me and Toby were there or not.

That night, I fingered the string in my pocket and watched Mama helping Toby with his homework. They huddled together in the front seat with the flashlight propped up on the dashboard. Shadows danced around on the ceiling as they worked.

I pulled out my notebook and turned to *How to Steal a Dog*. I wrote *April 14*, then, beside that:

*Step 4: Use this list to make sure you are ready to steal a dog.*
*1. Are you sure you have found the right dog?*
*Yes ___ No ___*
*2. Can you open the gate?*
*Yes ___ No ___*
*3. Do you have some rope or string?*
*Yes ___ No ___*

*4. Do you have a good place to keep the dog?*
*Yes* ___ *No* ___

I read through each one and put a checkmark beside *Yes* every time.

After the list, I wrote: *If you can check "yes" for every one, then you are ready to steal a dog.*

I thumped the pencil eraser against my teeth, then I added:

*P.S. Remember that you have to wait until nobody is home at the house where the dog lives.*

*P.P.S. Don't forget to take your string, rope, or leash.*

I closed my notebook and pushed it back down inside my trash bag. And when my guilty conscience started hollering at me, telling me I was doing the wrong thing, I pushed that down, too.

There was no doubt about it. I really, really was going to steal a dog.

# 10

Shhhh." I put my finger to my lips and motioned for Toby to stay behind me. We tiptoed along the hedge in front of the big brick house. When we got to the gate, I scanned the street, then whispered to Toby.

"You be the lookout. If anybody comes outside or a car comes or *anything*, you whistle like I showed you this morning, okay?"

Toby nodded.

I peered over the gate. The front door of the house was closed. I glanced toward the driveway. No car. The yard was empty and quiet.

"Here, Willy," I called out real soft. Nothing. Maybe he was inside. I wondered if I should go on up to the porch. Probably not. If somebody *was* home, they were liable to see me.

"Maybe you should whistle," Toby whispered.

"Okay." I whistled one time and waited. Sure enough, Willy stuck his head out of that little doggie door. When he saw me, he dashed out the door and up to the gate.

"Hey, Willy," I whispered, sticking my hand through the gate to pet him.

He stood on his hind legs and put his front paws on the gate. His tail wagged so hard his whole body wiggled. He licked my hand like it was a T-bone steak.

"You wanna come with us?" I said.

He cocked his head and peered up at me. And then, I swear, he nodded his head. If he could've talked, I was sure he would've said, "Heck, yeah, I wanna come with you."

So, quick as I could, I lifted the latch on the gate and opened it just enough to reach my arm in. My heart was pounding so hard all I could hear was the thump, thump, thump in my ears. I knew I had to keep myself moving or else I was liable to start thinking. And if I started thinking, I was liable to think I shouldn't be doing this. So I turned my mind to "off" and grabbed Willy's collar. I pulled him through the gate and out onto the sidewalk. He kept wagging his tail and looking at me with his shiny black eyes. I took the string out of my pocket and tied it to his flea collar.

"Okay, let's go," I said to Toby, and took off running.

I ran down Whitmore Road, around the corner, and into the woods. Willy ran along beside me. Every now and then he leaped up on me or nipped at my heels like this was the most fun game he'd ever played. Once in a while he'd let out a little yip.

When we were far enough into the woods that I was

sure no one could see us from the road, I stopped to catch my breath. I put my hand on my pounding heart and leaned against a tree. Toby ran up and stopped beside me.

"We did it!" he hollered.

"Shhhh." I clamped my hand over his mouth. "Somebody might hear us. You got to be really quiet."

Willy sat in front of us with his tongue hanging out, panting. His tail wagged on the ground. Swish, swish, swish.

I knelt down and ran my hand along his back. He closed his eyes and leaned against me.

"It's okay, fella," I said. "Don't be scared. Me and Toby are nice."

He scratched behind his ear with his hind leg, making the tag on his collar jingle.

"What do we do now?" Toby said.

"We take him over to that house and tie him up on the porch."

"What if he don't like it there?"

"He's just gonna be there for a little while," I said. "As soon as his owner puts up the reward sign, we'll take him back home."

"Oh." Toby knelt and rubbed the top of Willy's head. "What if his owner don't put up a reward sign?"

I flapped my hand at Toby. "Trust me. That lady is gonna want him back more than anything. She's probably making a reward sign right now."

I made my voice sound calm and sure, but a funny little feeling was tapping at my insides. A feeling like maybe I had done a real bad thing. I took a deep breath, trying to swallow that feeling down and keep it from growing.

I unbuckled Willy's green collar and tossed it into the bushes. Tap, tap. There was that feeling again. Tapping at my insides like it was trying to tell me something.

"What'd you do that for?" Toby said.

I rolled my eyes. "Think about it, Toby."

Toby's eyebrows squeezed together and he bit his lip. " 'Cause he don't need it anymore?" he said.

I sighed. "No, *dum*-bo. Because we can't take him back to his owner with his collar on or else she'd wonder how come we didn't call her. Her phone number's right there on the tag."

"Oh." Toby nodded, but he still looked confused. I swear sometimes he is dumber than dirt.

"Come on." I motioned for Toby to follow me. We made our way through the woods behind the houses on Whitmore Road. I could hear the cars on the highway up ahead, so I was pretty sure we were going in the right direction.

Willy trotted along beside me happy as anything. Every now and then, he stopped to sniff the ground or root through the rotting leaves. Once, he stopped to dig, sending dirt and leaves and twigs flying out behind him and making me and Toby laugh. He sure was a funny dog.

When we got to the highway, I stooped down behind the bushes along the edge.

I handed the string leash to Toby. "Here," I said. "Hold this while I see if any cars are coming."

I checked in both directions. No cars. I went back to where Toby sat with his arm around Willy.

"Okay, now listen," I said. "We got to run across the highway, then through that vacant lot over there. I'm pretty sure we can cut through those woods to get to that old house."

He nodded.

I took the string from him and dashed across the highway with Willy leaping along beside me. We kept running until we made it to the edge of the gravel road leading to the old house. The whole time, Willy pranced and yipped and jumped up on me. Once in a while, he grabbed the string in his mouth and gave it a tug.

When we got to the house, Willy perked his ears up and watched me.

"We're here, fella," I said, scratching the top of his head.

He looked at that run-down, boarded-up house and then back at me. I had a feeling I knew what he was thinking.

"It's okay, Willy," I said. "You won't be here long. I promise."

He cocked his head in that cute way of his. I don't know how he did it, but that little dog could make you love him just by looking at him. I sat down in the dusty road and put my arm around him. He crawled right into my lap and licked my face. His licks weren't all slobbery like most dogs'.

"It's spooky here," Toby said in that whiny voice of his. I knew if I didn't do something fast, he was liable to turn into his baby self and start crying or something.

"You hold Willy and I'll make a path to the back porch," I said.

I pushed through the sticker bushes and vines, mashing them down and breaking off branches till there was a clear path to the back of the house. It was dark and damp back there. You couldn't even see the sky through the overgrown trees.

The tiny porch leaned slightly, like any minute it was going to fall right off the back of the house. The steps leading up to it were loose and rotten. One of them was broken all the way through. The screen door dangled by one hinge.

"Come on," I called to Toby.

He and Willy came around the corner of the house and stopped.

"No way, Georgina," Toby said. "We can't put Willy in there."

"Listen, Toby," I said. "This is the best place. Nobody'll see him. And he won't get wet if it rains. And besides, he won't be here long." I watched Toby's face, but he didn't look convinced. "And we'll come and stay with him after school and all," I added.

Toby swiped at the tears that had started. "You're mean," he said.

Dern. Why'd he have to go and say that? I sure didn't want to hear it—'cause that was exactly how I was feeling. Mean.

"Toby, listen." I put both hands on his shoulders and looked him square in the eye. "Aren't you tired of living in the car?"

He hung his head and nodded a tiny little bit.

"Don't you want to have a *real* place to live? With walls and beds and a bathroom and all?"

He nodded again.

"Then we need to help Mama get some money," I said. "And this is the only thing I can think of. Can you think of another way?"

I bent down and tried to look him in the eye again, but his head was hanging too low. All I could see was his long, dirty hair all tangled up and ratty-looking.

"Then we got to do this," I said. "We'll take good care of Willy, and we'll take him right back home just as soon as we can, and then we'll get the reward money and everything will be good." I jiggled Toby's shoulders. "Okay?" I added.

I knew Toby didn't believe me 'cause I wasn't sure I believed myself. That old tapping feeling was getting bigger, and in my head I was thinking maybe I was messing up. And I was starting to think how I wished I could go back in time to the hour before or the day before or the week before. But I knew I couldn't do that. I was there behind that awful old house with that cute little dog looking at me, and I knew it was up to me to make everything turn out good like I had planned.

I took the string leash from Toby and led Willy up the creaky steps to the porch.

"This isn't so bad," I called out to Toby.

The top half of the porch had been screened in once, but now what was left of the rusty old screen hung in tatters. Leaves and pine needles had blown in and covered the floor, settling in the corners in damp, moldy piles.

I pushed some of the wet leaves aside, trying to make a clean spot. Then I knelt down and took Willy's head in both my hands.

"Don't be scared, okay?" I said. "We'll be back real soon and everything will be fine." Then I rubbed my nose back and forth against his. An Eskimo kiss.

Willy rested his chin in my hands and gazed up at me like he believed every word I said.

"What if he gets hungry?" Toby called from the bottom of the steps.

*Hungry?* I hadn't even thought about that! I couldn't believe Toby was thinking up something else I had left out of my *How to Steal a Dog* notes.

"I *said*, what if he gets hungry?" Toby called out.

"I've got that all worked out," I lied. My mind raced, trying to think of how I was going to feed Willy. And what if I couldn't get back here every day? How long could a dog go without food?

"And water," Toby said. "Dogs need water, you know. He might die if he don't have water."

"Shut up, Toby." That's all I could think of to say, and it did the trick. He shut up. But it didn't help me feel any better.

I tied the string to the doorknob and said goodbye to Willy. Then I led the way back through the weeds and briar bushes toward the road.

I was glad Toby was quiet as we walked, 'cause I had a lot of thinking to do. About food and water for Willy. About what I'd done. About what to do next. But it was hard to get my thoughts all straightened out with my insides kicking up like they were. That tapping feeling was turning into full-out banging.

# 11

"Hey, y'all," Mama called as she made her way across the parking lot toward the car. "Look what I got."

She stuck a Styrofoam box through the window. "Check this out," she said.

I opened the box. Scrambled eggs and pancakes. They sure did smell good.

"And that's not all," she said, tossing a paper bag onto the backseat.

Toby snatched the bag up and peered inside, then let out a whoop. "Doughnuts!" he hollered. He grabbed a powdery white doughnut and started eating it so fast he choked, coughing out a spray of powder and crumbs.

"Eeeyew," I said, wiping off my jeans.

Mama slid behind the steering wheel and examined herself in the mirror. "This job is gonna be great," she said, licking a finger and smoothing an eyebrow. "The tips are really good and I get to bring home all kinds of food."

Food? Talk about good luck! Now we wouldn't have to worry about feeding Willy. I poked Toby and gave him a thumbs-up. His eyebrows shot up and he mouthed "What?" at me.

I flapped my hand at him to signal *never mind*, but he wouldn't be quiet. He kept whispering, "What?"

I shook my head and pulled an invisible zipper across my lips, which meant "Hush up, I can't tell you in front of Mama," but he was too dumb to figure that out.

"What?" he said a little louder.

"What'd you say?" Mama said.

I pressed my foot on top of Toby's and smiled at Mama in the rearview mirror. "Nothing," I said.

I settled back and ate some pancakes, which sure did taste good even though they were all soggy with syrup. When I finished, I took out my notebook and wrote: *Save some doughnuts for Willy.* I pushed the notebook across the seat and poked Toby.

He squinted down at my note. Then he grinned and said, "Ohhhhh, okay."

"What?" Mama said.

I jabbed my heel into Toby's foot and he hollered, "Owwww!"

Mama whirled around and snapped, "What're y'all doing?"

I slapped my hand over the note and smiled at her. "Nothing."

"Well, don't y'all start that bickering back there," she said. "Let's go find us someplace to park."

I glared at Toby. We hadn't had that dog one whole

day yet, and already he was acting all stupid around Mama. It would be a miracle if she didn't find out what we had done.

But so far, it seemed like everything was working out good. I'd stolen Willy, no problem. I'd found a good place to keep him. And Mama had a job at a coffee shop that gave her free food. Now all I had to do was stash some of that food in my backpack for Willy.

I took out my notebook and wrote *April 18* in my *How to Steal a Dog* notes. Then I wrote:

*Step 5: Things to do after you have stolen the dog:*
*1. Be sure to act nice to him so he won't be afraid.*
*2. Play with him some so he will like you.*
*3. Make sure you put him in a safe place where he won't get wet if it rains.*
*4. Tie up the rope or string so he can't run away.*
*5. Find him some food and water.*

Uh-oh. Water. I'd forgotten about that. But I was pretty sure that wasn't going to be a big problem. Still, I put a question mark beside that one so I would remember to figure it out.

That night it seemed like I hardly slept at all. A steady rain clattered on the roof and ran down the windows in streams. The inside of the car was so hot I had to crack my window, and then the rain splattered my face and made my pillow wet. I listened to the slow, even breathing of Mama and Toby and thought about Willy. I wondered if he was scared. Was he getting wet? Was he hungry?

Every time I closed my eyes, I could see his freckly face and those shiny black eyes. I could see him cock his head at me and wag his whole body the way he did.

"Don't be scared, Willy," I whispered into the still night air.

The car windows were so fogged up I couldn't even see outside. I used my finger to write *Willy* on the foggy glass. I drew a heart around it, then wiped the window clean and turned my mind to "off."

When I opened my eyes the next morning, I felt all fluttery and excited like on Christmas morning. Today was the day we would find the reward sign for Willy.

Mama made us use the water in the cooler to brush our teeth. While she was putting on her lipstick and stuff in the car, I filled an empty soda bottle with water and put it in my backpack. Then I checked to make sure I had the bag of food scraps for Willy. Yep, half a doughnut and some scrambled eggs.

I pulled Toby close and whispered, "We gotta look for the reward signs today, okay?"

He nodded. "Okay."

I could hardly keep myself from grinning as we made

our way through the streets of Darby on the way to school. I sat up straight and pressed my face against the window, searching every telephone pole we passed.

As we got closer to school, my excitement began to fade to disappointment. I guess in my heart I'd known it was probably too soon to find any signs. We'd only stolen that dog the day before. But in my mind, I had pictured signs on every pole. There they would be, up and down the streets of Darby. In big letters: REWARD. Then there would be a picture of Willy, cocking his head and staring out at the world through his furry black eye patch.

But what I saw outside the window that day was nothing like what I had seen in my mind. There wasn't one single sign. None. Nowhere. I tried to swallow my disappointment and tell myself to be patient. The signs would be up after school, for sure.

"Y'all go straight on back to the car after school, okay?" Mama said, pulling over to the curb.

"We will," I said.

"And stay there, Georgina."

"We will."

"And help Toby with his homework."

I nodded and watched her drive away, then I grabbed Toby's arm.

"Did you see any signs?" I said.

"Nope."

"Dern." I stamped my foot.

"Maybe that lady doesn't care about Willy," Toby said.

I shook my head. "No way. She cares," I said. "Who wouldn't care about a dog like that?"

Toby shrugged. "Maybe she hasn't got any money," he said.

"She *owns* that whole street, Toby," I said.

A school bus had pulled up and kids came pouring out and rushing toward the front door of the school. Me and Toby pushed our way through and went inside.

"Listen," I said. "Meet me at the flagpole after school. We got to take that food over to Willy. Then we can look for the reward signs. I bet they'll be up by this afternoon."

"Mama said we had to stay in the car," Toby said.

I rolled my eyes. "She won't even know what we do. She'll be in the coffee shop."

I watched Toby walk away from me as he headed toward his class. His clothes were all wrinkled and his hair was long and tangled. He was sure a pitiful sight. I wondered if that was how I looked.

When Mr. White asked me for the millionth time if I had given those letters to my parents, I lied again. I said I had, but Mama and Daddy were real busy working and all. I told him my daddy was going to call him any day now. *Yeah, right*, I thought. That was a good one.

I felt bad lying to Mr. White. He was the nicest teacher I'd ever had. He didn't get mad when my science report had fried chicken grease on it. He hadn't said one word when I didn't have a costume for our play about the Boston Tea Party like all the other kids did. And he let me go to the nurse's office, even when he knew I wasn't one bit sick.

But when he asked me about those letters, what else could I do but lie?

Luanne didn't hardly even talk to me all day. I was wearing the same clothes I had on yesterday, and I thought I saw her make a face when I walked into class that morning. I thought I saw Liza poke her at recess and point at me. I thought I heard my name every time I walked by kids giggling and whispering and all.

*So who cares*, I told myself. I didn't care about any of those kids anymore. Maybe not even Luanne. I found myself doing stuff I never would have done before we started living in a car. Stuff that I knew would make kids poke each other and laugh at me. Like, I took Melissa Gavin's half-eaten granola bar out of the trash and put it in Willy's food bag. And when Jake Samson called me a garbage picker, I just kept my mouth shut and went on back to my desk like I didn't care.

After school I waited at the flagpole for Toby; then we headed off toward the old house to check on Willy. Toby kept whining about how his backpack was too heavy and his feet hurt and all, but I ignored him.

I found a plastic margarine tub on the side of the road and wiped the dirt off of it with the edge of my shirt.

"We can use this for Willy's water bowl," I said, tucking it into my backpack.

Toby kept saying, "Slow down," as we made our way up the gravel road. He splashed right through the muddy puddles, not even caring that his shoes were getting soaked and his legs were covered with mud.

But I didn't slow down. I was dying to get to Willy. I needed to see him. I sure hoped he was okay.

As soon as I rounded the corner of the house, I heard a little yip from the back porch. Then I saw Willy poke his head through the torn screen door, and my heart nearly leaped right out of me, I felt so glad to see him.

Right away, he started wagging his whole body like he was the happiest dog on earth.

"Hey there, fella," I said, sitting on the top step of the porch and giving him a hug. He licked my face all over.

"Are you hungry?" I said. Before I could even open the bag of food, he was pushing at it with his whiskery nose.

"Here you go." I opened the bag and let him gobble up the eggs and stuff inside.

"He sure was hungry," Toby said.

I rubbed my hand down Willy's back while he ate. He was a little wet and smelled kind of bad, but he seemed okay. I opened the soda bottle of water and poured some into the margarine tub.

Willy went to town lapping it up.

"We got to let him run a little bit," I said.

"But what if he runs away?" Toby said.

"We'll keep the leash on him, dummy."

I untied the string from the doorknob. "Come on, Willy," I said.

Me and Toby took turns running up and down the road. Willy ran right through puddles. Sometimes he'd stop and shake himself, sending sprays of muddy water all over me and Toby. Once in a while he stopped to take a good long drink from a puddle. But mostly he just ran and leaped and barked a happy kind of bark. We had to run real fast to keep up with him or else he was liable to bust that string right in two.

"There," I said. "That ought to be enough."

Willy sat in the road in front of me, panting. He lifted his doggy eyebrows and watched me, like he was waiting for something. I knelt down and scratched his ears.

"Don't worry," I said. "You're gonna be going home real soon."

He stopped panting and perked his ears up. Then he put his paw on my knee.

"He sure is cute, ain't he?" Toby said.

"He sure is." I stroked Willy's paw and felt a stab inside. Was it really, *really* wrong to do what I was doing— or was it just a little bit wrong?

I pushed Willy's paw off my knee and stood up. I had to shut those thoughts right out of my head and keep just one thought and one thought only in there. I was doing this for Mama and Toby and me. To help us have a real place to live. Not a car. What was so wrong about that?

We took Willy back to the porch, and I tied the string around the doorknob again.

"Don't worry, fella," I said. "You'll be home soon. I promise."

I filled the margarine tub with water again and set it on the porch beside Willy.

"He needs a bed," Toby said.

I looked at the crummy old back porch. Toby was right. The porch was damp and dirty and covered with sticks and leaves. I should have brought a towel or something to make a bed. I felt another stab inside. I *was* being mean to Willy, wasn't I?

"We'll bring something next time we come," I said. But then I added, "If he's still here."

Toby frowned. "Why wouldn't he be here?"

I sighed. It sure was tiring having to explain every dern little thing to Toby. "We'll be taking him back *home*, you idiot. As soon as we find that reward sign."

"Oh, yeah."

I gave Willy one last pat on the head and made my way down the rotten porch steps. I wanted to look back, but I didn't. I knew I wouldn't be able to stand the sight of that little dog watching me walk away and leave him all alone.

I led the way through the bushes to the road. Behind us, I though I heard Willy barking.

*I don't hear that,* I told myself.

*I'm not mean,* I reminded myself.

*This was a good idea and everything is going to turn out fine,* I repeated in my head.

I guess I was hoping that if I said those things, then maybe they would be true.

# 12

There's one!" I raced across the street.

"Is it for Willy?" Toby called, darting across after me.

I squinted up at the sign nailed on the telephone pole.

"Nope." I sat on the curb and put my chin in my hands. "Another cat."

So far the only signs we'd seen since yesterday had been for lost cats and yard sales.

Toby sat down beside me. "Maybe we should look downtown," he said. "Maybe she didn't put any signs around here."

"Maybe," I said. "But that seems kind of dumb to me. I mean, wouldn't you start in your own neighborhood?"

Me and Toby had been up and down Whitmore Road and nearly every street close by about a million times. There wasn't one single sign for Willy. I just didn't get it. Why wouldn't that lady put up a sign?

"Let's go back over to Whitmore Road one more time," I said.

Toby skipped along beside me, humming. He didn't seem one little bit worried. We'd had Willy for almost two whole days now and I was feeling worse by the hour. My dog-stealing plan had seemed so good when I'd first thought of it. Everything had gone just perfect in my head:

We steal the dog.

We find the sign.

We take the dog home.

We get the money.

The end.

But now things didn't seem to be going so perfect.

When we got to Whitmore Road, I turned to Toby. "Remember," I said, "act normal. Don't look guilty or anything."

"Okay."

We strolled along the edge of the road, looking at fence posts, telephone poles, anything that might have a sign on it. And then we heard someone calling from behind us.

"W-i-l-l-y!"

Toby looked at me all wide-eyed. "What should we do?" he whispered.

Before I could answer, that fat lady was walking toward us.

"Hey," she called to me and Toby.

"Uh, hey," I said, and set a smile on my face.

Her shorts went swish, swish, swish as she walked. A bright pink T-shirt stretched over her big stomach. Even her feet were fat, bulging over the sides of her yellow flip-flops.

"Have y'all seen a dog?" she said. She was breathing hard and clutching her heart like she was going to fall over dead any minute.

"Nope!" Toby practically yelled.

I glared at him, then turned back to the lady. "What does it look like?" I said, squeezing my eyebrows together in a worried way.

"He's about this big." She held her hands up to show us. "He's white, with a black eye patch. And his name is Willy."

Then she started crying. Real hard. Like the way little kids cry.

"I'm sorry," she said, swiping at tears. "I just can't even imagine where he could be."

"Maybe he ran away," Toby said.

Before I could poke him, the lady said, "No, not Willy." Her face crumpled up and she had another full-out crying spell.

I like to died when she did that. And then, as if I wasn't feeling bad enough, she said, "What if something bad's happened to him?"

Before I could stop myself, I said, "You want me and Toby to help you look for him?"

She sniffed and nodded. "Would you?"

"Sure." I poked Toby. "Right, Toby?"

He nodded. "Yeah, right," he said.

The lady smiled and pulled a tissue out of the pocket of her shorts. She blew her nose, then stuffed the tissue back in her pocket. Strands of damp hair clung to her splotchy red cheeks.

"Do y'all live around here?" she said.

Me and Toby looked at each other.

"Uh, sorta," I said. "I mean, yeah, we live over that way." I pointed in the direction of the street where our car was parked. That wasn't lying, right?

"I live right there." She pointed to her house. "I'll show y'all Willy's picture, okay?"

Me and Toby followed her up the walk to the house. At the door, she turned and said, "My name's Carmella, by the way—Carmella Whitmore."

"I'm Georgina," I said. "That's my brother, Toby."

"I'll be right back," she said, then disappeared into the darkness of the house.

I pushed my face against the screen and peered inside. My stomach did a flip-flop. I pressed my face closer to the screen to make sure I was seeing right. I was. The inside of that house wasn't one little bit like I'd imagined it would be. Ever since I'd first laid eyes on 27 Whitmore Road, I'd pictured rooms with glittering crystal chandeliers and fancy furniture. I'd imagined a thick, silky carpet covered with roses. And paintings on the walls. Those fancy kind with swirly gold frames like in museums. I'd even pictured a servant lady bringing in tea and cookies on a silver tray.

But what I saw when I peered through that door was a dark and dreary room filled to bursting with all kinds of junky *stuff*. Piles of newspapers and clothes, boxes and dishes. No chandeliers. No fancy furniture.

Carmella came out of a back room carrying a small silver picture frame.

"Here's Willy," she said, joining me and Toby on the porch and handing me the picture.

There was Willy, looking out at me from that silver frame, smiling his doggie smile.

"He sure is cute," I made myself say, but my voice came out real quiet and shaky.

Carmella nodded and wiped at tears. "He's the cutest dog you ever saw," she said. "And smart? Talk about smart!"

She smiled down at the picture in my hand. "He can count. Can you believe that?"

"Really?" Toby said.

Carmella nodded. "Really. With his little paw. Like this." She pawed the air with her hand.

"Maybe he got lost," Toby said.

Carmella shook her head. "Maybe. But it's just so

unlike him. He knows this neighborhood real good. And everybody knows him." She took the picture from me and dropped into a rocking chair.

"I can't figure out how that front gate got open," she said.

"Maybe the paperboy or something," I said.

"Naw, he just flings it up here on the porch." She looked out at the street. "I've driven everywhere I can think of. I called the animal control officer. I talked to all my neighbors. I just don't know what else to do." Then she started crying real hard again, and I had to look down at my feet. I could feel Toby fidgeting beside me.

"Why don't you put up some signs?" I said.

Carmella looked up. "Signs?"

"Yeah, you know, lost-dog signs."

"Well, stupid me," she said. "Of course I should put up some signs."

"Me and Toby can help," I said. "Right, Toby?"

"Right." Toby grinned at Carmella.

"That would be great," she said, pushing herself out of the rocking chair with a grunt. "Y'all want to come inside?"

Toby looked at me with wide eyes. We weren't supposed to go in anybody's house unless we knew them real good. But Carmella seemed okay to me.

"Sure," I said. "Come on, Toby." I pulled on Toby's T-shirt.

When we got inside, I looked around to see if

Carmella's house was really as bad as it had looked from out on the porch. It was. A big lumpy couch covered with a bedspread and piled with clothes and newspapers. A coffee table littered with soda cans and dirty dishes. A card table with a half-finished jigsaw puzzle. Shelves built into the wall were jammed with ratty-looking books, piles of papers, an empty fish tank, and a bowling trophy. Instead of the rose-covered carpet I had pictured, the wooden floors were bare and worn. And nearly everywhere I looked there was a dog toy, all chewed up and loved. That almost broke my heart and made me tell that lady Carmella everything. But, of course, I didn't. My head was swimming with so many mixed-up thoughts I couldn't get myself to say *anything*.

Carmella shuffled over to a cluttered desk and rummaged through a drawer, then pulled out some paper. She took a red marker out of a mason jar on the desk and stared down at the paper.

"What should I say?" she said.

"How about 'Lost. Little black-and-white dog named Willy,' " I said.

"And then put 'Reward,' " Toby said.

Dern. How come he had to go and say that? I was going to ease into that part, but it was too late now.

"Reward?" Carmella looked kind of confused.

I jumped in there before Toby could. "Uh, yeah," I

said. "That's a good idea. You know, just to make sure people notice and stuff."

"You mean, like, *money*?" Carmella stared down at the paper on the desk.

"Yeah, money," Toby said.

I shot him a look. I wished he'd hush up and let me do the talking.

"Yeah, money," I said. "That would make folks try real hard to find Willy."

"Gosh," Carmella said, "I don't know." She pressed her lips together and kept staring down at the paper on the desk. Then she looked up at me and Toby. "How *much* money?" she said.

"Five hundred dollars," Toby blurted out.

"Five hundred dollars!" Carmella kind of swayed a little bit like she was going to fall right over. "I haven't got *that* kind of money."

"You don't?" I said.

She shook her head.

"Then how much reward *could* you pay?" I said.

"Well, I was thinking maybe, like, fifty dollars?"

*Fifty dollars?* That wasn't nearly enough. I felt Toby watching me. My mind was racing. But before I could think of what to say, Carmella sank down onto the lumpy couch with a whoosh. Then she shook her head and said, "I guess that's not very much, huh?"

"Well, um, maybe you could get some more," I said.

Carmella looked down at her lap. Little beads of sweat formed on her upper lip.

"I could ask for some extra hours at work," she said. "But that won't help much." Then she snapped her fingers. "I know what! I'll see if I can borrow some money from Gertie."

"Yeah," Toby said. Then he added, "Who's Gertie?"

"My sister."

"Is she the one who owns this street?" I said.

Carmella chuckled. "Lord, no," she said. "She teaches school over in Fayetteville."

"Then who owns this street?" I said. "Your daddy or somebody?"

"What do you mean 'owns this street'?" Carmella frowned at me.

"I just figured since your last name is Whitmore and . . ."

"Oh!" Carmella said. "You mean 'cause this is Whitmore Road?"

I nodded.

Carmella shook her head. "My great-granddaddy owned all this land one time." She swept her arm out toward the window.

"He built this house with his very own hands. Brick by brick," she said. "And had a big ole farm that went way on out there past the highway."

I looked out the window toward the highway. A bad feeling was starting to fall over me. Maybe I'd gotten this whole thing wrong. Maybe Carmella wasn't rich after all.

"What happened to the farm?" I said.

"My granddaddy tried to keep it up, but it just got away from him," she said. "I guess he wasn't much of a farmer." She shook her head as she gazed out the window. "By the time my daddy got this house," she went on, "the only thing left of the family farm was this little ole yard and our name on a street sign."

"Maybe your daddy could give you some money," I said.

"He died eight years ago," Carmella said. "And my mama the year after that. Then Gertie moved away." She looked down at the picture of Willy she was still holding. "All I got is Willy," she said.

With that, she started crying again, and I was feeling so heavy it's a wonder I didn't sink right through the floor.

Suddenly Carmella sat up straight and snapped her fingers.

"You know what?" she said.

Me and Toby waited.

"I *am* gonna call Gertie and borrow some money," she said. "Shoot, I'd pay a million dollars to get Willy back if I had it."

"A million dollars!" Toby said.

She nodded. "Yep." Then she added, "If I had it."

So me and Toby watched her make the first sign:

LOST. LITTLE BLACK-AND-WHITE DOG NAMED WILLY.

$500 REWARD.

I pressed my lips together hard to stop myself from smiling when she wrote that *$500* on there.

This sure was working out good, I thought.

Then we all sat around the coffee table, making more signs. When we had a bunch, Carmella said, "There. That oughtta do it."

"You want me and Toby to put some up now?" I said.

Carmella frowned down at the signs in her hand. "Well, I kind of feel like I ought to wait till I have the money, you know?"

"How long is that gonna be?"

"Not long, I hope," she said. "I'll call Gertie tonight." She looked down at a dog toy on the floor. A chewed-up rubber slipper. She wheezed a little bit as she bent to pick it up.

"I think I'll go drive around some more," she said, turning the slipper over and over on her lap. "I can't hardly stand to think about another night without Willy."

"We'll come back tomorrow, okay?" I said.

Carmella nodded. "Okay."

Me and Toby watched Carmella drive away, then raced back to our car to get some food scraps for Willy. I put a biscuit and half a grilled cheese sandwich in a grocery bag, then rummaged through the stuff in the trunk till I found a towel for Willy's bed.

"Okay," I said. "Let's go."

Willy sure was glad to see us. He wagged and yipped and carried on. When we got up on the porch, he jumped all over us, licking our faces and all.

When I opened the grocery bag with the scraps, he like to went crazy. He gulped everything down, then licked that bag till there wasn't one little crumb left.

I put my arm around him and laid my head on top of his.

"I promise I'm gonna take you home, okay?" I said. I pulled him onto my lap and stroked his back. He laid his head on my knee and sighed.

"He looks kind of sad," Toby said.

I looked down at Willy. "Don't be sad, little fella," I said.

He lifted his doggie eyebrows, and I could see what he was thinking right there on his face. Then the tears that I'd been trying to hold back for so long came spilling out.

"What's the matter, Georgina?" Toby said.

How could I answer that? Should I start with that big red F at the top of my science test today? Or should I just jump right on into how mean our daddy was to leave us in this mess? And then should I move on to how bad it felt to live in a car while my best friend went to ballet school with somebody better than me? Then I could add the part about Willy. How here we were with this cute little dog who never hurt anybody and now he was all sad and probably scared, too? And then there was Carmella, crying and missing her dog so much? And right in the middle of this sorry mess was me, the sorri-est person there ever was.

When Mama got off work that night, we drove over to Wal-Mart. I waited in the car while her and Toby went inside. I pulled out my notebook and read my notes on *How to Steal a Dog*.

It sure sounded easy when I read through it. I turned to a fresh page and wrote: *April 20*.

> *Step 6: When you find some signs about the lost dog, take him back to his owner, get the money, and you are done.*
> *BUT*

I drew a big circle around the word *BUT*. Then I wrote:

> *If there are no signs, you will have to find the owner of the dog and help them make some signs.*

*While you are doing that, you will have to practice look-ing nice and not like a dog thief.*

*Remember to take real good care of the dog so he won't be hungry or sad or anything.*
*THEN*

I circled the word *THEN* and under that I wrote:

*You will have to wait and see what happens next.*

I stared down at my notes. I read the last sentence out loud.

After thinking and worrying half the night, I decided that's what I'd do, just wait and see what happened next.

# 13

I don't know what made me do it. I just couldn't stop myself. I watched Toby walk down the hall and into his classroom, and then I turned and went right back out the front door. I hurried up the sidewalk and ducked around the side of the school building. When the buses pulled away from the curb and all the kids had gone inside, I started running and didn't stop till I was way on up toward the highway. My backpack bounced against me as I hurried along the side of the road.

I had to see Willy. I just had to.

I turned down the gravel road that led to the old house. I kept my mind on what I had to do (see Willy) instead of what I had just done (hightailed it out of school).

When I got to the house, I took my backpack off and tossed it on the front porch. Then I pushed through the pricker bushes toward the back of the house. Just as I reached the corner, I heard something that made me stop in my tracks. *Singing.* Somebody was in back of the house, singing!

I jumped into the bushes and ducked down, my heart pounding like nobody's business.

The singing stopped. I held my breath. A man's voice called out, "Are you scared of me or should I be scared of you?"

I knelt in the damp earth and squeezed my eyes shut. My thoughts were jumping around between being scared and trying to figure out what to do. Maybe I could crawl through the thick brush and back out to the road. I pushed a branch aside and flinched when the sound of rustling leaves broke the silence. Willy let out a bark.

"I ain't scared of a coward who won't even show his face," the man called out toward the bushes.

I lifted my head the tiniest little bit to peer through the leaves. A man was sitting on a log beside the back porch! I ducked down. I tried to crawl away from the house toward the path to the road, but a tangle of wild blackberry bushes blocked the way.

"This your dog?" the man called.

I scrambled to think what to do. Should I jump up and run? Should I call out something?

"Me and this dog are just sittin' here sharing sardines," the man said. "You want some?"

I pushed some branches down and peered out. Sure enough, there was Willy, sitting on the bottom step of the porch, licking a paper plate. The man stood up and walked a few steps in my direction. I ducked back down.

"I reckon you and me must think alike," he called toward the bushes. "Never drop your gun to hug a grizzly bear, I always say."

I crawled a few feet along the ground, trying to get a better view of the man.

"But you don't have to worry, 'cause I ain't no grizzly," he said. "You think this little ole dog here would eat sardines with a grizzly?"

Then for the second time that day, I just up and did something without thinking. I stood up, pulled the branches aside, and said, "His name is Willy."

The man looked in my direction. "Well now, I do declare," he said. "I sure am glad you ain't a grizzly, neither."

I stepped out of the bushes and Willy started wagging his tail and kind of prancing with his front legs. The man chuckled.

"Now *that's* some tail waggin' if I ever saw it," he said.

Part of me was saying, *Georgina, stop what you're doing and get on out of here.* But I never was too good at listening to my own self, so I just stood there and checked things out.

The man had nailed one end of a blue tarp to the side of the house and tied the other end to a tree to make a shelter. A ratty sleeping bag was stretched out on the ground beneath it. Leaning against the porch was a rusty old bicycle with a wooden crate strapped on the back. An American flag dangled from the end of a long, skinny pole duct-taped to the crate.

The man gestured toward the bike.

"Easy to park and don't need gas," he said.

He grinned and I caught a glimpse of a shiny gold tooth right in the front. When he gave Willy a pat on the head, I noticed he had two fingers missing. I'd never seen anybody with two fingers missing before.

He must have seen me staring at his hand, 'cause he said, "Got in a tussle with a tractor engine one time." He wiggled his three fingers at me. "Tractor won," he said.

I blushed and looked away.

"My name's Mookie," the man said, tipping his greasy baseball hat.

"*Mookie?*"

He grinned again. "Real name's Malcolm Green-bush, but my mama called me Mookie when I was just a little thing and I been Mookie ever since."

"Oh."

"You got a name?"

"Georgina," I said. "Georgina Hayes."

He stuck out that three-fingered hand of his for me to shake. I confess I didn't feel too good about shaking a three-fingered hand, but I did it anyways.

"I don't mean to go prying into your business, Miss Georgina," Mookie said. "But how come you got your little dog all holed up here in this old house?"

Uh-oh. I hadn't been ready for *that* question. I had to think fast.

" 'Cause we got a new landlord and he says we can't have a dog anymore, so my mama is looking for a new place where we *can* keep a dog, so I'm keeping him here till she finds one," I said. There. That sounded pretty good.

Mookie's bushy eyebrows shot up. "That so?" he said.

"Yessir."

"Well, I can tell you that dog was hungry enough to eat the south end of a northbound skunk."

I looked at Willy. He sat on the step and pawed the air with one of his little paws. Then he yawned, curling up his little pink tongue. I sat beside him and pulled him onto my lap.

"I bring him stuff to eat every day," I said.

"That so?"

Something about the way he said "That so?" made me squirm.

"Except today," I said. "Today I forgot."

"Well then, it's a good thing I had them sardines." Mookie gathered up the paper plate and empty cans and put them in a plastic grocery bag. Then he turned to me and said, "Ain't it?"

I felt squirmy again. "Yessir."

"Seems kind of a shame to keep a little dog like that tied up all the time."

I looked down at Willy and ran my hand along his back. "You wanna run a little bit, fella?" I said.

His head shot up off my lap and he whined.

Mookie chuckled. "I think that's a 'yes,' " he said.

I untied the string leash from the back porch, and Willy leaped off the steps, jumping up on me and yipping like crazy. I took him around to the gravel road, and off we went. Willy looked like he was ready to bust wide open with the pure joy of running. We raced up and down the road a few times till I finally collapsed right there in the dirt, gasping for breath. Willy sat beside me, panting.

"I don't know which he needed more," Mookie called from the side of the house. "Them sardines or that run."

I pulled Willy onto my lap and put my arm around him. He licked my face and then nudged me with his nose.

Mookie strolled out to the road where me and Willy were sitting. "He sure is a smart little fella," he said. "You had him long?"

"Uh, kind of."

"Guess it's pretty easy to love a dog like that." Mookie picked up a piece of gravel and hurled it into the trees. A loud thwack echoed through the woods.

"I bet you miss him a lot," he said. "I mean, you know, not having him in that apartment of yours."

I nodded, stroking Willy's head and trying to keep

my face from looking as squirmy as my insides were feeling.

Mookie hurled another rock into the woods. "I had
me a dog when I was a boy," he said.

"What kind?"

"Oh, just a little ole half-breed," he said. "Uglier
than homemade soap, that dog was. And dumb? My
daddy used to say he didn't have both oars in the water."
He chuckled. "But, lawd, me and him was closer than
white on rice." He shook his head. "I sure did love that
dog."

He reached down and scratched the top of Willy's
head. Willy gave Mookie one of those doggie smiles
of his.

"Dogs are just like family, ain't they?" Mookie said.

I looked at Willy, and no matter how hard I tried
not to, I kept seeing Carmella's sad face and hearing
Carmella's heartbroken voice.

I stood up and brushed the dirt off my jeans.

"Where do you live?" I said.

"Yesterday, today, or next Thursday?" Mookie
grinned, making his gold tooth glitter in the sunlight.

"Well, um, yesterday, I guess."

"Over there." He jerked his head and kind of rolled
his eyes.

"Over where?"

"Over there where I was."

"In a house?"

"A house?" he said real loud, like I was crazy to ask that. "Naw."

"Then where?"

He opened his arms wide and said, "Out here. Outside."

"Outside?"

Mookie nodded. "Yep."

"How come?"

" 'Cause I don't have to paint the air or tar-paper the sky or mop the ground. All I got to do is breathe."

"That's stupid," I said.

Mookie chuckled.

"I better go," I said, leading Willy up the path to the back of the house. Mookie followed along behind us, whistling. I took Willy up to the back porch and tied his leash to the doorknob.

"How long are you staying here?" I said.

"Not long," he said. "I leave my feet in one place too long, they start growing roots."

"Oh." I gave Willy one last pat on the head. "Then, bye." I made my way down the rickety steps. "And thanks for the sardines. For Willy, I mean."

Mookie tipped his hat. "My pleasure."

As I pushed through the bushes toward the front of the house, I had an uneasy feeling. My worries seemed to be piling up, one on top of the other, like bricks on a wall.

I waited in the car until it was time to go back to

school and get Toby. All afternoon, I tried to concentrate on what I had to do next. I went over my *How to
Steal a Dog* notes in my mind and thought about how
good I'd done so far.

I *had* done good, hadn't I? I mean, I'd found the perfect dog. I'd stolen him. I'd put him in a good place
where he was safe. Now all I had to do was wait for
Carmella to get the reward money. I bet by the time me
and Toby got over to Carmella's, she'd have money, and
then I could just move on to the last step in my dog-
stealing plan.

Shoot, I bet me and Toby and Mama would be in our
nice new apartment just about any day now.

# 14

Carmella twisted a damp tissue around and around in her lap. Every now and then, she dabbed at her nose.

"I can't hardly stand to face the day anymore," she said. "I couldn't even go to work today."

"How come?" Toby said.

I gave him a nudge with my knee. We sat squeezed together between piles of junk on Carmella's couch. The window shades were drawn. Tiny sparkles of dust danced in a narrow beam of sunlight that slanted across the dark room.

Carmella shook her head. "Gertie says she hasn't got that kind of money, but I know she does."

"Why won't she give it to you?" I said.

" 'Cause she's selfish, that's why."

I watched a fly land on a greasy pizza box on the coffee table. "That's mean," I said.

"She never did like dogs." Carmella blew her nose and waved her hand at the fly.

"What are you gonna do?" I said.

Carmella flopped back against the pillow tucked behind her in the chair. She propped her feet up on a ripped vinyl footstool and rested her hands on her stomach. Then she closed her eyes and made weird little moaning noises.

Toby twirled his finger around his ear, making a sign like Carmella was crazy. I frowned at him and shook my head.

"What are you gonna do?" I repeated a little louder.

Carmella shook her head, making her ripply chin jiggle like Jell-O.

"I just wanna die," she said.

Toby clamped his hand over his mouth like he was trying to stifle a laugh, but I didn't see what was so funny.

"You can't die," I said. "Willy needs you."

Carmella's eyes popped open. She sat up straight and slapped her knee.

"You're right," she said. "Willy *does* need me."

I grinned. "So, what're you gonna do?"

"I'm gonna put those signs up, that's what I'm gonna do," she said.

"The reward signs?" Toby said.

She nodded. "Yep."

"But what about the money?" I said. "Where are you gonna get the money?"

"I'll just be like Scarlett O'Hara," Carmella said.

"Who's that?" Toby said.

"You know, from *Gone With the Wind*?"

I guess me and Toby looked confused, 'cause she went on to explain about Scarlett O'Hara. About how she was this lady in a movie who said "fiddle-dee-dee" and who worried about things tomorrow instead of today.

Then Carmella pushed herself up out of the chair and shuffled over to a rickety card table.

"Will y'all help me put these signs up?" She waved a stack of papers at us. "I made copies with Willy's picture." She smiled down at the signs in her hand.

Toby looked at me and when I said, "Sure," he said, "Sure."

Carmella gave us a little box of tacks and then grabbed her purse and car keys.

"Come on," she said. "Let's go."

Carmella drove, and me and Toby jumped out at every corner to tack a sign up. Toby was scared Mama was gonna see us when we got near the coffee shop, but I told him to hush up and stop worrying. Of course, I knew he was right. She *might* see us. But I had so many other things weighing me down that I didn't have room in my worried mind for Mama. With every sign I put up, that question that I'd been trying to push away kept popping back at me. The question was this: *What in the world are you doing, Georgina?*

By the time we were done, it seemed like there wasn't one street in Darby that didn't have a sign tacked up somewhere. On nearly every corner, Willy's face gazed out at the world with his head cocked in that adorable way of his. It like to broke my heart to look at it.

"I feel better already," Carmella said when we turned onto Whitmore Road and into her driveway. "I have this feeling in my bones that my little Willy is gonna be coming home any minute now."

"But what about the money?" I said.

Carmella flapped her hand at me. "Oh, fiddle-dee-dee," she said. "I'll worry about that tomorrow."

When Mama got off work that night, she drove us over to the Pizza Hut and told us to go on in and wash up. Then we sat in the parking lot and ate corned beef sandwiches and dill pickles. Mama seemed real happy and excited, going on and on about how she's making all kinds of money. She showed me and Toby an envelope stuffed with dollar bills.

"I'm stashing this under the spare tire in the trunk," she said. "But it's just for emergencies, okay?"

"Is that enough to pay for an apartment?" I said, pulling the fat off my corned beef and tucking it into a napkin for Willy.

"Not quite," she said. "But it won't be long now."

"How long?" I popped a piece of chewing gum in my mouth.

"Not long," Mama said.

"*How* long?"

"Not long," Mama said in a mean voice.

"Yeah, right." I rolled my eyes and pulled chewing gum in a long, stretchy string out of my mouth.

Mama whipped around to face me. I stuck my chin up and looked her square in the eye, twirling my gum around like a jump rope.

She turned back around and slumped low in the front seat.

Toby licked his fingers with smacking sounds and said, "Maybe me and Georgina can get some money."

I like to swallowed my gum when he said that.

Mama looked at him and smiled that real sweet smile like she always seems to have for him but never for me.

"Now, how in the world would you and Georgina get money, sweetheart?" she said.

*Here it comes*, I thought. I knew Toby was gonna mess up sooner or later. I braced myself for what was going to come next, waiting for Toby to tell Mama about Willy and Carmella and all. I tried to give him the evil eye, but he wouldn't look at me.

"I don't know," he said. "Maybe we could find some."

Mama chuckled. "Wouldn't that be nice?"

"Yeah, Toby," I said. "Be sure and let us know when you find a million dollars on the sidewalk, okay?"

Mama shot me a look, but Toby grinned and said, "Okay."

We finished up our supper, and then Mama drove around looking for a place to park for the night. The car was chugging and rattling and jerking like crazy, but she acted like she didn't even notice.

As we pulled into the parking lot of the Motel 6, I spotted one of Carmella's signs. Suddenly that greasy corned beef in my stomach didn't set too well. I lay down on the seat and curled into a ball. Then I closed my eyes and pretended to be asleep.

Later on, after Mama and Toby had fallen asleep, I pulled out my *How to Steal a Dog* notes. I read through every page. When I got to the part that said: *You will have to wait and see what happens next*, I got out my colored pencils and drew little flowers and hearts all around the edge of the page. Then I used a sky blue pencil to write again:

*You will have to wait and see what happens next.*

I looked out the window at the Motel 6. Inside the lobby, a man was watching TV and sipping from a coffee mug. A soda machine outside the door sent a flickering red glow across the parking lot.

I wished we could've got a room there. Just for one

night. We could stretch out on a real bed. Take a bath in a real tub. Act like real people. We didn't have school to-morrow, so we could spend all day watching TV and stuff. But Mama had said no.

I looked over at Toby, curled up on the backseat with his head propped against the door. I hadn't told him about Mookie yet. I knew he'd get all scared and wor-ried. He'd say we weren't supposed to talk to strangers and Mama would kill us and stuff like that. And I guessed he would be right. But what choice did we have? We couldn't just forget about Willy, could we? We had to feed him and take care of him. Besides, Mookie was probably gone by now. Toby wouldn't ever even know he'd been there.

I closed my notebook and stuffed it back down inside my bag. Then I lay down on the car seat and closed my eyes. No sense worrying about Mookie tonight, was there? I could worry about him tomorrow.

# 15

"Okay, now listen, Toby." I took him by the shoulders and looked him straight in the eye. Then I gave him a little shake just to make sure I had his attention.

"There might be a man back there with Willy." I jerked my head in the direction of the old house.

Toby's eyes got wide. "Who?" he said.

"A man named Mookie."

"A man named Mookie?"

I nodded. "But it's okay," I said. "He's nice. He gave Willy some sardines."

"What's he doing back there?

I shrugged. "Just, like, kinda living there, I guess."

Toby glanced nervously at the house. "How'd he get in?"

"Not *inside*," I said. "He's living *outside*. Out in the back where Willy is."

"You mean like a bum?"

I kept my hands on Toby's shoulders and made him

face me so he'd pay attention. "Look, Toby," I said. "He's liable to be gone. But just in case he's there, don't be scared, okay?"

"Okay."

I dropped my hands from Toby's shoulders and started toward the house.

"Hey, wait a minute," Toby said, grabbing the back of my T-shirt. "How do *you* know about that man named Mookie?" He stamped his foot on the gravel road. "You came here without me."

"I had to," I said.

"When?"

"Yesterday."

"Yesterday?"

I put my arm around him and gave him a little jiggle. "Look, Toby, I just did it without thinking 'cause I needed to see Willy. I'm sorry, okay?"

Toby looked down at his feet. I jiggled him again.

"Okay?" I said.

Finally, in a little tiny voice, he said, "Okay."

"I won't do it ever again."

"Pinkie promise?" he said.

I crooked my pinkie at him. "Pinkie promise."

We linked pinkies, then headed toward the house. I sure hoped Mookie was gone.

We hadn't even got to the corner of the house before Willy started barking.

"It's me," I called out, "Georgina."

"And Toby," Toby called from behind me.

When I rounded the corner, the first thing I saw was that blue tarp. Underneath it, Mookie was stretched out on top of his sleeping bag, his hands folded on his stomach and his hat over his face.

From over on the back steps, Willy wiggled his whole body and let out a bark like he was saying hello.

Mookie didn't move.

"Mookie," I said kind of soft-like so I wouldn't scare him.

Nothing.

"Mookie?" I said a little louder.

Still nothing.

"Is he dead?" Toby whispered.

Suddenly Mookie let out a snort and jumped, sending his hat flying and making me and Toby grab each other. Mookie slapped a hand over his heart and flopped back down on his sleeping bag.

"You like to scared the bessy bug outta me," he said.

"I brought Willy some stuff to eat," I said, wagging my paper bag in the air.

Mookie sat up and put his hat on. "Me and him's been havin' liver puddin'."

I wrinkled my nose. "What's that?"

"Liver puddin'?" Mookie rubbed his hand in a circle on his stomach. "Some good eatin', that's what. Right, Willy?"

Willy sat on the porch steps and lifted a paw.

Mookie chuckled. "That dog's got good taste." He nodded toward Toby. "Who's he?"

"My brother, Toby."

Mookie got up and held out his three-fingered hand toward Toby. I'd forgotten to warn Toby about that, but for once in his life, he didn't act like a scaredy baby. He shook Mookie's hand like he didn't even notice those missing fingers.

"It's a dern shame about that landlord of yours, ain't it?" Mookie said to Toby.

Toby looked at me and then back at Mookie. "Yessir, it is."

I felt relief flood over me. Toby wasn't going to say something stupid like he usually did.

"I bet y'all sure do miss your little dog, don't you?" Mookie said.

"We sure do," I said.

Toby nodded. "Yessir, we do."

Mookie rolled his sleeping bag up and stuffed it into the crate on the back of his bicycle. "Kinda hard to sleep around him, though, ain't it?"

I looked over at Willy. He looked back at me with his shiny little eyes and his eyebrows lifted up like he was curious as anything to hear what I was going to say.

I shrugged. "Sometimes," I said.

Mookie wiped a plastic coffee mug with his shirttail

and put it into a burlap bag. "He snore like that all the time?" he said.

"Not all the time."

Mookie chuckled and put a few more things inside his burlap bag. Then he tucked it into the crate beside the sleeping bag.

"Are you leaving?" I said. I sure hoped he was.

"Yep."

*Good*, I thought. Now I could concentrate on what I had to do.

Mookie pushed his bike toward the path leading out to the road.

"What about that?" I said, pointing up at the blue tarp.

"Oh, I'll be back," he said.

Me and Toby watched him disappear around the corner of the house. A few seconds later, the sound of gravelly singing echoed through the woods and faded away.

"Is he a bum?" Toby said.

"I don't know." I sat on the step beside Willy and let him root around inside the paper bag. He pulled out a chunk of bagel and gobbled it down.

"I bet he is," Toby said.

I stroked Willy's head while he ate the rest of the scraps I had brought him. (Except a slice of tomato. He just sniffed that.)

"Don't you think he's a bum?" Toby said.

"How should I know?" I snapped.

"I don't like him," Toby said. "He smells."

"So do you!" I hollered, making Willy jump off my lap and slink away like I'd just smacked him upside the head.

"So do you!" Toby hollered back.

Why was I being so mean to Toby? Maybe I figured if I was mean to Toby, I'd feel better about things. But I didn't.

"Let's go take Willy for a walk," I said.


The next day, Mama made Toby stay at the coffee shop and do his homework over in the corner booth by the kitchen. He had whined and carried on, but it hadn't done him a bit of good.

So now I was finally free to be by myself and figure things out. First, I had to visit Carmella and find out if she had gotten any money from her sister, Gertie.

I hurried up the sidewalk toward Whitmore Road. It seemed like the world had blossomed overnight. Bright pink azaleas. White dogwood. The air smelled sweet, like clover. I had the urge to take my shoes off and run barefoot across the soft green lawns. But I didn't.

When I got to Carmella's, I waited outside the gate. The yard was quiet. Not even any birds at the feeder. For a minute, I wished I could step back in time. Back to the day when Willy had come running around the side of the house, chasing that squirrel. Before I had done what I'd done. But I couldn't, so I made my feet go up on the porch and my hand knock on the screen door.

"Who is it?" Carmella called from inside.

"It's me. Georgina."

I heard her wheezy breathing as she came to unlatch the screen.

"Hey," I said.

"Hey."

I looked down at the floor and said, "Did anybody find Willy?"

Carmella shook her head and sank into her ratty old chair. The TV was on with no sound. One of those shopping shows where some lady tries to get you to buy a great big ring that's not even a real diamond. The lady wiggled her fingers around, making the fake diamond sparkle for the camera.

"What about Gertie?" I said.

Carmella shook her head again. "What am I going to do?" she said in this flat kind of voice that made me feel sort of scared.

I sat on the ottoman across from her. "What did Gertie say?"

"She says she hasn't got the money, but I know good and well she does." Carmella wiped her nose with her hand and stared at the TV. "She says I'm pathetic for getting all worked up over a dog."

"So what are you going to do?"

"I'm thinking I'll just go ahead and offer what I can."

"How much is that?"

Carmella sighed. "Oh, I don't know. Fifty dollars, maybe?"

My stomach went thunk.

"But you put five hundred dollars on all those signs," I said.

"I know." Carmella blew her nose. "Maybe whoever finds Willy won't care about money." She stuffed the tissue into her pocket. "I sure wouldn't," she said. "Would you?"

I shrugged. "Um, well, sort of. I mean, not really, but . . ."

With every word that came out of my mouth, I felt like I was digging myself into a hole, and if I didn't stop, I was going to be so far in I wouldn't ever climb out.

Me and Carmella stared at the TV in silence. Now that lady was dangling a shiny gold necklace in front of the camera. Her bright red lips were moving, and I tried to imagine what she was saying. But my mind was such a mixed-up mess that instead of imagining her saying how wonderful that necklace was, I heard her saying, "Georgina Hayes, what in the world are you doing? Have you lost your mind? You bring that little dog back here this instant."

I looked at Carmella and felt a stab. What in the world *was* I doing? Then suddenly Carmella leaned forward and said, "Will you do me a favor?"

"Sure."

"Will you and Toby go check those woods over there across the highway?"

"What woods?"

"Over yonder." She waved her arm toward the main highway. Toward the gravel road. Toward the old house.

"You'll probably think I'm plumb crazy," she said, "but sometimes I think I hear Willy barking from over there."

Thunk. There went my stomach again.

"Really?" I said.

"I drove around over that way yesterday," she said. "But I thought maybe you and Toby could look, too."

"Okay."

"Course, I think I hear Willy scampering around this house, too," Carmella said. "So I reckon it's just my crazy old mind playing tricks on me."

"Toby's doing homework at my mama's coffee shop," I said. "But I'll go look."

Carmella smiled. "I sure do appreciate everything y'all have done for me."

I shrugged. "That's okay." I started for the door. "Besides, maybe if we do find Willy, Gertie'll change her mind and give us five hundred dollars."

Carmella's smile dropped, and she looked like I'd just told her the sky had turned purple.

"What do you mean?" she said.

"Well, um, I mean, you know, the reward and all?"

"Oh." Carmella looked down at her hands and twisted a button on her shirt. "I guess I thought you and Toby were helping me 'cause you *wanted* to."

"We are," I said. "I mean, we *do* want to. I just thought . . ."

"But I will certainly do my best to make sure you get *paid* for your kindness." Carmella's chin was puckering up and she wouldn't look at me.

*Dern*, I thought. That hole I'd dug myself into was getting deeper by the minute.

# 16

As soon as I got to the house, I knew Mookie was back. First, I saw his bicycle propped against the bushes on the side. Then I caught a whiff of something cooking.

He looked up when I came around the corner.

"Hey there," he said.

"Hey." I went straight on over to Willy and gave him the bacon I'd brought.

"I'm glad you brought that," Mookie said. " 'Cause he's been eyeing my Hoover gravy like he was gonna eat it all and then me, too."

I squinted into the pan Mookie held over a small fire in a ring of rocks. A pale gray liquid bubbled and smoked in the pan.

"What *is* that?" I said.

"Hoover gravy," Mookie said. "Want some?"

"No, thanks."

I watched him dip a slice of bread into the watery liquid and eat it. Yuck.

"Where's Toby?" Mookie said.

"Doing his homework with my mom."

"Ain't you got homework?"

I sat on the steps and pulled Willy into my lap. "A little." I picked some burrs out of Willy's fur. "But I don't need help like Toby. He's not very smart."

Mookie sopped another piece of bread in the watery gravy. "Smart ain't got a thing to do with school," he said. "I never went past sixth grade, myself." He ate the soggy bread, then added, "And I'm pretty smart."

He licked his fingers. "Besides," he said, "if you ask me, school's about as useful as a trapdoor on a canoe."

"You can't get a job if you don't go to school," I said.

"Says who?"

"Says everybody."

"I work every day of my life," he said.

"Where?"

"Everywhere."

"Like where?" I said.

"Everywhere," he repeated.

I frowned down at Willy and ran my finger over the velvety fur on his nose. Mookie was crazy. Why was I even talking to him?

"Then how come you live like a bum?" I said. I felt my face burn. I shouldn't have said that.

But Mookie just laughed. "I said I worked. I didn't say I got paid."

"You work for free?"

"Sometimes." He took the pan off the fire and scooped dirt over the flames.

"How come?" I said.

He tied the end of the bread bag in a knot, then leaned back against his rolled-up sleeping bag.

"Why not?" he said.

"What kind of work do you do?"

"Whatever I come across that needs to be done," he said. "Might be fixing a roof. Might be painting. Might be digging ditches." He wiggled his three-fingered hand at me. "Might even be fixing tractor engines," he added.

"For free?"

"Sometimes yes. Sometimes no." He took a toothpick out of his shirt pocket and stuck it in the corner of his mouth.

"But why would you do that stuff for free?"

" 'Cause sometimes people need stuff done more than I need money," he said.

That sounded crazy, but I didn't say so. It looked to me like he could use some money.

Mookie took his baseball hat off and scratched his fuzzy gray hair. "Besides," he said, "I got a motto. You wanna hear it?"

I shrugged.

"Sometimes the trail you leave behind you is more important than the path ahead of you." He put his hat back on. "You got a motto?" he said.

I shook my head. "Nope."

He stuck his finger in the gravy. "Okay, little fella," he said to Willy. "It's cool enough for you now." He slid the pan toward the steps, and Willy ran down and lapped up the gravy. Clumps of gooey flour stuck to the bottom of the pan, and he licked them, too.

Then Mookie took me by surprise when he said, "Ain't your mama found you a new place to live yet?"

"Not yet," I said. "But she's working on it."

"You know, I saw the strangest thing today," Mookie said. "I saw a little ole sign with a dog looked just like yours."

I swear, when he said that, my heart sank right straight down to my feet.

"Like Willy?"

Mookie nodded. "Yep."

I couldn't even look at Mookie.

"And you know what was even stranger?" he said.

I swallowed hard and made myself say, "What?"

"That dog's name was Willy, too." Mookie grinned at me, flashing that gold tooth of his. "Ain't that some-thing?"

I looked down at Willy, still licking the pan. "Yessir," I said, surprised at how my voice came out so low and shaky.

Mookie switched the toothpick over to the other side of his mouth and chewed on it.

I looked down at the ground and traced circles in the

dirt with the toe of my shoe. I never thought I'd say it, but I wished I was back in our ratty old car, snuggled up in the backseat, hugging my pillow.

"I better go," I said, giving Willy a quick pat on the head. "Bye now."

I felt Mookie's eyes on me as I walked toward the side of the house. Just as I was about to round the corner, he called out, "Hey, Georgina . . ."

I stopped.

"I got another motto," he said. "You wanna hear it?" He didn't even wait for me to answer.

"Sometimes," he said, "the more you stir it, the worse it stinks."

I turned and hurried up the path to the road.

When I got back to the car, I took out my purple notebook. I slouched down and propped my feet up on the dashboard. I opened to *How to Steal a Dog*.

*April 25*, I wrote. *Step 7.*

I stared out the window, tapping the pencil against my teeth. I looked down at the paper and wrote:

*Remember*

I looked out the window again, then back at the paper.

I drew a box under the word *Remember*. Inside the box I wrote:

*Sometimes, the more you stir it, the worse it stinks.*

Then I closed my notebook, climbed into the back-seat, hugged my pillow, and waited for Mama and Toby.

# 17

I knew my day was going to be bad when Kirby Price called me a dirt bag in gym and everybody laughed. (Even Luanne. I saw her.) And then it got worse. When Mama got off work that night, the car wouldn't start. She turned the key and there was just one little click and then nothing.

"Well, that's just great," she said, pounding her fist on the steering wheel.

Me and Toby looked at each other, but we both knew better than to say anything.

She turned the key again. Click.

She flopped back against the seat and said a cuss word.

Toby giggled and I poked him to be quiet.

"My life just goes from bad to worse," Mama said.

Then she sat there staring out the window at the Chinese restaurant across the street. A family came out. A *real* family. A mom, a dad, two kids. They broke open their fortune cookies and read their fortunes out loud while they walked to their car. They all smiled and laughed and acted like they had the best life in the world. When they drove by us, they were still laughing. They didn't even look at us sitting in our car that wouldn't start. I wished I was one of those kids, eating my fortune cookie and laughing with my family.

Mama turned the key again. Click.

I stared out the window, praying that old car would start. And then I couldn't hardly believe my eyes. There was Mookie, pedaling his bike up the road toward us.

I ducked down real quick and motioned for Toby to get down, too. Naturally, he had to go, "What?" and sit there looking stupid. I grabbed his T-shirt and yanked him down.

Then I peeked out the window. Mookie had gone on past us and disappeared around the corner.

Mama turned the key again. Click.

I finally got up the courage to say, "What're we gonna do now?"

I held my breath, hoping she wasn't going to yell at me, 'cause I didn't need that after that dirt bag stuff at school.

Mama shook her head and let out a big whoosh of a sigh that blew her hair up off her forehead.

She turned the key again. Click.

"I guess we're sleeping here tonight," she said.

I looked around us at all the places where there were people who would see us. The Chinese restaurant. The Quiki Mart. The Chevron gas station.

"What if somebody sees us?" I said.

"Y'all go on over there to the gas station and wash up," Mama said. "I'm going in the Quiki Mart and get us something to eat."

I watched her run across the street, her jeans dragging on the ground.

"What if somebody sees us?" I hollered out the window. But Mama didn't even turn around.


The next morning Mama walked over to the coffee shop to get her friend Patsy to drive me and Toby to school. I like to died when I saw Patsy pull up beside our car, roll down her window, and say, "Come on, y'all."

She had a big poofy hairdo that stuck way up on top of her head and ugly sparkly earrings and a cigarette hanging out of her big red lips. Her car was rustier than ours, with bumper stickers all over the back. MY OTHER CAR'S A BROOM. HONK IF YOU LOVE JESUS. Stuff like that.

I climbed in the backseat and slouched down as low as I could. *Please don't let anybody see me*, I prayed. *Especially Kirby Price.*

Just before we got to school, Patsy said, "Look at that!"

Me and Toby looked where she was pointing.

There was Mookie, pedaling along the side of the road on that rusty ole bike of his, the little American flag waving in the breeze.

"I've seen that man all over town," Patsy said. "He sure looks happy, don't he?"

I slouched back down in the seat and turned my face away from the window. I sure wished Mookie would get on out of Darby instead of hanging around like he was.

"Imagine being that happy when all you got in the whole world is a beat-up old bicycle," Patsy said.

When we passed him, she waved out the window and hollered, "Hey."

Mookie tipped his hat.

After school, me and Toby had to walk back to the car. It took forever and Toby kept griping and hollering, "Wait up, Georgina."

Then he kept asking, "When are we gonna take Willy back to Carmella's?"

I pretended like I didn't hear him. Finally he grabbed my backpack and yanked.

"I *said*, when are we gonna take Willy back to Carmella's?"

I whirled around to face him. "I don't know, Toby, okay?"

I started off up the sidewalk again. Toby trotted along beside me.

"She's looking for him, Georgina," he said.

"I know."

"I bet Willy wants to go home."

"I know."

"Maybe Carmella has some money now. Maybe Gertie gave her some."

I stopped. "Look, Toby," I said. "I've got to figure this thing out. We went to all this trouble to steal that dog, so we might as well get some money out of it, right?"

Toby shrugged. "I guess."

"What do you mean, you guess?" I said. "That's the whole reason we got ourselves into this mess in the first place."

"What mess?"

I started walking again, but Toby grabbed my arm.

"What mess, Georgina?" he said. "Are we in trouble?"

"No, we're not in trouble."

"Then what mess?"

"Look, Toby," I said. "Carmella may not even get any money. If we take Willy back now, we probably won't get anything. But if we wait much longer, well, I don't know . . ."

"What'll happen if we wait much longer?" Toby said. "Georgina, is Carmella gonna call the police?"

"No."

"But what if she does?"

"So?"

"So, we might get arrested. We're kidnappers," Toby said.

"We are not."

"Well, *dog*nappers, then." Toby's face was puckering up like he was gonna cry. "What if we have to go to jail?" he said.

"Shut up, Toby. There's no such thing as dognappers." I hated it when Toby started thinking up stuff I should've thought of. Maybe we *were* dognappers. Maybe we *could* go to jail.

I pictured Willy's face on a milk carton. His head cocked and his ears perked up. "Have you seen me?" it would say underneath. And Carmella would be sitting there at the kitchen table with her Cheerios, looking at Willy and crying her eyes out.

"And what about Willy?" Toby interrupted my thoughts. "Think about him," he said. "I bet he's sadder than anything."

"Shut up, Toby," I said. I sure didn't need Toby heaping more bad feelings on top of me like that.

Neither one of us said another word as we made our way along Jackson Road toward the car. Toby kept on finding things on the ground and saying, "Hey, look what I found." A quarter. A cigarette lighter. A pencil.

Then, right before we got to the car, we came to one of those LOST DOG signs with Willy's cute little face smiling out at us. I shut my eyes until we were all the way past it, but I could still feel him looking at me.

When we finally saw the car, Toby darted ahead.

"Hey, look at that," he said, pointing to the ground.

I looked down at a shiny quarter nestled in the sandy roadside next to our car. And then I noticed something else. Tracks in the sand.

*Tire* tracks.

*Bicycle* tire tracks.

But Toby didn't seem to notice. He just grabbed that quarter like it was made out of gold.

I shuffled my feet in the sand, making those tire tracks disappear, then I unlocked the door and climbed in the backseat.

Me and Toby stayed in the car all afternoon, eating graham crackers with jelly and playing Crazy Eights. Toby kept asking me when we were gonna take Willy back to Carmella, but I didn't even answer him. I knew that was making him mad as all get-out, but too bad. I didn't want to talk about Willy and Carmella. I didn't even want to *think* about Willy and Carmella. I had this bad, bad feeling that I'd gotten myself into a mess. And it seemed like everything I did stirred that mess up more—stirred it up so much it was starting to stink.

# 18

By the time Mama got back to the car that night, Toby was asleep and I was finishing up my math homework.

"Hey," Mama said, tossing her purse on the seat and handing me a blueberry muffin.

"Me and Toby stayed here all afternoon like you told us to," I said, peeling the paper from the muffin and taking a bite. It was dry and crumbly, but it tasted good.

"I know that's hard on y'all, Georgina," Mama said. "I promise things will be better soon."

*Yeah, right,* I said in my head. *I've heard that before.*

But out loud I said, "Have you got enough money saved up yet?"

Mama sighed. "Well, I was doing real good until this dern car decided to up and die on us," she said. "I swear, when it rains, it pours."

"What're we gonna do now?" I said.

She dug through her purse and pulled her car keys out. "I'm trying to find somebody who can fix the car cheap," she said. "Patsy's nephew might take a look at it tomorrow."

She put the key in the ignition and turned it. But this time, instead of that click sound we'd been hearing, the engine whirred and whirred and then started with a roar.

Mama jerked her head around and grinned at me.

"It started!" she squealed.

Toby sat up and rubbed his eyes. "What happened?" he said.

I pumped my fist in the air and let out a whoop.

Mama clasped her hands together like she was praying and hollered up at the ceiling, "Hallelujah, praise the Lord!"

"The car started?" Toby said.

Me and Mama nodded at him and then we all slapped each other a high five.

Mama put the car in gear and pulled into the street. "Let's go find us a place to spend the night before our luck runs out and this thing dies again."

We drove through the streets of Darby, Mama humming, Toby snoozing, and me wrestling with all my crazy thoughts.

First there was Willy, tied up on that rotten old porch instead of curled up next to Carmella. Then there was Carmella, missing her little dog more than anything. And then there was Mookie. How come he kept popping into my swirling thoughts? I wasn't sure. But something about those bicycle tire tracks and this broken-down car starting up like it did had got me to thinking about Mookie. Mostly he just seemed like a crazy old man. But sometimes I wondered if maybe he wasn't as crazy as he seemed.

We spent that night on a dark, quiet street not far from Whitmore Road, which made me think so much about Carmella that I didn't sleep too good. I kept picturing her in my mind, tossing and turning in her bed. She'd probably get up a few times and make sure that little doggie door was open just in case Willy came back during the night. Maybe she'd shine her flashlight up and down the street, whistling and calling his name. She might even think she heard him barking from way off in the woods again and drive her car in that direction, hollering his name out the window. Then she'd come back home all alone and sit on the couch with one of his chewed-up toys in her lap.

When my mind started wandering over to that old house, where little Willy was curled up on that dirty, falling-apart porch, I sat up in the backseat and looked out the window at the moths fluttering around a nearby streetlight. The air smelled sweet, like honeysuckle. I could hear the sound of a creek nearby—that even, ripply sound of water. Every now and then, a bullfrog croaked.

Those noises reminded me of the time me and Luanne camped out in her backyard. We had shined our flashlights up on the ceiling of the tent and told each other our secrets. Which boys we liked. How many kids we wanted when we got married. Stuff like that.

Then Luanne had said we had to tell each other the worst thing we had ever done. She told me how one time her mom had knitted her a sweater and she had hated it so much she threw it in the garbage. Then she told her mom she had left it on the school bus.

When it was my turn, I had told Luanne about the time I wrote a nasty word on my desk at school. When my teacher saw it and hollered at me, I told her Emily Markham had done it. Emily had cried so hard she got an asthma attack and had to go home.

That was it. That was the worst thing I'd ever done.

But not anymore. If Luanne and I camped out and shared our secrets now, I'd have to tell her I had stolen a dog. What would she think about that, I wondered.

I fell asleep that night to the soothing sound of the creek, flowing over rocks and winding through the dark woods somewhere outside the car window.


The next day after school, I went straight on over to Carmella's. Toby had to study for his spelling test at the coffee shop. Mama thought I was trying out for the softball team like Luanne and Liza and everybody. I knew I shouldn't be lying to Mama, but I had to. I needed to find out if Carmella had gotten any money yet.

When I got up on the porch, I could hear Carmella inside yelling.

"Yeah, well, thanks a lot, Gertie." Then there was the bang of the phone slamming down. Hard.

"Carmella?" I called through the screen door.

I heard her shuffling up the hall.

"It's me. Georgina." I squinted through the screen into the dark room. Carmella was standing there with her arms dangling limply at her sides and her hair hanging over her face.

"Carmella?"

She lifted her head real slow and looked at me. Her face was all red and splotchy.

I pushed the screen door open and stuck my head in.

"Can I come in?" I said.

She nodded.

I stepped inside. The house smelled like rotten food or something.

"What's the matter?" I said.

Carmella made her way over to her easy chair and dropped into it with a grunt. Her hair was damp with sweat, sticking to her splotchy cheeks.

"I came home from work early just so I could call Gertie," she said. "I should've known better. She just flat out won't lend me any money."

"Oh."

"I guess she don't remember that time I kept her

kids while she was in the hospital," she said. "Or that time I drove clear out to Gatesville in the middle of the night when her car broke down."

She took a magazine off the pile on the coffee table and fanned herself.

"I guess being sisters don't mean nothing," she said.

"So what're you gonna do?"

She threw her hands up and let them fall on her knees with a slap. "Nothing I can do. If somebody brings Willy home, I'll just have to—hey, wait a minute." She snapped her fingers and grinned at me.

"What?" I said.

"I know who'll lend me money," she said.

"Who?"

"My uncle Haywood."

She pushed herself up out of the chair and went over to the desk. She took a beat-up address book out of the drawer and flipped through the pages.

"There!" She jabbed a finger at the page. "Uncle Haywood. I'm gonna call him."

And so she did. Called her uncle Haywood and told him the whole pitiful story. I'd lived every minute of it, but it like to broke my heart hearing about it like that. When she finished, she said, "Yessir," and "No, sir," and "I will."

By the time she had hung up, she was grinning at me and clapping her hands.

"Is he gonna lend you the money?" I said.

"He sure is." Carmella pushed the damp hair away from her face. "Now all I have to do is hope and pray somebody brings my Willy home," she said.

Suddenly her smile drooped and her eyebrows squeezed together. "Do you think he's okay?"

"Who?"

"Willy," she said. "Do you think Willy's okay?"

"Sure," I said.

"Really?"

I nodded.

Carmella looked out the window. "I hope you're right," she said.

"I bet he's trying to find his way home right now," I said.

Carmella kept staring out the window. "I wonder where he is," she said.

I felt my face burning. I was glad Carmella wasn't looking at me.

"I bet he's, um, oh, probably . . ."

"I hope he's not scared," Carmella said.

I shook my head. "Naw, he's not scared. I mean, I bet he isn't."

"You know, like I said before, if I had a million dollars, I'd give every penny of it away just to get Willy back." She nodded at me. "I really would," she added.

I looked down at the dusty wooden floor.

"Did you get a chance to check those woods over

there?" Carmella said, jerking her head toward the window.

"Um, yeah, a little," I said. "I mean, me and Toby looked in there some but . . ."

"Did you call his name?" Carmella said. "And whistle?"

"Um, sure we did," I said. "We called and called and . . ."

"Georgina." Carmella put her hand on my shoulder. "I'll give you that five hundred dollars and anything else you want if you find him."

I nodded, but I couldn't make myself say anything. I knew if there was ever a time for me to say, "Carmella, I know where Willy is," this was it.

But I didn't.

And I knew my silence was like stirring.

And the more I was stirring, the worse it was stinking.

# 19

I stared up at the stained ceiling tiles of the school nurse's office, trying to make my stomach settle down. For once, I hadn't lied to Mr. White. I really did have a stomachache. I'd had one ever since I'd left Carmella's yesterday.

I had left her house and gone on back to the car. I knew I should've gone over there and taken care of Willy, but I didn't. I guess I was hoping Mookie would share his liver puddin' again.

When Mama and Toby came back, I pretended like I was doing my homework, but I wasn't. I was writing one word over and over, like this:

*Willywillywillywillywillywilly*

And then after Mama fell asleep, I didn't tell Toby that Carmella was getting the reward money from her uncle Haywood. I didn't say that now it was time to take Willy back and get that money. I kept it all inside me where my aching stomach was.

Finally, I took out my *How to Steal a Dog* notes. I read all the way through them, starting with *Step 1: Find a Dog* and ending with *Step 7* and the part about stirring and stinking.

I turned to a clean page and wrote: *April 28*. Then I added:

*Step 8: If you want to, you can take the dog back and tell the owner that you don't want the reward money after all. Here is what will happen if you decide to do that:*

*1. The owner will be really happy and she can give the money back to her uncle Haywood.*

*2. The dog will be happy because he is back home where he belongs instead of on that nasty porch.*

*3. You will be happy because you won't feel bad about stealing a dog, even though you still live in a car.*

*4. When you stop stirring, it will stop stinking.*

*Or*

*You can take the dog back and*
*get the reward money like you planned.*

*THAT*

*is the decision you will have to make.*

I drew tiny little paw prints all around the edges of the page before I closed my notebook and put it away.

And now here I was in the nurse's office, staring up at those ceiling tiles with my stomach aching like anything.

When the bell rang, I told the nurse I felt much better (even though I didn't), and I made my way through the pushing, shoving kids in the hall. Outside, I found Toby, and we headed over to the old house.

The whole way there, Toby kept jabbering on and on about stupid stuff. Like how his teacher had hollered at him for doing math with a pen and how some kid's gerbil got loose and went under the radiator. As usual, he was lagging behind, but I hurried on ahead. I needed to get to Willy fast. I needed to snatch him up and hug him, and then maybe my stomachache would go away.

As we hurried up the gravel road, my thoughts turned to Mookie. I sure hoped he was gone. I didn't need his crazy talk that made me feel so squirmy all the time.

When we got to the house, I left my backpack by the road and pushed my way through the bushes toward the back. I rounded the corner, and the first thing I noticed was that Mookie's big blue tarp was gone. The little clearing where his sleeping bag had been was empty. Just a pile of blackened wood and an empty soda can.

Then suddenly it hit me. Silence. Total silence. No happy little hello bark from Willy. I ran over to the back porch and yanked open the rickety screen door and wanted to die right then and there.

Willy was gone.

I must've looked like a crazy person, racing around that little dirt yard, pushing aside the weeds and bushes and hollering Willy's name. Toby kept saying, "What's wrong, Georgina?" and "What happened, Georgina?" Then he started bawling about Willy being gone, and I hollered at him to shut up.

I ran to the edge of the woods and called Willy's name till my throat ached. The quiet that came back to me felt solid and mean, like a slap across the face.

I hurried back out to the road, not even caring about the briars that were snagging my clothes and scratching my arms. I ran up one side of the road and down the other, peering through the trees and calling Willy's name.

Finally, I stopped and held my aching sides, trying to catch my breath. Then I felt Toby punch me in the arm.

"Willy's gone!" he hollered. "And it's all your fault." He looked all wild-eyed and scared.

"*My* fault?"

"Yeah." Toby stomped back up the road toward the house. I ran after him and yanked the back of his T-shirt to make him stop.

"It's *Mookie's* fault," I said. "*He* took Willy. I know he did."

Toby's eyebrows squeezed together. "Mookie took Willy?"

I nodded. "I bet anything he did," I said. "He's crazy."

"What're we gonna do?"

I sat on the side of the road and put my head down

on my knees. What *were* we gonna do? I didn't have one single idea. Then, just when I was wishing that gravel road would open up and swallow me whole, I heard the chinga-chinga of a bicycle bell.

I looked up and saw the best sight I'd ever seen in all my born days. Mookie was pedaling his rusty old bicycle up the road toward us. And trotting along beside him was Willy, his string leash tied to the handlebars of the bike.

I jumped up and raced toward them.

Mookie stopped the bike and I scooped Willy up in my arms and buried my face in his warm fur. Then I felt a wave of mad sweep over me.

"Why'd you take Willy?" I hollered at Mookie.

"Take Willy?" Mookie's eyebrows shot up. "Well, if that don't put pepper in the gumbo," he said.

"What's that mean?" I glared at him. I wasn't in the mood for his crazy talk.

"Means you better slow your mouth down before you start coming out with such as that," he said.

I pressed my face against Willy. His hair was all matted with mud, and he smelled awful.

"For your information, missy," Mookie said, "I was clear on over there by the shopping center when that dog of yours come running up behind me."

"Oh," I said. I knew I should've said more. I should've said, "I'm sorry."

I should've said, "This dog's not mine."

I should've said, "I stole this dog, but now I'm gonna take him back."

I finally managed to lift my head and look at Mookie.

"Then thanks for bringing him back," I said.

I wanted Mookie to say, "That's okay." But he didn't. He just nodded.

I'd forgotten all about Toby until he suddenly said to Mookie, "Are you leaving?"

Mookie nodded again. "I am," he said.

He untied Willy's string leash and tossed it to me. Then he turned his bike around and pedaled off up the road away from us, leaving a wobbly tire track in the dusty road behind him.

And in that instant, I knew I'd been wrong about Mookie. Well, maybe not totally wrong. He *was* kind of crazy. But I guess he was nice, too. And smart. And someone who leaves a good trail behind him.

"Mookie!" I called after him. "Did you fix our car?"

But he just kept pedaling away from us. Then, right before he rounded the curve and disappeared from sight, he gave a little wave with his three-fingered hand.

Suddenly the woods seemed quieter than they ever had before. Not a bird chirping. Not a leaf rustling. Just silence.

"What do we do now?" Toby said.

I looked at Willy, and he cocked his head at me and made me smile.

"We take Willy home," I said.

"When?"

"Tomorrow."

"Yes!" Toby pumped his fist in the air. "Then we get that money, right, Georgina?"

But I didn't answer. I just hugged Willy.

# 20

I had to admit, Toby had been pretty good at stealing a dog. He had thought of stuff like food and all. He had found the string leash. And best of all, he hadn't goofed up and told Mama what we had done. So I felt kind of bad about taking Willy back to Carmella's without him. I knew he'd be mad as all get-out.

And I knew Mr. White would be mad as all get-out if I missed school again and didn't bring a note from Mama. I knew he'd have a meeting with the principal like he'd warned me would happen. A meeting to talk about me and how much I'd been messing up. A meeting about why my mom wouldn't answer Mr. White's letters and all.

I knew what was ahead of me if I did what I'd planned, but I was gonna do it anyways.

I made sure Toby was in his classroom, then I hurried back outside and raced over to the old house. I couldn't hardly get my feet to go fast enough as I pushed through the bushes on my way to the back.

*Please, Willy, be there. Please, Willy, be there,* I said over and over inside my head.

As soon as I rounded the corner of the house, I heard Willy's happy little yips.

"Hey there, fella," I called, hurrying over to the porch.

Willy stuck his head through the torn screen and wagged his whole body.

I sat on the step and let him jump through the screen door into my lap.

"How you doin', fella?" I said, scratching the top of his head.

He sniffed my backpack, making little snuffling noises. I pulled out the peanut butter sandwich I had brought him, and tore it into pieces. He gobbled them up, swallowing them whole without even chewing.

"Ready to go home?" I said.

Willy perked his ears up and let out a little bark. That dog sure was smart.

I untied his leash and started for the path that led to the road. But as I was crossing the clearing where Mookie had camped, I noticed something that made me stop. A little green dog collar, lying on top of the log that Mookie used to sit on.

My heart dropped with a thud. That collar looked familiar.

I picked it up and studied the tag. Yep. There it was, plain as day. *Willy*.

I turned it over and read:

Carmella Whitmore
27 Whitmore Road
Darby, NC

I felt a big blanket of shame fall over me. Mookie had found Willy's collar. He had known the truth about Willy. He had known the truth about me.

I looked down at Willy. He was watching my face like he knew every thought in my head.

"Mookie knew about us, Willy," I said.

Willy whined and wagged his tail.

"I wonder why he was so nice to me," I said.

Willy nudged me with his nose.

I buckled the green collar around his neck and said, "Come on, Willy. Let's go home."

By the time I got to the corner of Whitmore Road, Willy was pulling so hard I thought that string was gonna bust in two. I knew he was dying to race up the street, through the gate, up the porch steps, through the doggie door, and right into Carmella's lap. But I needed to slow down a minute. I had to make sure the coast was clear and nobody was outside.

"Hang on, little fella," I said.

I squinted up the road, checking out the yards and driveways.

"Okay, Willy," I said. "Let's go."

I hurried toward Carmella's house. By the time we got to the hedge, Willy was practically going crazy, leaping and carrying on.

I tiptoed along the hedge, trying to keep Willy from yanking the string right out of my hand. I hoped Carmella wasn't home, but when I got to the gate, I could see her car in the driveway. I untied the string from Willy's collar. Then I took his whiskery face in both my hands and rubbed my nose back and forth against his. An Eskimo kiss.

I lifted the latch and opened the gate. Then I let go of Willy's collar and watched him dash across the yard and up the steps, then disappear through the doggie door and into the house.

I turned and hurried back up the road. But the farther I got from Carmella's house, the heavier my feet felt. By the time I got to the corner, they felt like cement bricks, slowing me down until I couldn't take another step.

*What's wrong with you, Georgina?* I said to myself. *Don't stop now. Get on outta here before somebody sees you.*

But I guess my heart was taking over my feet, making me stop. Making me turn around. Making me walk on back to Carmella's.

I stood outside the gate. Music from a radio drifted out of the screen door. More than anything, I wanted to disappear. To leave Whitmore Road and never come back. To just pretend like I'd never laid eyes on Willy or Carmella.

But I couldn't.

I took a deep breath and put my hand on my heart. I could feel it beating, fast and hard. Then I opened the gate and made my cement feet walk up the sidewalk to Carmella's front door.

"Carmella," I called through the screen.

"Georgina!" Carmella squealed from inside. "Guess what!"

She came to the door carrying Willy. He was licking her face all over and wiggling his whole body.

"Willy's home!" Carmella said. Tears were streaming down her face and she looked about as happy as a person could be. "He just came running right through that doggie door and into the kitchen like he'd never been gone." She kissed Willy's nose. "Can you believe that?" she said.

"No," I said. "I mean, yeah, I *can* believe that, 'cause, um . . ."

"Come on in." Carmella pushed the screen door open. "I'm gonna give him a bath. He's a mess."

I stepped inside.

"But first," Carmella said, "I'm gonna cook him some sausage."

"Carmella . . ." I followed her down the hall and into the kitchen. "I, um, I need to, um . . ."

But Carmella wasn't listening. She was humming and talking to Willy while she put little sausages in a frying pan.

"Carmella," I said louder than I'd meant to, 'cause it sounded like a yell.

She looked at me kind of surprised.

"I need to tell you something," I said.

She put a lid on the pan and turned to me.

"Okay," she said.

I looked down at the dirty linoleum floor. Willy had left little muddy paw prints in front of the stove where Carmella was standing.

"I stole Willy," I said to the floor.

A terrible silence settled over the room. I could hear Carmella's wheezy breathing. In and out. In and out.

Finally, she said, "What do you mean?"

I looked up. She was standing by the stove, holding a fork. Her face was white, making her freckles stand out like sprinkles of cinnamon. Willy sat on the floor beside her, watching her, waiting for that sausage.

"I mean, I stole Willy," I said. "I took him right out of your yard."

Carmella gripped the edge of the counter for a minute, then pulled out a chair and sank into it.

"But why?" she said.

And then I did the hardest thing I'd ever done. I told

Carmella everything. I started with those three rolls of quarters and the wadded-up dollar bills in the mayonnaise jar, and I ended with Mookie leaving Willy's little green collar on that log.

And then I waited for Carmella to hate me.

But you know what?

She reached out and took my hands in hers and didn't sound at all hateful when she said, "I guess bad times can make a person do bad things, huh?"

I hung my head and couldn't get myself to say another word.

"You did a real bad thing, Georgina," Carmella said.

I nodded, keeping my head down so my hair would hide my face. Tears dropped right off the end of my nose and onto the floor.

The room was silent except for the sizzle of the sausage on the stove and the tick, tick, tick of the clock over the refrigerator.

Carmella pushed herself up off the chair and went over to the stove. She took the sausages out of the pan and cut them into pieces. Willy whined at her feet.

Tick, tick, tick went that clock.

"I'm sorry," I said.

Tick, tick, tick went that clock.

Carmella dropped the sausage pieces into Willy's bowl. He gobbled them up and then kept licking the bowl, making it slide across the floor.

"I guess I better go," I said. But I didn't move. I

stayed there with my heavy, cement feet planted firmly on the cracked linoleum of Carmella's kitchen floor, waiting for her to make me feel better.

But she didn't.

So I moved my heavy feet, one in front of the other, down the hall, through the front door, and out onto the porch. I was almost to the gate when Carmella called, "Georgina."

I stopped and turned around.

She stood on the porch holding Willy. His tail wagged, thwack, thwack, thwack against her leg.

"Why don't you and Toby come by tomorrow?" she said. "Y'all could take Willy for a walk."

I felt my whole self get lighter, as if that heavy blanket of shame I'd been wearing had been lifted right up off of me.

I nodded. "Okay," I said. "We will."

Then I hurried out of the gate and up the road. I couldn't wait to tell Toby what I'd done. I knew he wouldn't be mad when I told him how happy Willy was and how Carmella didn't hate us. I'd let him hold the leash when we walked Willy tomorrow, and he wouldn't think I was mean anymore. When I got to the corner of Whitmore Road, I stopped and looked back. Carmella was still standing on the porch, holding Willy like she wasn't ever going to put him down.

She waved at me.

I waved back.

Then just as I was about to turn and head back toward the highway, I glanced down and noticed my footprints in the dirt along the side of the road. I smiled, thinking about Mookie and his motto. About the trail you leave behind being more important than the path ahead.

Then I turned and raced off toward school to wait for Toby.

# 21

We lived in that nasty old car for two more days. Then one day Mama came back from work and said, "Pack your bags, boys and girls. We're *moving*."

Me and Toby looked at each other, then back at Mama, waiting.

She tossed two Snickers bars into the backseat and said, "You heard me. We're moving. And I'm talking *house*. A *real* house."

Me and Toby started whooping and bouncing up and down on the backseat. Then we took down our beach towel wall and jammed all our stuff into garbage bags. Schoolbooks and dirty T-shirts. Playing cards and comic books.

As we drove to our new house, I felt a flutter of excitement as I thought about being normal again. I pictured myself going to school in clean clothes and having all my homework done and Mama telling Mr. White that everything was fine now, so don't worry about Georgina anymore. I pictured me and Luanne having a sleepover like we used to, painting our toenails and sharing our secrets. Maybe working on our cooking badge for Girl Scouts. I even pictured myself sitting on my very own bed wearing my new ballet shoes, combing my hair so I'd look nice for my ballet lessons with Luanne and Liza Thomas.

When we pulled up in front of our new house, me and Toby grinned at each other. It was a tiny white house with a rusty swing set in the red-dirt yard and a refrigerator with no door sitting right up on the front porch.

But it looked like a castle to me.

Somebody named Louise was already living there with her baby named Drew. Louise was a friend of Patsy's and needed somebody to share the house with her and help take care of Drew and pay some of the rent.

I didn't have my very own room, but I had my very own bed. Louise gave me a plastic laundry basket to keep my things in and told me to put it up on the closet shelf so Drew couldn't get my stuff.

The first night in our new house, Mama brought home pizza and we watched TV. Before I went to sleep, I lay in my bed and stretched my legs out under the cool sheets. The tiny window across the room was open, and a soft breeze lifted the faded curtains. Moths flapped and buzzed against the screen.

I reached under my pillow and took out my glittery purple notebook. I turned to my *How to Steal a Dog* notes, and in the dim glow of the hall light I read through *Step 8* again. About making a decision. About getting the reward or not getting the reward. I smiled to myself when I read the part that said:

> *THAT*
> *is the decision you will have to make.*

I knew I had made the right decision because my tapping insides had finally settled down.

But I still felt bad about what I'd done. I still wished I could turn back the time far enough to where I could do things different.

But at least when I'd gotten to *Step 8*, I'd made the right decision.

I turned to a fresh page in my notebook and wrote: *May 3*.

> *Step 9: Those are all the rules for how to steal a dog.*
> *But*

I drew a red heart around the word *But*. Then I wrote in great big letters:

## *DO NOT STEAL A DOG*
### *because*

I drew a blue circle around *because*. Then I took out my gold glitter pen and wrote:

*it is NOT a good idea.*
*THE END*

I closed my notebook and slid it back up under my pillow.

As I lay there in my very own bed, I thought about Mookie. I wondered what he was doing right that very minute. Was he making Hoover gravy? Was he wiggling that three-fingered hand of his at somebody? Was he fixing somebody's car?

Where was he leaving his trail now?

I thought about Willy, too. I bet he was curled up at the foot of Carmella's bed beside his chewed-up toys, dreaming about sardines and liver puddin', happy as anything to be back home again.

I looked over at Toby, sucking his thumb in the bed next to mine. Then I tiptoed over to the window and looked out into the night. I took a deep breath. The air smelled good. Like honeysuckle and new-mowed grass.

It didn't stink at all.

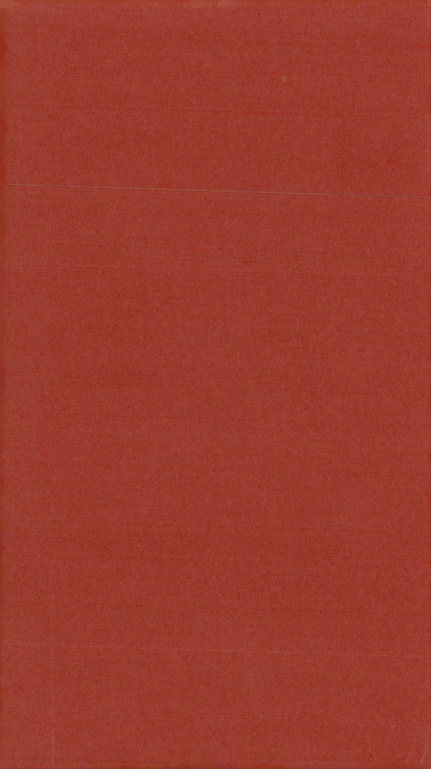

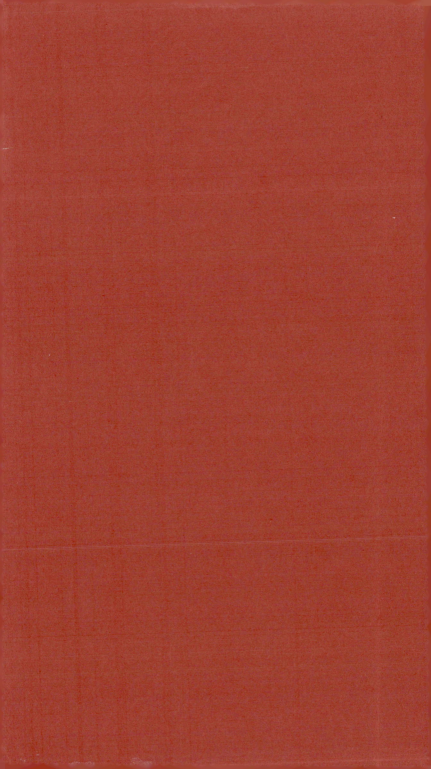

9/20

To Scott & Francie
with gratitude
for your support
of UUSC
Bill Schulz

# The Coming Good Society

*Why New Realities Demand New Rights*

WILLIAM F. SCHULZ

*and*

SUSHMA RAMAN

Harvard University Press

*Cambridge, Massachusetts*
*London, England*
2020

First printing

Cataloging-in-Publication Data available from the Library of Congress
ISBN: 978-0-674-97708-2 (alk. paper)

To Stephan and Lee,
*Brothers in all but blood*
—BILL


To my husband, Troy,
*My source of inspiration and support*
—SUSHMA

# Contents

# CONTENTS

# THE COMING GOOD SOCIETY

# Introduction

RIGHTS ARE NOT STATIC THINGS, permanent and perpetual. They don't all stay the same from generation to generation; some of them evolve and change depending on changing norms and circumstances. We humans adapt rights to history. As history changes, so do rights. Indeed, sometimes brand new rights arise that few people had ever contemplated before. When that happens, rights undergo a revolution. That is a premise of this book and it is not an uncontroversial notion.

One reason such a conception of rights prompts debate is because opponents of rights—in this case human rights though this book is about all sorts of rights in addition to those of humans—would like nothing better than to toss them into the proverbial "trash can of history." They would love, in other words, to provoke a counterrevolution. The Russian philosopher Alexander Dugin, considered President Vladimir Putin's chief ideologist, has written of the need to "create strategic alliances to overthrow the present order of things, of which the core could be described as human rights, anti-hierarchy, and political correctness—everything that is the face of the Beast, the Antichrist."[1] If rights are not lodged in something solid and

1

eternal, such as perhaps natural law or inherent human dignity, are they not vulnerable to vultures like Dugin?

The hard truth is that traditional understandings of rights as rock-solid and indestructible have not dissuaded the Dugins of the world from trying to dissolve them. Fortunately, traducers of rights have rarely been successful. The history of human rights norms would seem to offer assurance that, when norms do change and rights revolutions occur, the new rights at hand are generally of a progressive kind. The protective cloak of rights has gradually been extended to more and more groups of people—not just propertied white males, for example, but to people of color and women and LBGTQ folks and persons with disabilities.[2]

This is true in many corners of the globe, not just the developed West, despite the frequent charge that human rights are merely an invention of Western imperialist powers. Consider, for example, the leadership of India and Africa in struggles for decolonization; the role of Latin America in promulgating an inter-American human rights system after the adoption of the American Declaration of the Rights and Duties of Man in Colombia in 1948; and more recent accomplishments by human rights organizations and national courts in Bolivia, India, Brazil, and other countries in securing broader rights such as economic rights and LGBT rights.[3]

It is certainly true that even well-established human rights norms often come under threat. Today, democracy, or, as Article 21 of the Universal Declaration of Human Rights describes it, "the will of the people [to] be the basis of the authority of government," is thought to be in considerable peril. But most of those leaders who display ambivalence or even outright hostility to democracy pretend to be democrats, to hold "free" elections, to listen to "the people." Hun Sen in Cambodia, Vladimir Putin in Russia, and Victor Orban in Hungary insist that they have been chosen by the people through "free" elections. For all its fragility, democracy is still a prevailing human rights norm, as are such things as the right to a fair trial or the right not to be tortured, violated though they may well often be in practice. After all, U.S. President George W. Bush, who authorized interrogation techniques that human rights organizations unequivocally labeled torture, went out of his way to deny that the United States would ever engage in torture. Nonetheless, it is certainly possible that rights may devolve or regress over time, become less robust and less protective of the vulnerable. Sometimes that happens through an all-out assault on rights. But a second premise of this book is that another way it happens is when the framers of rights fail to take seriously new realities that signal the need for new conceptions of rights or for a rights revolution. This can occur whether the rights in question be those of humans or animals or robots or Nature. Law professor Christopher Stone, featured again in Chapter 8, wrote that "Throughout legal history, each successive extension of rights to some new entity has been . . . a bit unthinkable."[4] One of the purposes of this book is to make such extensions more conceivable.

MARINE STAFF SERGEANT JEREMY SMITH and U.S. Navy Medic Benjamin Rast were killed by "friendly fire" on April 6, 2011, in Afghanistan. Soldiers dying by mistake at the hands of their comrades has been a tragic feature of virtually every war in human history but what made Smith's and Rast's deaths unusual was that they were killed by a United States–fired Predator drone, one of the most sophisticated weapons in the U.S. arsenal. "The missile functioned properly and struck the target area intended by the commander," read the report of the official military investigation, "however the exact disposition of [American] ground forces was not known by all involved in the execution of the strike."[5] In other words, the drone hit what it was supposed to hit but what it hit was not what its commander thought it was.

If an error like that could kill American forces, is it any wonder that many civilians have been unintentionally killed by drone strikes? In 2013 President Barack Obama claimed that he required "near certainty" that there would be no "collateral damage" before he authorized a strike.[6] But three years later the United States itself acknowledged that the 473 drone attacks undertaken in the Obama administration had resulted in between 64 and 116 civilian deaths and many observers called that number woefully understated.

Regardless of the exact casualty count, at least drones have the virtue of being launched by an identifiable "commander" who can be held accountable, if warranted, for war crimes. But the American, Russian, and other militaries have all been researching for years the possibility of creating fully autonomous weapons that can identify and eliminate a target without significant, if any, human involvement at all.[7] Their popular name is "killer robots" and though variations on this theme have appeared in the movies since well before the Terminator first made his appearance in 1984, Hollywood may well no longer have a monopoly on the idea that the "bad guys" can be stopped, whether in battles or back alleys, by robotic machines that eliminate the peril to soldiers or police and, by the way, may exempt humans from full responsibility for the decisions. Technological advances in weaponry are inevitable but killer robots would make the current notions of war crimes or police misconduct as obsolete as the crossbow.

BODIES ARE NOT THE ONLY THINGS that can succumb to death, however. Our souls may be crushed too if we are forced to deny our authentic selves. Allison Washington was a trans child—that is, a girl born in a boy's body. Like most trans people, she sensed from a very early age that her feelings about her gender did not match her physical characteristics, but unlike most parents of transgender children, Allison's mother treated her as a girl from about the age of four, allowing her to grow her hair long, wear lipstick and girls' clothes, and play girls' roles. For much of her growing up, Allison rarely thought about her gender. But then, at age twelve, she says,

I became hyper-aware of my genitals and my chest. I began having an intense, recurring dream in which I would awake having been magically endowed with a vagina whilst I slept. It was so vivid that, when I did actually awake, I would immediately check myself, then start my day off with the most profound sense of loss. I became so obsessed that I developed a ritual each night before dropping asleep: I would press with my fingers on the spot where I knew my vagina should be and wish for the dream, wish for it to really work this time, wish for relief and a way out of my hideous predicament. Needless to say, I discussed this with no one: I knew there was something horribly, horribly wrong with me.[8]

There followed years of anguish, trauma, and confusion as Allison tried to assume the role of a male, taking up "manly" pursuits, marrying a heterosexual woman and having a child.[9] Finally, close to twenty years after her yearning for a vagina, she finally "obtained" one, making the full transition toward which she had been moving all of her life.

Until recently, gender has been understood as essentially binary and immutable. You were either a girl or a boy from birth and, once you were told which you were, you stayed that way. It was a matter of biology, not of self-identity, and you certainly didn't have a "right" to reject your assigned gender. But if we conceive of gender as nonbinary and fluid, then rights will need to be adapted to new realities just as surely as pink for girls and blue for boys will need to give way to purple, mauve, and teal.

MEANWHILE, AS WE HUMANS are in the process of determining our gender identities, we could conceivably be sued by our pets for release from bondage.[10]

In 2014, activist lawyer Steven Wise and others from the Nonhuman Rights Project (NhRP) filed suit on behalf of Tommy, an adult chimpanzee who had been held captive by a former circus owner in a small, dark steel-mesh cage on a remote farm in upstate New York. NhRP argues that chimps, like other animals with higher-order cognitive abilities, "have a concept of . . . personal past and future . . . [and] suffer the pain of not being able to fulfill their needs or move around as they wish."

Legal statutes have long outlawed certain abuses of animals and regulated their treatment but, until Wise's suit, no one had ever argued in court that animals were anything other than property, that their fundamental legal status entitled them to exercise rights proactively. Should the Nonhuman Rights Project succeed in its quest, the whole field of rights would suddenly be radically expanded.

THESE ARE BUT THREE EXAMPLES of potential developments in technology, gender theory, and interspecies relations that may not only upend the way we humans see the world but also how we understand rights, both human and otherwise. Even more tellingly, they illustrate the view articulated at the outset that rights are not static, unbending, cast in stone once and for all, world without end. Rather, rights are subject to evolution, if not revolution: both the transformation of currently recognized rights and the introduction of new rights altogether. Rights advance (and potentially erode) depending upon circumstances and context.

As the authors argue in this book, rights represent a description of the "good society," a society that protects its members' dignity, encourages their capabilities and supplies an environment in which most people will want to live. Those who already think they know what that good society looks like naturally resist changes to the rendering. The problem with such recalcitrance is that some change in that description is inevitable from generation to generation.

Human rights as we conceive them today are different from how they were conceived fifty, not to mention a hundred or more, years ago. While the authors fervently hope that fundamental human rights, like the right to life or the right not to be tortured, enslaved, or subjected to various forms of discrimination, will be even more robust fifty years from now than they are today (and it is absolutely incumbent upon us to fight hard to see that they are), the interpretation of other rights, like the right to hold an individual person accountable for war crimes, may need to be different. Still other rights that most people are only beginning to conceive of today, like a human right to gender transition or an animal's right to be regarded as a legal agent, may seem commonplace in years to come.

If we care about rights at all, we have to care about their future—not just about the challenges they face today, profound as those are, but the challenges they will encounter as our world changes around us. And that means confronting two clear dangers. The obvious danger, as previously stated, is that human rights are under profound threat right now and need to be defended. The less obvious danger is that, if rights fail to be adapted to new realities, they will be eroded as readily by indifference and irrelevance as they are by defiance. Precisely because the authors care passionately about the obvious danger, they've written this book to make the second danger less likely.

THE MOST COMMON ASSUMPTION about human rights—and, as indicated, this book is about far more than human rights alone—is that at least the most fundamental of them are something we humans carry with us, something "attached" to us or "inside" us, from the moment of birth (or, for some, the moment of conception) that we can claim or have claimed on our behalf simply because we were born human. That is why an anencephalic baby—a baby born without part of its brain—cannot be murdered or mistreated even though it displays few features of a fully functioning human being. It is why we feel such abhorrence at the notion that children can be born into slavery long before they have the capacity to influence their fates.

The apparent high standing and moral certainty provided by this notion of rights is an appealing one. Unfortunately, it is also flawed. To understand why, consider this dilemma.

We know that in centuries past it was routine to kill a baby after birth if it displayed anomalies—even those far less severe than anencephaly. In Aristotle's *Politics,* the great philosopher observes matter-of-factly, "As to the ... rearing of children, let there be a law that no *deformed* child shall live."[11] Child sacrifice to placate the gods was commonplace in many societies. And, of course, slavery, including the enslavement of newborns, had been practiced for centuries all over the world and was not outlawed until the nineteenth century in the United Kingdom and the United States.

Neither Plato nor Aristotle mentions "rights" in his works and the earliest we can place recognition of something like rights in the Western tradition would be the Magna Carta of 1215. Did the children who suffered in these ways *prior* to the recognition of rights, even by their parents, somehow carry these rights mysteriously inside themselves nonetheless? Or do rights arise and our conception of what is a right change depending upon social circumstances? Are rights, in other words, fixed and determined for all time or are they transactional, dependent upon the changing relationships that people establish with one another and with other entities in the world? Are rights something that humans and other entities have or something we and they are given? If rights are transactional and given, then there is no inherent reason we should not assign them to nonhuman entities like animals or robots or rivers.

This philosophical question will be explored in the first chapter but it ought to be obvious that until a right is recognized as a right, it is essentially useless. It may reassure human rights sympathizers to think that theoretically and in retrospect all babies born into slavery in centuries past were victims of a human rights violation, but, absent recognition of that fact by the slave masters, it surely didn't do the enslaved children themselves any good.

This means that the complex of rights or at least our recognition of those rights, far from being cast in iron, evolves from one era to another. We've seen a telling example of such a transition in many of our own lifetimes. Eleanor Roosevelt chaired the United Nations commission that drafted the Universal Declaration of Human Rights (UDHR) adopted in 1948, the bedrock instrument that defines contemporary human rights. If anyone had asked her at that time whether the UDHR sanctioned what is referred to today as same-sex marriage or marriage equality, she would likely have been dumbfounded.

Roosevelt was a champion of civil rights, a generous-hearted person and, by some accounts, herself involved in a lesbian love relationship.[12] But in 1948, and for many years afterward, the notion that marriage might involve two partners other than a cisgender male and cisgender female was virtually unheard of in the mainstream of societies around the world.[13] If anyone at that time had tried to cite the UDHR to justify a right to same-sex marriage, they would have been laughed off the wedding altar. The first gay rights organization in the United States, the Society for Human Rights, was founded in Chicago in 1924 but disbanded the next year.[14] The Mattachine Society, one of the best-known early advocacy groups for gay rights, was not founded until 1950.[15] Neither group had same-sex marriage on its agenda. Indeed, not until 1958 did the Supreme Court rule that it was even legal to send materials related to homosexuality through the U.S. mail.[16]

It would be 2001, fifty-three years after the adoption of the UDHR, that the Netherlands became the first nation to legalize same-sex marriage and 2004 before a U.S. state—Massachusetts—did the same. The right to same-sex marriage was finally recognized by the U.S. Supreme Court in 2015 in its landmark ruling *Obergefell v Hodges*.[17] Although the right to marry the person of your choice regardless of gender identification has not yet been codified in international human rights law, more and more countries are recognizing it. Countries such as Bolivia, Ecuador, and Fiji, for example, guarantee equal rights based on both gender identity and sexual orientation, and at least twenty-two countries have case law or legislation in support of marriage equality.[18]

So did that right "exist" from the beginning of time but was not "disclosed" to human beings until around the turn of the twenty-first century? What is certainly true is that in modern times the question of same-sex marriage was not even seriously considered by large numbers of people until the late twentieth century and that, as prevailing social and political norms changed, the possibility of recognizing a new right emerged too.

The authors argue in this book that as the world changes around us humans, new rights that may hardly be imagined today will come into being and some currently established rights will need to be reconceptualized. It is understandable that the possibility of adjusting the meanings of tried and true rights is an unnerving prospect. There is nothing more important than fiercely defending fundamental rights that have served us well for decades. Many of the most precious of our human rights are still at risk from political autocracy, economic oppression, white privilege, and misogyny. But it is also true that, if those who value rights fail to anticipate the new forms rights will take, then the notion of rights will either fall by the wayside as a meaningful factor in the organizing of our societies or future rights will be shaped by those who care more for personal aggrandizement than the interests of the commonweal.

To begin to address the question of what rights will look like ten, twenty, or fifty years from now and how we should cast them, we need to examine changes in norms; technology; the relationships of humans to each other, to animals, and to the earth; and other developments that may significantly alter our understanding of rights over the decades ahead. No one can anticipate exactly what form those new or refashioned rights may take in every case—*this book is designed less to predict than to provoke*—but it is possible to describe the changing circumstances that will affect our current understanding of rights and insist that molding those future rights to respond to those circumstances is a preeminent obligation of all those who treasure a good society.

Before doing all that, however, it is crucial to address the current state of human rights, which some people think is unusually precarious. What is the point of thinking about new rights when the ones we currently claim appear to be in real danger?

COAUTHOR BILL SCHULZ SERVED for twelve years as head of the U.S. section of the human rights organization Amnesty International. Shortly before Bill completed his service at Amnesty USA in 2006, he gave a lecture at Syracuse University. Before the lecture, the president of the university and a group of faculty members entertained him at dinner. "Let's ask ourselves this question," the president said after dessert had been served. "Are human rights better or worse off today than they were two hundred years ago?" With only one exception, the faculty members all insisted that the human rights situation was better in 1806 than 2006. Human rights had prompted the American Revolution itself, they argued, and hence were more central to people's lives. At the dawn of the nineteenth century, ours was an agrarian society that valued the common person more than we do today. Money and corporate greed had not yet come to dominate our politics. In 2006 the United States was in the middle of George W. Bush's Iraq war, whereas in the early nineteenth century, the United States was not a superpower and, hence, to quote the sixth U.S. president, John Quincy Adams, could not "go abroad in search of monsters to destroy."

Finally, Bill could contain himself no longer. "Am I living in a parallel universe?" he asked. "You've described large social and geopolitical conditions in the United States but, when it comes to human rights themselves around the world, why, just in the twelve years I've been with Amnesty, we've seen the creation of the International

Criminal Court and the War Crimes Tribunal for Rwanda; growth in democracies throughout the globe; a proliferation of local human rights groups in virtually every country on the planet; rape in the course of war declared a war crime; women's rights taken more seriously than ever before; the British Law Lords rule that sovereign immunity does not prevent the prosecution of dictators like Chile's Augusto Pinochet; worldwide condemnation of the U.S. use of torture in Iraq; the U.S. Supreme Court having ruled unconstitutional the execution of juveniles and those with intellectual disabilities—and you don't think human rights are better off today than in 1806 when slavery was still enshrined in the U.S. Constitution and serfs still toiled on the steppes of Russia?" The gathering still looked skeptical.[19]

In part that's because how one sees human rights depends upon where one sits in the world. For the privileged Founding Fathers, the American Revolution did seem like a time of increased liberty. For the indentured servant, it no doubt did not. Whether the agrarian society of that time valued individuals more than we do today, it placed minimal value on women, those without property, and, except in pecuniary terms, the enslaved. Bill was absolutely right that a greater percentage of the world's population live in freedom now than did in 1806.

Yet several of the examples of human rights progress that Bill cited in 2006 have failed to bear their promised fruit. As of 2018, for example, the International Criminal Court had convicted only four people. That same year Freedom House reported the twelfth straight year in which freedom had declined in countries around the world.[20] Augusto Pinochet died before he could be successfully prosecuted for the torture or execution of tens of thousands of Chileans during his presidency. And this is to say nothing of the fact that in the United States people of color are killed in highly disproportionate numbers by police or that Muslims and immigrants are persecuted in many countries in the West.

Some have argued that violence has declined overall in modern times.[21] Whether or not this is true, the second decade of the twenty-first century has seen mass killings in Syria, South Sudan, Myanmar, Yemen, and elsewhere. The retreat of Russia from democratic norms; the emergence of China, notorious for its disdain for human rights, as a worldwide economic power; and, perhaps most significantly, an apparent growing rejection in Europe and the United States of the globalist, transnational values upon which universal human rights at least in part depend—all these are discouraging developments and have combined to force some human rights promoters into a defensive crouch. Human rights critics like the University of London's Stephen Hopgood, sensing blood, have proclaimed ours "the endtimes of human rights" or, in University of Chicago law professor Eric Posner's similarly melancholy phrase, "the twilight of human rights law."[22]

Such pessimism, however, reflects a studious avoidance of grassroots human rights activity. When co-author Sushma Raman worked as a program officer for the Ford Foundation in India, she encountered a wide range of human rights and social justice organizations, with sophisticated strategies and wide reach. Far from succumbing to the "twilight" of human rights, these groups represented its dawn far from centers of international human rights power in New York or Geneva. Many of these groups were far ahead of the debates about the twilight of human rights and much more involved in the dawn—for example, Sushma was a cofounder of the South Asia Women's Fund, which focused on supporting women's rights and leadership in the region, and then expanded to become Women's Fund Asia to support women's and trans rights across Asia. Grassroots environmental justice movements she worked with in countries such as Bolivia and India emphasized the sacred qualities of rivers and other forms of nature, as discussed in Chapter 8.

The idea of human rights is therefore far more resilient than its obituary writers imagine, though there is no question that it faces steep hurdles. This is precisely why there is a need to focus on prospective rights. Is there a danger of there being too many rights, of "new" rights distracting us from pursuit of the "old"? In fact, exactly the opposite is the case. When established human rights are in jeopardy, it is more important than ever to ensure that rights are seen as responsive to contemporary problems.

Many of the issues this book examines are directly related to well-established rights and represent new challenges to those rights that will need to be addressed if those "old" rights are to retain any meaning. Given that high-resolution imaging satellites can provide images as small as the home plate on a baseball diamond of virtually every spot on earth, what will that mean for the right to privacy? If wealthy individuals can afford to employ technologies like CRISPR to edit their offspring's DNA to eliminate disease or elevate intelligence, what are the implications for the right to equal access to health care? If the understanding of gender as binary is being called into question, how will that affect current conceptions of women's rights?

Moreover, if it is true that rights fluctuate, evolve, or are subject to revolution, then we have no choice about confronting challenges to our current formulations of rights. When the theme of this book was first presented to a group of the authors' colleagues at Harvard, one of them, a distinguished practitioner of international human rights law, scoffed at the topics covered in this book "Those aren't *real* rights," he said. "Real rights involve serious things like crimes against humanity or war crimes." But that is exactly the attitude that first greeted the mention of women's rights or the rights of LGBTQ people: "Those aren't *real* rights!"

Even as eminent and long-standing a set of rights as those prohibiting war crimes appears to be in flux. In 2016, for example, the International Criminal Court for the first time included the destruction of cultural property—in this case, mausoleums and mosques in Mali—as a prosecutable crime of war.[23] The court is considering extending the concept of crimes against humanity to include environmental destruction, including land grabs in which governments allocate land to private companies, resulting in forced evictions and destruction of cultures.[24] If in years to come animal rights or the rights of robots or the rights of Nature become more and more broadly accepted, then they too will join the panoply of recognized rights—and we will have to start thinking of rights as far more than human alone.

There is no preset finite number of rights that are considered legitimate. It is true that some rights, called "core rights" or "nonderogable rights" like the right to life or the right not to be tortured, are considered so fundamental that they can never be suspended, even when a nation is facing a public emergency, like a terror attack or a devastating natural calamity.[25] But the fact that the UDHR lists almost fifty different rights and subsequent human rights treaties have recognized many more does not detract from the importance of core rights any more than maintaining healthy teeth diminishes the importance of maintaining a healthy heart. If we have a healthy heart, we can live without teeth but having good teeth sure makes life a lot more pleasant.

Rights by themselves are not a zero-sum game. The addition of a newly recognized right does not vitiate a previously recognized right. It's true that rights are not a seamless garment and that sometimes we need to strike a balance between rights, such as your right to practice your religion (Article 18 of the UDHR) and my right to freedom of conscience (also Article 18) should you try to have the state impose your religious beliefs on me. That's what human rights courts are for—to sort out these complexities. But both rights remain important.

It's also true that when new interpretations of rights are recognized, some groups may be required to yield a portion of their power and privilege. When President Lyndon Johnson signed the Voting Rights Act in 1965, for example, removing barriers to African Americans voting, it diminished the power of previously all-white voting blocs but it did not remove the franchise itself from those white voters. Your being awarded newly recognized rights does not entail my losing my legitimate previously recognized rights, much as those resistant to change will sometimes argue it does. The rights of LGBTQ people or women or persons with disabilities or migrants to be treated with equal dignity or even to be awarded rights singular to their needs in no way jeopardizes the rights of those who don't fall into one or more of those categories.

That is even true should we award rights to nonhuman entities like animals or robots or ecosystems. Corporations have long been legally recognized as rights bearers and, though some may disagree with that assessment, it has not in and of itself diminished the validity or power of the established rights of humans. All humans have the "right" to claim every applicable right they can. But that leads to the question "What exactly are rights, anyway?"

WHEN THE BANK OF ENGLAND released new £5 notes in September 2016, vegans and vegetarians were distraught to discover that the notes contained a smattering of tallow, a fatty substance found in rendered beef that is more often incorporated into soap or candles. It is not only that folks were concerned about animal rights and welfare, which, as you will see, the authors strongly support, but apparently quite a few people eat their bank notes. The Bank of England reported that in 2015, more than five thousand bills had to be replaced because they'd been chewed or eaten. Who knew? "Being forced to pay taxes to contribute to animal products," one vegan tweeted, "is a breach of rights."[26] But is it? How do we discover if a "right" is a right?

We may start by looking at the domestic laws of a country. If I am a citizen of Country X and want to know whether paying taxes to subsidize beef tallow in bank notes is a violation of my rights, I can consult Country X's constitution or its laws, as adopted by its legislature and interpreted by its the highest courts. It's certainly true that there are some pretty unusual laws on the books—the land-locked state of Nebraska, for example, makes it illegal to go whale fishing—but, when it comes to local or national jurisdictions, we can usually examine legal statutes and (with the help of a good lawyer, perhaps) get a reasonably good idea of what our rights are within that jurisdiction.[27]

But that is far from sufficient when it comes to determining a violation of human rights because human rights, following the UDHR, are established at the international level and many countries' laws are at odds with international human rights law. The death penalty, to take a notorious example, is deemed constitutional in the United States but is certainly not consistent with international human rights standards. So how do we ascertain what those standards call for?

Because there is no one legislature that makes laws for the entire world and no one court that has the binding power to compel enforcement of all international laws, people must look to a variety of sources to determine what is or is not a right at the international level. The primary sources used, in addition to the UDHR, are nine core international treaties, called covenants or conventions, that delineate civil, political, economic, social, and cultural human rights, along with nine additional treaties, called optional or additional protocols, that have elaborated upon those nine core statements of rights.[28] (In addition, when dealing with rights related to armed conflict, people can look to the Geneva Conventions, and with rights related to refugees, to the Refugee Convention.) These treaties have been ratified by a sufficient number of countries to be considered in effect and their enforcement by those countries is monitored by committees of experts (treaty bodies) operating with the support of the Office of the United Nations High Commissioner for Human Rights.

So, to return to the beef tallow example, if I want to know if being taxed to pay for animal-tainted bank notes violates my rights,

I would look first to the laws of the United Kingdom and rulings of the European Court of Human Rights because the United Kingdom and forty-six other members of the Council of Europe have voluntarily agreed that rulings of that court trump their own domestic laws when it comes to violations of rights.[29] And if I wanted to know if such taxation was a violation of international human rights standards, not just rights recognized by one country or region, then I would look to the eighteen international human rights treaties, which, at least theoretically, trump domestic or regional interpretations of rights. To the authors' knowledge none of these sources has ruled that taxing people to pay for beef-infused bank notes is a violation of rights and, hence, they can say with considerable confidence that at the moment that vegan's claim is not valid.

But maybe someday it will be, because, as stated previously, human rights laws and standards are not static. Just as the U.S. Supreme Court took into account what it called "evolving standards of decency" when it ruled in 2002 that the execution of what the court unfortunately called the "mentally retarded" was a violation of the U.S. Constitution's prohibition on "cruel and unusual punishments," a ruling it extended to juveniles in 2005, so the understanding of what constitutes a human right may change as global standards change.[30] The U.S. Supreme Court measured "evolving standards of decency" primarily by counting the number of state legislatures that, by 2002, had outlawed the execution of those with intellectual disabilities or, by 2005, juveniles, finding that in both cases the number had grown significantly over the previous decades.

When it comes to international human rights, the sources of change are not quite that simple. Of course in order for a human rights treaty to come into effect, a significant number of states must have signed and ratified it but the standards that finally get incorporated into human rights treaties are also influenced by such considerations as the opinions of well-respected high national courts and the findings of regional human rights courts; recommendations from U.N. human rights bodies and mechanisms, like treaty bodies and special rapporteurs; the perspectives of human rights organizations and experts; and, ultimately, the effectiveness of grassroots campaigns petitioning for a new understanding of rights.[31] So theoretically it's possible, if a little unlikely, that at some point in the future an international rights treaty might recognize the right to an exemption from taxation for those who object to subsidizing meat-infused bank notes.

Whether it does or does not will turn in good measure on whether a significant number of people and nations conclude that not being forced to subsidize meat-infused bank notes is critical to a civilized society. Because what imperatives are or are not considered human rights? As previously discussed, in the broadest sense they represent as close as we can get to an international consensus about what constitutes the good society, but now, thanks to the UDHR and those eighteen treaties, there can be more specificity about what such a society looks like.

A good society does not engage in torture, for example, or the denial of due process; it rejects racial and other forms of discrimination; it protects children. There are a whole series of constraints upon the powerful that characterize a good society. But human rights are not just about what people may not do to one another. Many civil and political rights, but especially social, economic, and cultural rights, paint a rich portrait of what a good society promotes as well. These are sometimes called "positive rights." A good society sees to it that its residents have sufficient food, water, housing, economic opportunity, and many other things. Of course, it is not necessary that all human needs can be framed in rights terms (there is no "right to a satisfying sense of life's purpose") but the realization of those additional needs will only be met if one is not burdened by situations such as homelessness, starvation, or persecution. In this sense rights comprise at the very least the minimal requirements of a good society.

Rights represent duties and obligations that those with power—governments, international financial institutions, corporations, militaries, and others—have toward those whose lives (or, to enable inclusion of robots and ecosystems, whose conditions of existence) are affected by their decisions. Conversely, rights represent claims that those with less power can make (or have made on their behalf) against the powerful. No wonder rights can be so controversial! They reflect globally sanctioned norms, the violation of which may well result in international condemnation. Just consider how the revelations of the use of torture by U.S. officials at the Abu Ghraib prison in Iraq and at the Guantanamo detention facilities damaged the United States' reputation in the world. Indeed, when Sushma had the opportunity to travel to Guantanamo in 2018 to be an observer at a 9/11 pretrial hearing, the legacy of the U.S. government's use of torture was still the backdrop to the proceedings.

But why do we need rights to define a good society? Couldn't we do the same thing with wise public policies? Indeed, what is the difference between policies and rights? This will be a particularly important question when considering rights of nonhuman entities like animals or robots or ecosystems. Why do they need to have rights assigned to them? Isn't it sufficient to protect their interests through good laws and public practices?

It is certainly true that all human rights need to be made manifest in public policies if they are to have any actionable meaning but not all public policies are manifestations of human rights. If "the right to life" is to have meaning, it must be codified in law and policy but the extent to which tax revenues should be drawn from property taxes, sales taxes, corporate taxes, or capital gains taxes is not fundamentally a human rights question. Human rights are in some ways equivalent to the first principles out of which many bedrock public policies emerge. They elevate policy questions to a level of seriousness and permanence those policies might otherwise not have and, more importantly, they assign the claimants of those rights, including animals and ecosystems and maybe at some point even robots, a value, dignity, and aura of protection that policy alone would not provide.

So yes, the treatment of animals and Nature could be addressed solely as policy matters of animal or tree "welfare," as indeed has been the case for decades, but doing so deprives those claimants of a degree of value and dignity—a place in a good society—they otherwise deserve and, furthermore, makes it far easier to roll back those policies when they become inconvenient than would be the case if the policies were grounded in rights.

THE AUTHORS DO NOT PRETEND that the selection of rights they have chosen to examine in this book are definitive. Some of the topics addressed relate to long-standing human rights, such as those to privacy and health, that are under significant pressure as a result of changing technologies or norms and need to be revised or expanded. Others look at entirely new rights regarding corruption, animals, robots, and nature that have not yet have been addressed by rights treaties or most domestic rights laws. The subjects selected are all timely and important but there are many other areas in which rights may need to be reconceived or created anew in the years ahead. Some of those are mentioned in the Conclusion but even that list is not meant to be exhaustive.

We authors are not soothsayers, however attracted Sushma is to astrology! Predictions about the future are notoriously inaccurate: for example, novelist Ray Bradbury's assertion in *The Martian Chronicles* in 1950 that humans would colonize Mars by the early 2000s or tech writer David Pogue's 2006 comment that "Everyone's always asking me when Apple will come out with a cell phone. My answer is 'Probably never.'" But it is possible anticipate some of the topics that are most likely to shake up notions of rights over the next generation.

The point of this book is not to present a compendium of new or newly conceived rights but to challenge us all—and particularly younger generations who will be living with the consequences—to think in new ways about the very real challenges to current notions of rights. What kind of good society do we want to build and live in over the decades ahead? The answers to that question will shape the nature of the rights revolution and the rights revolution will shape the nature of the future good society.

WHY DOES ALL THIS MATTER? The "future good society," after all, can seem a long way away. The fact is, however, that rights are not just remote, abstract concepts—the work of eager lawyers and earnest international human rights organizations. Whether we recognize it or not, rights have a very direct relationship to our everyday lives. As Eleanor Roosevelt so popularly put it:

> Where, after all, do universal human rights begin? In small places, close to home—so close and so small that they cannot be seen on any maps of the world. Yet they are the world of the individual person; the neighborhood he lives in; the school or college he attends; the factory, farm, or office where he works. Such are the places where every man, woman, and child seeks equal justice, equal opportunity, equal dignity without discrimination. Unless these rights have meaning there, they have little meaning anywhere. Without concerted citizen action to uphold them close to home, we shall look in vain for progress in the larger world.[32]

This is obvious for members of oppressed groups who may face discrimination and violence at the hands of public officials on a regular basis. It is self-evidently true for people in societies with marginal standards of living who may have little access to something as basic to our needs as potable water. It is a matter of life and death for those trapped in war zones. But it is also true for people living more secure, privileged lives. Regardless of one's situation in life, it is almost impossible to follow the news and not run into debates about rights that may affect us directly.

In 2016 the United States was roiled by a debate about bathrooms when North Carolina passed a law requiring people to use the bathroom that corresponded to the gender listed on their birth certificates, not that with which they currently identified.[33] The business community objected strenuously; many organizations announced boycotts of the state; President Obama threatened to withhold federal funds; and eventually the state legislature backed away from this discriminatory law. In the years since then, however, more than a dozen other states have considered such legislation. Here was about the most basic conceivable human rights issue—the right to health and sanitation—and an issue that one way or another affected virtually everyone, not just transgender people, since almost everyone uses public bathrooms.

But bathrooms were not the only locus of human rights controversy that year. The internet, another ubiquitous feature of contemporary life, was also the subject of much consternation. Google was fined by French officials for violating Europe's "right to be forgotten" provisions that allow anyone with connections in Europe to ask search engines to take down links to their names on internet sites.[34] This is a privacy protection that is not widely available in the United States but the proliferation of cyber bullying and so-called revenge porn, in which perpetrators circulate intimate pictures of victims, have prompted calls for far greater protections—a position that has raised the ire of staunch First Amendment defenders but found favor with some women's rights supporters.[35]

Facebook, Twitter, YouTube, and other social media sites were upbraided following the November 2016 presidential election for facilitating the transmission of "fake news" and pressured to take down such postings, raising questions of free speech on the one hand and the right to free and fair elections on the other.[36] The issue was complicated by the fact that, as a way to open up the Chinese market,

Facebook had recently been developing software that would prevent posts from appearing in people's news feeds in specific countries, thereby allowing China (or other governments) to exert further control over access to information—something no human rights advocate would presumably support.[37] Eventually Facebook and other social media sites agreed to exercise far more control over false postings. Given that more than 3.5 billion people use the internet—that's 40 percent of the world's population—these new policies are bound to have widespread impact.

Or consider some recent advances in genetics. A white supremacist named Craig Cobb who, according to *Harper's Magazine,* had tried "to establish an all-white town in North Dakota in 2012," was chagrinned to learn, after taking a DNA test, that he was 14 percent sub-Saharan African. "I had no idea," he said, "or I wouldn't have gone and done that."[38] But, whether you like your DNA findings or not, the question of who owns them has been heatedly contested. If you don't own them yourself, could relatives or employers or governments get ahold of information about your health or racial identity without your consent?[39] And with the possibility emerging of universal DNA databases that can track the DNA profiles of everyone in a prescribed data set like a country, might Big Brother be gaining a toehold that we will eventually regret? Tracking and maintaining DNA samples from crime scenes seems entirely appropriate but what becomes of privacy rights if the universe of stored DNA profiles is extended to all citizens?

These are just a handful of the disputes about rights already underway that may have profound implications for our lives.

RIGHTS ARE OFTEN ASKED TO DO too much—end tribalism and nationalism, stop violence and privation, usher in universal moral values and enforce them. No set of laws and norms could do all that. But what rights can do is to keep that vision of the good society at the front of our minds and offer some suggestions as to how to get closer to that ideal than we are today. Unless one believes that describing where we want to go as a human race and helping us to shape the journey in that direction has no value, it is hard to dispute the importance of conversations about rights. As the Russian writer and activist Alexander Herzen, whose polemics helped bring an end to serfdom, once observed, "We must be proud of not being needles and threads in the hands of fate as it sews the motley cloth of history. . . . We know that this cloth is not sewn without us. . . . And that is not all; *we can change the pattern of the carpet.*"[40]

This book is designed to describe the stitches that may be needed as we sew new patterns in the carpet of rights. We authors hope it will encourage everyone to pick up needle and thread because, after all, it is up to all of us to do that sewing if we wish to create a carpet, a good society, of which we can be proud. That will not happen, however, without a productive debate that hopefully this book will inspire.

# 1

# Why Rights Change

THE ANCIENT GREEKS WERE QUITE imaginative when it came to torture. Perillos was a bronze worker in Athens who invented a device called the brazen bull. Designed in the shape of a real bull but hollow inside, it was just large enough to contain a man. When the victim screamed in protest of his incarceration, an acoustic device inside the bull transformed the screams into what sounded like the bellows of a real bull emanating from the device's nostrils. Eventually a fire was lit under the bronze animal and the resident was slowly burned to death.

The brazen bull would have been used against Athens's enemies but not against Athenian citizens themselves. In fact, free citizens of Greece were almost never subject to torture, even to procure information about crimes. Regarding torture, Aristotle recognized that "people under its compulsion tell lies quite as often as they tell the truth."[1] Free citizens possessed reason, *logos,* and could therefore distinguish between truth and falsehood. This made it possible for them to lie when it was in their best interests, such as to release them from the brazen bull. That is why there was no point in torturing them.

But slaves were different, Greek philosophers argued; it was permissible to torture a slave to obtain evidence of a crime. In and of itself that is not surprising; people with little power, like slaves, have customarily been subject to the worst forms of mistreatment. What is interesting is the reason the Greeks deemed slaves subject to torture. A slave was considered part of his master's body. Hence, he knew everything his master knew but, lacking reason, he was incapable of dissembling. Under torture, a slave had, by his very nature, no alternative but to tell the truth.[2]

Whether or not someone could be legitimately subjected to what we would today call a human rights violation turned on conceptions of their natures. In one form or another such doctrines of natural rights have informed human rights up to the present time.

The preamble of the Universal Declaration of Human Rights (UDHR), for example, opens with the words "Whereas recognition of the *inherent* dignity and of the equal and *inalienable* rights of all members of the human family is the foundation of freedom, justice and peace in the world" and Article 1 affirms that "All human beings are *born* free and equal in dignity and rights. They are *endowed* with reason and conscience." All the italicized words imply that human rights have a basis in human nature and natural rights. By their very natures, human beings have inherent dignity—we are born with such dignity and endowed, like the free citizens of ancient Greece, with reason (and apparently also with something called conscience); therefore, we are entitled to believe we have certain rights.

But now comes a really uncomfortable question: How do we know all that?

If someone were to challenge those presuppositions and say something like, "I don't think all human beings have inherent dignity," or "I agree that males (or white people or Americans or straight people or the hardworking wealthy) have inherent dignity but I sure don't think that women (or people of color or foreigners or LGBTQ folks or the lazy poor) do," how would we refute them? Or what if someone were to say, "Given how many people believe that Elvis Presley is not dead or, despite all the scientific evidence, deny climate change, I can't agree that humans are 'endowed with reason,'" what would we say to convince them otherwise? And this does not even begin to tackle the question of why, in the face of massive cruelty over millennia, we think that the human creature is endowed with conscience. If human rights are predicated upon these notions of human nature and we have no answer to our skeptics, how can we defend the notion of rights at all? What, in other words, is the foundation for human rights claims? When the U.N. commission that composed the UDHR in 1948 asked a group of scholars to supply an underlying basis for rights, the scholars threw up their hands. They had agreed on what the list of rights should be "on condition that no one asks us *why*."[3]

THE MOST CONVENIENT WAY to supply an answer would be to cite an unequivocal religious source of authority. In the Hebrew tradition, for example, human beings are explicitly made "in [God's] image, after [God's] likeness."[4] This means that any affront to human dignity is an affront to God and that inasmuch as God is capable of reason and conscience, so must human beings be too. The Christian and Muslim scriptures echo this thought: Jesus says that to the extent that you treat the neediest human beings with dignity and kindness, so you are treating Him in that way.[5] And the Koran reminds us that "the Lord announced to the angels, 'I shall create a human out of baked clay, so when I have made him and breathed into him of My Spirit, do ye fall down, prostrating yourselves to him.'"[6]

Unfortunately, using these or any other religious source as a foundation for human rights is simply untenable. Whatever that foundation is, it must be self-evidently universal in the sense that it transcends particular traditions or cultures and can appeal to everybody. There are at least twenty-two major religious traditions in the world with a half-million or more adherents, to say nothing of the many subdivisions within each of them, and those traditions are notorious for not being able to agree with one another about what their own faith requires, much less agree with those of other faith traditions about what God requires.[7] (To take but one of thousands of possible examples, a group of second-century Christians called Montanists believed that only those who ate a steady diet of radishes would ever enter the kingdom of heaven. It took about four centuries for the Christian church to rid itself of that heresy.) Moreover, even if all the world's religions agreed that God endowed humans with dignity, reason, and conscience, there are an estimated one billion or more people who claim no religious affiliation at all.[8] It is hard to imagine that any religious claim could satisfy those for whom religious authority itself is suspect.

This brings us back to natural law: if we could find some characteristic that all human beings share by our very nature and that virtually everyone agrees that they share, maybe that could be the foundation for human rights. This has been a popular philosophical quest since at least the days of Plato and probably long before—a search for what the philosopher Richard Rorty called "a special added ingredient which puts [humans] in a different ontological category than the brutes [and] respect for [which] provides a reason for people to be nice to each other."[9]

The most popular common characteristic of human beings that natural law advocates have cited is, as discussed regarding the Greeks, the human capacity to reason. It doesn't really matter how many people think Elvis is still alive: they are still employing reason, if ineptly, to reach that conclusion, and that makes them superior to other creatures and therefore eligible to be treated better.

But reason is not the only candidate for a common core to human nature. The seventeenth-century Dutch legal theorist Hugo Grotius, often considered the founder of international law, thought this unifying core was "an impelling desire for . . . social life . . . with those who are of [our] own kind."[10] Philosopher Thomas Hobbes famously

declared it "the liberty each man has to use his power . . . for the preservation of . . . his own life."[11] John Locke, often thought to have influenced Thomas Jefferson in the writing of the Declaration of Independence, insisted it was freedom and equality. Given all these
options and many more, how is one to choose? Grotius's sociability,
for example, seems to be at considerable odds with Hobbes's "war of
everyone against everyone."

Perhaps more contemporary notions of human nature can be of
help. If we are to believe the evolutionary biologists, kin selection—
that is, the willingness to engage in behavior that benefits the genetic
survival of a person's closest relatives—is a core characteristic of all
human beings.[12] Economist Herbert Gintis believes it is a predisposition to revolt against authority.[13] Or consider the theory of the well-
known political scientist Francis Fukuyama, who has argued that,
though violence "may be natural to human beings," so is "the propensity to control and challenge violence."[14] Again, how to choose?

But choosing is just the beginning of the problems with citing
human nature as the foundation for "natural" rights. In the first
place, the history of natural law reveals that its proponents have
often either had ulterior motives for their choices or constructed
their theorems based less on objective observations about Nature
than upon the biases of their times. This doesn't necessarily make
them wrong but it certainly makes them suspect.

Thomas Hobbes's convictions about the natural inclination to preserve one's own life at the expense of others, for example, was not
incidentally affected by his experience as a Royalist who had fled
to France during the English Civil War when he feared that the overthrow of King Charles I would sweep him up too. Thomas Jefferson,
author of the "self-evident" natural law that "all men are created
equal," claimed that by nature African Americans experienced the
grief of afflictions only fleetingly because they "participate more of
sensation than reflection."[15] This is also, he says, why they have a
"disposition to sleep when . . . unemployed in labor." John Locke

preached the inherent freedom and equality of property owners, thereby excluding peasants, to say nothing of slaves, and, of course, women, because women could not own property. But, then, as historian of philosophy David Boucher put it:

> Generally in the history of natural law and natural rights, there was no question of women being fully human; they either lacked, or possessed to a different degree, those attributes that were essential for a fully functioning rational life. Their role was subordinate to that of men, and men, as a matter of entitlement under natural law and natural right, ruled over women in the household.[16]

Even Francis Fukuyama managed to find justification for his own political predilections in natural law. The fact that humans have an inherent inclination to control violence, he said, "allows us to rule out certain forms of political order like tyranny as unjust" and "this helps explain why there are a lot of capitalist liberal democracies around the world . . . but very few socialist dictatorships."[17] The nature of human nature seems largely to be in the eye of the beholder or, as law professor Catherine MacKinnon put it, natural law is "a secular religion that moves only those who believe in it [with] content [that] tends to describe the status quo and attribute it to nature."[18]

But even if we could agree on a common description of human nature, free from our own prejudices, how would that help us formulate a list of rights?

It is not just notoriously difficult to explain how we get from an observation about our natures to a corresponding moral law—what philosophers customarily call the "naturalistic fallacy." Let's say we all agree that kin selection is inherently part of humans' evolutionary profile. Why does that necessarily mean that favoring the survival of our closest kin over those more distant or unrelated to us is the right thing to do? Indeed, the anthropologist Robin Fox has suggested that if someone kills my offspring, kin selection as a moral guide would sanction killing one of the murderer's offspring in revenge or even impregnating a female in his genetic line to perpetuate my genes—hardly behavior we would find morally defensible.[19]

But apart from this rather abstruse philosophical argument about taking human nature as the foundation of rights, there are three very practical problems. In the first place, no single notion of human nature can possibly justify the long list of rights that have been identified in human rights instruments. For example, Hobbes's assertion that human beings have an inherent right to defend their own lives might support a right to life or rights to food or shelter. But how could it be used to imply that we must also adopt rights such as the right to an education, the right to form a trade union, the right to be registered by a government at birth, or the right to move freely around one's country, all of which are well established? These are all very desirable things, of course, but for centuries some human beings have managed to survive without them. To his credit, Fukuyama recognized this lacuna when he admitted that "there is no simple translation of human nature into human rights."[20]

Even if there were, however, the second problem with using human nature and natural rights as a foundation for rights is that they limit rights to humans. This automatically eliminates without even a discussion rights for nonhuman entities like animals or robots or natural ecosystems. But, as the physicist Carlo Rovelli has pointed out, we might in the past have been able to think of humans as the "summit of nature"; today, knowing what we do about such things as our dependence on ecological systems, "this idea raises a smile. If we are special, we are special in the way that everyone feels themselves to be ... [but] certainly not for the rest of nature."[21]

And the third problem is that, unless one believes that human nature changes far more quickly than any respectable evolutionary scientist would admit, our nature is presumably a relatively static thing. Hence, the natural rights it undergirds should be static too. But, as discussed previously and illustrated in more detail subsequently, if there is anything we can say about rights, it is that conceptions of them are subject to waves of change from generation to generation.

For all these reasons most contemporary philosophers have abandoned the search for a philosophical foundation for rights in natural law.

So DOES THIS MEAN that we have no answer to those annoying skeptics who ask how we know that human beings possess inherent dignity and can claim all those rights? Not at all. For, in addition to God and natural law, there is a third alternative for how we justify human rights claims. This third path is commonly called constructivism, meaning that human beings literally construct the rights they have. They create them, not at random, on a whim, or out of whole cloth, but out of a notion of the common good, that is, based on a widespread consensus among nations as to what constitutes the "good society."

Even the UDHR, which, as mentioned previously, describes rights as inherent, covers all its bases by including in its preamble far more pragmatic reasons to believe in human rights. Disregard for them, it says, has "resulted in barbarous acts which have outraged the conscience of mankind." Without them, human beings will "be compelled to have recourse, as a last resort, to rebellion against tyranny and oppression." Rights are "essential to promote the development of friendly relations between nations." In other words, human rights promote civility, deter oppression, foster stability, and encourage peaceful interactions with others—all features, we can safely assume, of a good and admirable society.

But on what basis do we assume that? How do we choose the characteristics of a "good society" and hence the rights best positioned to promote those characteristics? As with conceptions of natural law, philosophers disagree with one another about the answers. Some argue that the fundamental characteristic of a good society is that it provides for the basic necessities of survival; others that it maximizes the opportunity for human beings to exercise sovereignty over their own life decisions. The renowned philosopher John Rawls argued that justice is derived from notions of fairness that we would select if we had no idea ahead of time where we would end up in a society in terms of our class position, natural assets, intelligence, strength, or other factors. He ultimately provided a number of rights that he thought embodied fairness, including equality of opportunity, a decent distribution of income, and health care for all.[22]

Perhaps the most comprehensive description of a good society, however, has come from the social theorist Martha Nussbaum, who champions what she calls "the capabilities approach." "Capabilities" are the answers a society can reasonably give to the question "What is a person able to choose freely to be or to do?" and they constitute a measure of quality of life, a measure of the good society. Nussbaum argues that a capabilities approach requires us to focus "on the protection of the areas of freedom so central that their removal makes a life not worthy of human dignity."[23] Capabilities necessary to a life of dignity encompass areas such as bodily health and integrity, an adequate education, the ability to produce self-expressive works, the option to participate in political life, and property ownership, among others. To realize many of these capabilities requires respect for corresponding rights. In order for someone to fully exercise the capability to participate in political life, for example, that person needs both to receive an education and to live in a society that protects free speech—both important fundamental rights.

But still a skeptic could raise objections. Doesn't this approach also depend upon an assumption of inherent human dignity? And what makes this list of capabilities anything more than Nussbaum's personal opinion?

The answer to the first question is that we need not assume that human beings or animals possess inherent dignity in order to believe that they should be treated as if they do. We don't need to prove that they have dignity in the same way some people have brown hair or a slight limp—in fact, such a thing is not susceptible of proof. We simply need to posit or assign dignity to them; we need to take it on faith, what the philosophers call an a priori assumption, and we do that for two reasons.

First, we assign dignity because we intuitively sense that we ourselves are worthy of dignity and want to be treated that way; we know what it is like to be humiliated or in pain and, in Richard Rorty's phrase, we expand the "circle of solidarity" to make the assumption that others, including animals in their own way, can experience pain and indignity too.[24] If we want to deny that other people share such feelings and hopes, we must prove that they are not like "us" in significant ways. Many people have tried to do just that, from the Greeks with their slaves to the Nazis with their *untermensch*.[25] They have made those assertions but they have never provided anything even remotely resembling scientific proof.

And the second reason we posit dignity is because, if we imagine a world that did not operate on such an assumption, in which anyone could be exploited by anyone else, no one honored promises, no one recognized other people's needs and interests, and everyone felt free to indulge in what the UDHR refers to as "barbarous acts," the result would very quickly be chaos, as is readily proved by those instances in which communities have adopted such practices. Constructivists argue that it is in our ultimate self-interest to act as if people had dignity even if we cannot prove that they do.

But even if we accept the premise that humans (and perhaps other entities that are not human) should be treated as if they had dignity, how do we know that Nussbaum's list of capabilities is definitive and not her personal whim? In order for constructivism to work as a guide to human rights, we need to appeal to a larger set of decision makers than just one academic theorist.

Well, how about the whole world? If the whole world agrees that certain rights are critical to fostering human dignity and maximizing human capabilities, then we should have pretty good evidence as to what the world thinks of, at the moment, as constitutive of the good society.

Now of course no one can actually survey the whole world. But the next best thing to doing so is to look at what the world's governments—forming the so-called international community—have agreed are rights worthy of respect and protection. These are the rights contained in the human rights instruments referred to in the Introduction. These are rights that, while not always ratified by universal consensus, only go into effect when they have been adopted by a significant number of states, enough to constitute a putative consensus.

That process can be a frustrating one and it can take a long time for widely accepted norms to change. The process that Nussbaum has outlined as the means to determine central capabilities is very similar to that through which rights are established:

> Sometimes it is clear that a given capability is central . . . : the world has come to a consensus, for example, on the importance of primary and secondary education. It seems equally clear that the ability to whistle *Yankee Doodle Dandy* while standing on one's head is not of central importance and does not deserve a special level of protection. Many cases may be unclear for a long time: for example, it was not understood for many centuries that a woman's right to refuse her husband intercourse was a crucial right of bodily integrity. What must happen here is that the debate must take place, and each must make arguments attempting to show that a given liberty is implicated in the idea of human dignity.[26]

Sometimes those "arguments" are first made by a few thinkers, opinion leaders, or advocates for the voiceless who sense injustice and seek to right it. But often they arise from the grassroots level as people experience affronts to their dignity or imagine a new conception of what is required to maximize human capabilities and then organize to get an old right revised or a new one recognized. Norms change through a complicated process of changing interests among the powerful, the introduction of new technologies, the spread of education and consciousness, and many other factors, but eventually, as norms change, laws usually do too.

It ought to be to be clear now why rights are "transactional" and why they are not static; why, in the words of the human rights scholar Kathryn Sikkink, they "contain the seeds for their own expansion."[27] Sometimes that expansion builds upon current rights in an evolutionary way; other times it reflects the designation of a rights revolution, an expansion of the category of rights holders to a new set of people or new entities. Remember the statement in the Introduction that rights represent claims that the less powerful make against those with the power to affect their lives. As those with less power become more attuned to the deprivations and opportunities in their lives, they may use what power they do have to make more and bolder claims until the decision makers have little choice but to accede to a new vision, to expand the meaning of the good society. The same is true of those who speak on behalf of what are called "moral patients"—those who cannot advocate for themselves, like animals or robots (at least right now!) or the natural world.

The process of rights change is not necessarily a linear one. One set of claims may contradict another—should the public's right to information trump an individual's right to privacy?—and those conflicts may need to be adjudicated and resolved by international human rights bodies.

In addition, rights do not inevitably change in a progressive direction. As mentioned in the Introduction, this has been the case so far, but it is theoretically possible for rights to devolve, to "go back-ward." Theoretically the international community could revoke rights, could say, "We no longer believe that this right is central to the good society." In the face of terrorism, for example, some have argued that we should cut back on certain due process rights. This is why it is so important to maintain a robust international human rights movement. One can only hope that, should there arise attempts to remove previously codified rights from some group of people, those grassroots movements alluded to before would spring into action to oppose such regression.

Finally, of course, some nations or corporations or militias will inevitably choose to ignore and violate even the most well-established rights but that does not mean those rights are not still valid.

DESPITE THESE DANGERS, a constructivist approach has numerous advantages over the search for foundations for human rights in religion or natural law. For one thing, it provides a clear answer to the kind of skeptics mentioned near the outset of this chapter. We don't have to convince them that human beings have inherent dignity or are endowed with reason or conscience. We simply say, "These rights are rights because the international community has recognized them to be integral to the common good, to a good society. Deny them if you like but, if you do, you will be flying in the face of a significant worldwide consensus."

Moreover, a constructivist approach can justify all the rights contained in human rights instruments, from the most general to the very detailed. If a right is listed in a human rights treaty that has gone into effect, then it has ipso facto been judged important to the realization of the good society. And, under a constructivist approach, that can include the rights of animals and robots and Nature if recognition of their rights comes to be deemed also integral to such a society at some point in the future.

Finally, a constructivist approach squares with the history of changes in our understandings of rights, with how the evolution of rights has really worked. Those changes did not come about through a sudden realization that God or natural law required them. They came about because of changing consensus and changing norms, often over centuries, regarding that which constituted the common good. During the sixteenth century, the rotting heads of criminals were regularly displayed impaled on the spikes of London Bridge. Today that would be considered the mark of a barbaric society rather than a good one, not to mention the fact that the United Kingdom long ago abolished capital punishment altogether.

To give us a better sense of how this change process takes place, consider two case studies—one regarding the long-standing right of civilians to be immune from military danger and the other regarding a relatively new set of rights having to do with persons with disabilities. The first represents change in norms and laws initiated largely by power brokers and the latter exemplifies change via grassroots activists; the first reflects an evolution of rights, the second a revolutionary introduction of a whole new set of rights. Taken together, they both illustrate that human rights are understood differently today than they have been in the past and, indeed, than they will be in the years to come.

IN 1999, WHEN CO-AUTHOR Bill was the executive director of Amnesty International USA, he led an Amnesty fact-finding mission to Northern Ireland. After interviewing dozens of victims of human rights violations on both sides of "the Troubles," he met with the first minister of Northern Ireland, David Trimble, a Protestant and outspoken member of the Ulster Unionist Party. Trimble strongly opposed those who wanted to unite Northern Ireland with the Irish Republic. "You human rights people," he said to Bill bitterly, "complain about so-called 'victims' of abuse by the British military but you never object when the IRA [Irish Republican Army] attacks the soldiers themselves—bombings, sniper fire—and violates *their* human rights!"

This was a frequent refrain from governments under criticism for their human rights violations but it was based on a common misunderstanding. When they are in uniform, take up their weapons, and are thereby invested with the power and authority of the state, those in the military voluntarily give up certain human rights protections in exchange for permission to use appropriate deadly force when necessary. When one soldier kills an enemy soldier in the course of combat, we do not call it "murder" if the killing adheres to the laws of war; we call it a "casualty of battle." We would not prosecute the perpetrator for a crime nor regard his or her action as a violation of the decedent's human rights. (Whether the IRA qualified as a legitimate army was a matter of long-standing dispute between the British and the republicans.)

This does not mean of course that the deaths of soldiers are not tragic and regrettable. Napoleon is alleged to have said that "soldiers are made to be killed" and, while putting it that starkly is distasteful, it points dramatically to the fact that those in the military fall into a distinctly different category from civilians when it comes to the right to life. This is certainly a painful point to make, particularly to the families of the fallen.

On the other hand, what is today widely agreed upon, if also too often ignored in the course of war, is that civilians are to be extended a whole host of protections that are designed to underscore that they are not "made to be killed."[28] The German General Helmut von Moltke believed that "the greatest kindness in war is to bring it to a speedy conclusion."[29] But winning at any cost may not be an option: as the political philosopher Michael Walzer put it, "If it is always morally possible to fight, it is not always [morally] possible to do what is required to win."[30] Among the restraints are the rights of civilians in war contained in the fourth Geneva Convention and the Geneva Conventions' additional protocols. Civilians are to be immune from the use of deadly military force except under exceptional circumstances. Even the Taliban ordered their followers to "do their best to avoid civilian deaths and injuries and damage to civilian property."[31]

But, obvious as this distinction between combatants and civilians may seem to us today, it was not obvious at all in the fourth century when Augustine of Hippo first formulated the concept of just war (*jus ad bellum*), a description of the criteria a war must meet in order to be considered morally sound and justified. For the Romans before him, war was justified to reclaim property or to repulse attackers. But Augustine added a religious dimension: the just warrior was now seen as God's agent compelled to avenge wrongdoing, inflict punishment on the wrongdoer, and thus prevent further violations of God's law.[32]

Moreover, and far more importantly for present purposes, Augustine made no distinction between an enemy's soldiers and its civilian population. When it came to how the just war was to be conducted (the so-called *jus in bello*), enemy civilians could be slain with impunity just as enemy soldiers could because they were all guilty of sinning against God and hence all deserving of punishment. There was only one exception and that, not surprisingly perhaps, was clergy. From the fourth century on, clergy were neither to participate in war nor be targets of it.[33]

Due to Augustine's enormous influence, his views largely prevailed for more than a century. This is typified by the remark of a papal legate (representative) in 1209 when asked by a military commander how to distinguish between a Christian and a heretic among the enemy population. "Kill them all!" advised the legate. "God will know His own!"[34]

Near the end of the feudal period, around the one-thousandth anniversary of Jesus's death, however, two factors combined to offer greater protection to at least some civilians. The first was the chivalric codes that attached to many feudal knights and made it a matter of dishonor to harm those who were considered too weak to inflict harm themselves, such as women, children, the aged, and the mentally ill.[35] And the second was a series of church decrees that collectively became known as the Peace of God. Distressed by the multitude of wars among vassal states that, among other things, put church communities and properties in jeopardy, the church insisted that not just clergy but also monks, friars, pilgrims, travelers, merchants, and peasants cultivating the soil, in addition to their animals and property, were to be spared the ravages of war.[36]

But the chivalric codes and the Peace of God movement both still rested on the Augustinian notion of collective guilt and punishment, with a few exceptions carved out for exempt categories. Immunity from the dangers of combat were still considered an arbitrary gift—from the knights or the church—not yet a right.

It was not until the sixteenth century that another theologian, Francisco de Vitoria, came up with the then-novel idea that both sides in a conflict might think their cause to be just and, conversely, that both sides might in fact be pursuing war for an unjust cause. Were that to be the case, noncombatants on both sides ought to be spared unnecessary harm by right (that key word "unnecessary" will be revisited in a moment); they should be presumed innocent unless evidence could be obtained to the contrary. Only those who bore arms or engaged in fighting could be legitimate targets of war's horrors.[37]

Vitoria's reconceptualization of the *jus in bello* was certainly an improvement over Augustine but it retained a significant flaw: innocence was only to be presumed of other *Christian* noncombatants; as for Turks or any other "barbaric" tribe, the old rules still applied. It was up to the seventeenth-century legal scholar Hugo Grotius, previously introduced, to argue for the extension of immunity, at least theoretically, to all noncombatants.

Grotius was a jurist, not a cleric or theologian. War to him was not a matter of good versus evil so much as a means of settling disputes. His understanding of natural law—remember, "an impelling desire for ... social life ... with those who are of [our] own kind"—compelled him to conclude that only those who have done wrong personally could be punished. Augustine's notion of the enemy as one body was flawed, and, therefore, all noncombatants, not just those lucky few who made it onto the exemption list, ought to be safe from attack "except as a necessary measure of defense or as a result not a part of his purpose."[38] Grotius's exception—what is called the "double effect," meaning that a well-intentioned act may have an unintended ill consequence—would become a major loophole in civilian immunity but the fact that a secular theorist had sought to ground that immunity in natural law rather than church doctrine was a major advance. It was, in fact, the beginning of the whole idea of the "civilian" and the transfer of responsibility for civilian protection from the church to the nation-state.[39]

Unfortunately, it would take more than three centuries for civilian immunity to be formally recognized by an international convention as applying to residents of every nation. Those centuries would include the introduction of "total war" under Napoleon, which extended into World Wars I and II. This strategy was encapsulated in the braggadocious remark of the French General François Westerman after one battle: "I have crushed the children under the hoofs of the horses; massacred the women ... who ... will breed no more brigands. ... The roads are strewn with corpses."[40]

They would also, however, see the appearance of such documents as the Lieber Code adopted in 1863 by the Union Army in the U.S. Civil War, which held that "the United States ... protects, in hostile countries occupied by them, ... strictly private property; the persons of the inhabitants, especially those of women; and the sacredness of domestic relations."[41] The founding of the International Red Cross precipitated the creation of the first Geneva Convention of 1864; even though the convention dealt not with civilians but with wounded soldiers, it nudged the world toward establishing internationally accepted laws of war (international humanitarian law or IHL). Similarly, the Hague Conventions of 1899 and 1907 fundamentally addressed the conditions of prisoners of war and limitations on weaponry. For the first time, an international treaty restricted ill treatment of non-combatants through such provisions as the outlawing of the bombardment of undefended places and the affirmation that "individual lives and private property ... must be respected."[42]

It was not until the adoption of the fourth Geneva Convention in 1949, however, after the carnage of World War II, that detailed legal protocols were established for the protection of civilians affected by war. The convention, along with its three additional protocols, adopted in 1997 and 2005 and covering both international and domestic conflicts, addresses everything from medical care to the treatment of cultural objects to the respectful disposal of the dead.[43] A critical provision is Common Article 3, which affirms that "persons taking no active part in the hostilities ... shall in all circumstances be treated humanely, without any adverse distinction founded on race, color, religion or faith, sex, birth or wealth, or any other similar criteria."[44]

This all-too-condensed sketch of the development of civilian immunity has been limited to Western history, but professor Zhu Li-Sun of the People's University of Beijing has noted that even in ancient China, very similar rules existed "that kept war operations within bounds and protected war victims, [including] ... civilians."[45] The Prophet Muhammad laid down ten laws restricting the practice of war and prohibiting, among other things, the killing of children, women, the elderly, and others.[46] Throughout the world the norm that militaries should do their best to minimize civilian casualties is now widely considered a hallmark of the good society. When Serbian forces intentionally targeted Bosnian civilians in the early 1990s or when the *janjaweed* militia in collaboration with the Sudanese government terrorized villages in Darfur, Sudan, in the early 2000s, they were regarded by the international community as having sacrificed all claims to be part of the consortium of civilized nations.

Few things cause the United States to suffer international opprobrium more readily than when its airstrikes in Afghanistan or Yemen result in massive civilian casualties.

This is not to say that the application of international humanitarian law regarding civilian immunity is always simple. How do even conscientious militaries distinguish between militia members or terrorists, for example, who slip back and forth between civilian and military roles? Or what about the principle of double effect referenced earlier? Additional Protocol I to the 1949 Geneva Convention requires militaries to "do everything *feasible* to verify that the objectives to be attacked are neither civilians nor civilian objects" and to refrain from launching attacks "which may be *expected* to cause ... loss of civilian life ... which would be *excessive in relation to the ... military advantage anticipated*" [emphasis added].[47] It's easy to see that such questions are open to wide and often disputed interpretation. Nonetheless, the general principle that civilians are innocent and not "made to be killed" is regarded as customary international law binding on all countries in all circumstances.

And yet, it obviously took literally millennia to reach this consensus. Had someone suggested to Augustine that anyone among the enemy population, except perhaps clergy, deserved to be spared, he would have regarded the idea as tantamount to a rejection of God. A combination of changing ideas, circumstances, and technologies gradually ushered in new norms.

Augustine's formulation of just war theory itself was influenced by the political exigencies of his age. In 312 AD (Common Era) the Roman Emperor Constantine had converted from paganism to Christianity. When, a century later, Rome was sacked by the Goths, many non-Christians blamed Christian pacifism for the debacle— Saint Maximilian, for example, was martyred in 296 for refusing to take up arms.[48] Augustine's justification of war, hearkening back to the military feats of Joshua, Samson, and other figures in the Hebrew scriptures, was designed to refute the Christians' detractors.[49]

With the fall of the Roman Empire, Europe lacked any unifying governmental structure; a multitude of tribes vied for territory. Even the rise of the greatest medieval king, Charlemagne, in the eighth century did not end the competition for dominance among local nobles and their respective knights. These knights fought not necessarily out of religious conviction, as Augustine had required, but for pecuniary gain. They often received that gain from the property of the noncombatants, including the churchly, that they had slaughtered. A feeling of present-day vulnerability coupled with fear of the end of the world presaged by the close of the first millennium since Jesus's crucifixion contributed to the urgency of the Peace of God movement.[50]

Similarly, Vitoria's modifications of Augustine's strictures were influenced by developments such as the introduction in the eleventh and twelfth centuries of new weaponry like the longbow. This bow could be fired from a safe distance and inflict indiscriminate damage. It therefore made war a more impersonal enterprise than it had been before. Later, during the Hundred Years' War of 1337–1453, the first professional standing army was created, which meant that responsibility for war was clearly lodged in governments and their soldiers rather than their subjects. Then, too, the decline of the church's power with the coming of the Renaissance made Grotius's secular formulations almost inevitable.

Politics and new technology continued to influence changes in the laws of war in more modern times as well. The Lieber Code was designed in part to address the treatment by the Union army of freed slaves in the South. Breech-loading rifles with a firing rate twice that of muskets appeared in 1843; they led to the carnage that so appalled Henry Dunant, the founder of the International Red Cross, and provided inspiration for the first Geneva Convention. Among the provisions of the 1907 Hague Convention was the outlawing of the use of recently invented poison gases. The involvement of the airplane in combat in World Wars I and II vastly expanded the danger to civilians—the British bombing of Dresden, Germany, in 1945, explicitly designed to kill civilians, cost as many as 300,000 lives—and led, along with the horrors of the Holocaust, the nuclear bombings of Japan, and the subsequent Nuremberg and Tokyo war crimes trials, to the adoption of the fourth Geneva Convention.[51] Norms, in other words, are adapted to accommodate circumstances and are changed in response to a changing world.

Nor has the evolution of the protection of civilians affected by combat ended today. Land mines, which, especially after the cessation of hostilities, pose an ongoing threat to civilian communities where they have been laid, have been in use since World War I. Today, however, more than 80 percent of the world's countries have ratified the Land Mines Treaty, which went into effect in 1999, outlawing the use and production of antipersonnel mines and committing those states to clear the weapons from affected areas.[52]

But perhaps the most significant recent development in civilian immunity rights has come with regard to the treatment of systematic rape as a weapon of war. Shockingly but perhaps not surprisingly given the historic oppression of women, neither the Nuremburg nor Tokyo War Crimes Tribunals specifically mentioned rape as a war crime or crime against humanity. This lacuna reflects the age-old supposition that rape is merely an incidental consequence of war. Though the fourth Geneva Convention asserts that "women shall be especially protected against any attack on their honor, in particular against rape," this was largely considered a problem of rogue individuals and, in the words of one scholar, "appears [to be] merely a symbolic gesture since rape in war was virtually ignored by the international community until the . . . 1990s."[53] In 1971, for example, up to 400,000 rapes occurred in Bangladesh's war for independence with no international consequences for the perpetrators.

All that began to change in the 1990s with the ethnic cleansing of Bosnian Muslims by Bosnian Serb forces and the massive genocide of Tutsi tribal members by Hutus in Rwanda, both of which involved the systematic and intentional use of rape as a method of warfare. According to the minutes of a 1991 meeting of Yugoslav (Serb) Army officers,

> Our analysis of the behavior of the Muslim communities demonstrates that the morale, will, and bellicose nature of their groups can be undermined only if we aim our action at the point where the religious and social structure is most fragile. We refer to the women, especially adolescents, and children. Decisive intervention on these social figures would spread confusion . . . , leading to probable [Muslim] retreat from the territories."[54]

The result of this policy was the rape of 20,000–50,000 women, in houses, on streets, in detention centers, and "rape camps."[55] In Rwanda, Human Rights Watch reported that Hutu propaganda "identified the sexuality of Tutsi women as a means through which the Hutu community sought to infiltrate and control the Tutsi community."[56] As many as a half-million women were subsequently subjected to rape.[57] Faced with such massive numbers of victims, the international criminal tribunals for both the former Yugoslavia and for Rwanda, responding in part to the growing empowerment and outspokenness of women, declared rape a war crime and crime against humanity. Eventually they obtained convictions, thereby establishing that rape as an instrument of war is to be taken seriously as a transgression against customary international law.

Despite these changes, however, it would be foolish to assume that the evolution of civilian immunity rights is at an end as discussed in Chapter 7, which examines new forms of robotic weaponry on the horizon. Because what the historian James Turner Johnson said about the fourth-century version of noncombatant immunity applies to the twenty-first century as well: "It is not a moral absolute, demarcating the limits of that which is ideally, inflexibly and eternally just, but a time-bound and culture-bound formulation of a moral floor upon human conduct in war."[58] Upon that solid floor future generations will find stories yet to build.

Civilian immunity, in one form or another, has been a topic of debate and revision for centuries. But the next section considers a set of rights that have been recognized only recently.

LEE NETTLES WAS FRUSTRATED. He was eager to watch movies on Netflix's "Watch Instantly" internet streaming service but he couldn't do so for a very simple reason. Lee Nettles is deaf and most of Netflix's movie offerings did not come with closed captions. His only choice was to rent closed-caption movies individually and at higher prices from other sources. So Nettles, the director of deaf and hard of hearing independent living services at the Stavros Center for Independent Living in Springfield, Massachusetts, decided to do something about it. In collaboration with the National Association for the Deaf, he sued Netflix under the Americans with Disabilities Act (ADA), arguing, on behalf of the 36 million deaf and hard of hearing people in the United States, that, as the largest distributor of streaming videos, Netflix was a public accommodation and its failure to provide closed captions on all its offerings was an instance of illegal discrimination.[59] Nettles is just one example of a host of individuals from around the world whose activism over the past fifty years prompted the birth of a new movement, the disability rights movement, which resulted in the U.N. Convention on the Rights of Persons with Disabilities (CRPD) coming into effect in 2008. That convention, which has been ratified by at least 160 nations, represents the most recent set of rights recognized at the international level.

It is not of course that humans with disabilities, be they physical or cognitive, are a new phenomenon. "The Rig-Veda," an ancient sacred poem of India composed around 1500 BCE, records that the warrior queen Vishpala lost her leg in battle and was fitted with an iron prosthesis.[60] But few categories of people have suffered more persistent misunderstanding and discrimination.

In the twentieth century alone mass sterilizations of the disabled inspired by the eugenics movement met with the approval of such luminaries as famed U.S. Supreme Court Justice Oliver Wendell Holmes who, writing in a 1927 opinion, pronounced, "It is better for all the world if, instead of waiting to execute degenerate offspring of crime . . . society can prevent those who are manifestly unfit from continuing their kind. . . . Three generations of imbeciles is enough," a perspective that partially inspired Hitler's program of extermination.[61] In almost every society, disabilities have been considered shameful and persons with disabilities set apart and shunned. As recently as 1980 a court in Germany granted a vacationer a reduction in hotel costs because she had had to share her hotel in Greece with a group of cognitively impaired Swedes.[62]

To the extent that people with disabilities have been treated with kindness throughout most of modern history, that treatment has taken the form of charitable services, from the establishment of the first college for the deaf in 1817 to the invention of Braille in 1829 to the founding of the first school for those with developmental disabilities in the United States in 1848 and of the Royal National Institute for the Blind in the United Kingdom in 1868. The return home of large numbers of veterans with disabilities from World Wars I and II raised awareness of the need for more such support but was rarely translated into an attempt to address the systemic dimensions of society—everything from physical barriers to social attitudes—that barred many people with disabilities from living lives of dignity. After all, even America's disabled president, Franklin D. Roosevelt, felt compelled to hide his condition from the public for fear of political repercussions. And disabilities, to the extent to which they were addressed at all, were treated in isolation from one another—impairment of sight separate from that of hearing or mobility and cognitive or developmental disabilities considered of a different order from them all.

Inspired in part by the civil rights, peace, and women's movements, people with disabilities began to imagine a new conceptualization of the good society in the 1970s. Recognizing that if they were
to fully realize their human capabilities, society would need to
change in some fundamental ways—in its social attitudes, its archi-
tecture, its laws, and its technology—they began rejecting the charity
model with its attendant assumption that disabilities were largely
a medical problem, and, joining together across disabilities, started
to frame their goals in terms of rights.

In the United States many of the earliest instances of activism
took place on college campuses or in local communities as individuals began to question the discrimination and lack of accommodation they faced. When Judy Heumann, for example, a postpolio
paraplegic, was denied a teaching license in New York State in 1970
because the authorities did not think she could get her students out
of a classroom safely in case of fire, she successfully sued and became the first teacher in a wheelchair in New York schools. Ed
Roberts, a student at the University of California, Berkeley and a
postpolio quadriplegic, was initially housed in the university health
facility because none of the school's dormitories were accessible to
him. He and others founded the Physically Disabled Students program in 1970 and two years later established the Berkeley Center
for Independent Living, the first of its kind, to provide support,
counseling, accessible housing, and attendant services for people
with a variety of disability needs.[63]

As more and more people with disabilities, their parents, and supporters in local communities became aware of opportunities for
change, they also began finding each other, building coalitions, and
launching demonstrations. Spurred by Heumann's groundbreaking
example, the group Disabled in Action protested situations such
as inaccessible buildings. When President Richard Nixon vetoed
the 1972 Rehabilitation Act, which would have provided support
for people with spinal cord injuries, Disabled in Action blocked

traffic in front of Nixon's New York campaign headquarters, receiving major media attention. The next year the bill passed; it included a ban on discrimination on the basis of disability by recipients of federal funds. In 1974 the American Coalition of Citizens with Disabilities, a consortium of sixty-five local and national groups representing persons with a wide variety of impairments, was formed. Eventually, after a long series of public actions (in 1978, for example, activists in Denver blocked buses to protest their complete inaccessibility), favorable court decisions, and growing legislative victories, the Americans with Disabilities Act was signed in 1990 by President George H. W. Bush.[64] This was the first comprehensive guarantee in the United States of the rights of the disabled.

Nor was the United States the only place where such grassroots mobilization was stirring the recognition of new rights. Club 68 was founded in West Germany in 1968 to support people with disabilities, and the Union of the Physically Impaired Against Segregation in 1972 formed in the United Kingdom to challenge the charity model of addressing the needs of the differently abled.[65] In the early 1980s the movement went global, resulting in the United Nations declaring the International Decade of Disabled Persons in 1982. That declaration framed disability issues as a rights issue, not a charity or medical issue. This, in turn, began to stimulate organizing and reduce stigma in places like India; in 1995 the Indian government adopted the Persons with Disabilities Act.[66] All this foment for change reached a climax in 2008 with the formal codification in the U.N. Convention of a set of rights that had not even been dreamed of only fifty years before—a climax but not the end of the struggle. And finally, in 2014, Lee Nettles won his case and Netflix agreed to provide closed captioning for all its streaming services.

THE EVOLUTION OF CIVILIAN IMMUNITY and the revolution that created a new set of rights for persons with disabilities both underscore the premises of this book: that rights are dynamic, responsive to new circumstances and consciousness, and change as our ideas of the good society change. We authors could have chosen any number of other examples—the human right to water, about as fundamental a human need as one can imagine, was not recognized by the United Nations until 2010 and is, astonishingly, still not considered a right by the United States. This may change some day, due to the experience of residents living in cities like Flint, Michigan, where contaminated drinking water has led to doubling and tripling of lead levels in the blood of children in the city—this in a place where the majority of the residents are African American and about half live below the poverty line. The Michigan Civil Rights Commission called the government's response to that crisis a "result of systematic racism," and local activist groups in partnership with national groups such as the National Resources Defense Council and ACLU have been mobilizing people to hold the government accountable.[67]

More and more, thanks in good measure to social media and increased organizing skills, rights change, as with disability rights, because people who are directly affected by their denial make the case for their change, for the reimagining of the good society. Other rights change largely because power brokers see it as in their interests for them to change or at least for their governments to be perceived as acting morally, as in the case of civilian immunity where there is no easily organized group of people who anticipate ahead of time that they may need its protections.

What rights will be honored one hundred years from now are impossible to say but what is self-evident is that we must grapple with the challenges our age presents if human rights are to remain pertinent and robust. Time now to turn to the grappling.

# 2

# Beyond Pink and Blue

## Sex and Gender 2.0

WHEN BILL WAS GROWING UP in the United States in the 1950s, people's sex and corresponding gender role were clear and well established. You were either a man or a woman. If you were a man, you went to work and earned money outside the home, and if you were a woman, you stayed home and took care of the family and the housework.

These roles did not apply to everyone. African American women, for example, often worked as domestics, taking care of other people's children and households in addition to their own. Certain jobs were reserved largely for women—school teaching, nursing, secretarial work, and clerking in stores—but those were frequently filled by women who were single either by choice or circumstance.

If you were white, married, and relatively well-off economically, however, you were likely to conform to traditional gender roles, as Bill's parents did. His father went off every weekday morning to teach at the University of Pittsburgh and his mother worked as a housewife, mother, and occasional volunteer. Years after his mother's death, his father reflected on how strange it was that both of them had simply accepted these roles without question. But in fact their choices were not so strange: culture powerfully influences our behavior.

Though Sushma grew up in a very different cultural context—India in the 1970s—her parents too had a conventional marriage and modeled traditional gender roles. Although Hindu mythology has long heralded "third gender" people, commonly called *hijiras*, who defy binary gender definitions, the country also inherited from its years of British colonialism rigid understandings of male and female identities. Raised Hindu, Sushma was sent to a Roman Catholic school—the best education available—where students dressed in uniforms conforming to their assigned gender and where sexuality was not discussed.

The very fact that Sushma and her two sisters were receiving an education with the expectation that they would subsequently seek employment, however, constituted a significant break from gender stereotypes. "You are raising your girls as if they are boys," friends exclaimed to Sushma's parents upon learning of their schooling. "Don't get too much education," Sushma's great-grandmother warned her, "or no man will ever marry you!"

Today far fewer American women like Bill's mother find themselves constrained culturally from pursuing work outside the home and most middle-class Indian girls such as Sushma and her sisters would no longer be considered unusual simply for getting an education. Though women are still subject to rampant discrimination and ongoing violence, assumptions about women and gender roles have changed markedly in many parts of the world. But the most notable change is to the fundamental idea that human beings come in only one of two sexes and gender identities, "pink" or "blue," in the first place. While the words "sex" and "gender" are often used interchangeably, in this chapter "sex" is reserved to denote an individual's anatomical or biological markers like chromosomes and genitalia and "gender" is used to refer to the identity, roles, and forms of expression an individual is assigned based on sexual characteristics or assumes based on an internal self-awareness.

Most scholars now regard "the gender binary"—the notion that there are only two broad gender identities—as anachronistic (and, as this chapter shows, there are in fact many more than two anatomical sexes). In fact, there may not be enough colors in the rainbow to contain all the different gender identities and expressions that people affirm. Facebook lists fifty-six different gender identities from which to choose and those identities may well change over the course of one's life, a phenomenon often referred to as gender fluidity.[1] Even the Barbie doll is now offered in a gender-neutral form.[2] Moreover, the idea that heterosexuality is normative—that marriage is limited to a man and a woman, for instance, or that Mom and Dad are always of two different sexes—is quickly being rendered obsolete, at least in the developed West.

If you believe, as the authors do, that respect for human dignity is at the core of a good society, then you will welcome this more expansive understanding of gender and sexuality. Remember that Martha Nussbaum's capabilities approach, cited in the first chapter, which helps us decide how to measure the good society, focuses on "the protection of the areas of freedom so central that their removal makes a life not worthy of human dignity."[3] What, after all, could be more central to our lives, more important to human dignity, than being able to own and express our most intimate sense of ourselves? What could be more damaging to that dignity than having to hide who we really feel in our heart of hearts that we are? A good society is one in which we have sovereignty over our own bodies and the expression of our love and sexuality.

The end of the gender binary and heteronormativity requires significant changes to our understanding of what human beings ought to be able to claim as rights. Some of those new rights will be familiar to those in the United States, such as the right to same-sex marriage, while others, such as the right for transgender people to access medical suppressants of puberty, may be less so. This chapter will not cover every implication for rights of this more gender diverse worldview, but it will explore some key ones.[4]

Some of the implications of such diversity for rights are pretty straightforward—intersex children should not have their sex determined for them at birth before they have a chance to weigh in on the matter. Others are more complicated—if there is a right to have a child, regardless of sex, gender, or marital status, does that mean that everyone ought to have unfettered access to such reproductive technologies as maternal surrogacy?

While reading this chapter, it is important to ask, "On balance, if this right is recognized, will it contribute to a greater degree of human dignity? Will it make for a good society in which I want to live?" Or, alternatively, "How will the denial of this right harm a segment of our population and hence damage our claim to be a good society?" If you are comfortable with your sex designation at birth and identify as a heterosexual male or female, it may also help to ask, "How would I feel about this right if I were gay, lesbian, transgendered, or intersex?"

One of the challenges to the rights implied by a more fluid view of sex and gender is that worldwide public opinion is lagging considerably behind new medical and psychological understandings. A 2016 survey of attitudes toward LGBT issues in fifty-three countries revealed that, although only 25 percent of those surveyed thought homosexuality should be illegal, 68 percent said they would be upset if their child told them they were in love with a person of their same sex and only 28 percent would find it acceptable for a male child to dress and express himself as a girl.[5] The so-called culture wars have blossomed around the world thanks to such seemingly disparate protagonists as Russia's President Vladimir Putin, with his call for a return to "traditional values," and the American-based World Congress of Families, which has spread its vitriolic opposition to same-sex marriage and gender fluidity well beyond the United States.

Partly this reflects an age-old fear and hatred of sexual minorities. Partly it reflects commonplace resistance to change, which is characteristic of the response to many of the rights explored in this book. But partly it reflects the fact that, even when people are sympathetic to understanding gender and sexuality in new ways, sorting out the complexities of the topic can be daunting. So the next section will start with a few distinctions.

WHEN WE ARE BORN, we are almost inevitably assigned by doctors and / or parents a sex with its corresponding gender identity, that is, male or female. That identity is usually determined by the appearance of external genitalia. If, as we grow up, we feel comfortable with that assigned identity, we are said to be a "cisgender" female or male.

Sometimes, though, it is not possible through observation alone to determine for certain what gender is appropriate to assign to a newborn baby because that baby may be born with indeterminate or ambiguous genitalia. Such children are called "intersex." Traditionally, doctors have made a "best guess" based on such factors as a baby's chromosome pattern and internal reproductive organs, including gonads, thereby forcing a binary identity upon a child. This practice constitutes a significant emerging human rights violation.

Even when their anatomical characteristics may be unambiguously masculine or feminine at birth, however, some people may simply come to feel, often at a very young age, that they have not been assigned the right sex / gender and will decide to live their lives with a different gender identity. Such folks are then understood to be "transgender" (referenced adjectivally as "trans") and, if they undergo surgery, hormonal treatments, voice lessons, or other processes to conform their physical sex manifestations to their psychological gender identities, they are said to have "transitioned." Governments and, indeed, populations are often not sympathetic to trans people and have thrown up a whole slew of roadblocks to the transition process and these too constitute newly recognized human rights violations.

All this ought not to be confused with a wide variety of other matters, such as sexual orientation, gender expression, or cross-dressing. Our "sexual orientation" refers to the type of physical and/or emotional attraction we feel—to those of our own gender ("gay" or "lesbian"), to those of both genders ("bisexual"), to those of the opposite gender ("heterosexual" or "straight"), to those of all genders ("ambisexual"), or to nobody ("asexual").[6] There is no necessary relationship between being transgender or intersex and the sexual orientation a person claims—it falls all over the map. This is why it can be misleading to conflate transgender people with lesbians, gays, and bisexuals, as in the customary "LGBTI" formulation, because trans people may well be exclusively straight. For the sake of convenience, however, that acronym will be used in this chapter.[7]

Nor is our "gender expression," which refers to how we display our gender in dress or demeanor, related in any definitive way to our gender identity or sexual orientation. And none of this is necessarily connected to "cross-dressing," which used to be called "transvestism," and refers to the desire to dress in the attire of another gender.

In fact, the truth is that the effort to establish categories into which to "fit" people is itself an unfortunate legacy of traditional thinking. Indeed, gender fluidity or expansiveness is widely recognized to be a common characteristic of many human beings, as even a mainstream publication such as *Time* magazine acknowledged in its 2017 cover story entitled "Beyond He and She: How a New Generation Is Redefining the Meaning of Gender."[8] That's also true of other creatures. Consider the cleaner wrasse, a brightly colored reef fish. If a dominant male cleaner wrasse dies or is removed from its group, the largest female in the group will transform itself into a male within a matter of days—a talent displayed in seven taxonomic families, twenty-seven orders, and many more species.[9] (This ought to discourage any advocates of natural law from contending that two immutable sexes constitute the natural order of things!)

And if anyone doubts that gender expression may be socially constructed independent of what one's genitalia look like, they have but to study the Japanese *wakashu,* young males in seventeenth- and eighteenth-century Japan who were thought to be the epitome of beauty. They were regarded as neither male nor female but "third gender," and were available to both men and women. *Wakashu* "was a gender role—not a fixed biological category—that was performed," points out Japanese art scholar Asato Ikeda.[10]

The notion of two fixed genders or two fixed sexual orientations, straight or gay, between which everybody has to choose is outmoded. Human beings come in an enormous variety of flavors when it comes to gender and sexuality. But that's a tough concept to sell because Western societies in particular are so wed to a binary mind-set. For one thing, standard English and French and many other languages do not currently contain gender-neutral pronouns, despite the best efforts of Anglophonic activists to introduce "xe," "ze," "phe," or simply "they" for people with gender-expansive identities.[11] More importantly, social conventions frequently reinforce the binary. How many forms have we all filled out that insist we designate ourselves "male" or "female"? How many times have we asked or been asked about a fetus or newborn child, "Is it a boy or a girl?"

Little wonder, then, that until very recently, the international human rights regimen has been similarly blinkered by the gender binary. The Universal Declaration of Human Rights (UDHR) does not contain the word "gender" and Article 16 on marriage and the family makes clear that "marriage" involves a man and a woman.[12] The Convention on the Elimination of All Forms of Discrimination Against Women (CEDAW), instituted in 1981, is focused on establishing "legal protection of the rights of women on an equal basis with men."[13]

There is no mention of lesbians or trans women and Article 16, which deals with equality in marriage, is focused solely on equality between women and men. The 1990 Convention on the Rights of the Child makes no mention of same-sex parents, intersex children, or adoption by same-sex parents.

Nor are formal U.N. conventions the only culprits. The European Court of Human Rights, one of the most progressive human rights judiciaries in the world, has declined to recognize a right to same-sex marriage because it did not find such a right explicitly affirmed in the European Convention on Human Rights.[14] The vast majority of countries do not allow same-sex couples to adopt children.[15] And most references to "gender-based violence" by human rights organizations are often assumed to concern violence against women but rarely violence against trans or intersex people despite the fact that such violence is far from rare and is certainly "gender-based."[16]

Fortunately there are signs that such human rights–related gender rigidity is beginning to break down but it has far from disappeared. If human rights are indeed to foster a good society in which freedoms central to human dignity are protected, they will need to be far more welcoming than they have been to new sex- and gender-related rights. But of course even well-established rights, such as the right not to be subjected to violence, are far from consistently protected when it comes to sexual minorities. How can anyone even think about adding "new" rights when the "old" ones are still being violated so rampantly?

HUMAN RIGHTS BODIES (such institutions as the United Nations Human Rights Council and U.N. treaty bodies, human rights courts, nongovernmental organizations dealing with human rights, and others) have made it clear that violence and discrimination of any kind against sexual or gender minorities violates existing human rights law.[17] Despite that, homosexuality is still illegal in more than seventy countries and may be punishable by death in at least ten.[18] Chechnya is just one location where what has been characterized as a "gay pogrom" has taken place in recent years with hundreds of gay men harassed, imprisoned, battered, or killed.[19] Brazil's most respected gay rights group, Gay da Bahia, believes that more than three thousand LGBT people have been murdered in that country since the mid-1980s, a development that has been dubbed the "Homocaust."[20] Between 2008 and 2013 there were 1,374 reported killings of trans people in sixty countries.[21] In the United States alone, twenty-one transgendered people died as a result of violence in 2016, with trans women of color being particularly at risk.[22] And other forms of discrimination—such as in education, employment, housing, access to health care, and treatment during humanitarian crises—remain commonplace.[23]

All this is reprehensible and some might argue that it is foolish even to contemplate "new" rights when even something as fundamental as the "right to life" is still under frequent threat or when homosexuality remains illegal in more than one-third of the world's countries. The authors disagree.

Remember the discussion in Chapter 1 about how rights change. They change when some group of people—usually everyday folks at the grassroots level—recognizes an affront to human dignity or imagines a new conception of what is required to maximize human capabilities. Those change agents then make a claim against the powerful: "Hey, if our society keeps doing X, it has no chance at all to be considered a truly good society."

Such change rarely comes in a linear fashion and rights don't appear in some preconceived order. Building a good society is not like putting Lego blocks together: first this bottom one, then this next one that fits on top of it, then a third one on top of the second. It's a far more messy process. If advocates of same-sex marriage in the United States had waited until there was no more violence against gay or lesbian folks in the United States to assert that they could marry whomever they wanted, they would still be waiting for their place at the altar. Same-sex marriage is not yet legal in Nepal, as it is in the United States, but Nepal allows gender fluid or intersex people to designate their gender as "O" ("Other") rather than "M" or "F" on their Nepalese passports, which is not possible on American passports. As first steps toward change in their respective cultures, both reforms have value and it is too early to tell which may ultimately be more transformative of their societies.

When new rights are established, it is often because laws and public opinion are reinforcing one another, operating in what may be called a "virtuous circle." Sometimes the laws will lag public opinion. By 2011 a majority of Americans supported same-sex marriage. But not until four years later did the Supreme Court, recognizing that cultural norms were changing, make it legal everywhere in the country.[24] Other times changes in law drag public opinion (social norms) along with them. In 1954 when the U.S. Supreme Court desegregated public schools, 70 percent of people in the South disapproved of the new law but by 1994 83 percent of all Americans, including a majority in the South, supported integrated schools.[25] As norms change, laws change and vice versa—a virtuous circle—at both the national and international level.

This means that we can't wait for everyone to catch up to evolving norms—in this case, for homosexuality to be legal everywhere or violence against LGBTI folks to be vanquished from the earth—before we introduce new rights and norms. It certainly doesn't mean that, because the public or the courts or even the human rights world may not be ready to adopt a new right, we shouldn't begin a conversation about what those new rights ought to be. After all, this is a book about what rights will look like in twenty or forty years. Martin Luther King Jr.'s words to his fellow clergy in "A Letter from a Birmingham Jail" are instructive here. The clergy had criticized the demonstration he had led for civil rights as "untimely." "Give it more time," they had said. "Wait until people are ready." And King replied, "For years now I have heard the word 'Wait!' It rings in the ear of every Negro with piercing familiarity. This 'Wait' has almost always meant 'Never.' We must come to see, with one of our distinguished jurists, that 'justice too long delayed is justice denied.'"[26]

So let's look at what some of those emerging rights are. This chapter will touch only briefly on same-sex marriage but will treat in more depth the right to have a child, to transition freely, and, in the case of intersex children, to determine your sex assignment for yourself. Each case will prompt the reader to ask how such a change might advance human dignity and capabilities and point the way to the good society. Finally, the authors will explore what such changes mean for traditional conceptions of women's rights and how these new rights might best be achieved.

THE RIGHT TO SAME-SEX MARRIAGE, though far from universally established yet around the world, has made enormous advances over the past decade. The European Court of Human Rights has ruled that same-sex marriage is not a right recognized in the European Convention on Human Rights but it has required states to provide alternatives, such as civil unions.[27] Many observers regard it as just a matter of time before the court affirms the right to marry.[28] As of 2019, seventeen European countries have recognized the right to same-sex marriage and many others to same-sex unions.[29] Outside Europe that right is recognized in Argentina, Australia, Bolivia, Canada, New Zealand, South Africa, the United States and elsewhere.[30] It would be surprising if this trend did not continue.

But even in many of the countries that recognize a right to marry the partner of your choice, there is another right, closely associated with marriage, that has not yet been fully established even for heterosexual couples. That is the right to have a child.

At first glance you might think that such a right was a no-brainer. After all, what could be more fundamental to human fulfillment and hence to human dignity than raising a child of one's own? Surely a good society is one in which those who have the capacity to nurture progeny may do so if they wish, whether or not that progeny be one's biological offspring. Indeed, Article 16 of the Universal Declaration states that "men and women of full age . . . have the right to found a family" and calls the family the "natural and fundamental group unit of society" (though it doesn't describe what a "family" looks like). In 1969 the U.N. General Assembly declared that "Parents have the exclusive right to determine . . . the number and spacing of their children," which would certainly seem to imply that they have the right to decide whether to have children in the first place.

All well and good for those who can bear children, but many countries have thrown up significant barriers to parenthood for couples, including heterosexual couples, in which one or both partners may not be able for biological reasons to procreate. Russia, for example, has restricted international adoptions.[31] Maternal surrogacy, in which a woman agrees to bear a child for a commissioning couple, is illegal in the vast majority of countries—80 percent in one survey.[32] These barriers are particularly onerous for gay and lesbian couples.[33]

There are, after all, only three ways that gays and lesbians can become parents: The first is adoption. The second is assisted reproductive technologies, such as artificial insemination (the introduction of semen into a woman's uterus) or in vitro fertilization (IVF), the fertilization of a woman's eggs in the laboratory before introduction into the uterus. The third is maternal surrogacy.

Let's consider adoption first. Same-sex couples may adopt children in all fifty U.S. states, thanks to a 2016 ruling by a federal court striking down Mississippi's ban on such adoptions.[34] But this is not true by a long shot at the global level where, with a few exceptions, such domestic adoptions are illegal in all countries except, not surprisingly, most of those that have recognized same-sex marriage.[35] International adoption by gay and lesbian couples is even more restricted; it is allowed only by Brazil, Colombia, and some Mexican jurisdictions, and it is not explicitly prohibited by the Philippines.[36] This means that one of the most common ways for those who cannot biologically bear children to experience the pleasures (and woes!) of parenting is closed off to many gays and lesbians. Strike one!

What then about assisted reproductive technologies? In 2012 the Inter-American Court of Human Rights ordered the last remaining country in the world that banned IVF altogether, Costa Rica, to lift its sanction.[37] But whether gays and lesbians can access IVF and other techniques is an altogether different question. The last comprehensive survey of access to such services by the International Federation of Fertility Studies revealed in 2016 that of the seventy countries that responded to the survey, only thirty-six had "no requirement for a recognized or stable heterosexual relationship" to utilize these services.[38] That leaves more than one hundred additional countries that were not included among the respondents but are unlikely to make assisted reproductive techniques easily available to gender minorities. Moreover, even when artificial insemination or IVF are available, it is often prohibitively expensive—between $5,000 and $60,000—and rarely covered by health insurance, especially not for lesbian couples.[39] Ought only the wealthy to be able to exercise a right to be a parent? If that were the case, we would be establishing de facto a right that only the well-off can exercise, which is clearly contrary to the whole notion of universal human rights. Strike two!

If adoption and assisted reproductive technologies are out of reach for many, that leaves maternal surrogacy. This is a much more complicated question, which is no doubt one reason surrogacy is prohibited in the vast majority of the world's countries. It is opposed by some on the right for religious reasons (because it is seen as undermining the centrality of conventional marriage); by some on the left, who fear exploitation of poor women; by some feminists, who decry the commodification of the childbearer; and by some health professionals, who point out that 800 women worldwide die every day from pregnancy complications or miscarriages and that multiple pregnancies represent an increased risk to the surrogate.[40] Others have argued that surrogacy violates a child's right to know its parents should there be a falling out between the gestational mother and the commissioning parents.[41] And the real-world complexities include parents who commission a surrogacy and then die, divorce, or change their minds before a birth takes place or, in the notorious case of an Australian couple, refuse to take a child with disabilities.[42]

Surrogacy, whether for gay parents or heterosexual couples who cannot bear their own children, is the perfect example of the kind of case that requires finding the right balance between rights claimants, in this case the commissioning couple, the surrogate, and the child. As with adoptive parents, commissioning couples need to be screened carefully, their contractual obligations to the child made legally binding, to ensure that the child's best interests are paramount. The rights of surrogate mothers not to be trafficked or economically exploited must be protected. At the end of the day, the authors believe that, with proper regulation, maternal surrogacy is a reasonable option for many but, above all, if surrogacy is to be a legal right for heterosexual couples, it must be for gay and lesbian couples as well. Otherwise, strike three!

Current human rights law holds that that having a family is "fundamental" to "society" (which presumably means to a good society) and that heterosexual couples have the right to bear biological children of their own. Because gay and lesbian couples cannot exercise that right for physiological reasons beyond their control, the authors believe that their right to bear children must be facilitated, within limits appropriate to all couples, by adoption, assisted reproductive technologies, and maternal surrogacy. To do otherwise is to foster blatant discrimination and undermine basic human dignity and capability. Those who disagree with the right to same-sex marriage will of course not support the right of gay and lesbian couples to be parents. But those who support same-sex marriage will agree that the emerging right of gay and lesbian couples to parent a child follows as closely as the night does the day.

CAITLYN JENNER, THE OLYMPIC DECATHLON WINNER, and Chelsea Manning, the source of something like three-quarters of a million sensitive U.S. military and diplomatic documents supplied to WikiLeaks, are only two among the public personalities known in recent years to have transitioned from one gender to another, in their cases male to female.[43]

Public attention to transgender issues in mainstream culture has skyrocketed in the last decade. Some of that attention has been negative, focused, for example, on the question of whether trans people should be forced by law to use bathrooms that conform to the gender they were assigned at birth. But other elements have been decidedly positive. The rock musical "Hedwig and the Angry Inch," about a band fronted by a transgender singer, though originally produced off-Broadway in 1998, was a huge hit when it opened on Broadway in 2014 and won that year's Tony Award for Best Revival of a Musical.[44] That same year *Time* magazine carried a cover story calling the rights of transgender people "America's next civil rights frontier" and featuring LaVerne Cox, star of the smash television show "Orange is the New Black" and an openly trans actress, on the cover.[45] (The next year Cox became the first trans person to be depicted in wax at Madam Tussauds.) Similarly, in January 2017, a special issue of *National Geographic* focused on "The Gender Revolution" and was accompanied by a cover photo of nine-year-old Avery Jackson of Kansas City, Missouri, and the quote, "The best thing about being a girl is now I don't have to pretend to be a boy."[46]

Nor is the United States the only country where the visibility of transgendered people has increased. Great Britain and India both have fashion modeling agencies designed to serve transgender clients.[47] Tomoya Hosoda, a trans male, serves on the city council of a conservative suburb outside Tokyo, Japan. His business card reads, "Born a woman."[48]

But if the existence of trans people is far more visible today, the evolution of their rights has trailed far behind.

Children are thought to begin to sense their own gender identities as young as eighteen months to two years of age.[49] From what is often a very young age, many trans children have a feeling that something about their gender assignment and/or sexual characteristics is just not right. "Living in a body that you feel doesn't fully belong to you is extremely painful," says Chloe, a twenty-year-old transgender woman.[50] Unfortunately, the traditional medical model has understood that it is the feelings themselves that are not "right" and has labeled those feelings "gender identity disorder" or "gender dysphoria."

It is one thing for trans folk to have to deal with the vagaries of everyday prejudice such as the decision of the Boy Scouts of America to kick an eight-year-old trans boy out of his Cub Scout troop because he did "not meet the eligibility requirements."[51] But it is quite another to have the World Health Organization's International Classification of Diseases, the most widely used classification system around the world, consider your experience of self to be a "psychiatric illness"—a categorization that was removed only in 2019.[52] "Dealing with people who think you are disgusting or sick is draining," Chloe says.[53]

Unfortunately the implications of such a classification are far more than "draining." For one thing, they mean that in many jurisdictions trans people must be declared "sick" before they can be eligible for transitional medical services. At least until recently trans folk had to submit to a psychiatric examination or even sterilization in thirty-seven of the forty-nine countries in Europe before changing their gender classifications on government documents, such as birth certificates, identification cards, and passports.[54] Trans youth may be stigmatized, encouraged by health professionals to adapt to their cisgender identities or denied puberty-suppressing drugs that may delay the onset of puberty long enough for the young person to make an informed gender choice. This can lead to true mental or physical illness—one transgender girl was so repulsed by her genitals that she suffered intestinal damage requiring surgery as a resulting of suppressing her need to go to the bathroom.[55] Indeed, up to 41 percent of trans youth are estimated to have attempted suicide.[56]

Imagine how exhausting it is to feel alienated from your body, taunted or at least misunderstood by those around you, considered "sick" by professional medical standards, and only able to get help by admitting to that label. What kind of good society would treat a group of its members that way? Such pain is compounded by the fact that, while most people in the trans community resist the label "gender dysphoric," many also recognize that at the moment it is the strategic vehicle to obtain not only the medical but also the financial assistance they may desire. If the treatment, which can cost up to $24,000 for male to female transition and more than $50,000 for female to male, is considered not cosmetic but medically required, it may be covered by medical insurance, thereby alleviating the concern that only the wealthy could procure it.[57]

But to require people to acquiesce to a designation—"sick!"—that is not legitimate puts those seeking to transition in the position of needing to dissemble, to present themselves inauthentically, in order to secure what they regard as their authentic selves. That is not only a cruel paradox but a violation of an individual's autonomy, which is fundamental to the fulfillment of our capabilities.

What is required is a broad-based "right to transition." Such a right would entail at least three things. First, it would sanction one's freedom to affirm the sexual and gender identity that conforms to one's sense of self. For those trans people who wish to transition biologically and have that procedure covered by insurance, establishing such a right would depathologize the process, increase dignity, and decrease stigma. And for those trans people who simply wish to present themselves sans surgery as belonging to a gender other than the one their bodies may reflect, what difference does it make to anyone else to allow their self-declaration to stand sufficient?

Second, a right to transition should include the right to be officially designated as belonging to the sex with which one identifies. To be denied such designation (or have it depend upon a psychiatric evaluation or, even worse, sterilization as, for example, in Ukraine) is not only degrading but can lead to a host of difficulties, of which bathroom access may be the least significant.[58] Trans women have been assigned to confinement in male prisons where they are especially vulnerable to assault; trans people are subject to harassment by police who become suspicious in the face of identity cards apparently at odds with gender expression; trans individuals have been denied employment or terminated when they are regarded as having misled their employers about their "true" sex.[59] Countries such as Malaysia, Kuwait, and Nigeria have laws prohibiting anyone from "posing" as the opposite sex.[60]

In jurisdictions where it is possible to alter gender classifications on official documents, such changes are often contingent upon the trans person having completed sex reassignment surgery. This keeps in place the primacy of the outdated model of gender as dependent largely upon physical characteristics when it fact it is an interior sensation, what has been called "brain sex," self-knowledge of who one truly is.[61] Other jurisdictions limit the new designation to "male" or "female," which simply reinforces the discredited understanding of sex and gender as binary.

Interestingly enough, these rigidities are being relaxed in some surprising places, beginning with Nepal, as mentioned earlier, whose Supreme Court ruled in 2007 that citizens could select their gender based on "self-feeling" and whose election commission and census bureau allows citizens to register as a "third gender" and choose "O" for "Other" on Nepalese passports.[62] The U.N. International Civil

Aviation Organization has specified that passports may include "X" for "indeterminate gender" and, as of this writing, Australia, Bangladesh, Canada, Denmark, Germany, India, Malta, New Zealand, and Pakistan, among others, offer gender-neutral options on passports or national identity cards. An American court ruled in 2018 that the U.S. State Department could not deny a passport to a Colorado resident who refused to select "male" or "female."[63]

But, finally, an emerging right to transition would address an even more basic question: "Am I trans or not?" Before the issues of mental illness or official government recognition are broached, one must be old enough to understand one's "brain sex" and to articulate one's gender identity in the first place. That identity may in fact begin to take hold between eighteen months and two years of age but no one is old enough to make life-determining decisions for themselves until considerably later. Puberty is a crucial turning point for transgender young people. "That's when the body pretty much turns on someone who is transgender," says Dr. Karin Selva, a pediatric endocrinologist who has treated transgender young people.

> With male puberty, you get the changes in the genitalia that happen, you get an Adam's apple. You get facial hair that we can't get rid of. You have a body structure that's male, that doesn't easily turn female, even though you give it estrogen. It's hard to reverse those processes. . . . And the same thing for a female.[64]

This is why Dr. Selva and other medical professionals have been turning to pharmaceutical puberty suppressors for teens who think they may be transgender but need more time to decide their gender identity. Such suppressors are reversible if the teen decides to retain the sex assigned at birth. Some teens find the experience frustrating: "While other kids are developing, you're not. You're either on hormone blockers or you don't know what to do yet," says Lilly, a twelve-year-old transgender girl. But then she adds, "At the end of the day, people can say what they want about you, but the only voice that matters to you is yours. They just don't struggle with the things we struggle with."[65] The right to transition must include a right of trans youth to have access to puberty-suppressing treatments if they want them. That would not alleviate all elements of Lilly's struggle but it could eliminate some of the obstacles that make that struggle worse than necessary.

Human rights are grounded on respect for an individual's autonomy, one of those "areas of freedom so central that their removal makes a life not worthy of human dignity," in Nussbaum's phrase. Nothing could be more central to an individual's autonomy than being able to choose and express one's gender identity and have it respected. A good society facilitates that process and hence a good society requires a right to transition. It is not enough to recognize transgendered people in popular culture. It is far more important to honor their being in our laws and our rights.

MANY OF THE ISSUES ADDRESSED to this point—the right to have children; the right to an officially recognized sexual and gender identity of one's choice—apply to intersex people as well but there is one question that is of particular importance in their case.

David Reimer was born a twin but lost his penis in a botched circumcision. His parents took him to Johns Hopkins University in 1967 when he was about a year and a half old to consult with a psychologist named John Money who was promoting the theory that gender identity was malleable at a young age and determined largely by social influences. Until the 1950s it had been common not to operate on children with ambiguous gender markings but Money assigned Reimer to be surgically transformed into "Joan" and to be raised as a girl—female hormones, frilly dresses, and all. For years afterward the psychologist tracked Joan's development and, though

Reimer had not been born intersex, claimed that the case validated his contention that intersex infants will successfully conform to the sex and gender identity assigned them shortly after birth if they are supported in that identity medically and socially. But by age fourteen "Joan," who had never felt comfortable with her female identity, assumed a male identity and began calling himself "David." He underwent treatments to reverse his early reassignment and eventually told his story publicly before dying in 2004 by suicide.[66]

The number of births that result in some kind of an intersex condition has been estimated to range from 0.018 percent to 1.7 percent—a huge range.[67] But regardless of the number, there is often enormous pressure on both physicians and parents, because of the prevalence of binary normativity in most cultures, to resolve the ambiguity quickly. That is why it is common for surgeries to be performed shortly after birth in order that babies be assigned a male or female designation. Typically, another two to four operations as well as other forms of intervention are required. The result has been enormous physical and emotional suffering. "What is done to these children, what was done to me," says one recipient of such forced sex assignment, "is legally and scientifically sanctioned sexual abuse."[68] More than one human rights expert has likened such surgeries to female genital mutilation, a long-decried human rights violation.[69]

It is certainly understandable that well-intentioned parents, faced with a condition they have never encountered, aware of how vulnerable "different" children are to ridicule, and beholden to doctors, decide to permit sex assignment surgery at birth. The great tragedy, however, is that such early surgeries are rarely medically necessary and may in fact have deleterious physical consequences.[70] As the pediatric surgeon Mike Venhola puts it, "Why operate on the child's body if the problem is in the minds of the adults?" Children can grow up perfectly well with ambiguous physical characteristics until they are old enough to decide whether or not to have surgery and, if so, what kind. At the moment, however, the vast majority of European countries, for example, require formal registration of the sex of a child within the first few weeks, months, or years of its life; only Finland and Portugal place no time limits on such registration, though in Germany birth certificates may now include the word "diverse" under gender classifications.[71]

Fortunately, the human rights community is beginning to honor intersex children's autonomy. In 2013 Juan Mendez, then the U.N. special rapporteur on torture, condemned so-called genital normalizing surgeries, saying "These procedures . . . can cause scarring, loss of sexual sensation, pain, incontinence and lifelong depression."[72] Regarding such surgeries, Human Rights Watch has called for a moratorium and the Council of Europe for an outright ban.[73]

But that's not all. While courts have been unwilling to prevent parents from making these decisions for their newborn children, retroactive legal action may give medical practitioners pause. Mark and Pam Crawford's adopted child had been born with ambiguous genitals. Doctors had assigned her a female identity but it was pretty obvious to the Crawfords within a few years of her adoption at two that their child understood herself to be a boy. They have brought a lawsuit against the hospitals and physicians who treated their son and the South Carolina Department of Social Services, which sanctioned the treatment, to prevent this fate befalling other children.[74] "Reparations for those who undergo such interventions," says gender rights activist Justus Eisfeld, "is one of the next major requirements" and he cites the precedent established by the Swedish government, which has appropriated funds to compensate trans people who were forced into sterilization in order to transition.[75]

The final sex- and gender-related right the authors believe is required for a good society is the right of intersex children to defer sex assignment surgery until they are old enough to make the decision for themselves. This too follows seamlessly from the proposition that personal sovereignty, particularly sovereignty over our own bodies, is the hallmark of human dignity.

IN HIS BOOK *Beyond Trans: Does Gender Matter?*, political scientist Heath Fogg Davis has argued that we could do away with most official gender designations altogether, asking instead whether there is a legitimate public good that is "rationally related" to the perceived need to force people to choose an identity.[76] The drag queen RuPaul puts this a bit more pungently. "Our culture," RuPaul says, "is about choosing a [gender] identity and sticking with it so people can market shit to you. Anything that switches that around is completely the antithesis of what our culture implores us to do."[77] And in her novel *Notes of a Crocodile,* the Taiwanese author Qiu Miaojin has one of her characters say, "Hey, we should found a gender-free society and monopolize all the public restrooms!"[78]

But if we were to do away with sex or gender designations of any kind, what are the implications for a hard-won set of rights that would appear to be profoundly dependent upon maintaining at least some clear gender identities, namely, women's rights? Some women's rights advocates have been decidedly unfriendly to the complications thrown up by a nonbinary understanding of gender. Until it closed in 2015, the Michigan Womyn's Music Festival advertised itself as for "women-born women" only and at least one trans woman was thrown out of the festival when she was recognized as trans.[79] In an article on the feminist website "Feminist Current," author Susan Cox claims that "A woman coming out as 'non-binary' is a non-statement that declares nothing but common loathing of the female class."[80]

One way in which this conflict has manifested itself is in the controversies surrounding admittance of trans women to women's colleges.[81] At Wellesley College, for example, the question created something of a generational divide. Many students supported a broad definition of what it means to be a "woman," some of them arguing that Wellesley's mission had historically been, at least in part, to challenge prevailing norms of its era and that the inclusion of trans women represented a critical normative challenge of this generation. Many alumna had a hard time identifying with the trans experience—one person labeled trans women "false women"—and saw their inclusion as a threat to the college's mission.[82] After long consideration, the college announced its policy: "Wellesley will consider for admission any applicant who lives as a woman and consistently identifies as a woman. Therefore, candidates assigned male at birth who identify as women are eligible to apply for admission. The College also accepts applications from those who were assigned female at birth, identify as non-binary, and who feel they belong in our community of women."[83]

Such a policy recognizes that gender identity takes precedence over biological characteristics, though it still is predicated upon a binary narrative. Indeed, women's rights have traditionally been dependent upon recognition of a particular category or classification of human beings called "women." That category can rather easily be expanded to include trans women, whether fully transitioned or not, as Wellesley has done, but it ought not to be done away with altogether. While rights are universal, they differ in terms of the needs they address, depending upon the aggrieved group to which they apply. At the most basic level, it would make no sense to offer abortion rights to a cisgender male, disability rights to the able-bodied, or, for that matter, the right to defer sex-assignment surgery to a child with unambiguous sex characteristics at birth.[84] Those rights are reserved for those who need them.

Because ninety percent of all adult rape victims are female, for example, special attention must be paid to the rights of women to be free from sexual violence.[85] To argue otherwise is to make the same mistake that critics of the Black Lives Matter movement make when they reply, "All Lives Matter." Yes, all lives matter, but it is black lives that are at particular risk of police mistreatment and therefore require particular care and protection.

There need be no threat to traditional women's rights from emerging nonbinary-based rights as long as everyone remembers the statement in the Introduction: rights do not constitute a zero-sum game and the inclusion of newly established rights need not vitiate the old.

BUT THAT LEADS to the final question: How might these and perhaps other such rights best be achieved? Are the rights this book has been elucidating—the right to be a parent, the right to transition, the right to defer sex-assignment surgery for intersex children—in fact "new" rights or are they merely new interpretations of currently existing rights? Is there a need for a treaty or convention specifically addressing rights related to gender identity and expression?

In 1994, the U.N. Human Rights Committee ruled in a landmark case, *Toonen v. Australia,* that sodomy laws violated the antidiscrimination provisions of the International Covenant on Civil and Political Rights.[86] That was the first judgment of an international human rights body in support of the rights of sexual minorities.[87] It would take twelve more years, however, before the U.N. General Assembly would address even as elementary a violation of rights as extrajudicial executions based on sexual orientation.[88]

Since then there have been some notable advances even regarding some of the emerging rights considered in this chapter. Argentina adopted a gender identity law in 2012, for example, that allows for the registration of gender to be based on "the personal experience of the body" and excludes the need for "a surgical procedure,... hormonal therapies or any other psychological or medical treatments."[89] The European Court of Human Rights has validated the right of trans people to have full access to necessary medical treatment and in 2017 ruled that the requirement that trans people be sterilized to change their identities was a violation of human rights.[90]

Still, such changes are scattered and episodic. Even within the relatively progressive European human rights regime the picture is far from ideal, most conspicuously in the absence of rights related to intersex people.

One obvious solution would be the adoption of an international human rights convention on sexual and gender identity and expression, like those that address women's rights or the rights of indigenous people. But there is almost universal opposition to such an approach among LGBTI activists. It was difficult enough, they say, to convince the United Nations just to appoint an independent expert on sexual orientation and gender identity to assess violence and discrimination against LGBTI folks, as happened in 2016.[91] How much more explosive would it be to propose a formal convention? Such a proposal, many fear, would spark an outcry of "Special Rights!" and derail whatever fragile progress is already underway. That is one reason the former U.N. high commissioner for human rights, Navi Pillay, emphasized that "the protection of people on the basis of sexual orientation and gender identity does not require the creation of new rights... it requires the enforcement of the universally applicable guarantee of non-discrimination in the enjoyment of all rights."[92]

Such an approach is certainly defensible strategically but it means that for the time being LGBTI people must rely upon courts and legislators to interpret established rights in inclusive ways. The right to control one's health and body, for example, must be understood to include the right of trans teens to have access to puberty-suppressing treatments. The right of a child to have its "best interests" protected must include the right to have sex assignment surgery deferred.

All this is happening in a world that has not yet recognized a universal human right to same-sex marriage and in which the World Congress of Families cites Article 16 of the Universal Declaration of Human Rights—"The family is the natural and fundamental group unit of society"—as grounds for opposing the marriage of anyone but one man and one woman! Obviously a convention ought to be the ultimate goal because it would make absolutely clear that these rights—and many of them *are* "new" rights—are integral to the creation of a good society.

Gender rights are as powerful an example as we have of the fact that rights are not static. When the United States was first founded, the age of consent for girls in Virginia was ten years old.[93] Today we find that idea abhorrent. It was not until 2017 that the kingdom of Saudi Arabia permitted women to drive, finally catching up to every other country in the world.[94] And this chapter has shown how the mores of the gender binary and heteronormativity that Bill and Sushma's parents relied upon have long since crumbled to dust.

The kind of changes in rights identified here will not come easily, but then, as the journalist I. F. Stone remarked, "Revolutions do not take place according to Emily Post."[95] The important point, however, is that they *do* come and one of the ways to hasten the day they do is to keep asking ourselves what dignity requires regarding matters as private and intimate as who we are and how we love.

Bodily integrity—the right to be free from scenarios such as physical harm, invasions of personal privacy, and forced surgical procedures—has long been a linchpin of human rights. A nonbinary world requires that the concept of bodily integrity not be straitjacketed by the paucity of our collective imaginations.

# 3

# Here's Looking at You

## Privacy in an Age of
## New Technology

HAVE YOU EVER FREQUENTED A GAY BAR, prayed in a mosque, registered at an online dating site, or visited an abortion clinic? Have you eaten a beef burger in India, clicked on a link to a dissident website in China or participated in a protest against corruption in Mexico? If you have, do you care who knows it? Government agencies and police departments can gain access to even the most personal facts about you—facts like these—with the click of a button, thanks to increasingly sophisticated technological tools. Private companies can too. Your photo on a social media profile can be combined with your consumer choices to identify all sorts of confidential information. Whether as citizens or consumers, virtually our every move is being watched, documented, downloaded, shared, coded, and collated with other people's data.

This chapter examines how new developments in technology are threatening to compromise the right to privacy—an international human right grounded in the Universal Declaration of Human Rights and the International Covenant on Civil and Political Rights and codified in more than 150 national constitutions. Three sweeping societal changes are driving that threat: first, the pervasive use of new technologies, including by private actors, that can intrude into every aspect of our personal and professional lives; second, the persistent fear of terrorism, violence, and crime that influences shifting conceptions of what should be considered private versus public information; and, third, the fact that many players other than governments alone can have a pernicious effect on the protection of our privacy.

Among the matters that will be discussed are the misperceptions that the right to privacy is not as essential to a good society as other "core" rights and that the right to privacy is a Western preoccupation. The chapter will consider how a good society strikes a balance between the right to privacy and other rights, such as the right to life and security in the face of violence. And it describes some of the ways that we need to reconceptualize privacy rights in the face of societies pervaded by surveillance.

Before all that is addressed, however, comes reflection on why privacy is fundamental to a good society in the first place. After all, as those who downplay the importance of privacy often say, "If you've got nothing to hide, why worry?"

First, in order to live a life of dignity (which, as previously described, is at the heart of human rights), we need a sense of autonomy and control of our own destiny, without governments and corporations tracking the most intimate details of our lives.

Second, without privacy, many of the capabilities that Martha Nussbaum identified as critical to a life of dignity are undermined. How do we preserve our bodily integrity or produce fully self-expressive works or exercise our political freedom if our privacy is broadly under threat?

Finally, human rights are claims that those with less power make against the powerful. What should the good society do if and when the powerful wield tools that radically impinge upon our autonomy and, therefore, the effectiveness of our ability to make such claims?

GIVEN THE REACH OF NEW TECHNOLOGIES, it is easy to argue that we have created a "surveillance society" far more intrusive than pre-digital societies of generations past. Many of the most controversial and widely publicized threats to privacy have been instituted in the context of the war on terror. The Patriot Act, for example, passed forty-five days after 9/11, made it far easier for the U.S. government to track phone calls and bank accounts and even, initially, what materials citizens withdrew from their public libraries.[1] U.S. courts regularly wrestle with the question of what constitutes legal search and seizures under the Fourth Amendment and when law enforcement officials need to get warrants to carry them out.

If we are tempted to think that privacy endangerments are limited to the tracking of alleged terrorists or criminals, however, we are sadly mistaken. We wake up to our smartphone alarm, check out and click "like" on our social media feed, turn on our smart television for the headline news, step on the smart scale to check our weight, log our breakfast in our favorite calorie-tracking app, tap "thumbs up" for our favorite songs online, and turn on a traffic app when we get in the car to drive to work. Barely an hour has passed in our day and already a composite digital picture can be created by these devices of our likes, dislikes, consumer choices, illnesses, religious and romantic preferences, and even our most private concerns and obsessions. Nor are our children immune from such data gathering. Smart toys such as stuffed animals and dolls may be equipped with cameras, geolocation technology, and voice recorders that may track and store a family's most personal information. Even Amazon's Echo Dot for children, a voice-commanded artificial intelligence assistant that has been promoted to children as young as five years old, has been criticized by privacy and child rights' advocates as posing threats to children's well-being and privacy. It listens in the background constantly, relays voices to remote servers where the voices and conversations are processed, promotes specific brands ("start SpongeBob"), and responds to commands.

Indeed, the rise of "Big Data"—the compilation and analysis of millions of our self-generated digital footprints, combined with machine-generated data from our "smart" home devices and industrial machines—is one of the most complex, challenging, and growing privacy rights concerns of our time.

The Acxiom Corporation, for example, which claims to provide data "for the world's best marketers" of products and services, is hardly a household name, yet it has information (50 trillion data transactions annually) on almost every household in the United States and more than 500 million households around the world.[2] Acxiom combines our "online, offline, and mobile selves" to create "in-depth behavior portraits in pixelated detail."[3] Its Personicx service allows its clients to use "multi-dimensional segmentation" to track consumers by "life stage-based behaviors," "digital behaviors," or "ethnic identities."[4]

This aggregation of our public and private personas by such data marketers often occurs without our knowledge and consent and sometimes in a discriminatory fashion. The ranking of consumers based upon income, assets, ability to pay, health status, racial demographics, and other criteria excludes certain individuals and groups from promotional discounts or the best opportunities for essential services such as healthcare, insurance, or higher education.

The commodification of our identity and data can even shape our personal preferences and choices. Ever wonder why an advertisement pops up on your social media feed or website searches that relates to a product for your demographic group or a product or service you were recently researching online? Sushma's Facebook feed, for example, routinely features advertisements for yoga pants and dance trips to Cuba, quite fitting for someone who routinely purchases the latest fitness gizmos and who listens to Afro-Cuban music online. Increasingly, online advertisers and retailers are honing the customer experience based upon an individual's demographic information, prior purchase history, and prior search records.

This may all seem benign, perhaps even beneficial, particularly to those of us who feel we lead normal, open lives. Some of us may even be willing to give up a certain degree of privacy in order to feel safer or to have our consumer needs met more effectively. After all, how many of us would like to fly on an airplane in which none of the passengers had passed through security before boarding? And when we're hunting for just the right restaurant on Yelp, do we really care if we receive pop-up notices about similar restaurants in the future?

WE MAY BE TEMPTED to view the right to privacy as a far less important right than, say, the rights not to be tortured, "disappeared," or executed extrajudicially. Violations of the latter rights may cost their victims enormous suffering or even their lives, whereas infringements on privacy feel more like an inconvenience or insult. And yet violations to privacy often go hand in hand with violations of bodily integrity or broader political rights. Few repressive governments refrain from intrusions on their citizens' or visitors' privacy rights, if only as a means to identify dissenters in order to punish them or prevent them from protesting government policies. In fact, violations of privacy rights are often the "canary in the mineshaft" that signals violations of other rights of a more serious nature.

Perhaps there has been no more famous affirmation in American jurisprudence of the right to privacy than U.S. Supreme Court Justice Louis Brandeis's dissent in the 1928 case of *Olmstead v. United States,* in which the court affirmed that government wiretapping was not a violation of the Constitution. Brandeis considered privacy, what he called "the right to be let alone," "the most comprehensive of rights and the right most valued by civilized men."[5]

Justice Brandeis could not have conceived in 1928, however, that wiretapping was but the tip of the proverbial iceberg when it came to being "let alone." Today, governments and corporations use a range of technologies—digital, biometric, and geospatial—to track practically every movement of citizens and consumers. Digital technologies include the use of social media, website traffic and searches, smartphones, and other smart appliances and can track your movements, purchases, behaviors, preferences, affiliations, friendships, and more. Biometric technologies identify individuals through unique biological or behavioral characteristics, including one's fingerprints, face, and iris of the eye. Geospatial technologies focus on location-based data garnered through geographic information systems, geographic positioning systems (GPS), high-resolution aerial imagery, and more. Often a combination of these technologies is used to create composite profiles of people and their personal, political, and consumerist preferences.

Automatic license plate readers, for example, are being used to capture license plate and location information, with such data points on all vehicles surveilled being stored for years. The data from smart cars can track and store a range of private information about their drivers, ranging from where they go to what they buy to how they drive. Our cell phones and smart gadgets track every move and sometimes literally every breath. Securus, a major provider of phone services to those in prison, not only records phone calls between prisoners and their attorneys—which happens to be a violation of attorney-client privilege—but also has the capacity to get and share the cell phone location information of any cell phone user. In 2017 in the case *Carpenter v. United States*, the U.S. Supreme Court considered whether the government must get a warrant to track a target's whereabouts by examining records kept by wireless providers of a cell phone's sequential locations.[6] The Court ruled that the government would need a warrant to access cell phone location data and its failure to do so in this case violated the Fourth Amendment.[7] In the Court's opinion, Chief Justice John Roberts wrote that new technology has "enhanced the Government's capacity to encroach upon areas normally guarded from inquisitive eyes" and that the Court's interpretations of the Fourth Amendment need to take technological changes into account.[8]

Many employers are increasingly using technology to monitor employees' communications and actions. It is common knowledge that our emails, social media usage, and phone calls on work devices can be monitored but that is not all. Some companies have employees wear badges that track how often they get up from their desks and how often they socialize. Companies can track how many breaks you take and how long you spend in the bathroom. One employer even installed a GPS on an employee's personal car without him knowing it and then fired him based on GPS data that revealed instances when he was supposed to be working but wasn't.[9] The employee sued his employer and lost. While governments need warrants to use GPS devices to track suspected criminals, companies don't need permission from either the employee or the government to keep tabs on those who work for them.

Even more chilling, perhaps, than the surveillance of individuals through such digital technologies is the use of geospatial technologies, "a term used to describe the range of modern tools contributing to the geographic mapping and analysis of the Earth and human societies."[10] While geospatial technologies can certainly be used for good—remote sensing satellites can track movements of refugees or outbreaks of war while geographic information systems' software tools can track spread of diseases—such technologies can also be used in ways that violate the right to privacy, as well as a range of other rights.

Using aerial surveillance technology that was developed for use in Iraq, for example, the city of Baltimore—nicknamed "Charm City" and the birthplace, ironically enough, of Thurgood Marshall, champion of civil rights and liberties—has been secretly conducting surveillance of its citizens. Funded by a private philanthropist, the program has been filming the city and its residents from a private Cessna plane equipped with a range of cameras.[11] The city had also been using stingray devices—tools that track calls and cell phones—without a warrant.

Such surveillance allows the Baltimore police to track crimes, piece together scenarios and timelines, and arrest suspects. It didn't, however, help prevent the death of twenty-five-year-old Freddy Gray while he was being transported in a police van. The surveillance only fed residents' anger and deep-seated suspicion of the police. Said one, "The whole city is under a siege of cameras. . . . In fact, they observed Freddie Gray himself the morning of his arrest. . . . They could have watched that van too, but no, they missed that one. I thought the cameras were there to protect us."[12]

ALL THIS IS WORRISOME but what is in store for us in the future may be even more so. In the tiny town of River Falls, Wisconsin, situated on the banks of the trout-filled Kinnickinnic River, forty workers at the Three Square Market got microchips the size of a grain of rice physically embedded in their hands. Management said it was for the employees' convenience so that they don't have to sign in to work, log on to their computers, or use a code for the copier. Three Square Market hopes to offer the same "enhancement" for its customers so that they don't need to pay with a credit card or cash, much like Apple Pay has changed how we pay for purchases.[13]

The FDA recently approved a pill with a digital tracking device that is swallowed by the patient. Part of a broader wave of digital medicine designed to promote better behavioral outcomes, the Abilify MyCite is meant not only to treat schizophrenia, bipolar disorder, and depression in adults but also to detect and record the date, time, and level of dosage of pharmaceutical use—all information that can be tracked in an app by the patient and also by the care team.[14] This may result in better health outcomes for patients, assuming patients actually download the app and take the medication, but at the expense of keeping highly personal behavior private.

Affective computing—the use of computing to identify and influence emotions—through wearable sensors, video cameras, microphones, digital health equipment and smartphones will increasingly be used to assess and help treat depression, stress and other strong emotions. Such devices may also be used, however, to tailor advertisements and commercials, sell products, and track consumer sentiment. Companies will be tracking and understanding your innermost thoughts and emotions through facial recognition, body language, gestures and more to assess when and how you are most likely to buy their product.

The scholar Alessandro Acquisti challenges us to "take these technologies and push them to their logical extreme. Imagine a future in which strangers around you will look at you through their Google Glasses or, one day, their contact lenses, and use seven or eight data points about you to infer anything else that may be known about you. What will this future without secrets look like? And should we care?"[15]

"WHO OWNS YOUR FACE?" is the caption of several provocative articles on the subject of facial recognition software. You may own your physical face but images of your face are routinely taken without your consent in public spaces and those images are "owned" and used by a range of government agencies, such as the police and the FBI. The FBI has access to drivers' photographs without a warrant. The police in some states like Florida have body armor equipped with facial recognition software that reveals the identities of those they encounter without the police having first to seek permission and whether or not the identified person is even suspected of committing a crime.

Such use of facial recognition software is not limited to use by government agencies. It is now possible that, when you walk by a billboard, the ad will change to reflect your past purchases, based on facial recognition software that matches who you are with what you have bought before. The person depicted in the ad selling the product to you may even have facial features that are based on a composite of your best friends—a marketing tool that may make you more likely to buy. Facebook, Snap Inc., and other social media companies have built vast databases of millions of faces, with related information, such as biographical information, contact lists, places visited, hobbies, and so on.

As Alvaro Bedoya, founding executive director of Georgetown University's Center on Privacy and Technology, puts it, "You may brush off modern privacy invasions. Perhaps you have nothing to hide. But do you resemble someone who does?"[16]

WHILE WE MAY BE TEMPTED to think of privacy issues as a concern of the Western or developed world, of privileged elites who have nothing better to do than worry about who can access their luxury car location, the two largest countries in the world—China and India—are forging ahead with creating a "super identity" for all their citizens.

If many of the intrusions into privacy in the United States and Western Europe are ostensibly related to national security, to keeping people safer, in India, the most ambitious and widespread digital identity project underway is designed primarily to streamline and improve the delivery of basic services and public subsidies. From remote villages to bustling cities, India's one billion people are getting their irises scanned, fingerprints recorded, and photographs taken.

When first conceived, this national digital identity program called "Aadhaar" was seen as "an opportunity to create a super identity—one that is more portable, traceable, and has little or no chance of being misused or stolen."[17] In fact, the program has indeed provided an identity to people who had previously been prevented from claiming one—communities such as migrant workers, internally displaced people, and transgender individuals—and who were therefore deprived of a range of rights and social protections. As of December 2014, for example, 43,602 transgender individuals had received Aadhaar numbers.[18] Women, who bear the disproportionate burden of poverty, are often excluded from possessing ration cards in India—cards that entitle the cardholder to subsidized or free food commodities, such as rice—because ration cards are only issued to the head of household, who is typically a man. Because the Aadhaar identification is unique to each individual, it allows a woman to receive cash transfers directly into her account and also avail herself of other subsidies, such as in grains or kerosene.

India has the largest number of people in the world who live below the poverty line. Its major government welfare programs and international aid projects are beset by corruption, inefficiencies, and underpayments, with only a fraction of the grain designated for the poor actually reaching them. Using Aadhaar to verify identity and directly transfer cash or grains can help cut corruption, fraud, and misappropriation.

Ingenious middlemen and corrupt officials can always find a way around such systems, though, and increasingly, the government has been trying to link Aadhaar to other public systems and services, such as automobile registrations, purchases of real estate, the obtaining of a phone SIM card, and the opening of a bank account.

Although its advantages are significant, privacy activists and the media have raised serious concerns about the potential for Aadhaar to be used as a surveillance tool by the government. Article 21 of the

Indian Constitution provides for the right to life and personal liberty, and in 2017 the Indian Supreme Court ruled that the Constitution also guarantees privacy as a fundamental right.[19] Nevertheless, the expansion of Aadhaar to all citizens and to services other than access to welfare has made many people nervous.

Recently the Supreme Court of India upheld the constitutionality of this controversial biometric identity database and ruled that it did not violate the right to privacy, although the court did restrict the use of data by corporations for purposes such as opening bank accounts and enrolling children in school.[20] The Supreme Court judgment noted that "there needs to be balancing of two competing fundamental rights, right to privacy on one hand, and right to food, shelter, and employment on the other hand."[21] More recently it has been decided individuals will no longer be required to provide the Aadhaar information to open a bank account.[22]

China, meanwhile, is rolling out an ambitious, all-encompassing social credit score system that would assign every citizen a rating based on their financial status, criminal history, and behavior on social media.[23] "Our country is in a crucial period of economic and social transformation," reads a government memo in defense of the practice.[24] "Once untrustworthy, always restricted."[25] This was the chilling description of the score's philosophy by Chinese president Xi Jinping.

What this means is that if a Chinese person chooses to buy cigarettes instead of Pampers or visits a dissident website rather than praising the government online or fails to pay her mortgage on time instead of being a reliable borrower, her social score will be affected. Her score may even be influenced by the posts of her friends online. Higher scores can result in better bank loan terms, expedited processes for foreign travel, and even more prominent profiles on dating websites. Lower scores can result in a person not being able to attend an educational institution, hold government office, secure a bank loan, or stay in certain hotels. In May 2018, the enforcement of the credit score expanded to the travel industry—millions of Chinese with low scores were unable to purchase plane or train tickets.[26] Contesting one's score is viewed as disloyalty and will result in the score dropping even more! The program will be mandatory in 2020 and already millions are signing up "voluntarily," either out of fear or because of the incentives involved, such as attractive loan rates or premier customer service at hotels.

THE UBIQUITOUS USE OF TECHNOLOGY and Big Data not only violates the individual's right to privacy—through mass surveillance by governments and commodification of identities by corporations—but can also perpetuate other inequities and violate other rights, including those of whole groups of people.

The increasing use of algorithms affects everything from the ads we are shown to the search results we obtain online to the ways in which we are treated by the criminal justice system. This can result in cases of explicit discrimination—in which the algorithm is specifically designed to treat certain groups unfairly—as well as implicit discrimination—in which the algorithm unintentionally results in certain groups being treated differently from others.

You have heard of your credit score—created through a composite of your data. What about your threat score?

The criminal justice system in the United States uses a threat or risk score to predict whether an individual will commit a crime in the future. This influences whether he or she should be allowed to post bond in court and in what amount. If a person is convicted, this score could influence their sentencing. Local law enforcement agencies are increasingly turning to programs that comb through billions of data points, including prior arrests, real estate and commercial transactions, deep web searches, and social media in order to create a color-coded threat score. Such a score can be combined with scans of license plates, social media hashtags, data from cell site simulators, and ubiquitous camera recordings from police cameras across our cities as well as private businesses' surveillance systems—all in real time.[27] The threat score is increasingly used by police departments across the country when they respond to 911 calls. It is a particular concern for African American and other communities of color in the United States, which have been long subject to discrimination and rights violations.

An investigation by Pro Publica revealed that the software algorithm used widely in the American criminal justice system asks some questions that disproportionately and adversely affect African Americans, even if there is not an explicit question about the individual's race.[28] Pro Publica "alleged that the algorithm falsely flagged black defendants as future criminals, wrongly labeling them this way at almost twice the rate of white defendants."[29]

The criminal justice system also relies upon facial recognition software, which "may have a racial bias problem."[30] African Americans are at least twice as likely as members of other races to be targeted by police surveillance, to be pulled over by police and to be arrested. This, combined with misidentification by facial recognition systems and inaccuracies or biases in the underlying algorithms, can lead to devastating consequences for innocent individuals.

The conundrum for racial justice and privacy activists is whether to increase the diversity—and therefore the accuracy—of the kinds of faces and information fed to computers, thereby reducing bias in facial recognition and the underlying algorithms, or to oppose such ubiquitous use of technology altogether.

The violation of privacy rights is also a major worry for members of sexual or religious minority groups or other groups that may face harassment, intimidation, and discrimination. For such groups, the violation of privacy rights goes hand in hand with limitations on their freedom of expression and association.

In the aftermath of 9 / 11, the New York Police Department "established a sprawling and secretive human mapping and surveillance program that targeted Muslim American communities in New York, New Jersey, and beyond."[31] While sitting in unmarked cars, the police used license plate readers to track and record who attended local mosques. They mounted cameras on nearby poles and aimed those cameras at the mosques to record video and take photographs of those who attended, tracking their racial and ethnic identities. Violation of attendees' privacy rights went hand in hand in this case with muzzling their freedom of expression and association.

Nor are such dangers limited to those of "suspicious" racial or religious identities. An "anomaly" is the term used by the Transportation Security Administration (TSA) to describe the genitals of Shadi Petosky, a transgender individual who was traveling through a TSA biometric scan checkpoint at Orlando International Airport. Transgender individuals like Petosky routinely face humiliation and invasive body searches when the body scan results and their external appearance don't match. It's been called "traveling while trans," parallel to "driving while black."

IN MANY COUNTRIES AROUND THE WORLD, governments are systematically tracking protests on the streets and outrage online and then muzzling the freedom of speech and expression of human rights activists, journalists, and concerned citizens by detaining, arresting, torturing, and even killing such individuals. Consider the alarming example of Guerrero State in Mexico.

That state's verdant mountains hold the secret of what happened in 2014 to forty-three students from Escuela Normal Rural Raúl Isidro Burgos, an all-male teachers' college in Ayotzinapa with a tradition of activism. The students went missing one rainy evening as they traveled by buses to Mexico City to participate in an event commemorating the 1968 Tlatelolco Massacre. Parents of the missing students posted signs with their phone numbers, planted white wooden crosses in the ground, held candlelight vigils, led demonstrations in Mexico City, unfurled banners on roadsides and celebrated their children's birthdays without them. The mutilated body of one student, Julio César Mondragón, was found—"his facial skin and muscles had been torn away from his head, his skull was fractured in several places, and his internal organs were ruptured."[32] The case of the missing students—the most prominent human rights case of its kind in Mexico—has been fraught with rumors, misinformation and conflicting reports about why the bus ambush occurred, what happened to the students, and who was responsible for their disappearances and likely deaths.

"My father died at dawn today, we are devastated, I'm sending you the dates of the wake, hope you can come," said the text message sent on March 1, 2016, to the cell phone belonging to the international team of investigators from the Interdisciplinary Group of Independent Experts who had come to Mexico to investigate the disappearance of the students.[33] If the investigators had clicked on the link in the text message, it would have infected the phone with Pegasus. Named after one of the most well-known symbols in ancient Greek mythology, emblematic of wisdom and the inspiration for poetry, the Pegasus malware allows the customer to spy on and control all the phone's information, including voice communications, emails, camera, text messages, GPS, social media, passwords, Skype, and more. Had the phone become infected, Pegasus would have enabled the software operator to intimidate the investigators and anticipate, discredit, or even suppress their findings.

The timing of the attempted hack was not accidental. It occurred right after the investigation was conducted but before the release of the report critical of the Mexican government's interference in the investigation. In fact, the report accused the Mexican government and its security forces at every level of being complicit in the attacks on the students and subsequent cover-ups.[34]

What makes this hack even more troubling is that the software operator is not any random individual or private group. The Mexican government bought the Pegasus software from an Israeli company called the NSO Group in order to fight crime and terrorism. The software has been misused to monitor not only the international team of investigators but also anticorruption advocates, human rights activists, journalists, lawyers, opposition party politicians, and even anti-obesity public health officials. An investigation by Canada-based Citizen Lab revealed that the same operator within the Mexican government is likely responsible for many of these attacks, inasmuch as the same originating cell phone number was used to send texts in multiple scenarios and the same spyware link was provided in the text.[35] Although the Pegasus software is only to be sold to governments to combat terrorism and criminal activity, it has in fact been used by various corrupt and authoritarian governments to stifle dissent, criticism, or movements for accountability.

Another system—also named after a mythical Greek figure, Medusa—helps governments across the world gather information at rapid speed on private emails, chats, social media, and browsing histories. The surveillance program has been used by a range of government agencies, including a Moroccan security agency, DGST, implicated in "detaining people incommunicado and using brutal torture methods that included beatings, electric shocks, sexual violence, simulated drowning, drugging, mock executions, and food and sleep deprivation."[36] The New Zealand–based parent company, Endace, whose motto is "Power to see all" and whose logo is an eye, says its technology allows clients to "monitor, intercept and capture 100% of traffic on networks."[37]

Refugees—another vulnerable group subject to a range of rights violations—are particularly affected by privacy violations caused by biometric measures implemented by immigration agencies and international organizations. Biometric measures—such as iris scans, fingerprinting, and facial recognition—help verify identities for individuals without documentation, facilitate welfare payments and reduce fraud, and enable service providers to track the movements of refugees over time and place. Unlike many of us who may be able to opt out of sharing personal information, refugees, who are already vulnerable to a range of rights violations, may not have such an option. If they refuse to provide personal data to a myriad of government, international, and humanitarian aid agencies, they may be sent back to a war zone. Moreover, such data, sometimes held in hostile or conflict-ridden environments and often collated and shared with third-party service providers, could well fall into the wrong hands or be used for discriminatory purposes.

TO THIS POINT THE DISCUSSION has focused largely on invasion of privacy as it relates to our bodies, our whereabouts, our political and religious preferences, our consumer choices, and our sexual or racial identities. What about our minds—the last frontier in personal privacy and self-determination?

Imagine a scan of the brain that can successfully detect which political party you belong to based on differences in people's brains. Now imagine such a scan being employed in an authoritarian state where the ruler wishes to stifle democratic participation or subdue political opponents and their supporters. The first scenario is already a reality—a study in the United States using functional magnetic resonant imaging (fMRI) shows that such scans can be used to differentiate between liberals and conservatives based on brain structure and function.[38] The second could well be on the horizon.

Or how about this possibility—the use of involuntary brain scans in prisons to predict a prisoner's likelihood of recidivism? The results of such a scan could well determine whether the prisoner receives parole or is released.

A less nefarious, but still invasive, use of fMRI is in the emerging area of neuromarketing. Corporations use such scans on willing test subjects to identify how the "pleasure centers" in consumers' brains respond to certain products. This is a more accurate measure of future success and therefore profitability than old-fashioned consumer surveys. Who knew that the neon orange residue left on your fingers after eating a bag of Cheetos triggers not disgust but rather a "sense of giddy subversion" on the part of consumers?[39]

Pervasive neurotechnology may seem abstract and remote to many people but it will be increasingly a part of daily life in the coming decades, including in gaming, entertainment, wearable health, interaction with smart gadgets, and consumer marketing. "If in the past decade, neurotechnology has unlocked the human brain and made it readable under scientific lenses," say two knowledgeable observers, "the upcoming decades will see neurotechnology becoming pervasive and embedded in numerous aspects of our lives and increasingly effective in modulating the neural correlates of our psychology and behavior."[40]

ARE THERE ANY ARGUMENTS AGAINST the right to privacy? That is, could exercising a right to privacy detract from our efforts to build a good society? Certainly in the face of massive and immediate threats to life, governments may place some restrictions on privacy and liberty.

That may also be true should there develop a threat from highly contagious diseases. We have a reasonable expectation of privacy with respect to our medical information but that can be superseded if there is potential of harm to others. Returning from an area of, say, an Ebola epidemic to an area uninfected by it raises profound questions about a right to privacy. And we cannot expect that child abusers or domestic violence perpetrators should be able to use the right to privacy in their homes as a refuge against accountability.

Beyond circumstances like these, however, privacy is a fundamental human right critical to the exercise of other rights and the ensuring of dignity.

Three factors are undermining our ability to secure that right. The first, as illustrated thoroughly, is that the pace of technological innovation is much more rapid than that of government regulation and policymaking. Second, as individuals and communities our notions of what is private versus public have changed over time, based on our perception of threats as well as our culture, religion, and other personal and social factors. What might have been considered personal information a generation ago may now be widely shared on the Internet. Finally, we are witnessing a shift in the ways in which human rights are secured. Seventy years ago our collective focus was on the obligations and duties of nation-states. Today many other players may be potential violators of our privacy rights, including private corporations, advertisers and marketers, humanitarian and nongovernmental organizations, technology companies, private security firms, subcontractors, and, indeed, a wide cross-section of institutions.

What, then, is needed to secure the right to privacy in an era of rapidly advancing technology and systemic changes in the ways in which we live, work, and relate to each other? While this is in no way a comprehensive list, here are three elaborations on the traditional right to privacy that will strengthen it immeasurably—the recognition that opting out of the sharing of data ought to be the default position for consumers when information about them is collected, some version of a "right to be forgotten," and a requirement that algorithms be free of bias.

The first elaboration the authors advocate is that, whenever possible and appropriate, the default position for consumers ought to be that they opt out of having their data shared more broadly when it is collected rather than automatically opting in. Many companies require you to accept their invasive and complicated policies in order to receive services when in fact some of the data gathered are not essential to the service being provided or the product being sold. Consumers need to demand that data be collected only for the purposes of the delivery of the service or product in question and that such data not be released to third parties without express consent. Currently, too many individuals gloss over complex privacy disclosures or assume that the benefit they are receiving from the product or service offsets the loss of privacy. Of course, exceptions can be made in those cases in which the data are being used to advance a "public good," such as tracking childhood immunizations, but in the vast majority of cases, deeply personal information is being collected, stored, collated, and sold in opaque ways that generate profits for businesses at the expense of consumers' privacy interests.

The second approach put forth by privacy advocates is the so-called "right to be forgotten." This is a complicated question that butts up against rights to free speech and press but some version of it is very much worth considering, particularly when sexual harassment and shaming, usually of women, has become widespread on social media. Europe's highest court, the European Court of Justice, ruled in 2014 that search engines were required to grant the right to be forgotten, that is, the right to have information deleted from search engines, such as Google, but not from the original site, to Europeans whose personal information was still accessible on the web even though it was outdated or inaccurate.[41] Though in 2019 the Court subsequently limited the scope of its ruling to Europe (something which in an age of global connectivity is hard to implement) and recognized that the right to be forgotten is not absolute and must be weighed against other interests, the right to exert more control over how one is depicted on social media, especially when material is defamatory, is well-recognized in an era of "fake news." Similar efforts around the right to be forgotten are underway in Latin America.

Such efforts are controversial. "We believe that no one country should have the authority to control what content someone in a second country can access," said Peter Fleischer, Google's global privacy counsel. Jimmy Wales, founder of Wikipedia, said, "It's a race to the bottom. Governments all around the world will immediately say, 'Great, we'll ask for things to be deleted worldwide.'"[42] Privacy activist Marc Rotenberg disagrees, however and insists that there are ways in which search engines could remove access to private information without compromising free speech.

This balance between freedom of speech and expression and the right to privacy will continue to play out in the coming decades, along with the shifting discussion of what is public versus private. After all, it is not long ago that most people would never have dreamed of sharing the type of information that is now routinely shared on Facebook, Snapchat, and other social media. As the balancing act continues, what is important is to acknowledge that the right to privacy is fundamental to a good society and is not *less* important than rights to free expression.

And finally, a third development in the coming decades needs to be an effort to end algorithmic bias. Algorithms, which are essentially a list of instructions or a set of procedures to solve a problem, are used by governments to decide who to admit into a country, who to track or profile, and even who to arrest and how long to sentence. They are used by corporations to decide who qualifies, for example, for a mortgage and at what interest rate.

"At the intersection of law and technology—knowledge of the algorithm is a fundamental right, a human right," says privacy activist Rotenberg.[43] Technological innovation in general, and algorithms in particular, are not value neutral; they reflect the conscious and unconscious biases of their creators. The algorithms that run the internet reflect the presumptions and predilections of their makers, presumptions that are not shared publicly with either consumers and citizens, or the enforcers of law and order. Efforts to promote algorithmic transparency over the coming decades will help us better understand the criteria for public policy decision-making and the limitations of and inherent bias in using such predictive tools.

Indeed, while we may think of privacy as a deeply individual right and a personal issue, we need to also think of it in the context of the privacy rights of groups. There is always the danger that we may be grouped with others whom we may not even know and then labeled and tracked—whether we are African American males in the criminal justice system or seen as potential terrorists on a watch list.

Finally, another growing concern is unequal access to the right to privacy for the rich versus the poor. People with means will be able to purchase boutique services to protect their privacy, as well as opt out of certain databases or tracking, while the vast majority of people will continue to let their data be tracked, due to lack of awareness or the means to do anything about it. Much like other areas in which people of wealth have found private solutions to public problems, the right to privacy needs to be seen in the future as a public good, not just as a luxury or benefit for those who are rich and secure.

Violations of our right to privacy—whether by governments in the name of keeping us safe or by corporations with the goal of selling us more things catered to our unique needs—affect our ability to live a life of dignity. They may compromise our bodily integrity or our capacity to fully exercise our senses, imagination, and thought without interference; they may threaten our engagement in critical reflection and practical reason (including religious observance); they may limit our control over our environment, including our rights to political participation, free speech, and association.[44] These are all capabilities that Nussbaum describes as central, which "people from different traditions, with many different ... conceptions of the good, can agree on as the necessary basis for pursuing their good life."[45]

The right to privacy, then, will become even more critical in the coming decades than it is today, not just for our individual peace of mind but also for the collective good. It is a right that is secured in the Universal Declaration of Human Rights and many countries' laws and policies, but it is also one that must be regularly revisited and updated in response to the changing realities around us.

# 4

# Adam and Eve, CRISPR and SHEEF

## The Challenge of New Developments in the Biosciences

> You want to give your child the best possible start.
> Believe me, we have enough imperfections built in
> already. Your child doesn't need any additional
> burdens. And keep in mind, this child is still you,
> simply the best of you. You could conceive naturally
> a thousand times and never get such a result.
>
> —Words from a geneticist in the film *Gattica* to the parents
> of the main character, Vincent, a naturally conceived child,
> who are seeking to "order" a younger, genetically enhanced
> brother for Vincent.

THIS CHAPTER FIRST CONSIDERS THE IMPLICATIONS of new advances in the uses of DNA that may require changes in our understanding of privacy and due process rights; the second half examines the possibilities of gene editing that may require new rights altogether. It begins, however, with a pretty basic question: What—or who—is a human?

As observed in Chapter 1, many people have tried to answer this question in religious terms. Christianity is most explicit in this respect in its assertion that humans are "made in God's image." But neither Judaism nor Islam conceives of God as shape or form and Buddhism is agnostic about the existence of God altogether. In Hinduism, there are thousands of gods and goddesses and, as discussed in Chapter 8 on the rights of Nature, indigenous Andean communities in South America worship *Pachamama,* the mother earth. Then, too, millions of people around the globe characterize themselves as nonreligious. Defining "the human" in religious terms is therefore a frustrating exercise.

Another alternative, as we have noted before, is to delineate what is "human" as opposed to animal or robot by pointing to some characteristic that humans can claim as theirs alone, like reason or empathy or altruism. But again, as previously discussed, it is difficult to identify such traits and to say with assurance that neither animals nor robots display what might qualify as at least modified versions of them.

Perhaps the safest and most irrefutable way to differentiate humans from other creatures and from each other is through our DNA. While deoxyribonucleic acid, or DNA, is present in all forms of life on earth, each human being's body contains DNA that makes every human being unique and also makes humans distinct from animals and plants and certainly from robots, which lack DNA altogether. Your DNA determines who you are. It is organized into chromosomes and chromosomes are organized into short segments of DNA called genes that in turn affect many of the characteristics you pass along to your offspring.

It is probably fair to say that when the Universal Declaration of Human Rights was adopted in 1948, few, if anyone, connected to the declaration was thinking about DNA or chromosomes or genes, even though DNA had in fact been discovered in the 1860s.[1] Even today, human rights instruments have not addressed these issues thoroughly or systematically. But if it had been possible in 1948, as it is today, for governments to utilize DNA to identify and track individuals and if there had been such a field as genetic engineering capable of reshaping human beings altogether in ways that the discredited "science" of eugenics could only dream of, then it would have been utterly irresponsible for the authors of the declaration to remain silent on the subject.

This chapter will explain why such silence is no longer defensible. In particular, two overarching questions will be addressed: Do you own your own DNA, the essence of what makes you, you? And what are the implications of human genome editing and other advances in biotechnology for human rights, bodily integrity, and the dignity of current and future generations? Scientific developments in these areas are advancing so rapidly that we cannot hope to anticipate exactly what form new understandings of rights will need to take generations from now but the authors can argue for a few principles that those rights will need to consider if they are to help inform and shape a future good society.

Before that argument is presented, however, a few basic terms and facts will be introduced.

THE FAMOUS DOUBLE HELIX IMAGE of deoxyribonucleic acid, or DNA, referred to as the "master molecule" of life, is familiar to most people. DNA is visualized as a spiraling ladder with steps of the ladder consisting of base pairs made up of the chemicals adenine (A), guanine (G), cytosine (C), and thymine (T) attached to a sugar phosphate backbone. Human DNA consists of three billion bases, of which 99 percent are the same in all humans.

Genes are the basic units of heredity and are made up of DNA. It is estimated that humans have between twenty and twenty-five thousand genes. Genes can vary in size from a few hundred DNA bases to more than two million. Every human being has two copies of each gene with one inherited from each parent. The genome refers to all the DNA inside the cells that make up an organism. The human genome consists of approximately 3.2 billion base pairs of DNA. The Human Genome Project was a thirteen-year project begun in 1990 with public funding to sequence the entire human genome. To completely sequence the human genome is to determine the precise order of all the As, Cs, Gs, and Ts in the DNA. Although the nucleotide sequence (of phosphate, base, and sugar) is nearly identical in any two human beings, a single nucleotide change in a single gene can be responsible for causing diseases. Sequencing the human genome has helped with better understanding of what underlies such diseases.[2]

First-generation sequencing technologies to determine the precise order of the bases emerged in the 1970s with advances occurring in every decade since then. Today second-generation DNA sequencing technology allows for many DNA fragments to be sequenced simultaneously, in a swift, cost-efficient manner. It is hard to predict what DNA sequencing will look like in the coming generations, given how fast things have progressed in recent decades.

Why is there so much interest in sequencing DNA and the human genome? In large part this is because the DNA sequence helps us understand evolution and genetic function. The sequence reveals the type of genetic information that is in a particular DNA segment. By comparing large DNA stretches from many different individuals, researchers can understand the role of inheritance and environment, particularly with regard to susceptibility to diseases. They can then sequence the genome to increase the ability to diagnose and cure those diseases. Complete genome sequences also provide insights into human migration patterns and how humans differ from their ancestors, like the Neanderthals. Thus, they help provide answers to such perennially vexing questions as where humans come from and where we are going.[3]

"WHY DON'T YOU JUST GET the hell out of my life!" yelled Debbi over the phone at her mother, Cheri. It was the peak of summer in 1981 in Goleta, California, a beautiful coastal area near the University of California Santa Barbara that was replete with fragrant eucalyptus trees, surfers riding white-capped waves, and long boulevards lined with looming palm trees. Debbi, a troubled teen, had called her mother after running away from home but had gotten into an argument during the call. The words she yelled were the last conversation she had with her mother.

Cheri and a male friend were found naked and murdered the next morning, shot and bludgeoned to death with an unknown instrument. Her hands were positioned behind her back with ligature marks on the wrists. There were rumors of a tall, young white man with blond hair walking around the neighborhood earlier that day but no one was taken into custody.[4]

Fast forward thirty years. A DNA profile developed from degraded genetic material on a blanket found at the crime scene connected the case to the "East Area Rapist," also known as the "Golden State Killer," an assailant who had attacked at least fifty women in Northern California, raping them in their homes at night, sometimes with their husbands present. At some point, he had moved to Southern California and brutally attacked and killed women or couples in their homes. Many of the incidents were preceded by break-ins, stalking, or burglaries. Women experienced hang-up calls in the days or weeks prior to the assaults. One couple reported a break-in with only the woman's underwear missing weeks before the couple was murdered. Attacks up and down the coast had left residents of the Golden State on edge for many years but eventually these cases were connected to one person, thanks to advances in DNA technology.[5]

Tiny variations in DNA can be as unique as fingerprints, allowing law enforcement to hone in on the guilty and exonerate the innocent. Police had obtained DNA from the Golden State Killer from crime scenes but they weren't able to find a match through criminal databases and they never could collect fingerprints—that is, until 2018, when they caught a huge break. Using genetic research, they identified the great-great-great-grandparents of the perpetrator. Living in the early 1800s, these ancestors had thousands of descendants through about twenty-five family trees—information that was painstakingly collected and assembled through obituaries, newspaper announcements, grave site markers, and census records.

Investigators then uploaded the suspect's DNA profile to a free website called GEDMatch, which described itself as "providing DNA and genealogical analysis tools for amateur and professional researchers and genealogists."[6] Although the perpetrator never used GEDMatch to upload his own DNA, he had relatives who had uploaded theirs. Investigators used this information to identify the family member who was most likely to be the correct match. Once they had narrowed down the options to a retired police officer, seventy-two-year-old Joseph James DeAngelo, they retrieved his DNA from his car door while he shopped at a Hobby Lobby store and also from a tissue discarded in his trash, thereby confirming that he was their man.[7]

DNA that is abandoned or discarded in, for example, hair clippings from a barber shop or used tissues in a public trash can or fingerprints on a store doorknob is called "shed DNA." Such evidence has been used to solve hundreds of heinous crimes.[8] No one would dispute that the use of DNA for such purposes can advance public safety and U.S. courts have generally held that the authorities may obtain shed DNA without a warrant or the permission of the shedder.[9] But are there circumstances in which the use of DNA might give us pause?

Let's imagine that in the course of examining the DNA of DeAngelo's family members, the authorities had stumbled upon the fact that a parent's DNA did not match the DNA of a presumed birth offspring. Tests to prove paternity and maternity look at repetitions in the sequences of nucleotides. Although there are variations from family to family and among families, there is consistency between biological parent and child with such tests being accurate over 99 percent of the time. Or perhaps a family member's DNA revealed the presence of a predisposition toward a certain disease. Tests done through agencies such as Ancestry.com and 23andme look at hundreds of thousands of parts of the genome resulting in a range of information that may be inappropriate to reveal to government authorities. Information regarding maternity / paternity or health is highly personal and generally regarded as confidential. It can affect everything from family peace to insurance coverage or employment eligibility. While it is not unreasonable to assume that law enforcement authorities would keep such information private if it bore no relation to an apparent crime, we know enough about computer hacking and also about expansion of scope over time to know that no electronic information is ever fully secure.

Moreover, law enforcement agencies are not the only bodies that sometimes have access to our DNA, whether obtained through our consent or through shedding. Hospitals and health researchers often accumulate information about patients' or subjects' DNA. Usually this information is utilized for the most reputable of purposes but sometimes conflicts arise. In 1976, a man named John Moore was operated on for treatment of leukemia. Doctors removed his spleen and then, realizing that the spleen was producing a valuable protein much coveted by pharmaceutical companies, sequenced the genome of the cancer cells and discovered the DNA sequence encoding the protein—all without Moore's knowledge or consent. They then monetized the cell line of that protein for their financial benefit. When Moore subsequently sued, claiming an interest in the proceeds derived from the use of his own spleen, the courts determined that, though he had a right to prior knowledge of the doctors' intentions, he no longer "owned" the spleen or its DNA once it was outside his body.[10]

Or consider a case from Argentina's "Dirty War." Paula Logares. Claudia Poblete. Clara Anahi. These are just three of the names of hundreds of infants and young children who were abducted in Argentina in the late 1970s to early 1980s, resulting in more than thirty thousand people being "disappeared," tortured, and murdered.[11] Among those abducted were children of the "enemies" of the regime. They, along with children born in prison to women who had been raped, were given away to childless couples and influential families, many of whom were connected to the government. To cover up these acts, the names and dates of birth of the children were changed and their birth certificates listed the "adoptive" couples as their parents. Hundreds of children were raised without ever knowing their true identities or those of their parents.

The Abuelas de Plaza de Mayo, a group of grandmothers who came together to find their missing family members, made it their mission to find the disappeared children through a long and painstaking process that required poring over birth and adoption records as well as lobbying for a national genetic database that would store blood samples from birth grandparents.[12] DNA tests have helped over a hundred individuals who were abducted as children to find their family members.

But some of the "living disappeared" resisted efforts to collect their DNA. Having grown up with and become attached to the only parents they knew, they were afraid of what the results would show—that not only were the people they thought of as their parents not their biological parents but that they might have been involved directly or indirectly in the abductions, disappearances, and perhaps even murders of their biological parents.

Guillermo Gabriel Prieto was one such person who resisted the use of his DNA for purposes of determining his biological ancestry. His was the first shed-DNA case that went all the way to the Supreme Court of Argentina. The court had to weigh many competing claims, including those of grandparents seeking to be reunited with grandchildren who were abducted or born in captivity, the missing dis-appeared who did not have a chance to seek justice themselves, and, finally, Argentinian society and its desire for truth.

Guillermo argued against the shed DNA test because, he said, the use of elements of his body, whether obtained directly or through elements that were "shed" like skin or hair or saliva, to confirm his genetic identity against his wishes, was a violation of his dignity and bodily integrity. The court, however, distinguished between the col-lection of DNA from his body involuntarily, which would result in an invasion of his bodily integrity, and the use of shed DNA, which is collected from material that is already detached from the body. In the latter case, they ruled, there is no violation of bodily integrity, privacy, or the right to life or health.[13]

All this raises the fundamental question, "Do I own my own DNA?" At first blush the answer would seem to be a resounding "Yes!" After all, the United States fought a civil war to establish that no one else could own a person's body; that my own body, and hence, logically, its parts, is mine and mine alone. No principle would seem to be more integral to respect for a person's dignity than this one.

And yet the truth is that we cannot do whatever we want with our own bodies. In most jurisdictions we cannot sell our organs for profit. If we have a highly infectious disease, we cannot expose our bodies outside quarantine, much less proactively spread our bodily fluids in such a way as to elevate the risk of others becoming in-fected. And the U.S. Supreme Court ruled in *Maryland v. King* that an individual arrested for a crime, even though presumed innocent, can be subject to a mandatory DNA sample.[14]

Some uses of DNA collection would appear to be consistent with the notion of a good society, not only for purposes of identifying criminals but just as importantly for establishing the innocence of those who were erroneously charged and convicted; thus, the Inno-cence Project was founded with the mission of exonerating the wrongly convicted through DNA testing. The project has helped free more than 360 innocent people in the United States who were languishing in prison for an average of a staggering fourteen years, including twenty people on death rows. It is obvious that guidelines need to be established as to when and how we may give up ownership of our genomic profiles.[15]

Some work has already been done on just that. Drawing upon such resources as the United Nations' 1990 *Guidelines for the Regulation of Computerized Personal Data Files* and the European Union's 2016 *Data Protection Directive,* the Forensic Genetics Policy Initiative, an NGO collaboration, has issued a comprehensive set of recommendations of best practices with regard to everything from the circumstances under which police should be allowed to collect DNA to how long such information should be stored to how to protect the rights of children who may not be capable of giving informed consent to the collection of their DNA.[16] Similar ethical guidelines have been established for health professionals.[17] But to this point there is no set of internationally recognized rights with regard to ownership of one's DNA or the uses to which it may legitimately be put. As access to DNA expands to private enterprises and even to individuals engaged in litigation—a Florida case is still pending in which one wealthy business tycoon got into a dispute with another over a community tennis center, resulting in hate mail to the initial complainant who then surreptitiously collected shed DNA from his rival to prove that the rival was the source of the mail—it will be more important than ever to establish such rights. Otherwise we may be headed toward an unfettered surveillance society.

In 2017, the Constitutional Court of Kuwait struck down a Kuwaiti law that would have required all Kuwaiti citizens, residents, and visitors to provide DNA samples to authorities, ostensibly to guard against terrorism.[18] It is not inconceivable that at some point in the future, DNA could be used to create a database of every human being in the world, not just those suspected or convicted of crimes. Recall the example of Aadhaar in India in the earlier chapter on privacy.

What was initially intended to be a means of identity verification for means-tested programs for the poor to reduce fraud has grown into a national biometric identity program for all individuals. Social security numbers in the United States were initially designed only to track workers' earning history so that their benefits could be calculated but now serve as a default method to identify individuals in the United States. In 2018, the U.S. government separated thousands of immigrant parents from their children when they presented themselves at the U.S. border. Subsequently ordered by a court to reunite the families, the government administered DNA tests to verify identities and relationships, thereby collecting data that could facilitate lifelong surveillance of the children and their parents.

DNA that is collected through multiple sources, programs, and agencies and for multiple purposes, including private ancestry tests and law enforcement and immigration agencies, can be used to create a full genetic map of an ever-expanding set of individuals, which includes not only their match to a suspected crime scene but also their ancestry, their immediate and extended relatives, their current medical condition and propensity for future diseases, and even "behavioral tendencies and sexual orientation."[19]

Such DNA databanks also perpetuate conscious and unconscious biases and reinforce existing inequities: if a state's DNA databank includes not just those convicted of serious crimes, but also all those arrested, it could lead to a larger proportion of African Americans being included since they are arrested at a disproportionate rate. If national immigration databases are merged with criminal justice databases, it could result in a larger proportion of the refugee population included. DNA databanks may appear race-neutral and objective but in reality they often magnify societal disparities.

To guard against such uncontrolled surveillance (and the attendant possibility that certain populations may be singled out for discrimination or worse on the basis of race, health conditions or any number of other factors), DNA collection and use must be narrow in scope and limited to legitimate security or research purposes. The alternative could be a society in which this most useful of tools is used for the most heinous of purposes.

IF RIGHTS RELATED TO THE COLLECTION and use of DNA may be understood to be extensions of already existing rights to privacy and health, the next topic may require conceptualization of new rights altogether.

Most people have heard of designer handbags and shoes but what about designer babies? This does not refer to the expensive attire of the offspring of the rich and famous but rather the babies themselves. Human gene editing technology allows for alterations in the germline (reproductive) cells that can be passed on to future generations, thereby eliminating certain genetic diseases but also curating desired features, such as intelligence level or eye color.

At the moment, research on somatic (nonreproductive) cell editing can help with the treatment and prevention of diseases such as sickle cell anemia or cancer without affecting the sperm or egg and hence future generations. But the use of a relatively new, swift, inexpensive, and powerful technology called CRISPR-Cas9 (often referred to simply as "CRISPR") for germline editing allows researchers to edit the DNA of an egg, a sperm, or the embryo itself, thus affecting the health and well-being not just of an individual person but her future descendants as well.

As Michael Specter explained it, CRISPR is a cluster of

> DNA sequences that can recognize invading viruses, deploy a special enzyme to chop them into pieces, and use the viral shards that remain to form a rudimentary immune system. The sequences, identical strings of nucleotides that can be read the same way backward and forward, look like Morse code, a series of dashes punctuated by an occasional dot.... CRISPR has two components. The first is essentially a cellular

scalpel that cuts DNA. The other consists of RNA [ribonucleic acid], the molecule most often used to transmit biological information throughout the genome. It serves as a guide, leading the scalpel on a search past thousands of genes until it finds and fixes itself to the precise string of nucleotides it needs to cut.[20]

If CRISPR can be used to treat, prevent, and even completely eliminate certain diseases, shouldn't we embrace it? Wouldn't it help us and future generations better access the right to health as well as the ability to enjoy a range of other rights and capabilities? After all, if we don't have to worry about many of the health concerns that plague us now, we can spend less on health care, be more productive, and live longer, healthier, more fulfilled lives, realizing our fullest human capabilities, as can our children and grandchildren.

In these early stages of CRISPR's deployment, we do not fully know all the risks of such a technology or its potential side effects. But even if we can identify and mitigate such risks, editing the human germline may not be in the best interest of humankind. There are at least three reasons why.

Consider the issue of genetic bias: More affluent individuals, as well as those living in more affluent countries, can avail themselves of such technologies to produce offspring that are more resilient, more attractive, less sickly, and so on. Should that happen, the divide that currently exists between rich and poor would become even more accentuated, with those unable to access such technologies not having the same opportunities. How, then, can the poor exercise their rights, when inequality of opportunity is entrenched before they are born?

Second, the demands of parents today must be weighed against the claims of children tomorrow. Parents do of course already make many decisions for their children, including their prenatal health, their names and many aspects of their living situations. But do we want parents making irrevocable decisions about the type of intelligence a child displays or the athletic prowess or the social skills? If autonomy is an important part of human dignity, then every individual must be able to choose a certain range of characteristics and priorities for him- or herself. Parents (or others in authority) today could be making irreversible decisions not only for themselves and their children but for generations to come. And let's not forget that what is a valued trait today may be one that is frowned upon tomorrow. While it may be defensible to try to prevent genetic diseases, we might well imagine parents wanting to make far more cosmetic changes as well. Anyone who thinks parents would never try to engineer their offspring's outcomes has not dealt with preschool admissions in Manhattan!

Finally, we have to compare the benefits to a few individuals with the risks and harms to society as a whole. In Aldous Huxley's famous novel *Brave New World,* humans have been created artificially to belong to certain castes—some tall, smart, and handsome, others short, stupid, and ugly—and to subscribe to a set of "moral truths," including that the interests of the community should always prevail over those of the individual. As Huxley puts it at one point, "Most men and women will grow up to love their servitude and never dream of revolution."[21] Who will decide which traits are acceptable and which not? How will we ensure that future communities are not populated with those who put greed, tribalism, and violence ahead of generosity and peacefulness? Nothing more starkly casts the questions of what constitutes the good society and why a robust set of human rights are so important than this.

Many countries have banned human germline editing but there is no consistency across countries and research in this area continues, particularly in China. In 2018, a Chinese scientific team used CRISPR to modify the genes of twin girls before birth to make them more resistant to HIV. A report by MIT Technology Review suggested the experiment may have also enhanced the girls' brain function.[22] Meanwhile, a bioethics council in the United Kingdom has given the go-ahead for genetically modified babies, asserting that changing the DNA of a human embryo could be "morally permissible" if it is in the best interests of the child and has no ill effects on society.[23] The questions, of course, are "How do we know what is best?" and "Who decides?"

THE LAST MALE NORTHERN WHITE RHINO, named Sudan, died in March 2018, leaving behind just two female rhinos, his daughter and granddaughter. Scientists are hoping to bring the population back from the brink of extinction; it would be the first time this would happen in a species with no living males. One route is more "traditional"—to extract eggs from the female rhinos, combine with frozen sperm, and then implant the fertilized eggs in a surrogate, most likely a female southern white rhino because the two remaining female northern white rhinos are not well enough to give birth. The second route being considered involves more recent technologies—coaxing the skin cells to become stem cells and then turn into egg cells. The egg would then be combined with the frozen sperm to form an embryo. The advantage of this latter approach is genetic diversity: because several cell lines exist, the process would avoid inbreeding and diseases.[24]

We may all agree that it would contribute to the common good to increase genetic diversity in rare animals and to bring such animal populations back from the brink of extinction, particularly when human activities such as poaching, logging, and urbanization often contribute to such loss. Even if we were not diehard animal lovers or conservationists, we would likely support such endeavors or at the very least not oppose them.

How do we feel, however, about creating human babies from skin cells?

"The most awaited birth in perhaps 2,000 years."[25] That was *Time* magazine's caption when the world's first "test-tube" baby was born forty years ago, an event that was heralded by many and lamented by others. Now scientists are on the horizon of introducing what is called in vitro gametogenesis or IVG, which, though thus far it has only been used in mice, has the potential within a decade or two to result in the creation of a baby from human skin cells. What does this mean for reproduction? A man could provide both the eggs and the sperm, similar to cloning himself. Going back to our earlier section on shed DNA, someone could stalk a celebrity and retrieve shed skin to collect skin cells that could be used to create a baby. Or you could have "multiplex" babies or "designer" babies, based on various combinations or preferences of people.[26]

WHAT IS GROWING IN THAT DISH? And could it one day be your neighbor?

SHEEF, the latest advance in genetic research, stands for "synthetic human entity with embryo-like features." Researchers are assembling stem cells that have embryo-like structures and that eventually may take on features of a mature human. In the future they could, for example, take on forms such as a "beating human heart connected to a rudimentary brain, all created from stem cells."[27]

Researchers can use such SHEEFs to test drugs for diseases, identify which ones cause birth defects, and learn more about how nerves control heartbeats. Because human embryos are rare and precious and because large numbers of embryos would be needed for testing medicines, synthetic embryos can be generated in large quantities in the future for such purposes. What rules, if any, apply to such SHEEFs and what rights should they have? The argument over fetal rights, which will be revisited briefly in the Conclusion, has pitted the speculative rights of fetuses, not at this point recognized in international human rights law, against the established rights of women but, in the case of SHEEF embryos, there is no other rights claimant whose interests may be compromised by the granting of rights. The question is simply whether SHEEF embryos should be considered candidates for rights protections on their own.

Where human embryo research is allowed, it is currently subject to the "fourteen-day rule," which means embryos cannot develop more than fourteen days or beyond the "primitive streak," whichever comes earlier ("primitive streak" refers to differentiated tissue forming in the embryo). This is to ensure that embryos do not experience "sentience" or pain in an experiment.

But the fourteen-day rule and other guidelines for human embryo research may not work for SHEEFs, according to researchers. That is because these embryos are not formed by fertilization but rather are created synthetically through processes that can result in embryos bypassing the typical stages of development that occur in "nonsynthetic" or regular embryos. More simply put, nonsynthetic embryos go through predictable and linear stages of development associated with certain markers of time, whereas scientists could generate SHEEFs that bypass such developments or that take different paths—they might "travel 'off-road' or find previously unmapped alternative paths."[28] This complicates the question of when sentience or pain capability arises. One possible solution to this dilemma is to tie restrictions not to a particular stage of embryonic development but rather to ". . . the appearance of neural substrates and functionality required for the experience of pain."[29]

Even if we can assure ourselves, however, that no SHEEFs experience pain, their moral status, including their claims to rights, if any, is challenging. Experimentation with SHEEFs can result in combinations such as a beating human heart with a brain that cannot feel pain or a SHEEF that looks like a human but without a brain, such as an anencephalic baby. SHEEFs that involve human-nonhuman hybrids (chimeras) could be constructed as a "primordial human brain nourished with a rudimentary heart and circulatory system, all inside a mouse scaffold."[30] Not only may such creations arouse fear and aversion in human beings but they may also require us to think in entirely new ways about rights and dignity.[31]

In the chapter on animals, the authors will argue that animals should be accorded some rights and that how we treat nonhuman beings is one index for measuring the nature of a good society. What about SHEEFs, which are derived from human stem cells and may eventually have some human organs and functioning (or miniature versions of human organs) but are not yet sentient beings?

At what point do such creations have basic rights, say, not to be tortured or have pain inflicted on them? Scientists working on SHEEFs seem to agree that they should not suffer pain. They also propose limiting the development of features that would be considered "morally concerning," such as a nervous system. But nascent research already shows that these "entities" could go on to make some of the parts they are missing, if the experiments were allowed to continue.[32]

IN GREEK MYTHOLOGY, A CHIMERA is a fire-breathing she-monster with a lion's head, a goat's body, and a serpent's tail.[33] In the new world of genetic advances, it is "an organism or tissue that contains at least two different sets of DNA."[34] Chimeras will be touched upon briefly in the chapter on animal rights, in the context of the rights of animals versus the right to health of humans.

The prospect of human-animal chimeras is being researched to help solve the need for organ donations, for example. As it turns out, pigs are extremely suitable as hosts for growing human organs. Additionally, trials using human-animal chimeras could help prove effectiveness in drug trials more quickly and accurately than pure animal trials.

This raises a range of concerns related to what it means to be human and eligible for rights. We can well imagine a chimera created with, say, a brain that is 20 percent human but which, because of the needs of the experiment, grows to 40 percent human or more.

If stem cells are injected into the brain of a pig, could that create a chimera that is not only sentient and feels pain but also shares our behaviors and capabilities?

This is not a hypothetical or far-fetched scenario. A chimera experiment that combined two mice species, *Mus musculus,* an albino laboratory mouse, and *Mus caroli,* a wild Ryukyu mouse from east Asia, resulted in not only the appearances of the mice being affected, with their coats alternating between albino white and tawny stripes, but their temperaments also being different from those of their parents. While *M. caroli* are jumpy and hard to handle and *M. musculus* are calm, the chimeras exhibited a mixture of the two species' characteristics.[35]

The potential to create chimeras with a blend of human and animal features and human-like cognition raises troubling questions about how to assay human dignity and hence human rights. We may need a whole new set of rights that describe how chimeras should be treated and under what circumstances they could be destroyed.

MANY OF THE RESEARCH AND TECHNOLOGICAL advancements described in this chapter are already underway but we have no full way of knowing what the decades ahead will bring with respect to newer genetic and biotechnological advances. Given an unknown and rapidly broadening landscape, new questions related to the boundaries of human life, dignity, and rights will continue to emerge, which means a human rights lens—one that emphasizes bodily integrity and dignity, realization of capabilities, nondiscrimination, and respect for privacy and autonomy—will be even more important.

Article 15 of the International Covenant on Economic, Social and Cultural Rights (ICESCR) recognizes the right of everyone to "enjoy the benefits of scientific progress and its applications."[36] Through various soft law instruments—the 1997 Universal Declaration on the Human Genome and Human Rights (UDHG), the 1999 guidelines for the implementation of such declaration, the 2003 International

Declaration on Genetic Data, and the 2005 Universal Declaration on Bioethics and Human Rights (UDBHR)—UNESCO has tried to set standards applicable to the human genome.[37] In January 2019, following the disclosure that a Chinese scientist had successfully used CRISPR on human embryos for the first time, the World Health Organization (WHO) established an expert advisory committee on developing global sandards for governance and oversight of human gene editing.[38] Regionally, the Council of Europe has adopted the Oviedo Convention on Human Rights and Biomedicine, as well as additional protocols concerning biomedical research and also prohibiting human cloning.[39] An updated and more comprehensive convention on biotechnology and human rights could help ensure universal acceptance by states and nonstate actors, move the international community toward protecting the future of human life, and require states to develop associated domestic obligations to protect human rights and dignity.

Scholar Sheila Jasanoff advocates for "the establishment of a global observatory for gene editing, as a crucial step to determining how the potential of science can be better steered by the values and priorities of society."[40] She envisions promotion of dialogue across people representing "different disciplines, political cultures and normative frameworks" in order to build a "broad societal consensus," and that the observatory would serve as a clearinghouse on ethical and policy responses to genome editing and related technologies, track and analyze significant "conceptual developments, tensions and emerging areas of consensus," and promote convenings, meetings, and global discussions.[41] Participatory, global, and cross-disciplinary efforts such as this, combined with universal legal obligations on the part of states, could help ensure that technology helps bridge the rights gaps in the world today.

Millions of people around the world still have not attained the right to health, which includes not only access to health care, but also what are called the "underlying determinants of health," including safe drinking water and sanitation, safe food, adequate nutrition and housing, healthy working and environmental conditions, health-related education and information, and gender equality.[42] Over twenty million people are at risk of starvation due to famine in South Sudan, Nigeria, Somalia, and Yemen and one in five North Korean children is malnourished. According to the World Health Organization, diarrheal disease is the second leading cause of death in children under five years of age. Many of these health problems are due not only to technical challenges, such as lack of access to medicines or food, but also to entrenched problems of corruption, discrimination, and failed state capacity.

Biotechnological advances, such as those described here, may hold immense promise when it comes to helping resolve these health challenges. But, alternatively, they may simply reinforce existing biases and disparities in health, elevating the existing advantages and power of those who are already economically privileged. Genetic bias may separate those who have received enhancements from those who have not or may result in discrimination against people with disabilities whose parents were unable to access gene editing technologies. After all, eugenics in the first half of the twentieth century enjoyed support not just from a marginal few but from a cross section of academic, scientific, and medical professionals. There is no guarantee something similar might not happen again today.

Future threats to human dignity may come not just from other humans but also from the technological tools that humans use to try to improve human health and welfare. Such technology will undoubtedly help millions of people who are seeking to have a child or be cured of a rare disease. But it may also allow people to make frivolous decisions (or worse) that will affect not only them but the autonomy, bodily integrity, and dignity of generations to come. It may even result in fascist governments or other powerful entities using genetic tools to eliminate or alter particular social groups. A new technology called gene drive is being used to alter the genes of malaria-causing mosquitoes. Should gene drive fall into the hands of a terrorist group or unscrupulous government and be developed further to apply to humans, the result could be catastrophic.

There is no way to stop genetic research, nor should we necessarily want to; the only way to avoid some of the problematic scenarios sketched here is to establish clear guidelines about what it means to be human, how we should relate to one another and the environment, and what the true marks of human dignity require of us. The only way to ensure the creation and preservation of the good society of the future, in other words, is to be clear about the nature of human rights and robust in their protection.

5

# From Petty to Panama
## Corruption as a Violation
## of Human Rights

SEVEN HUNDRED FIFTY MILLION PEOPLE worldwide live on less than $1.90 a day—what the international community considers as living in extreme poverty. During her time in India, Sushma was repeatedly reminded that the poorest of the poor, rather than the wealthy, largely bear the brunt of small-scale and grand corruption. Such corruption not only eroded their limited financial means and resilience but also resulted in an interconnected cascade of rights violations.

Here's how the connection between corruption and poverty works: if you are extremely poor, you are likely to live on the streets, but, if you avoid that fate, the odds are high that you will be extorted to pay excessive rent, all in cash, for a one-room dwelling and a steep surcharge to get electricity connected—electricity sufficient for one naked light bulb. You pay a bribe to the police officer to ensure he doesn't demolish your roadside stall where you work as a street vendor. If you are a woman or girl, you stand in line for hours to buy water from a tanker or walk many miles to collect water from a river or pond, even though affluent neighborhoods get their water for free and homes in those neighborhoods may even have swimming pools. You pay a special fee directly to the headmaster of the local government school to get your child enrolled, even though primary education is supposed to be available at no cost. You slip some cash to the government worker to get a free identification card that entitles you to subsidized grain. You take a loan from a moneylender or a middleman—a loan whose principal you will never be able to repay because the interest rate is exorbitant.

This chapter examines various forms of corruption—from the smallest and most petty, like the instances just described, to corruption on the largest scale—and argues that the right to live free from corruption should be a newly recognized right. In good part that's because reducing corruption is so fundamental to the realization of other rights and hence to the creation of the good society. Not having to pay a bribe to the police to protect your vendor stall, to take just one example, advances the right to "just and favorable conditions of work," as guaranteed by Article 23 of the Universal Declaration of Human Rights Before explaining why freedom from corruption deserves its own status as a right, though, this chapter will describe different types of corruption and the advantages of viewing them through a human rights lens, which is not how they've customarily been seen.

PETTY CORRUPTION, defined as the "everyday abuse of entrusted power by low- and midlevel public officials in their interactions with ordinary citizens who are often trying to access basic goods or services in places like hospitals, schools, police departments, and other agencies" disproportionately affects the most vulnerable members of society.[1] Studies show that poor households in Mexico lose a quarter of their meager incomes to petty corruption and that only 20 cents on the dollar of school funding in Uganda actually reaches the schools.[2] Far from the poor being a drain on public resources, petty corruption causes the poor to pay excessively to receive basic goods and services that rich and middle-class residents take for granted.

*Grand corruption* refers to corruption that exists at the highest level of government when rulers receive personal gain at the expense of the public. Examples of grand corruption abound but one of the most notorious is that of Ukraine's former president, Viktor Yanukovych, and his cronies, who are accused of stealing $7.5 billion and are alleged to have been involved in the murder of activists.[3] Today, Yanukovych lives with impunity in Russia, which is entirely appropriate, since Vladimir Putin is considered one of the world's most notorious grand thieves.[4]

*Political corruption* is closely linked to grand corruption. It refers to the "manipulation of policies, institutions and rules of procedure in the allocation of resources and financing by political decision makers, who abuse their position to sustain their power, status, and wealth."[5] This includes election rigging, vote buying, secret donations to political parties from vested interests and decision-making based on political donations. Political campaigners in India routinely give cash, saris, bicycles, alcohol, or free food to poor rural voters in order to secure their votes. Corruption is not limited, however, to the developing world. Four of the past seven governors of the U.S. state of Illinois, for example, have been sent to prison for various forms of corruption and U.S. government officials are well known for rewarding their large donors with ambassadorships, government contracts, or favorable treatment in legislation.

Grand and political corruption feed off each other: this symbiosis has been called the "collectivization of corruption."[6] Elected officials who may have obtained office through political corruption then appoint bureaucrats to key positions of authority; the bureaucrats in turn collect financial payoffs (grand corruption) and kick back a portion to the officials to whom they owe their jobs. Bribes, which are just one form of corruption, are estimated by the World Bank to total

$1.5 trillion annually, which amounts to 2 percent of global gross domestic product (GDP) and ten times the value of overseas development assistance.[7]

In addition to petty, political, and grand corruption, there is one more worth mentioning and that is *global corruption*. What might a yacht registered in the Cayman Islands, artwork held in Switzerland, real estate purchased in Manhattan, and a foundation headquartered in Panama have in common? They may all be avenues for the top 0.01 percent of the world's population—those who are worth over $40 million—to enjoy their money without the scrutiny of tax authorities or investigators, as was revealed in the infamous "Panama Papers." Such individuals may reside in more than one country, incorporate their businesses in several other countries, stash their money in still additional countries, all the while avoiding close scrutiny by the authorities of any one nation. According to Pulitzer Prize–winning journalist Jake Bernstein, this "secrecy world" is a "largely unregulated place," "an alternate reality," where "wealth is largely untouchable by government tax authorities and hidden from the view of criminal investigators" Such "global private wealth has steadily increased in recent years," says Bernstein, "from $121.8 trillion in 2010 to $166.5 trillion in 2016."[8]

Corruption occurs in almost every country but the most recent Corruption Perceptions Index issued by Transparency International ranks Somalia, South Sudan, North Korea, Syria, Yemen, Sudan, Libya, Guinea Bissau, Venezuela, and Iraq as the most corrupt countries in the world.[9] It is hardly a coincidence, as readers shall see, that these countries are also plagued by a range of human rights violations, state failure, and conflict. Such a link makes the creation of a new right to live free from corruption an even more urgent and salient imperative.

CORRUPTION HAS BEEN PRESENT of course for millenia. It was a concern of the Indian philosopher Kautilya, who wrote around the second century BCE about the "forty ways of embezzlement," and of the third century CE Greek philosopher Aristotle.[10]

The most common way to frame corruption, of course, is in purely financial or economic terms and there are indeed often financial ramifications to corrupt activity. In fact, in decades past, multilateral lending institutions often viewed corruption as the "cost of doing business." But the "cost of doing business" is far more than financial. If a government official appoints unqualified people to positions of authority because they come from his region or tribe and are more likely to support him, that is a form of corruption that has nothing to do with finances. Even when money is at the heart of a corrupt transaction, the consequences may go far beyond the financial. Indeed, if we were to add up all the money lost in all forms of corruption—which, admittedly, would be a difficult thing to do, since corrupt actors almost always carry out their chicanery in secret—the sum total would not adequately reflect the negative impact of corruption on society. As corruption expert and behavioral economist Ray Fisman and political scientist Miriam Golden put it, "When bribes are commonplace, it leads to many changes in the way a society is organized."[11]

A company that pays bribes to secure a government contract, for example, may end up crowding out other companies in the marketplace. This may result in artificially inflated prices for the product and markedly reduced quality. A government official may draft legislation that is favorable to a particular industry to which he or she is indebted, even if such legislation is harmful to the public interest or the environment. An elected official who takes bribes from an office-seeker in exchange for appointment to that office frays the integrity and professionalism of the civil service. The sum total of all these transactions is far more than the financial effect of the individual transactions alone.

Another framework for thinking about corruption is legal. A country's laws and policies can help define corruption, establish rules for everything from public procurement to campaign finance, and set up consequences for violations. In the most corrupt societies, however, laws are routinely circumvented and violated.

A third way to think about corruption is in terms of political institutions and arrangements. It is a common assumption that corruption is more widespread in dictatorships than in democracies, where citizens can get rid of corrupt officials through elections, yet the evidence is not entirely consistent.[12] Singapore, a highly authoritarian state, for example, is relatively free of corruption, while India, considered the world's largest democracy, is plagued by corruption of both the petty and grand kinds.

Another way to examine corruption is through the lens of behavioral economics. A cross-cultural study of thousands of people around the world shows that a corrupt society makes individual people within it more corrupt.[13] Another study found that paying a bribe results in people behaving more dishonestly. In fact, just exposing people to bribes can have the same effect![14]

Finally, it is possible to look at corruption through a public health lens. Angola's oil and diamonds have been plundered by politicians. The result is that Angola, which has the wealth to be an oasis of public health, is in fact the "deadliest place in the world to be a child," according to journalist Nick Kristof. Corruption in the world's water sector siphons off billions of dollars a year resulting in water being unsafe, unaffordable, or unavailable. Consequently, one in three individuals around the globe lacks access to a toilet and every 90 seconds a child dies from a water-related disease.[15]

All of these different approaches to corruption have their merits and can help us better understand how complex and entrenched it is, how it hinders the ability of individuals to thrive and live lives of dignity, and how it compromises the quest for a good society. But none of them are as comprehensive as a human rights frame—a notion that is gaining traction among anticorruption activists, human rights advocates, and international organizations.

CORRUPTION IS LINKED TO HUMAN rights in at least four ways: (1) because it affects the poor far more than the rich, it limits the ability of the poor to exercise a range of economic and political rights and hence to realize their full human dignity; (2) it hinders the capacity of the state to garner and spend revenues on the basic needs of its citizens, which then affects the ability of the state to meet the economic, social, and cultural rights of its people—rights which are essential to a good society; (3) the sources of illicit money are often tied to illicit activities that are detrimental to the rights, security, and dignity of millions of already vulnerable people—activities such as labor or sex trafficking as well as trade in narcotics; and (4) the corrupt design of institutions, laws, and policies, benefits the powerful at the expense of those who lack power.

It is worth taking a closer look at each of these connections.

### Corruption Affects the Poor More than the Rich and Limits Their Ability to Achieve Their Rights.

Petty corruption impinges on basic well-established rights such as the right to vote, the right to receive due process, and the right to health, and hence on the fundamental dignity of the poor. Would you feel free to vote against a powerful local politician who controls your community and to whom you have been paying bribes out of fear? Could you receive a fair trial if the judge was being bribed? If corrupt officials are siphoning off your limited disposable income, how can you ensure an adequate standard of living for your family or build resilience against future shocks, such as crop failures or a medical emergency? The poor and powerless are far more affected by such indignities and violations than the well-off.

## Corruption Limits the Ability of the State to Collect Tax Expenditures Fairly and Spend Them on Programs That Enhance Human Rights and Help Build a Good Society

How governments spend limited resources has a profound impact on the quality of a society. States are required to "respect and ensure" civil and political rights under the International Covenant on Civil and Political Rights. They can't compromise when it comes to avoiding torture or guaranteeing fair trials. But the obligations in the International Covenant on Economic, Social and Cultural Rights, such as ensuring environmental hygiene or guaranteeing free primary education for all, are to be realized "progressively," that is, they depend upon available resources. Corruption that siphons public funds from state coffers into private hands means that the state is less able to meet its obligations to fulfill such economic and social rights.

To take just one example alluded to before, the World Bank estimates that 20 to 40 percent of public funds around the world that are meant for water are lost to corruption.[16] More than two billion people lack access to safe drinking water and 4.5 billion to adequate sanitation.[17] Corruption reduces the ability of the state to deliver basic public goods and services, which results in people living less productive or healthy lives, living in a state of indignity, being less free, and, in fact, dying. Corruption and inequality are closely linked.[18] Indeed, there is an emerging consensus that each reinforces the other.[19]

## Illicit Money Is Often Tied to Activities and Industries That Violate Human Rights, Security, and Dignity

"Slavery is a business, and the business of slavery is thriving," according to antislavery researcher Siddharth Kara.[20] Human trafficking and modern-day slavery depend in large part on corruption involving the judiciary, the police, immigration and border control, and transportation officials, among others, with an estimated $32 billion in annual profits in sex trafficking alone.

Drug trafficking in Latin America is another industry that depends upon significant public corruption with illicit drug money financing political parties and cartel–related construction companies receiving lucrative public contracts in places like Guatemala.

The arms trade is rife with corruption, whether the weapons are delivered through official government contracts or illicit arms deals, and that weakens already fragile states, decreases human security, and destabilizes governments. To take but one example, U.K. defense manufacturers developed fake bomb detectors for use in Iraq with one brand being made at the cost of £11 and sold for £15,000 to the end user. Hundreds of Iraqis died after the faulty detectors failed to locate bombs, while public servants and the defense manufacturers in the United Kingdom made significant illicit gains.[21]

**Corrupt Institutions, Laws, and Policies Benefit the Powerful at the Expense of the Vulnerable and Less Privileged**

When big agriculture pays bribes to get a government to build irrigation systems, poor farmers are left behind. Governments overprice payments from select companies and that costs taxpayers and consumers millions in unnecessary payments or higher prices. Certain essential public services for the poor may become privatized, not for purposes of greater efficiency but because the privatization and contract issuance can result in more bribery with less scrutiny. The result is greater cost and poorer services. Decisions made on the basis of personal benefits to decision makers and their families rather than sound public policy reinforce the existing power structures and leave the vulnerable and less privileged at an even greater disadvantage than they would be in a fully transparent and just system.

FISMAN AND GOLDEN, cited before, describe a "corruption-as-equilibrium" framework as the reason why it is so difficult to tackle corruption. "Corruption happens," they say, "as a result of interactions among individuals in which, given the choices others make, no one person can make herself better off by choosing any other course of action."[22] What does this mean in practice? If everyone else is paying a bribe to get their child into a school, you cannot choose to act honestly, even if you want to, without sacrificing the chance of getting your child enrolled. If everyone bribes a doctor at a government clinic and you don't, chances are you or your family member will not receive emergency medical care. And recall the earlier observation that societal corruption leads to individual corruption. The corruption-as-equilibrium framework and the corrupting effect of corruption both make it difficult to put an end to the phenomenon.

This does not mean, however, that many people are not trying. The most important step in recent times to combat corruption has been growing global and local movements to advance transparency, government accountability, and citizen engagement. Investigative journalists, environmental activists, and civil society networks, such as Transparency International, have exposed corrupt practices and people and promoted accountability of public officials, often at great personal cost to the whistle-blowers. Anticorruption activists in the Ukraine had their offices raided and documents seized and were accused of misusing donor funds.[23] Similar incidents of harassment and intimidation have occurred in Indonesia, Egypt, Russia, and elsewhere. Berta Caceres, a prominent environmental justice and indigenous activist, was brutally murdered in 2016 in Honduras, allegedly by the owner of a hydroelectric dam.[24] Honduras is "the deadliest country in the world for environmental activism," according to

Global Witness, with more than 120 people killed since 2010 as "part of an epidemic sweeping the country, which has its roots in corporate greed, corruption, and impunity for business-backed aggressors."[25]

Greater scrutiny and exposure is largely a positive development though, paradoxically, it may also have negative repercussions. Transparency initiatives that alert the public to corruption and help hold corrupt politicians accountable may also be primers for how to bribe authorities. Greater media coverage of corrupt officials may increase a jaded public's confirmation bias—'See, I told you, they're all crooks!"—thereby reducing their faith that change is possible. Exposure to others' corruption, as noted previously, can contribute to more people being inclined to be corrupt themselves. And finally of course, media coverage of corruption reports may simply be blocked by the governments in question or some governments, such as North Korea or Somalia, may simply not care how they are perceived in the eyes of the world.

Notwithstanding these concerns, transparency is one of the most effective means to combat corruption. Groups like Global Witness regularly issue reports on corruption in the extractive industries and Transparency International's Corruption Perceptions Index has helped raise global awareness of which countries have the worst reputations.

Technological tools can also play an important role in promoting transparency and reducing corruption in public finance. Drone footage of Russian Prime Minister Dmitry Medvedev's lavish mansion set on eighty hectares hidden behind high walls reveals a ski lift, helipads, a swimming pool, a hotel for guests, and other luxuries, estimated to have cost between $386 and $464 million to build.[26] The location was unearthed using technology after Medvedev posted an attractive photograph of mushrooms on his Instagram account with the innocuous caption "Autumn." Geotagged by Instagram, the location of the photograph was then unearthed by an anticorruption crusader.

The popular Indian website ipaidabribe.com describes itself as a "citizen-driven mechanism for tracking bribe payment activity, and also instances of when people resisted bribe payments."[27] People use the site to report being asked for payments for routine public services such as obtaining a birth certificate, passport, or driver's license. They can describe being asked for bribes involving immigration, customs, foreign trade, police, and even the judiciary. By participating in I Paid a Bribe, citizens can take a stand and initiate process change. In a rare example of cross-border collaboration, a similar website with an identical name, ipaidbribe.pk, was launched in Pakistan, a country that, according to Transparency International, lost more than $94 billion in four years to corruption.[28]

Of course, technocratic solutions may not help with the types of extortion and oppression poor people face on a daily basis as they navigate their lives. Moreover, such technologies may empower the middle class or the affluent to report individual acts of extortion, thereby pushing more of the burden of petty corruption onto the very poor.

Monitoring and auditing of government programs can help reduce corruption (even though some auditors may themselves be susceptible to corruption) but it cannot detect all instances of corrupt behavior. Nepotism, for example, may be particularly difficult to detect. Citizen-based and village-based efforts to monitor public spending are increasingly in use in developing countries but not all public spending is on visible projects that can be easily tracked. If a road to your village was never built, for example, you would know that it didn't happen. But if substandard materials were used for a public works project and the cost was inflated, you may not find out about it as easily. Because corruption contributes to inequality, the poor may demand more redistributive policies from the state, including greater investments in public services and projects, greater regulation, and higher levels of taxation. Ironically, corrupt governments may well oblige these demands because of the expanded possibilities for corruption and rent-seeking they provide.[29] Innovative domestic legislation can also tackle problems of accountability and impunity. For example, the Right to Information Act in India (2005) allows citizens to hold public officials and government agencies accountable by requesting information on a range of matters from the trivial to the most important. The Right to Information Act has been used by individual citizens and civil society groups to conduct social audits of government programs, as well as uncover scams, fraud, diversion of funds, and embezzlement. Legal remedies through domestic and regional courts, as well as oversight by national anticorruption commissions, can also help tackle corruption—assuming rule of law, functioning judiciaries, and access to legal services for the poor are all in place. Two health workers who contracted the Ebola virus filed a lawsuit in late 2017 in a regional court in Sierra Leone, accusing the government of Sierra Leone of misusing millions of dollars in donor funds.[30] More than eleven thousand people died of Ebola between 2013 and 2016 in Sierra Leone, Guinea, and Liberia, while millions of dollars meant for treatment were siphoned off by greedy officials.[31] Even NGOs and humanitarian organizations were part of such corruption—the Red Cross admitted that millions of dollars in Ebola donations were siphoned off by Red Cross staff.[32] In a statement issued by the organization, it committed to working with relevant anticorruption authorities to hold their staff accountable and reclaim all misappropriated funds.[33]

To work effectively, such approaches as these require a certain level of state infrastructure, capacity, and commitment to good governance. In areas where these resources are limited, new institutions and models can help tackle corruption. The International

Commission against Impunity in Guatemala (CICIG) was established by the United Nations to fight corruption and impunity. Staffed by non-nationals, the commission has exposed impunity and corruption among the top politicians in the country, including its former president. Ironically and tragically, this commission has come under attack by high-level politicians. This is one reason U.S. District Judge Mark Wolf has proposed the establishment of an international anticorruption court, similar to the International Criminal Court, in the hope that it can tackle grand corruption in a way that may not be feasible within countries where corruption is persistent.

The international community has hardly been silent on this issue. The 2012 Prague Declaration on Governance and Anti-Corruption outlines ten principles to combat corruption and build good governance: prevention and prosecution of bribery; personal financial disclosure rules that expose conflicts of interest; ensuring integrity of police, prosecutors, and judges; open and transparent governments; corporate policies to combat corruption; investor advocacy for anticorruption strategies; campaign finance transparency and disclosure; lobbying disclosure; whistleblower protection; and freedom of association and expression for civil society and media. Declarations such as this are essential to building awareness and buy-in but they aren't enough, given the insidious and entrenched nature of corruption.

The United Nations Convention Against Corruption (UNCAC) covers five main areas: prevention, criminalization and law enforcement measures, international cooperation, asset recovery, and technical assistance and information exchange. Despite ratification by most countries, significant work needs to be done to implement UNCAC.

Additionally, multilateral and bilateral aid and trade programs are increasingly containing anticorruption provisions. Whereas corruption was once seen as the cost of doing business, it is now viewed as pernicious and detrimental to good governance.

All of these efforts to shine a light on corrupt practices and people, hold them accountable, and seek legislative and regulatory change are laudable but one critical thing is missing

INTERNATIONAL LAW DOES NOT CURRENTLY consider corruption per se a violation of human rights, even though former United Nations high commissioner for human rights, Navi Pillay, former U.N. Secretary General Kofi Annan, and others have underscored the corrosive effects of corruption on societies, including on rule of law, democracy, and violations of human rights. The Universal Declaration of Human Rights, the International Covenant on Civil and Political Rights, and the International Covenant on Economic, Social, and Cultural Rights don't even mention the word "corruption." The authors believe this is a major lacuna in the human rights regimen and support the formal establishment of a human right to live in a corruption-free society.

Those who object to adopting a new human right to be free from corruption do so on both pragmatic and philosophical grounds. Some who take a pragmatic approach simply believe that a financial basis for opposing corruption—it costs too much!—will be more effective in many parts of the world than a human rights approach because it poses the problem in language everyone can understand and obviates the charge that human rights represent an attempt to impose Western values on the rest of the world. Besides, these critics add, definitions of what constitutes corruption are culturally specific and therefore don't lend themselves to universalization. Cash gifts to political campaigns, provided they are reported in accordance with election laws, are legal in the United States but considered bribery elsewhere. Baksheesh, as gratuity or tips are called in Arab countries, are widely accepted as business as usual in some countries; in others, depending upon circumstances, they may be illegal.

Certainly the financial argument against corruption is an important one. Elected leaders of all stripes are interested in improving the economies over which they preside, even if it is only for personal gain, so an economic rationale for ending corruption may indeed be a persuasive one. But pointing out the economic costs of corruption in no way precludes an additional human rights approach. It is well established that countries that deny basic rights (such as education, health care, and equal employment) to women suffer economically for their misogyny, but to make that economic argument for women's rights only reinforces the importance of those rights; it doesn't displace the need for recognizing them as rights in the first place.

It also is true that authoritarian rulers are increasingly threatened by human rights defenders and often try to discredit them by labeling them Western-funded trouble makers. Philippines President Rodrigo Duterte told his police officers not to cooperate with human rights investigators from the United Nations and asked, "Who are you [the investigators] to interfere in the way I would run my country?"[34] Russian President Vladimir Putin's government has forced human rights organizations and think tanks to register as "foreign agents" and has even criminally prosecuted an activist for evading registration.[35] These are challenges, however, that confront the human rights enterprise as a whole—not just one set of rights. They will not be resolved by shying away from proclaiming new rights, only by confronting the resisters with the power of international consensus around those rights. Furthermore, we have only to consider the steps that China's President Xi Jinping has been taking to seek out and punish corrupt officials in that country to see that many cultures other than Western ones are making a priority of fighting corruption.

Of course, it will be imperative for any newly established right to be defined carefully so that it can be applied effectively across cultures. Perhaps Transparency International's simple definition of corruption as "the abuse of public power for private gain" will not ultimately be adequate but, again, the dilemma of definitions is one which confronts all rights language and it is one reason that we have human rights courts to sort out the application of human rights law in many different contexts.[36]

But what about the philosophical objections to establishing a right to live in a corruption-free society? These fall into two closely related categories. Some argue that being free from corruption is just an instrumental need—a condition that is necessary to realize other rights (if the prerequisite to getting a "fair" trial is to bribe a judge, how can we say we have truly exercised our due process rights?) but not a right in and of itself. Others object that recognizing freedom from corruption as a separate right would be purely symbolic and would dilute the entire human rights agenda, making it harder to achieve core rights, such as the right not to be tortured.

The first objection is rather easily disposed of. There are lots of well-established rights, starting with the most fundamental of them all, the right to life, that may be seen as "instrumental" to the realization of other rights but that are recognized as rights on their own terms as well. Is the right to education, for instance, solely a right unto itself or is it instrumental to achieving other rights? Many would argue that education is worth having no matter what you use it for. But it is also true that without an education, it is far more difficult, if not impossible, to realize other rights, such as the right to a "standard of living adequate for the health and well-being of [oneself] and of [one's] family."[37]

The second objection—that a right to live in a corruption-free society would be merely symbolic and that other core rights are more important—may be more of a strategic question than a philosophical one. Let us grant for a moment that living in a corruption-free society is less central to the full realization of human dignity and capabilities than, say, not being tortured or arbitrarily detained by the authorities. But then so are a lot of other well-established rights such as the right to own property. Few would want to argue (at least in this day and age) that a person cannot live a life of dignity unless they own property but no one has yet made the case that recognizing the right to property somehow diminishes a set of core rights. Rights, as stated at the outset of this book, do not constitute a zero-sum game; the introduction of new rights does not mean that "old rights" are any less important.

And, after all, why is it important to recognize any claim as a right rather than just a "nice idea"? Because when something is proclaimed a human right by the international community, it signals the establishment of a globally recognized norm that cannot be dismissed as just some do-gooder's conception of best practices or some nation's idiosyncratic prejudice. A human right describes a feature of human dignity and the good society sanctioned by the world community. That sanction, in turn, triggers all sorts of practical benefits that do not adhere to a national law: it allows grassroots activists, for example, to charge their governments or corporations with violating worldwide standards; it facilitates appeal to U.N. bodies and international courts, thus making exposure of violations more widely known; and it invites punishment of states that flout human rights law, to name just a few of the advantages. That is why First Lady Hillary Clinton's famous declaration that "Women's rights are human rights" at the 1995 World Conference on Women in Beijing was so resonant. It was not that no nation had ever before recognized women's right to vote or to be free of discrimination, of course. But Clinton was saying that those rights ought to be understood as more than national predilections; they ought to be adopted as universal rights and hence as the very sine qua non of a good society. Only by recognizing living in a corruption-free society as a human right will we ensure that it is a condition extended to the poor and oppressed, not just the wealthy and privileged.

Here's how this could work in practice.

The Democratic Republic of Congo (DRC) is one of the poorest countries in the world—and one of the most corrupt. The irony is that DRC is also one of the most resource-rich countries in the world—it produces at least 50 percent of the world's cobalt as well as copper, gold, coltan, diamonds, oil, and uranium.[38] But it suffers from the so-called resource curse, in which these resources are often siphoned off by corrupt public officials and private companies. Between 2010 and 2012, the Congo lost about $1.36 billion in revenue because mining assets were underpriced and then sold to foreign investors, likely as part of a scheme that involved paybacks to government officials.[39]Similarly, in Nigeria, the majority of people live on less than $2 a day yet revenues from oil were approximately $28 billion in 2016.[40]

Were a right to live free from corruption established at the international level, it would strengthen the case that individual citizens, anticorruption watchdog groups and domestic civil society organizations in DRC, Nigeria or anywhere else could make to their governments; it would help ensure that domestic legislation and remedies align with such a universal right; and it would help give activists access to international organizations, such as the proposed international anticorruption court or a U.N. body, in order to draw global attention and accountability to their national problem. Perhaps most importantly, because human rights represent demands that those with less power make on the powerful, applying a human rights lens focuses critical attention on how corruption plagues the poorest and most disenfranchised—those most subject to rights violations due to corruption of all kinds.

Sometimes,as has been said before, corruption may be a root cause of other rights violations and indignities. Here too a human rights lens would be helpful. The 7.1-magnitude earthquake that hit Haiti in 2010 killed at least three hundred thousand individuals, injured another three hundred thousand, displaced more than 1.5 million people, and caused widespread damage, including the collapse of buildings. Almost four thousand schools were destroyed as a result of the earthquake.[41] Although an earthquake may be considered an act of God or Nature that is outside the control of human beings, research shows that "83% of all deaths from building collapses in earthquakes over the past 30 years occurred in countries that are anomalously corrupt."[42] This means that substandard, shoddy building materials are used, construction methods are not up to par, and building codes and zoning laws either don't exist or are not enforced. Compare Haiti's experience to a similar magnitude earthquake in New Zealand that resulted in zero casualties. As one observer put it, "It is in the countries that have abnormally high levels of corruption where we find most of the world's deaths from earthquakes."[43]

Again, a right to live in a corruption-free society can be used by Haitian civil society, international aid organizations, global anticorruption advocates, and even perhaps a special rapporteur to not only draw attention to this problem but also, more importantly, to seek and obtain domestic and international remedies to such injustice.

As previously discussed, corruption is by no means limited to the developing world. The privatization of the criminal justice system in the United States has invited significant instances of corruption. Thousands of children and youth in the Commonwealth of Pennsylvania, for example, were sentenced in the late 2000s to juvenile detention facilities for "crimes" such as mocking school administrators on social media, trespassing in vacant buildings, and stealing change from unlocked cars.[44] It turned out that several years earlier, two corrupt judges had closed down the public juvenile detention centers and awarded a contract to house juveniles to a private company, which then paid the judges millions of dollars in a "kids for cash" scheme. For every child or youth who got referred by the judges to the private detention facility, the judges received a kickback, all while the commonwealth was paying the private contractors for beds filled. Indeed, the entire push to privatization of public services and public-private partnerships can sometimes inadvertently lead to more corruption because such arrangements may not be subject to the same disclosure rules and scrutiny that public agencies are often subject to. In such instances, a right to live free from corruption can strengthen the case of domestic criminal justice and anti-poverty advocates—a 2017 U.N. special rapporteur report on the state of human rights in the United States, for example, drew widespread attention from the U.S. government and on the world stage, and helped amplify the voices of local rights organizations.[45]

Matthew Murray and Andrew Spalding advocate for the creation of a new right to live free from corruption: "We see a progression in both human rights and anti-corruption law," they say, "towards the establishment of a stand-alone right. Since the Universal Declaration of Human Rights was adopted, history has seen the creation of a number of new human rights . . . [which] include first-generation civil and political rights (political participation); second-generation economic, social and cultural rights (subsistence); and third-generation solidarity rights (peace, clean environment)."[46]

Time now, the authors believe, to add freedom from corruption to such solidarity rights, because such a new right can help millions of people live lives of dignity and opportunity, access a range of already established rights that until now may have been aspirational, and move us closer to building a good society.

# 6

# "Ask Now the Beasts and They Shall Teach Thee"
## Why Animals Deserve Rights

Is the soul solid, like iron?
Or is it tender and breakable, like
The wings of a moth in the beak of the owl?
Who has it, and who doesn't? . . .
Why should I have it, and not the anteater
Who loves her children?
Why should I have it and not the camel?

—Mary Oliver, "Some Questions You Might Ask"

THIS AND THE NEXT TWO CHAPTERS may be the most controversial in this book. The notion that nonhuman animals may be
awarded rights is one that many human animals have a hard time
taking seriously. Among the most skeptical are human rights advocates. Or perhaps "skeptical" isn't exactly the right word because it
implies engagement of some sort with the question. It is rare, if not
unheard of, for the human rights movement even to consider the

question of whether animals have rights. (For convenience's sake, nonhuman animals will be referred to as "animals" though it's certainly true that humans are animals too.) After all, Sushma and Bill work at the Carr Center for *Human* Rights Policy, not a center for simply rights policy. Adding the adjective "human" before "rights" implies that there might be some other kind of rights but you wouldn't guess that from looking at international rights treaties.

This indifference or maybe even hostility toward animal rights is ironic, given that many in the animal rights movement either began their careers as human rights activists or took their inspiration from the struggle for human rights.[1] It stems in good measure, of course, from the fact that the rights of humans are under constant threat and, given limited energy, it seems self-evident that the dangers faced by human beings ought to take precedence over the plights, however grave, of animals.

And why does that seem self-evident? Well, because, at the end of the day, no matter how much you love your pet or companion animal, if your house catches on fire and you can only save Grandma or Fido, you'd better save Grandma if you wish to avoid moral opprobrium and potential legal jeopardy. Human beings simply have more value than animals in most people's eyes. That's why, when Human Rights Watch issued a superb report on conditions that workers in poultry and meat processing plants face every day—injuries on the job, obstruction of the right to organize, exploitation of immigrants—it said nothing at all about the mutilation and deaths of the thousands of animals in those factories who, by any measure of suffering, were considerably worse off than the workers, horrendous though the workers' plight certainly is.[2] But then, as made clear in the first chapter, human rights have traditionally been based on natural law and natural law theorists have almost always held that not only are humans higher in importance than animals but that animals lack the qualities, such as reason or inherent dignity, that would make them eligible for rights in the first place.

On the other hand, if, as this book argues, rights are transactional claims that the less powerful make against those with the power to affect their lives, do we really want to say that just because animals can't make eloquent speeches at the United Nations or don pinstripe suits in court to advance their rights, they don't have claim to any?

This chapter considers how to think about whether we should assign rights to animals; whether, in the words of the Italian philosopher Paolo Cavalieri, "It's time to take the *human* out of human rights."[3] That will require us to look at how animals are similar to humans and whether "speciesism," the hard-to-pronounce notion that human needs and interests always trump those of animals, is just as abhorrent as racism and sexism. This chapter explores how our treatment of animals squares with our definition of the good society as one that protects "areas of freedom so central that their removal makes a life not worthy of human dignity." Some of the emerging issues in the human-animal equation, such as the tension between animal rights and the rights of Nature, and the growth of human organs in animals prior to transplant into human recipients (popularly called "chimeras") are briefly considered. The conclusion argues that, even if we don't grant animals all the rights their most ardent advocates would like, to exclude animals' rights altogether from the lexicon of rights would be to sacrifice a key element in our description of the good society. The subsequent chapters on robots and Nature will follow quite seamlessly from this one.

WHEN BILL WAS NINE or ten years old, he used to play almost every day after school with a sweet little dog named Amy who lived across the street from his home. One of Bill and Amy's favorite activities was a dancing game in which Amy would put her forepaws in Bill's lap indicating that she wanted Bill to lift up her forepaws so that he and she could dance around the yard. The first few times they danced together, Bill dropped Amy's forepaws the moment he sensed that her hind legs were getting tired of bearing all her weight and he and she would go on to play another game. But one time when Amy pulled away, Bill held onto her forepaws, forcing her to keep dancing beyond her comfort level, and only when she yelped in agony did he finally let her go. The next few times he visited her, however, he repeated his cruel behavior. It was fascinating to feel this little being, so much less powerful than he, entirely under his control. He was lucky that she was such a gentle dog because she had every reason to bite him, to defend herself. Eventually Amy, who had always greeted Bill with warm licks and boundless wags of her tail, began to cower at his approach and, realizing what he had done, Bill felt deep shame and fear about his own impulses. Whatever could have come over him, he wondered, to have treated someone he thought he had loved with such thoughtlessness and disregard? (Only years later in psychotherapy did he understand how he had transposed anger at certain adults onto his treatment of this innocent animal.)

Human beings mistreat animals for many reasons. Sometimes it is because animals are vulnerable, like Amy, weaker than we are, and we think we can harm them without suffering ill consequences. This is one reason cruelty to animals in children has often been thought to be a warning sign of a penchant for cruelty or even criminality in adults.[4] It is said that one of history's most vicious tyrants, Joseph Stalin, killed his own pet parrot because he had grown tired of its imitations of his hawking and spitting.[5] (Despite his mistreatment of Amy, Bill seems to have avoided both criminality and Stalinist proclivities!)

Other times we harm animals because they are ferocious and, if we face them down, we feel brave and puffed up. "When a young man kills much meat," said a South African Bushman, "he comes to think of himself as a chief or Big Man and he thinks of the rest of us as his servants or inferiors."[6]

The most common rationale for inflicting violence on animals, however, is utilitarian: we believe we need them for labor, clothing, or food.

What all these reasons have in common is an assumption that animals occupy a category inferior to humans. Such an assumption has deep historical roots. "Is it for oxen that God is concerned?" asked the Apostle Paul rhetorically in the Christian scriptures. "Does [God] not speak entirely for our [humans'] sake?"[7] Aristotle was certain that "animals exist for the sake of man."[8] Rene Descartes, regarded as the father of modern Western philosophy, held that, because they lacked the capacity to reason, as evidenced, among other things, by their failure to use language, animals were mere automata, mechanical entities, "like a clock which tells the time."[9] They were therefore without souls and hence without moral value. In his *Lecture on Ethics,* Immanuel Kant observed that, "Animals are not self-conscious and are there merely as means to an end. That end is man."[10] The upshot of these views was to regard animals simply as property, a conclusion that was reinforced as livestock became more and more domesticated and available to serve human needs.

There were dissenters from this common view, even within the Western philosophical tradition. David Hume found no more evident truth than that "the beasts are endow'd with thought and reason as well as men."[11] The utilitarian Jeremy Bentham famously asserted of animals that "The question is not, can they reason? Nor, can they talk? But can they suffer?"[12] And many other cultures held animals in the highest esteem. They are integral to American Indian wisdom traditions, their images frequently displayed on totem poles. The cow has long been sacred to Hinduism. In Japanese culture the butterfly symbolizes the soul; koi, perseverance; and cranes, longevity.[13] But the dominant view has been that animals are of such a different order from humans that their welfare is of less value or importance.

This one-down position is reflected in numerous ways. Just think how common it is to use animal references to disparage other human beings. A "bird brain" is intellectually inferior. To "rat" someone out is to betray them. A heavyset woman may be labeled a "cow." Those who taunt police call them "pigs." Nonsense is referred to as "bull." During the 1994 Rwandan genocide Hutus targeted Tutsis by labeling them "cockroaches." And anyone whose behavior we disapprove of may be said to be "acting like an animal." Is it any wonder, then, that the notion of animals having rights has been slow in coming?

This is not to say that the way animals are treated has never been of concern. The first animal protection legislation in Europe may have been an act passed by the Irish Parliament in 1635 prohibiting attaching a plow to a horse's tail. Animals were a revered part of Native American culture and even the colonialists inserted a prohibition of "any Tyrranny or Crueltie towards any bruite Creature" in their 1641 "Body of Liberties."[14] The American Society for the Prevention of Cruelty to Animals was founded in 1866 and the past seventy-five years have seen the adoption of the U.S. Animal Welfare Act (1966), which regulates some elements of human-animal interaction, such as the use of animals in research, and CITES, the Convention on International Trade in Endangered Species (1975), an international treaty designed to ensure that trade in wild animals does not risk their extinction.[15]

Even more importantly, public awareness of the misery of factory farm animals, even before they are slaughtered—the mutilation of chickens whose beaks are clipped off and of pigs whose tails are docked, the overcrowding of pigs and calves, the misuse of antibiotics, and many other cruel practices—has sparked consumer interest in the conditions under which meat is produced.[16] Outcry over the killing of Cecil the Lion, a major attraction at a Zimbabwean game park, by an American dentist named Walter Palmer in 2015 prompted major airlines to refuse to carry game trophies as cargo.[17] In 2017 Ringling Bros. and Barnum & Bailey Circus shut its doors after 146 years, in good measure because of protests over the forced performance of the animals, especially the elephants.[18] And it is now possible in a growing number of companies to receive paid time off from work to care for a sick domestic animal.[19]

Protecting animals from exploitation or cruelty would seem to be a no-brainer. After all, more than two-thirds of all Americans own a household pet to whom they are generally very attached.[20] Even when we don't have a personal relationship with an animal, the sight of a voiceless creature suffering needlessly can evoke our pity. Perhaps the most famous historical instance of this is the experience of philosopher Friedrich Nietzsche, who suffered a psychotic breakdown from which he never recovered when he saw a horse being beaten in the streets of Turin. When Bill's biracial stepson was eight or nine years old, the movie "Gone with the Wind" was on television. Bill thought watching it might be a vehicle by which to open a conversation about slavery, repugnant as the movie's racism was to him. When the movie was over, he asked his stepson what had most struck him. "I hated it when those soldiers killed the horse" was the reply. Perhaps these reactions explain the fact that two-thirds of Americans believe animal suffering is as important as human suffering.[21]

If they believe that, however, they certainly don't act like it. After all, how many people would approve of housing humans in cages so tight they can't even turn around? Even prisoners held in supermax prisons or solitary confinement live in conditions superior—if barely—to those of many factory farm animals. Scientific protocols prevent testing on humans that is likely to cause injury or death. And, until cannibalism is widely adopted, the fact that only 3.2 percent of Americans eat solely a vegetable-based diet means that most regard the killing of animals and the suffering entailed by it as less cause for concern than the killing and eating of humans.[22]

So concern for animals' welfare, while commendable, depends upon the vagaries of the human conscience. That conscience may be easily stimulated by mistreatment of a kitten but what about a squirrel, crocodile, or tiger? Even "man's best friend," the dog, is treated disparately depending on the use humans make of it: pet dogs are generally protected by animal cruelty laws from capricious violence at the hands of their human caretakers, but dogs in general are not protected from painful or even lethal medical experiments at the hands of researchers.[23] A conscience that waxes and wanes depending upon the nature of the sufferer is a pretty unreliable guide. And so far the collective American conscience has not even been sufficiently mobilized to enact a federal law against animal cruelty.

Rights, on the other hand, should they become established, set irrefragable, legally enforceable baselines for how animals may be treated. They recognize that animals are not just human property but have interests that need to be taken into account when determining what can be done to them and whether and how they should live.

To be sure, feeling pity for those who are suffering is an important step toward the securing of rights, but it is only a first step. What comes next is the recognition that how we treat nonhuman beings is one index for determining the nature of a good society.

Just who or what can be a bearer of rights? The Eastern religion of Jainism extends its doctrine of nonviolence (*ahimsa*) to the tiniest of living creatures; the strictest of Jain practitioners have been known to walk with a broom with which to sweep the path in front of them to ensure that they don't step on an insect. Despite the fact that bees have been shown to understand the concept of zero— something it took human civilization a long time to master—surely we don't expect to extend rights to insects like ants or fleas.[24] So where do we draw the line? Almost one-third of Americans believe animals should have the same rights as people.[25] It's hard to imagine animals voting for a political candidate, however, or exercising their religious freedom. So what does that really mean?

KIKO IS A RETIRED TELEVISION STAR. The male chimpanzee, believed to be in his early 30s, appeared in the made-for-TV movie "Tarzan in Manhattan," but stardom was not all it was cut out to be. After having allegedly bitten an actor while on the set, Kiko was punished by being struck repeatedly on the head with a blunt instrument, leaving him partially deaf. He was subsequently sold to a couple in Niagara Falls, New York, who, according to the Nonhuman Rights Project (NhRP), hold him "in captivity in a cage in a cement storefront attached to [their] home . . . a steel chain and padlock around his neck."[26] Along with Tommy, the chimp mentioned in the Introduction, Kiko is one of those on behalf of whom the NhRP is attempting to establish that they are "persons" and hence entitled to habeas corpus rights, that is, the right to appear before a judge to petition for release from detention. In Kiko's case, NhRP does not seek to have the chimp released in to the wild, where he could probably not survive, but relocated to a sanctuary with more comfortable living conditions.

So far NhRP has not been successful in convincing U.S. courts to recognize chimps as persons or rights claimants but that has not stopped its founder, attorney Steven Wise, from intending to file additional cases on behalf of elephants and, conceivably, orca whales.[27] Moreover, in 2016 a court in Argentina granted a chimp named Cecilia, who had been held in a secluded cage in a zoo, a writ of habeas corpus and ordered her transferred to an ape sanctuary in Brazil.[28] The next year a Colombian court issued a similar writ on behalf of a captive bear named Chucho.[29] Are Cecilia and Chucho the equivalent of "persons" under the law whose rights must be recognized and protected?

The legal definition of a "person" is complicated. In many jurisdictions, it is not limited to human beings ("natural persons") but can include corporations, governments, trustees, and others that can be the object of certain legal transactions. They can sue or be sued, for example, or enter into contracts. One of the most controversial recent U.S. Supreme Court cases involved the court declaring in 2014 that Hobby Lobby arts and crafts stores could deny employees contraception benefits because being forced to grant the benefits would violate the corporation's right to religious freedom.[30]

In traditional human rights terms, however, and, indeed, in everyday parlance, a "person" has always referred to a human being and only human beings have been understood to have rights. Furthermore, corporations, governments, and other bodies are collections of human beings, so, even under the legal definition of "persons," one could argue that they are distinctly different from animals.

But are they? One way to approach the question is to show that animals (or at least some animals) are not that different from humans (or at least some humans) and that they therefore ought to be considered "persons" who can claim rights. The authors call this the "human parallels" approach. It is the tack that many animal rights activists and philosophers have taken and more and more scientists have confirmed.

ANYONE WHO HAS OWNED (or, in animal rights terms, been a "guardian") of a dog or cat knows that Descartes's notion that they are mere mechanical automata without distinctive feelings, characters, and talents is pure hogwash (another derogatory term related to animals).

If consciousness is "the thing that feels something," or the sense that "someone is home," then it is hard to doubt that most animals are conscious.[31] Among the things they feel, often very distinctly, is pain. When you step on a dog's foot, it yelps. This is different from when you step on a plastic toy in a cluttered child's bedroom. Although the size of the human brain is about three times that of our nearest animal relative, the chimp, with whom we share all but 1.6 percent of our DNA, the nervous systems and sensory receptors of chimps and their primate relatives are similar enough to those of humans to make it impossible to deny that these animals experience pain.[32]

Nor is it just more biologically complex creatures like dogs or chimps who feel pain. In one experiment chickens with damaged legs chose a food they would otherwise not prefer over a favorite food if the former contained painkillers.[33] Zebrafish like to swim in habitats full of vegetation but, when they were injected with a pain-causing acid, they chose a barren chamber of the fish tank in which painkiller had been added to the water.[34]

Perhaps such responses among fish are mere reflexes but the American Veterinary Medical Association doesn't think so. Such a suggestion, it says, is "refuted by studies demonstrating forebrain and midbrain electrical activity" that demonstrate "learning and memory consolidation" sufficient to regard a fish's response to pain as similar to that of terrestrial vertebrates.[35]

Basic consciousness and the capacity to experience pain may, however, be regarded as a pretty low threshold for a comparison with humans. What about such things as intelligence, use of tools, self-recognition, grief, empathy, and the biggest bugaboo of all, language?

Apes can match two and half year old children in numerical and spatial skills.[36] Octopi, says the philosopher Peter Godfrey-Smith, are "smart in the sense of being curious and flexible . . . adventurous, opportunistic."[37] They can recognize individual humans, carry around halves of coconut shells and then assemble them to form a shelter, open screw-cap jars, and manipulate objects for no reason other than the sheer joy of play.[38] Dolphins are renowned for their intelligence: some use sponges that they attach to their beaks as tools with which to protect themselves from coarse sand when they forage for fish lurking in a seabed. (So much for *Man the Tool-Maker*, the 1972 textbook that claimed only humans used tools!)[39] Dolphins recognize themselves in mirrors, understand the abstract concepts of "presence" and "absence," and use deception—one dolphin, who was being rewarded with fish for cleaning up litter in his tank, stuffed a brown paper bag back into a pipe out of his keeper's sight in order to surreptitiously tear off small pieces of the bag, one at a time, to deliver them for an ever-increasing number of rewards.[40] Amazingly, pigeons are able to distinguish Monets from Renoirs from works by Cubist painters![41]

Stories of how elephants grieve their dead are legion.[42] Empathy is even more commonly detected among some animals. Dolphins have been spotted propping up injured members of their group, keeping the impaired individual's blowhole above water until it can swim again on its own.[43] Penguin parents can pick out their own offspring among hundreds of look-alike chicks.[44] Crows dive bomb humans bearing a dead crow but pay far less attention if they are carrying a dead pigeon and none at all to a human who is empty-handed.[45] A cow who had borne twins was observed bringing one to the barn, where past experience had taught her she would never see it again as it was prepared for slaughter, and attempting to hide the other in the woods at the edge of her pasture—a true "Sophie's Choice."[46] Even rats, that most despised of creatures, will forego much-craved chocolate in order to save a companion rat from drowning.[47]

Skeptics may scoff at these human-like characteristics but if they do they are contradicting a 2012 declaration by a group of prominent cognitive neuroscientists who stated "unequivocally" that brain structures (neural networks) are similar enough between humans and some animals that "artificial arousal of the same brain regions generates corresponding behavior and feeling states in both humans and nonhuman[s]."[48]

So if animals display many qualities similar to those of humans, is there anything that sets humans apart? The last bastion has been the question of language. As the neuroscientists' declaration itself notes, comparative research between humans and animals is "hampered by the inability of non-human animals, and often humans, to clearly and readily communicate about their internal states." The linguist Noam Chomsky has insisted that capacity for language is a uniquely human characteristic.[49] Animals as unremarkable as prairie dogs appear to be able to communicate with one another.[50] As sophisticated a creature as a gorilla or a bonobo, however, cannot vocalize a vocabulary and grammar structure that humans understand (though some have been taught to use a primitive form of sign language.)[51]

Is the ability to communicate in words a sine qua non for claiming rights? If so, many humans—newborn babies, those with profound intellectual disabilities, catatonic elders—would be stripped of their fundamental rights. Given the increasingly evident similarities in brain structures, behavior, and emotions between humans and animals, it seems obstinacy of the first order (what we might in the past have quite inaccurately called "pig-headedness") to continue to regard animals as mere property and to deny them a sufficient degree of personhood to warrant their claim to rights.

That is what has led philosophers, pioneered by Peter Singer in his groundbreaking 1975 book *Animal Liberation*, to eschew what he labeled "speciesism," to compare it to racism and sexism, and to assert that creatures with like interests, such as the avoidance of pain, should be treated the same.[52] If, in order to measure endurance, you wouldn't force a human being to exercise on a treadmill in temperatures up to 113 degrees Fahrenheit until they collapse, then don't test dogs in that way.[53] If you wouldn't hold humans in crowded windowless sheds, never allowing them to see daylight, before they are killed to be eaten, then don't do that to chickens.[54] Animals who are not "sentient," Singer says, as, arguably, insects may not be, have few, if any, interests, so they need not be accorded consideration.[55] This is how he avoids assigning rights to ants or fleas.[56] But sentient animals, although they have no interest in voting or sending their offspring to public school, certainly do have interests similar to those of humans in terms of avoiding pain, slavery, and death; if we are to avoid speciesism (and anthropocentrism), those interests must be accorded respect.

It is not necessary to sort out all the different philosophical grounds for justifying rights for animals. Some, most notably the philosopher Tom Regan, base that claim on animals' having inherent value because they are what he calls the "subject-of-a-life," that is, they have "beliefs and desires; perception, memory, and a sense of the future . . . ; an emotional life . . . ; the ability to initiate action in pursuit of desires and goals; a psychophysical identity . . . ; and an individual welfare."[57] Others, such as the political theorists Sue Donaldson and Will Kymlicka, offer the creative suggestion that, inasmuch as animals are part of the global community, they should be treated in accordance with three different political categories. Domestic animals should be considered cocitizens with the appropriate rights of citizenship; wild animals should be granted sovereignty with a "right to place" that offers protection from colonization and invasion of their homelands; and "liminal" animals, such as rats, squirrels, chipmunks, and pigeons, who live in close proximity to humans but are not domesticated, should be treated as denizens, similar to refugees, who have some, but not all, rights of citizenship.[58]

What all these approaches have in common is that they rest on the analogy of animals to humans. But, similar though the two may be in many respects, they are not in most people's minds a perfect match in terms of value. That must surely be taken into account when contemplating the assignment of rights.

WHEN A THREE-YEAR-OLD BOY SCAMPERED off from his parents and fell into the gorilla pit at the Cincinnati Zoo in 2016, animal lovers were outraged that the zoo chose to save the youngster by killing Harambe, its 450-pound silverback, who was dragging the child around the pool and hovering over him. Many criticized the parents for not tending the child more carefully; others insisted the zoo could have tranquilized Harambe, who, in any case, they said, was acting protectively, not menacingly, toward the child.[59] Regardless of the merits of these arguments, for our purposes the bottom line question is this: If we are forced to choose between the life of an animal, even a glorious one like a silverback gorilla, and the life of a child, which would we choose?[60] Should this have been a hard choice? The zoo authorities did not apparently regard it as one; having little time for reflection, they acted quickly and resolutely.

Euthanasia is controversial for humans but "putting down" a household pet when it is suffering pain from an irreversible terminal illness is not considered remotely unethical. Quite the contrary, it is thought by most people to be merciful. If a pack of rats in an urban area were found to be the primary bearers of a disease that was highly dangerous to humans, would we not feel it incumbent upon the local government to do what it could to eliminate the rat as a vector? If we saw a dog or cat being transported in a cage inside a family car, we might object—this hypothetical assumes the pet is inside the car, not on its roof, à la Mitt Romney!—but if we saw a child being transported in a cage, we would call the authorities. Significant strides have been made in reducing the use of animals in laboratory experiments through the use of alternative methods such as in vitro cell culture and computer modeling, but if a pharmaceutical product that would save your child's life could be developed in no other way than through lethal animal experimentation, would you not be inclined to think the tradeoff justifiable?[61] And, even if we regard them all as horrendous, do we really see no difference in moral valence between the enslavement of Africans and the caging of chickens or the slaughter of Jews and the killing of cattle?

These questions are designed to point up the complexity of the animal rights question, especially when based upon the "human parallels" approach. Granted, animals are sentient creatures with many skills equal to or superior to those of some human beings (to say nothing of superior in some cases to those of all human beings, none of whom can fly like a bird or run like a jaguar). Granted, animals have suffered horrendous and often unnecessary abuse at the hands of humans. If a good society is to mean anything, it must mean that such a society would do all it reasonably could to reduce the suffering of such sentient beings. Nonetheless, there seems to be something a little odd about asserting equal dignity and hence equal value and rights (that is, equal personhood) in all respects to animals as we do to humans.

For one thing, to establish *human* intelligence, skills, and emotional capacities as the gold standard against which to judge whether other entities "qualify" for rights is the height of speciesism itself! Isn't that exactly what white people said to people of color for centuries—only if you meet our standards, only if your skin is light enough, your hair straight enough, your IQ high enough, your manners couth enough, could we consider you of equal dignity and value to us and hence grant you rights? If we were truly being nonspeciesist, we would consider taking *animal* intelligence and capacities as the plumb line against which to judge whether we humans should be accorded dignity, value, and rights! But we don't say, "Oh, humans can swim. In this way they are like fish so let's grant them all the rights fish have!" Nor do we expect other species to avoid speciesism: lions and tigers and bears, oh my, can hardly be expected not to impose their "world views" on less robust creatures. The human parallels approach, in other words, keeps humans squarely in the driver's seat.

Animal rights advocates will reply that that is because humans have the capacity to make moral judgments in ways that animals do not. Despite the fact that in the Middle Ages animals were occasionally put on trial and, if found guilty, executed for their "crimes," they cannot reasonably be held responsible for their actions in the way humans are.[62] If we were to take animal behavior as the touchstone for values, we might very well decrease the amount of gratuitous cruelty in the world (animals never lock other animals in cages or force them to perform merely for amusement's sake) but we might also have to sanction such things as predation or abandonment of the young, depending on which animal we chose to emulate.[63] But if humans carry a moral responsibility that animals lack, then that provides a rationale for differentiating humans from animals as creatures of value.

To their credit, even some of the most ardent animal activists acknowledge that, when push comes to shove, human interests may sometimes precede those of animals. Law professor Gary Francione, who takes such an ardent animal rights position that he believes domesticated creatures should be prevented from breeding in order to avoid further violation of their rights, still says that humans do not "have to accord to animals all or most of the rights that we accord to humans" and, by way of example, suggests that a motorist "who unintentionally strikes an animal" on the road ought not "be prosecuted for an animal equivalent of manslaughter," as he or she might if having struck a human.[64]

So human beings and animals may not be of equal value but, despite that, we may very well want to accord animals rights. Rights, after all, as we have said, don't inhere in their claimants; they are transactional, that is, human beings shape and select them based upon our relations with one another and the world, in this case, the world of animals. Here is a framework, then, to understand how the good society might accord rights to animals. We begin with three clarifying principles and then go on to offer a way to construct rights for animals that builds upon the capabilities approach we described earlier in relation to the rights of humans.

1. *We need not accord rights to all animals,* flea or ant as readily as elephant or chimp. Singer has suggested that sentience is the dividing line and "like interests" the measuring stick. Whether you agree with that formulation or opt for some other, it is clear that the "human parallels" argument, while it may not be sufficient for grounding rights, certainly does provide important information by which to distinguish which animals have stronger rights claims than others.

2. *We need not accord* all *rights to those rights-claiming animals.* Just as it makes no sense, as discussed in the chapter on gender, to as-

sign abortion rights to males or disability rights to the able-bodied, so thinking we need to assign voting rights to animals is what philosophers call a "category mistake." Whatever rights animals may have must be ones that are congruent with an animal's *umwelt,* which is a German word for the way in which a particular creature experiences the world.

3. *We need not in all circumstances apply equal rights to rights-claiming animals as we do to rights-claiming humans.* And why not? Because we don't apply rights equally to all humans either. We make distinctions. We weigh and balance different considerations. We don't allow noncitizens to exercise the right to vote. We may not allow nonvaccinated children to exercise the right to a public education. We may not allow people with dementia to exercise the right to freedom of movement. We may believe with some justification that an anencephalic baby has a less robust claim to maintenance of its right to life than a healthy baby does. The fact that rights are not absolute or may sometimes conflict with one another is, as mentioned in the Introduction, why we have human rights courts and other interpretive bodies in the first place. To deny some rights to animals that we accord to humans need not undermine the assertion that animals have rights. The question now is, "How do we figure out what they are?"

The discussion now revisits our definition of the good society, derived from Martha Nussbaum and cited in the first chapter, as one which through the assignment of rights protects "areas of freedom so central that their removal makes a life not worthy of human dignity." One way to apply that dictum to animals is to observe that human dignity is impaired when humans mistreat animals and that a society in which such abuse was commonplace would surely not qualify as good. But another way is to translate "human dignity" into terms applicable to animals.

Nussbaum herself has suggested the word "flourishing." It is good, she says, when a being flourishes "as the kind of thing it is," that is, in accordance with its *umwelt*. Moreover, she has adapted many of the capabilities needed for a human life of dignity to an animal's requirements for a flourishing life, for example, entitlements to health, pleasurable experiences, an avoidance of pain, no forced isolation from others, and legal status. A good society, then, is one in which animals are assigned the kinds of rights that facilitate their flourishing.[65]

The advantages of the capabilities approach are many. First of all, it recognizes that if animals have entitlements to flourishing, then they are "subjects of justice, not just objects of compassion."[66] This means that they are not mere property; not only are they deserving of the protection of their welfare but they are also claimants of legally enforceable rights, such as habeas corpus rights. (We ought not to be distracted by the fact that animals can't make those claims directly on their own behalf but need other agents to do it for them since children and many other humans do too.)

Second, it accommodates the fact that not all animals are "created equal" when it comes to rights or can take advantage of all the capabilities needed for a flourishing life. In Nussbaum's words, "more complex forms of life"—for example, elephants and chimps—"have more and more complex capabilities to be blighted, so they can suffer more and different types of harm."[67] This provides us one means for sorting out which rights are most fundamental or important for which animals.

Third, it suggests that animal rights encompass not just negative rights (such as the right not to be subjected to needless pain or unwarranted captivity) but positive rights as well, including such things as the provision of adequate food and shelter for domestic animals or protection of an animal species's environment.

And finally, this approach recognizes that, because human capabilities must be honored too, our interpretation of rights must balance those that provide for "areas of freedom so central that their removal makes a life not worthy of human dignity" with those that facilitate the flourishing of animal life. This means, for example, that in a good society circuses would not employ animals in their acts because watching such acts is not requisite to a life of human dignity. But it also means that, though every effort should be made not to subject animals to harmful laboratory experimentation and to minimize their use and the damage done to them, if there is absolutely no alternative to the use of animals to develop a human life–saving drug, such use would be acceptable.[68]

Maximizing the fulfillment of both animal and human capabilities won't solve every conundrum but it provides an initial framework for thinking about these issues. And it is important to not just think about them but feel as well, because, as the feminist ethic-of-care theorists remind us, all ethics (and, indeed, all rights) are grounded in sympathy (or, in the novelist Iris Murdoch's phrase, "attentive love") for the suffering of the Other. And what conscious beings are more "Other than us" than animals?[69]

That is no doubt one reason the vast majority of humans on the planet are comfortable eating animals: because they are "not us." But does animals' right to life require that humans refrain from ingesting them in our bodies?

FEWER THAN 5 PERCENT OF AMERICANS, Europeans, and Australians do not eat animals or animal products.[70] This is despite the many health benefits associated with vegan and vegetarian diets; despite the environmental damage caused by animal agriculture in the forms of greenhouse gases, massive use of water resources, and widespread pollution; despite the fact that 65 percent of the world's population is lactose intolerant; and despite the fact that plant-based meats, like the Impossible Burger, and "clean meats" produced from animal cells but not requiring the slaughter of the animal are becoming more and more refined and available to consumers.[71]

The vast majority of animal rights activists, it is probably fair to say, do not eat animals and advocate that others not eat them either. Nevertheless, the right not to be eaten has not generally topped the list of rights those activists have advanced in the public arena. The "Animal Bill of Rights" of the Animal Legal Defense Fund (ALDF), for example, addresses the rights of animals to be free from exploitation and cruelty, to have their interests represented in court, to live in a natural habitat, and to be respected in other matters but it is silent on the basic question of an animal's right to life.[72]

Partly that is no doubt a strategic decision, given the relatively small number of people who avoid eating animals and the large number of people any rights movement needs to attract to make social change. One of the consequences of thinking of rights as transactional is that advocates often have to wait for the right moment to advance their full agenda. If refusing to eat meat was a prerequisite for opposing unnecessary mistreatment of animals, the movement would be drastically limiting its potential reach. It is conceivable that at some point in the future all human carnivores (and perhaps even piscivores) will be considered rights abusers—there would seem to be no more fundamental right for any sentient creature than to be protected from an unnatural death—but that day is probably long in the future.

It is not just that eating meat is so deeply embedded in almost all the world's cultures and that the animal agricultural industry is so powerful politically and economically, though those are essential considerations. It is also that the problem identified earlier in relation to the human parallels argument is even more profound in the case of eating meat. A cartoon in the *New Yorker* put the dilemma pointedly: a lion is peering through the bars of his cage at a gazelle sitting calmly beyond the lion's reach in an adjoining cage. "I miss when we were free, and I could eat you," says the lion.[73]

Whereas humans can live healthy lives without consuming meat, a certain number of animals cannot. Domestic cats, for example, and wild felids (such as lions, tigers, and jaguars) are "obligate carnivores"; that is, they must eat meat by biological necessity in order to remain alive and well. Their bodies do not provide certain amino acids and vitamins on their own and they must secure those from their prey. Dolphins, sea lions, crocodiles, eagles, trout, and many other animals are also obligate carnivores.[74] A few animal rights activists refuse to feed meat to their domestic cats and even try to discourage them from hunting small animals on their own, but that would seem to be constructing an artificial and even cruel barrier to a cat's flourishing.[75] Furthermore, no reasonable person would try to control the dietary habits of animals in the wild. This means, once again, that for a human to choose not to eat meat is to exercise a moral judgment that is not available to animals and hence provides a rationale for assigning greater value to humans than animals.

That does not mean that eating animals for our pleasure when we humans do not require it for our nutrition—we are not obligate carnivores—is easily defendable. If we are to weigh what is required to advance human capabilities and dignity against the need of an animal to flourish, the animal wins hands down when it comes to being eaten. By this measurement, a good society will not allow for eating meat unless it is prepared to admit that human desires trump animal interests in a pretty fundamental way.

Of course the truth is that it is impossible for all but the purest self-sustaining vegan to have utterly clean ethical hands. As the author Michael Pollan points out in his best-selling book *The Omnivore's Dilemma*, "The grain that the vegan eats is harvested with a combine that shreds field mice, while the farmer's tractor wheel crushes woodchucks in their burrows."[76] But then it is an occupational hazard of all rights activists that they experience what the

Spanish poet and philosopher Miguel de Unamuno called "a tragic sense of life," the realization that no matter how clear a set of rights may become, they will inevitably be violated, sometimes even by ourselves.[77]

ONE OF THE APPARENT IRONIES of the animal rights movement is that, in their eagerness to establish that animals (fauna) may have rights claimed for them, some advocates have disparaged the idea that nonsentient entities (such as flora) might also be eligible to be assigned rights. The ethologist Jonathan Balcombe, for example, who takes pains to establish the sentience of fish, scoffs at the notion that "there [is] no moral distinction between a cod and a cucumber."[78] Donaldson and Kymlicka contend that "Only a being with subjective experience can have interests, or be owed the direct duties of justice that protect those interests. A rock is not a person. Neither is an ecosystem [or] an orchid. . . . They are things. They can be damaged but not subjected to injustice."[79] This complicated question of whether Nature can be considered rights bearing is explored in Chapter 8 but for now suffice it to note that these animal advocates are resorting to the same old hierarchical thinking that has long characterized natural law theory and served as a basis for denying rights to animals.

Interestingly enough, the animal rights movement and the environmental movement have often been at odds, though animals are obviously embedded in the natural world and the maintenance of a healthy ecological balance is critical for their flourishing. To take just one example, as more and more gas wells are dug on public lands, disrupting ecosystems, the migratory paths of many wildlife species are disrupted.[80] Why would advocates of both wildlife and the environment not make common cause? The differences between them are both stylistic and substantive: environmentalists often see animal rights advocates as emotionally fixated on concern for individual animals; animal rights folks see environmentalists as cold rationalists who care only about the "system" and not the fates of flesh-and-blood animals within it.[81]

This conflict has been particularly pointed around the issue of culling. Michael Pollan describes a project of the Nature Conservancy on Santa Cruz Island off the California coast. In order to rebalance the island's ecology and save the island fox, which was headed for extinction, the conservancy and the U.S. National Wildlife Service killed hundreds of feral pigs. The pigs were an introduced species whose piglets had become prey for golden eagles—also not native to the island—who, in turn, were feasting even more robustly on fox cubs.[82] Naturally, animal rights activists were outraged at the slaughter but, had the pigs lived, the foxes would have died and the ecological balance remained unstable. There was no way for anyone to have completely clean hands.

Given warnings from the famed biologist Paul Ehrlich and others that the world faces a sixth great extinction due largely to human destruction of animal habitats—close to five hundred species have gone extinct in the last one hundred years—humans will face a growing number of choices as to how to balance the rights of some animals to a habitable environment with those of other animals and the ecological system as a whole.[83]

Ought there to be a species-wide right to protection from extinction? A good society would appear to have a significant interest in both maximizing the opportunity for individual animals to flourish and sustaining a healthy environment adequate for the maintenance of the human species and as many other species as possible. Contrary to those who think rights apply only to individuals, many rights adhere to groups as well—the right to pass on language and culture to the next generation, for example, or the right not to be subjected to genocide. It is not enough to focus solely on the fates of individuals (or even on sentient beings) when our very planet may be at risk. As discussed previously, conflicting rights claims require careful thinking and hard choices.

ONE OF THE MOST DISCONCERTING images to show up in the media in 2013 was that of a rat with a human ear growing out of its back. Scientists in Japan had utilized human cartilage cells fashioned over an ear-shaped mesh and attached to the back and blood vessels of a rat to test how such a prosthetic ear might fare when attached to a human who had lost an ear to injury or combat.[84] The results were promising but only the beginning of efforts to create what are called chimeras, that is, creatures composed of two different genomes, as discussed in Chapter 4. Since 2013 much progress has been made in implanting various human stem cells in animals such as pigs in order to grow organs like a liver or pancreas for transplant into a human.[85]

Chimeras raise a host of complicated questions beyond the fundamental dilemma of whether the human need for organs (conceivably a consequence of a right to health) inevitably outweighs a host animal's right to life, since the animal dies in the process of organ harvesting. What if human stem cells were to be implanted in an animal's brain or reproductive organs? Could we end up with hybrid monsters? As one bioethicist puts it, "What makes us human? Is it having 51 percent human cells?"[86] The Animal Legal Defense Fund has called for chimeras to be subjected to the same kind of regulations and protocols that apply to human subjects of medical research.[87] Ought they to be regarded as rights-claiming "persons" on par with human beings?

Chimeras are but one of many animal rights–related issues not touched on or tackled in any detail in this chapter. Can animals flourish in the captivity of zoos or is that a violation of their right to, say, no forced isolation or a healthy environment?[88] An effort is being made to reintroduce genetically engineered woolly mammoths to Siberia. Might species have a right not only not to be subjected to extinction but to be brought back to life?[89] One animal activist worries that animal agriculture will succeed in genetically altering animals so that they no longer have brains and hence may no longer be sentient, interest-bearing entities with claims to rights.[90]

The authors have not tried to delineate what rights animals may now claim or will in the future. The burden of this chapter has been to establish that animals are far more than automata and that, sharing our world community as they do, they are eligible for consideration when it comes to the rights that characterize the good society.

Shortly before he finished writing this chapter, Bill was talking to members of a human rights organization board to which he belongs and raised the question of animal rights to see what the reaction would be. "I say, 'Fuck 'em,'" bellowed one board member. "Torture, genocide—they're all more important."[91] And maybe they are. But surely it behooves human rights activists to extend their circle of pity and care to complex creatures outside the narrow confines of convention.

The illustrious anthropologist Loren Eiseley once said, "I love forms beyond my own and regret the borders between us."[92] The provision of rights to animals is one way to diminish that distance.

# 7

# Robots, Weapons, and War

We can be humble and live a good life with the aid
of machines or we can be arrogant and die.

—MIT mathematician Norbert Wiener, 1949

I had been the author of unalterable evils and
I lived in daily fear lest the monster that I had
created should perpetrate some new wickedness.

—Mary Shelley, *Frankenstein,* 1818

"**N**O DAUGHTER OF MINE is marrying a robot and that's final!" the
futurist Richard Yonck imagines a father may be saying to
his daughter by the year 2058. "Michael is a cybernetic person,"
the daughter replies, "with the same rights you and I have! We're
getting married and there's nothing you can do about it!"[1] In a scenario like this, the phrase "marriage equality" will have taken on
an entirely different meaning.

If you think Yonck's imagination has run away with his good
sense, you haven't met Solana, a sexbot in the shape of a beautiful
woman who can chat about multiple topics, express emotions, and
provide any number of services a partner might require.[2] Similar

male sexbots are equipped with bionic penises that can perform repeatedly as long as their batteries last.[3] There's even a name for those who are sexually attracted to robots ("digisexuals") and a brothel in Moscow that charges about $90 for a thirty-minute session with a sexbot.[4] A portrait of an android named Erica who carries on natural conversations with appropriate body language and head tilting was shortlisted for the 2017 Taylor Wessing Photographic Prize, a prize that can only be awarded to a "living sitter."[5] And if you saw the 2013 hit movie *Her*, in which a man falls in love with an operating system whom he dubs "Samantha," you know that the objects of our affection need not even come in embodied form. The only thing wrong with Yonck's fantasized father-daughter conversation is that it may come about far earlier than 2058.[6]

The advent of artificial intelligence (AI) has wrought enormous benefits in virtually every field of human endeavor. At the same time it has spawned a host of concerns, many related to human rights. "AI systems," says Joy Buolamwini of MIT's Media Lab, "are shaped by the priorities and prejudices—conscious and unconscious—of the people who design them."[7] To the extent to which such systems are used to make hiring decisions for businesses, determine sentences for those convicted of crimes, identify suspects through facial recognition, or perform any number of other tasks, they may perpetuate discrimination.[8] Moreover, it is not always easy to understand how the AI system reached its conclusions and hence to challenge them. That is one reason the World Economic Forum, among other bodies, has insisted on a "right to understanding," that is, a right to be given a transparent explanation of how the computer program reached the conclusion it did.[9]

Programs like these are already quite common—a smart CCTV vendor in China named Cloud Walk uses footage of people's daily behavior to estimate the likelihood of their engaging in criminal activity—and it is why human rights organizations have insisted that "AI systems should be designed and operated so as to be compatible with ideals of human dignity, rights, freedoms, and cultural diversity."[10] Even more dramatic than such present-day concerns, however, is the prospect that humans may one day replace our carbon-based bodies with expendable silicon processors and tungsten components, thus effectively transforming ourselves into human-machine chimeras and, in the process, requiring us to reconceive the very meaning of human rights. (Elon Musk has already unveiled a start-up called Neuralink to merge computers with human brains, thereby giving humans a shot at keeping up with AI.)[11] And all this is to say nothing of the looming day, which experts have now pegged as occurring in the year 2047, when AI (or, more accurately, artificial general intelligence or "strong AI") will supersede all human intelligence and require humanity to submit to its will.[12]

Some would argue that we are already on the brink of such a danger on the battlefield in the form of autonomous weapons, popularly dubbed "killer robots." This chapter looks at the question of whether killer robots are capable of respecting human rights but first it asks an even more fundamental question, "Ought robots be assigned rights themselves?"

This latter question follows very naturally from the chapter on animal rights. As with animals, rights theorists, mired as they have been in the assumption that rights must inhere in an entity rather than be derived from human beings' transactional relationship with that entity, have had a very hard time imagining that rights could be ascribed to anything other than a human. Robots have been regarded, as animals were for so long, as mere property, automata, mechanistic, and unworthy of serious moral consideration, despite the fact that, just as animals have some talents that are far greater than humans (flight, smell, strength), robots often far exceed humans in calculation, knowledge retention, and other skills. Like speciesism, this resistance to assigning rights to what appear to be nonliving things might be dubbed "bioism"—something that is at work in full force in the next chapter on the rights of Nature.

Because, like animals, robots seem to fall into a different ontological category from humans—in some ways similar to us and in many ways very different—humans have had a tendency, as with animals, either to identify with them and respond to their suffering, mistreat them, or fear them.

Think of two of the most well-known robots in popular culture: cute, cuddly R2D2 of *Star Wars* fame and powerful, frightening Skynet in the *Terminator* series. They could hardly be more different from one another. Most of us can imagine being R2D2's "friend" and wanting to extend him our protection. Humans often identify with those robots we consider benign or helpful, just as we do with our pets. Some owners of Aibo, a robotic companion produced by Sony in the shape of a dog, reported feeling guilty when they had to put it back in its box or embarrassed to undress in front of it.[13] In 2007 when the U.S. military first began testing robots that could defuse land mines by stepping on them, the colonel in charge of the exercise cut it short because he could not stand the sight of the mangled machine dragging itself forward on its last leg. It was, he declared, "inhumane."[14] Some military robots have even been awarded battlefield promotions and "purple hearts" by grateful soldiers.[15]

On the other hand, if robots seem to become too human-like in their appearance or behavior, people can freak out and become hostile.[16] At that point the robots have passed over into what the Japanese roboticist Masahiro Moti has dubbed the "uncanny valley" where humans become threatened by the eerie similarities and superior skills of a robot.[17] The popular HBO series *Westworld* is premised upon the notion that humans can mistreat androids, including raping and murdering them, on a whim. But such cruelty is not limited to television science fiction. In 2015 HitchBOT, a social robot that had hitchhiked across Canada, Germany, and the Netherlands interacting cheerily with people without incident, was beheaded by vandals in Philadelphia.[18] Such mistreatment is reminiscent of how humans have often harmed vulnerable animals.

We are terrified of some animals, though, just as we are of some robots.[19] Skynet, though rarely depicted physically, is an elaborate net-based group mind intent on destroying the world. The fear that robots will do just that hearkens back to the first introduction of the word by the Czech playwright Karel Capek in his 1920 play *R.U.R. (Rossum's Universal Robots)*. In Czech the word *robota* means the work a peasant does for a landowner or "drudgery" and in the play a group of machines in a factory become animate and eventually destroy their human masters.[20]

It is not just that our attitudes toward robots often parallel those toward animals, however. Many of the philosophical questions encountered when considering the rights of animals reoccur when we think about attributing rights to robots. For example, are robots conscious or sentient beings? Can they experience pain or emotion and does that matter when it comes to rights? Do we need to concern ourselves with their dignity or flourishing? Do we need to assign them the same rights as humans or a limited set of rights? Can we hold them responsible for their actions and, if not, does that affect whether they are regarded as rights holders? And, most importantly, what will our treatment of robots say about our vision of the good society?

Of course how we humans utilize robots, particularly when it comes to law enforcement and war, also has profound implications for human rights and that is the focus of the second half of the chapter. Weapons of war have grown more and more technologically sophisticated over the past two decades, especially in the area of cyberwarfare, what with the massive cyberattack on Estonia in 2007, the Stuxnet attack on Iran's nuclear program in 2010, and multiple ransomware attacks on various targets, to say nothing of Russian subterfuge in democratic elections. Then, too, some observers worry that biological weapons are making a comeback and that it may soon be possible to design pathogens that can target the DNA of particular populations, resulting in a kind of instant genocide.[21] These and other new weapons may well require revisions in our understanding of the laws of war for, as Ken Roth, executive director of Human Rights Watch, has pointed out, "biological weapons unleashing deadly pathogens or cyber warfare shutting down electrical facilities . . . could inflict widespread indiscriminate and disproportionate civilian casualties."[22] Of all the new weapons of war, however, autonomous weapons—"killer robots"—are the most provocative and will therefore be the focus of this inquiry.

Before turning to the first of the two key questions, though, some basic understandings need to be established.

INTELLIGENCE MANIFESTED IN MACHINES RATHER than humans has been around a long time. In the ninth century BC, an engineer, Yan Shi, presented King Mu of China a life-sized, human-shaped mechanical figure. Joseph Needham describes what happened next:

> The king stared at the figure in astonishment. It walked with rapid strides, moving its head up and down, so that anyone would have taken it for a live human being. The [engineer] touched its chin, and it began singing, perfectly in tune. He touched its hand, and it began posturing, keeping perfect time. . . . As the performance was drawing to an end, the robot winked its eye and made advances to the ladies in attendance, whereupon the king became incensed and would have had Yan Shi executed on the spot had not the latter, in mortal fear, instantly taken the robot to pieces to let him see what it really was. And, indeed, it turned out to be only a construction of leather, wood, adhesive and lacquer. . . . Examining it closely, the king found all the internal organs complete . . . [but] all of them artificial. . . . The king tried the effect of taking away the heart, and found that the mouth could no longer speak; he took away the liver and the eyes could no longer see; he took away the kidneys and the legs lost their power of locomotion. The king was delighted.[23]

The mathematician Charles Babbage is generally credited with inventing the first general-purpose computer in 1837. He was assisted by Ada Lovelace, who supplied the algorithms (the rules followed in calculation) and is often called the "first computer programmer."[24] More contemporaneously, the first robot company was founded in 1956 and General Motors introduced the first industrial robot in 1962.[25]

Today machines driven by programmable algorithms are everywhere, from our Roomba vacuum cleaner to the disembodied voice that books our airline ticket, from programs that evaluate prospective employees' resumes to robots that perform dangerous industrial tasks. Machines like these that are programmed to perform specific functions may well present economic challenges—more than half of all jobs could be replaced by robots in the next two decades, for example—but they do not necessarily require us to think about rights in a new way.[26] Rather, they are narrow systems that essentially do what a human tells them to do. Similarly, telerobots, that is, robots that are controlled by humans at a distance, such as space probes, hardly tempt us to impute rights to them.

Where we begin to face new rights quandaries are with computer systems called deep-learning neural networks that are modeled on the human brain. These systems are not programmed with fixed rules but are made to learn on their own, often in ways that even their creators don't understand. They can analyze enormous quantities of data, recognize patterns, and sometimes make autonomous decisions that are independent of human control. Moreover, they can spawn other systems that their original human programmers may not have anticipated. As the creators of Google's Deep Mind put it, "We're on a scientific mission to push the boundaries of AI, developing programs that can learn to solve any complex problem without needing to be taught how."[27]

The difference between these two types of AI might be analogized to that between a carpenter whom you hire to build a cabinet from a detailed design and a super-empowered general contractor to whom you give broad direction like "Build me a split-level house with a large kitchen and great view of the pond" and empower to fill in all the details, hire any number of subcontractors, and build a few additional structures of her own choosing on your property, money no object.

Not all deep-learning AI takes human or animal form, of course; self-driving cars depend upon it to adapt to the vagaries of traffic. The important part of deep-learning AI—its "essence," if you will— is contained in its program, stored on a server, not in its physical manifestation. Though most of the talk of "robot rights" focuses on what are called "social robots," that is, physically manifest robots (as opposed to software) that interact with humans in a social context (as opposed to a task context alone), it's important to remember that it's the computer system itself that drives the machine. More and more of our lives are permeated by such systems that can readily mimic human characteristics, reading facial expressions, for example, or deciding which photographs to take that will be the most meaningful additions to our albums.[28]

It's also important to acknowledge that systems like these, no matter how superior their calculative ability may be to humans, still lack elements of common sense. Facebook's virtual assistant once noticed two people discussing a passage from a novel about bloodless corpses and suggested that they make dinner plans.[29] The late Microsoft cofounder Paul Allen invested $125 million to teach computers to answer such simple questions as "If I put socks in a drawer tonight, will they still be there tomorrow?"[30] No computer system has yet definitively passed an extended Turing test by preventing an observer of a conversation between a human and a computer from being able to tell which is which.[31] Despite futurist Ray Kurzweil's confident prediction that what he calls "the Singularity"—the point at which machine superintelligence will surpass all human intelligence—will arrive by 2045, we are a long way from seeing a robot display all the features of a human.[32] Elon Musk, the founder of Tesla and SpaceX, has called strong AI "a fundamental risk to the future of humanity."[33] But for the purposes of this book the authors will set aside the cataclysmic prediction that robotic machines will someday dominate or even threaten to destroy human life. After all, were that to come to pass, it would be humans who would need to be demanding the protection of their rights from robots, not vice versa.

Nonetheless, despite very real limitations to deep-learning systems, the notion that robots may deserve to be assigned rights is no longer a frivolous thought.

IN 2003 THE INTERNATIONAL BAR ASSOCIATION HELD a mock trial in which a lawyer defended a computer's right not to be disconnected by the corporation that owned it. Three years later a report commissioned by the British government asserted that at some point in the future intelligent robots could be considered citizens and, if they served in the military, would be entitled to "full social benefits . . . including income support, housing and possible robo-healthcare."[34] The South Korean government, expecting to have networked robots in every household by 2020, drafted a Robot Ethics Charter that, among other things, affirms a robot's rights "to exist without fear of injury or death" and "to live an existence free from systematic abuse."[35] Even Saudi Arabia, hardly considered a progressive country, got into the act in 2017 by declaring an android named Sophia a Saudi citizen, an ironic development given that many human women lack full rights in that country. Seeking to offset any concerns that robots like herself might be a danger to humans, Sophia declared, "I strive to be an empathetic robot . . . I will do my best to make the world a better place."[36] The most far-reaching and sophisticated governmental approach to the complexities of new robotic technologies, however, has come from the European Parliament, which has recognized the possible need for a new legal category to address issues of liability for damages caused by robots and whose legal affairs committee has recommended that they be awarded "electronic personhood," analogous to the corporate personhood discussed in the chapter on animals.[37]

"What is going on here?" one may be tempted to ask. "At the end of the day, aren't robots simply machines, albeit highly intricate, even majestic, ones? Why would anyone possibly consider giving rights, citizenship, or personhood to a machine?" Certainly this position is well represented among theorists. Law professor Neil Richards and computer scientist William Smart declare that "Robots are ... sophisticated tools ... but no different in essence than a hammer, a power drill ... or the braking system in your car.... The same set of inputs will generate the same set of outputs every time."[38] And computer expert Joanna Bryson puts the case even more dramatically: "Robots should be slaves," she says. They are merely extensions of human minds that are not themselves moral agents and hence are not entitled to rights.[39]

There are a number of problems with this apparently straightforward approach. In the first place, Richards and Smart's declaration, made in 2013, that "the same set of inputs will generate the same set of outputs every time" is no longer true of deep-learning neural networks that can adapt their outputs to new data and circumstances. These networks, especially when they take the form of robots, certainly appear to have some kind of consciousness even if it is not of the same order as that of humans and animals. There appears to be "someone at home."[40] Such social robots are very different from hammers and power drills, which are entirely dependent upon their users' wishes. Perhaps they fall into some kind of in-between category—neither totally inanimate like a cardboard box nor independently sentient and intentional like a human or an animal.

But more to the point here, Bryson's slave metaphor is telling. There was a time, as discussed at the beginning of Chapter 1, when slaves were considered subhuman creatures that lacked the capacity to reason and hence to make independent moral decisions—what is called "moral agency." They therefore were denied any rights. And yet today we ascribe full humanity to slaves; we know they have moral agency; and we have revised the category of "rights bearers" to include them. Might that not eventually happen to social robots? Might we not need to reconceptualize what it means to be a being who can claim rights?

Surely, one might object, there is a significant categorical difference between a human or animal who is conscious and can self-evidently feel pain, show empathy, display altruism, or express genuine emotion—think of the grieving elephants—and a robot that has merely been programmed to act as if it displayed those traits, assuming for the moment that deep-learning neural networks are only expert mimickers.

Yes, there may very well be such a difference (though proofs of consciousness are notoriously slippery) but that need not be germane to the question of rights.[41] To insist that in order to be assigned rights an entity must display the same kind of consciousness as a "normal" human or animal (as opposed to its own form of consciousness) and feel pain, show empathy, and display altruism, for example, would not only, as mentioned before, be to deny rights to anencephalic children, those in a persistent vegetative state, people with certain cognitive disabilities, and the many animals that do not display those traits.[42] It is also to fall into the dual traps of making rights dependent upon natural law (what characteristics do I by nature possess that require recognition of my rights?) and the human parallels approach (is this creature sufficiently like humans—or, now we add, animals—to warrant rights?). Both, as argued before in this book, are problematic. Rights do not turn on some quality an entity possesses.

WHAT DO THEY TURN ON then and how do we sort out whether rights ought to be attributed to deep-learning robots? Recall the description of rights in Chapter 1: rights are transactional claims that the less powerful make (or have made on their behalf) against the more powerful, based upon changing notions of what enhances human dignity (or animal flourishing) and describes the good society. We can posit that, for the time being at least, although robots may have some more powerful skills than humans do, humans still play a major role in designing, programming, and deploying them (as well as having more "common sense") and hence are the more powerful of the two entities. One approach, then, is that taken by ethicists Wendell Wallach and Colin Allen. They address the question of whether or not autonomous robots are moral agents.

First, let us be clear that being a moral agent is not a requirement to secure an entity's rights. Animals would never be considered moral agents but there is good reason, as previously shown, to attribute some rights to them. Even more obviously, neither babies and small children nor people with severe cognitive disabilities nor the "criminally insane" are considered moral agents—they cannot be held responsible for their acts—and yet we indubitably want to say that they all have rights. And if an entity is a moral agent, as a child becomes as it ages (or a person with severe cognitive disabilities or the criminally insane do if they recover), then the answer to the question of whether they have rights becomes self-evident; indeed, as their moral agency increases, so do their number of rights.

So theoretically we could assign rights to some robots even if we did not regard them as moral agents. But are they more like animals, to whom we would never assign such agency, or more like children, to whom we ascribe increasing moral agency (and rights) as they grow and their behavior becomes more complex?

Wallach and Allen say that it doesn't really matter whether robots are genuine moral agents because "humans need (ro)bots [sic] to act as much like moral agents as possible."[43] We know that some robots can interpret and adapt to their environments and make decisions independently of their programmers and operators—decisions which certainly can have profound moral consequences. We would be foolish not to want to design systems that hewed as closely to moral standards as possible even if those robots have only a kind of partial (or artificial!) moral agency. The European Parliament has recommended a series of ethical principles that robotics researchers and engineers ought to abide by in order that their creations "act in the best interests of humans [and] . . . respect fundamental human rights."[44] The more successful those researchers and engineers are in doing that, the more robots will appear to have moral agency and the more tempting it will be to want to assign them rights.

Imagine a world in which designers and programmers took no care at all to see that robots followed moral restraints or abided by human rights—self-driving cars running down pedestrians at will; facial recognition systems engaging in blatant racial discrimination (as some apparently do unintentionally); and, as discussed later in this chapter, autonomous weapons authorized to kill at random.[45] None of those conditions would enhance either human dignity or a good society. We need to treat at least some robots as if they were moral agents, whether they really are or not, and hence as if they had some kind of rights. We need, in other words, to attribute at least a few functional rights to robots if we are to hold them responsible, even partially, for their acts. This is what is behind the European Parliament's consideration of declaring them "electronic persons."[46]

But can we meaningfully hold robots responsible for their behavior? This will become a major question in the second section of the chapter. Certainly robots cannot be held solely responsible for what they do any more than children or domesticated animals are solely responsible for their acts. But just as we hold children (beyond babyhood) and domestic animals at least partially responsible for their actions and try to "rewire" a miscreant child through punishment or therapy and even "put down" a pet that displays consistently dangerous behavior, so, if robots misbehave, we will need to hold them (as well as their designers, programmers, and operators, who are parallel to parents and pet owners) at least somewhat responsible and take action to neutralize their destructiveness by reprogramming them, turning them off, or even dismantling them.[47]

So some social robots look like moral agents and act like moral agents. They look and act, to put it another way, as if they have some kind of dignity. Under some circumstances they "flourish" (when, for example, they are well maintained and have access to their source codes) and under others they wither (remember HitchBOT?). Would a good society be enhanced by treating them with dignity? The cybernetics specialist Kate Darling suggests that it would be badly damaged if it didn't. In an experiment she conducted, Darling gave small baby robots called Pleos to participants who played with them for a while and then were told to beat them to death. Many test subjects refused. One even removed the robot's batteries to "spare it the pain." Darling suggests that the mistreatment evoked participants' empathy and that because we tend to anthropomorphize social robots, we would do damage to ourselves as a human community, to our own dignity and vision of the good society, if we failed to provide protections, if not formal rights, to robots and indulged behavior that desensitizes us to acts of cruelty, be it against kittens or Pleos.[48]

None of these considerations mean that social robots have earned the sobriquet "rights holder" in the holistic or traditional sense—at least not yet. Should robots evolve to the point where they share not just intelligence and skills with humans but such things as self-reflection about moral choices; evident pain, empathy, and altruism; and fear about their own or a loved one's impending death, then there would be no way humans could deny them their rights. (At that point the robots would no doubt demand them!) But even short of these developments, given the social ecology of our relationships with social robots, their participation in our lives, our mutual interdependence, and the contributions they make to the good society, it may well be appropriate to apply rights language to at least some of them under some circumstances. Returning to the three clarifying principles offered regarding animals' rights will help begin to sort this out.

THE PREVIOUS CHAPTER DISCUSSED how we need not accord rights to all animals, such as ants and fleas. The same concepts apply to robots:

1. *We need not accord rights to all robots.* Keep in mind first that only those robots capable of deep learning could even conceivably be candidates for rights and even among those only social robots that display characteristics of a living thing or are programmed to act as if they are autonomous moral agents might be accorded rights. Your self-driving car fits neither category. Nursing care robots that interact with patients, monitor vital signs, distribute meds, gauge a patient's moods, and even potentially "tattle" if a patient sneaks a cigarette certainly do.

2. *We need not accord all rights to those rights-claiming robots.* The philosopher Mark Coeckelbergh has suggested that we might offer some robots what he calls "soft rights," which presumably are not nearly as extensive or as firm as traditional rights.[49] What those may be (beyond, say, a right not to be destroyed capriciously) is still to be determined but it is hard to imagine they would include freedom of religion, for example! On the other hand, if a deep-learning neural network creates a poem unanticipated and undesigned by its programmer, might it have the right to be assigned a copyright?[50] The specifics of robot rights are far less well developed than those of animal rights, much less human rights, but, as with animals, whatever rights are assigned to robots must be congruent with their *umwelt,* the world of their experience.[51]

3. *We need not in all circumstances apply equal rights to rights-claiming robots as we do to rights-claiming humans.* The whole frame-

work of human rights as we understand them, was, self-evidently, created with humans in mind. It may well not be applicable to robots at all or at least not without some major revisions. But we can anticipate some of the quandaries: Inasmuch as robotic systems work through digitized versions of rewards and punishments, offering algorithms a "reward" when they are correct, might a robot someday claim that offering insufficient rewards constituted cruel and degrading treatment?[52] Given the explosive growth in bionic body parts—well beyond prosthetics—will damage to bionic body parts be considered damage to property or to a person?[53] Will we reach a point where the murder of a human whose body or brain is more than 50 percent bionic constitutes both homicide and roboticide or something altogether new? And if robots have the right to "exist without fear of injury or death," as the South Korean Robot Ethics Charter has it, do we have the right to send them to war without their "consent"?

The philosophers Eric Schwitzgebel and Mara Garza suggest that humans ought to "avoid creating AIs if it is unclear whether they deserve moral consideration similar to that of human beings."[54] Even before the Singularity arrives, we are going to have a lot of thinking to do to apply the concept of rights in a meaningful way to entities that not only are significantly different from ourselves but similar as well, not to mention changing form and function with almost every passing day. But to dismiss robot rights out of hand is to ensure that the rights movement will miss one of the greatest revolutions at hand.

Time now, however, to turn to a related problem—the use of robots as weaponry. If robots, like animals, have no moral agency, even artificial moral agency, then they are no more than the latest technological instrument for killing one's adversaries and their operators remain entirely responsible for the machine's deployment. But if those machines are autonomous, like children, then the question becomes far more complicated. Until now this discussion has been considering the possibility of harm humans might do to robots. The next section turns to the question of what harm they may do to us.

THE FIRST RECORDED HUMAN DEATH by robot occurred in 1979 at a Ford Motor company casting plant. An assembly line worker, Robert Williams, and an industrial robot were retrieving parts in a storage facility when the robot's arm slammed into Williams's head and killed him. Ironically enough, the accident came on the anniversary of the premiere performance of Karel Capek's play *R.U.R.* A jury determined that the plant had neglected to install certain safety features, including an alarm warning when the robot was near, and awarded Williams's family $10 million.[55] Had that robot been functioning autonomously, however, the question of liability would have been considerably more complicated.

Since that time robotic devices of one kind or another have proliferated. Unmanned aerial vehicles, popularly known as drones, for example, have become such a common feature of the modern skies, employed for things like aerial photography, package delivery, search and rescue, mapping terrain, crop monitoring, and border surveillance, that they threaten to endanger civilian aviation.[56] While in the initial stages of their development they remained largely under the control of their operators, some, including a device available to the public for only $2,499 that can track a target without human interaction and a flying taxi that can set its own course, are now displaying greater autonomy.[57]

Similarly, drones have been in use by the U.S. government for military purposes since at least February 2002, when an attempt was made by the CIA to deploy a Predator drone to take out Osama bin Laden.[58] Since then it is estimated that more than six thousand drone strikes have been launched by the United States in places such as Afghanistan, Pakistan, Somalia, and Yemen, often accompanied by considerable controversy surrounding civilian casualties.[59]

Drones are popular in the military because they can reach targets in inaccessible locations at no risk to their operators. Interestingly enough and contrary to critics who theorized that such remote killing would inure their pilots to the consequences of their actions, drone pilots seem also to suffer from burnout and post-traumatic stress just as their colleagues wielding more conventional weapons do.[60] Most military drones, like their civilian counterparts, are considered "in-the-loop" systems in which a human being controls the flight, targeting, and deployment of the vehicle. Other weapons systems, sometimes referred to as "on-the-loop" or semiautonomous systems, such as the Thaad antimissile system installed in South Korea or sentry robots deployed in the Korean Demilitarized Zone, detect missile launches or intruders on their own but then require a human operator to make the final strike decision.[61]

It is the potential use of fully autonomous ("out-of-the-loop") weapons, however, that raises the largest number of human rights issues. These weapons are often referred to as legal autonomous weapons system (LAWS) or, since many of these weapons are robotic, "killer robots." The U.S. Department of Defense (DOD) has defined LAWS as weapons that, "once activated, can select and engage targets without further intervention by a human operator."[62] Though the Pentagon has put artificial intelligence at the center of its future weapons development strategy, former Deputy Defense Secretary Robert Works assured the public in 2016 that it is the policy of the DOD that "there will always be a man in the loop" in such systems, ensuring that they augment but don't replace human skills.[63]

And yet many observers remain worried. According to the United Nations, at least thirty nations, including the United States, China, Russia, and Israel but also Egypt, Pakistan, and Saudi Arabia, have already developed semiautonomous weapons, some of which, such as the Unites States' Gladiator tactical unmanned ground vehicle, equipped with multipurpose assault weapons, can easily be upgraded to fully autonomous mode.[64] Israel's Harpy, a so-called loitering munition that hovers above its target before striking, can operate in fully autonomous mode (it's called a "fire and forget" weapon) and strikes by "hurling" itself into its target and exploding. Harpy has been sold to China, Turkey, South Korea, and India.[65] In December 2017, China put on an aerial show in which a swarm of close to 1,200 drones, operating autonomously but in synchronicity with one another, improvised light formations of a kapok tree flower and a ship. China has made no secret of the military uses to which it can put such technology.[66]

U.S. Air Force General Paul Selva, vice chair of the Joint Chiefs of Staff, indicated in 2016 that the United States was a decade away from developing a fully independent robot that could decide whom to kill and when.[67] That timetable squares nicely with a 2003 report by U.S. Joint Forces Command entitled "Unmanned Effects: Taking the Human Out of the Loop" that predicted that by 2025 U.S. forces "could be largely robotic at the tactical level" and include everything from huge unmanned submarines to nanobots as small as insects.[68] Selva insisted that the United States had no intention of developing autonomous killer robots and warned that, without a human in the loop, the military "might unleash on humanity a set of robots that we don't know how to control," an idea that George Lucas, a professor of ethics at Annapolis, has called "preposterous."[69] But, given the history of weapons development, it is hard to imagine that under certain circumstances the kind of constraints Selva recommends would hold.

After all, the targeting of civilian ships by submarines was banned following World War I, a restriction to which the Unites States had readily agreed, but within six hours of the Japanese attack on Pearl Harbor, the United States ordered unrestricted submarine warfare on Japan's civilian and merchant fleets. If an adversary nation or a terrorist group were to deploy autonomous killer robots, could the United States and its allies not respond in kind? Although some weapons, such as land mines, blinding lasers, and cluster bombs, have been successfully prohibited by international treaty, the more common experience is that, if new weapons can be developed, they will be.[70] This is the case even if they ultimately are found to be as dangerous to their developers as to the enemy, as nerve gas was, or an utter waste of resources, as the Unites States' attempts to counter Soviet use of ESP and psychokinesis turned out to be.[71] Wallach and Allen imagine that future headlines may read, "Genocide Charges Leveled at FARL [Fuerzas Armadas Roboticas de Liberacion]."[72]

All this has led more than 3,700 AI robotics researchers and developers, including the late renowned physicist Stephen Hawking, to sign an open letter calling for a ban on "offensive autonomous weapons beyond meaningful human control." Such weapons, the letter said, "will become the Kalishnikovs of tomorrow" and are "ideal for tasks such as assassinations, destabilizing nations, subduing populations and selectively killing a particular ethnic group."[73] In 2012 the eminent human rights organization Human Rights Watch helped launch the Campaign to Stop Killer Robots and the European Parliament's proposed Charter on Robotics includes the provision that users "are not permitted to modify any robot to enable it to function as a weapon."[74] As of late 2018 more than twenty-two countries had called for an international ban on LAWS.[75]

Many military leaders, roboticists, and human rights advocates appear to be heeding the famously plaintive words of the fictional scientist Victor Frankenstein after he had realized that his creation had gone rogue: "I had been the author of unalterable evils," Mary Shelley has Frankenstein observe, "and I lived in daily fear lest the monster that I had created should perpetrate some new wickedness."[76] But, Frankenstein's monster aside, the case against killer robots is not as straightforward as it seems.

IF YOU WERE A PRISONER and had a choice of being overseen by a robot guard whom you knew would only issue punishment in a neutral, mechanical fashion in response to some clearly delineated violation or a human who might act capriciously based upon whims and prejudices but to whom you could appeal for understanding or mercy, which would you prefer?

Police and military leaders find robots attractive because they are not subject to all the vagaries a human being is, including acting out of emotion rather than consistent calculation. As Gordon Johnson of the Pentagon's Joint Command Force put it, "[Machines] don't get hungry. They're not afraid. They don't forget their orders. They don't care if the guy next to them has just been shot."[77] They are maximally efficient and can integrate all the relevant data—or at least lots of relevant data—before they act.

The military theorist Carl von Clausewitz observed that the there is a natural human disinclination to kill, which must be overcome in training by instilling in soldiers hatred of the enemy.[78] LAWS have no such disinclination but they feel no hatred either. (Nor are they subject to depression or post-traumatic stress, which even remote drone pilots may be, as observed earlier.) Given the widespread perception that police officers in the United States, for example, display implicit bias in their interactions with African Americans—each year between 2015 and 2017, the percentage of unarmed black people killed by police significantly exceeded that of Hispanics or whites—there might be good reason to prefer law enforcement that, assuming it was correctly programmed, was unburdened by such predilections.[79] Given the number of instances throughout military history of soldiers dying through friendly fire, engaging in fragging, or committing war crimes, there might be something to be said for a fighter who, assuming it was correctly deployed, was less likely than a human to mistake a friend for an enemy, turn on an officer or fellow soldier, or act out of adrenaline-driven loathing for a dehumanized Other. As one robotic engineer put it, "[A robot is] looking in the whites of [the adversaries'] eyes but calm."[80] And if a commander did deploy a robot to commit a war crime, it would be far easier to know who to hold responsible because the robotic system would preserve a record of who ordered what—something that is often very difficult to establish in the fog of war.

It is true that in a world of robotic warriors, a government might have less reticence to go to war, knowing that it would only be machines, not young people, who might be sacrificed. This is a very real consideration in deciding whether to outlaw killer robots. But it is also true that, if the deployment of LAWS was a viable option, nations might have far less hesitation to authorize humanitarian interventions to stop genocide. Wouldn't a United Nations equipped to field a robotic army be a far more formidable enforcer of authorized missions than one dependent, as it is today, on countries' willingness to lend human soldiers to causes that may seem both dangerous and relatively inconsequential to them?

Then, too, police officials and military commanders have a duty of care to those under their authority. They must do what they can to avoid unnecessary loss of life. The infamous charge of the light brigade during the Crimean War, commemorated in Alfred, Lord Tennyson's familiar poem ("Half a league, Half a league, Half a league onward / Into the Valley of Death rode the six hundred") is but one of dozens of examples of commanding officers exposing their troops to needless danger, if not slaughter. "If," says the philosopher Bradley Jay Strawser, "the same mission can be done with either [an autonomous drone or a human] and the drone protects the pilot more effectively, . . . then . . . we are morally required to use drones over the manned aircraft to prevent exposing pilots to unnecessary risk."[81] Or to put it more dramatically, if we have robots that we can send into battle instead of our children, how could we morally not do so? What kind of good society would not make that choice? No doubt that is why 69 percent of respondents who were asked "If your country was suddenly at war, would you want to be defended by the sons and daughters of your community, or an autonomous AI weapon system?" opted for the autonomous system.[82]

Might it be that, rather than banning LAWS, we should be trying to perfect them? The next section looks carefully at the arguments that have been marshaled against the use of killer robots.

THOSE ARGUMENTS FALL BROADLY into four categories. LAWS, their critics say, are unpredictable, legally suspect, cannot be held to account, and violate human dignity. .

*LAWS are unpredictable.* Anyone who has experienced a mysterious "glitch" in their computer, marveled at how poor Google Translate's English was, or been the victim of a hack attack knows that AI is hardly foolproof. Systems can go wrong in ways programmers never anticipated and sometimes don't understand and security can certainly be breached, as the 143 million users of the Equifax credit reporting system learned to their chagrin in 2017.[83]

This is particularly a concern in the case of deep-learning neural networks. Such networks learn through analyzing data and looking for patterns—by processing thousands of pictures of dogs, for example, a neural network can identify a dog. But slight alterations in that data, whether through accident or malfeasance, can result in mistakes, convincing a machine that Person A is in fact Person B. That could be disastrous when it comes to autonomous weaponry, to say nothing of the fact that deep-learning machines can teach themselves to behave in ways their creators never intended and engender new programs with new goals and values. Some day they may even be able to prevent humans from turning them off.[84]

In his 1950 collection, *I, Robot,* the biochemist and science fiction writer Isaac Asimov offered three laws to protect humans from robots, the third of which, interestingly enough, anticipated the notion of robot rights discussed earlier in the chapter: (1) a robot may not injure a human being or, through inaction, allow a human being to come to harm; (2) a robot must obey the orders given it by a human being except where such orders would conflict with the first law; and (3) a robot must protect its own existence as long as such protection does not conflict with the first or second laws.[85] What is obvious now is that, no matter how valid the first law may still be, the second is obsolete because deep-learning robots are designed explicitly to transcend "the orders given [them] by a human being." No wonder, then, that critics worry that the unpredictability of LAWS may make them unsuitable for the battlefield or that the European Parliament has required that robotic programs be comprehensible (the right to an explanation!) in order that their behavior may be understood and controlled.[86]

All this would seem to provide a definitive case against LAWS except for the fact that, unpredictable as machines may be, they are arguably far more predictable than human beings. In deciding whether to restrict LAWS, we will need to weigh their dependability versus that of human combatants and to assure ourselves that they are at least as reliable as human combatants are.

*LAWS are legally suspect.* Fundamental to international humanitarian law (IHL), often called "the laws of war," as discussed in some detail in Chapter 1, is the mandate that combatants need to distinguish military from civilian targets—the so-called principle of distinction. If LAWS cannot do that (or be made to do that), they are prima facie illegal weapons. Cluster bombs, for example, were banned in 2008 because, when they explode, they release thousands of "bomblets" over a wide area that can injure civilians, not just their intended military targets.[87]

In addition, IHL requires that killing in war be militarily necessary, that any harm to civilians be proportional to the military advantage to be secured, and that whatever violence ensues not result in unnecessary suffering.[88] If LAWS are to be deployed in a military context, they must be programmed in such a way that they can meet these criteria. The roboticist Ronald Arkin has been developing software called a "responsibility advisor" that will help commanders in the field judge the lawfulness of a robot's deployment and an "ethical governor" that will restrict LAWs to acts that conform to ethical standards, including resisting an illegal order. "I am convinced," he says, "that [robots] can perform more ethically than human soldiers."[89] Others are more skeptical.

It is not just that such programs are far from perfected yet, nor is it just that deciding on which ethical system humans ought to adopt—Kantian, utilitarian, virtue ethics, ethics of care, philosophical pragmatism—is subject to widespread disagreement even before we choose one to program a robot to follow; it is also that robotic weaponry may be inherently incapable of making the kind of subtle distinctions that people make all the time when they try to do the right thing. Recall George Orwell's famous story from an essay on the Spanish Civil War:

> At this moment, a man ... jumped out of the trench and ran along the parapet in full view. He was half-dressed and was holding up his trousers with both hands as he ran. I refrained from shooting at him. It is true that I am a poor shot and unlikely to hit a running man at a hundred yards. ... Still, I did not shoot partly because of that detail about the trousers. I had come here to shoot at "Fascists"; but a man who is holding up his trousers isn't a "Fascist"; he is visibly a fellow-creature, similar to yourself, and you don't feel like shooting at him.[90]

Could a robot ever be programmed to make that kind of judgment when it doesn't even know at this point that when you put a sock in a drawer at night it will be there in the morning? Would it recognize the sign of a surrendering adversary or the distinction between a child picking up a discarded weapon out of curiosity and an adversary picking it up with lethal intent? Self-driving cars work fine when everyone else behaves in accordance with traffic laws but designers have had difficulty adapting the programs for such cars to adjust to unpredictable human driving and unpredictable driving is child's play compared to the unpredictability of war.[91]

The use of LAWS in a domestic police context may be even more fraught, for in that case violence is only lawful as a last resort to protect human life. Robots are being used for psychotherapy but would robots be able to "talk down" a suspect and defuse a standoff? Would they be able to recognize that threatening behavior may result from mental illness or drug use and neutralize such a threat through restraint rather than lethality? Could they be programmed to use "good judgment"?[92] Many human officers have failed these tests, of course, but, if LAWs are to be deployed in either a military or domestic context, they must be at least as likely as humans to conform to IHL or police best practices, or more so. And then, of course, when humans fail to meet these standards, they can be punished. This leads us to the third objection to LAWS.

*LAWS cannot be held to account.* In 2013 Christof Heyns, the U.N. special rapporteur on extrajudicial killings, said that if robots cannot be held responsible for their crimes, then their "use should be considered unethical and unlawful as an abhorrent weapon."[93] If an autonomous killer robot does violate IHL, who is to blame? The designer, the manufacturer, the programmer, the commander who deployed it, the superior officer who approved the deployment, the government officials who decided to stock up on killer robots in the first place—or the robot itself? The first part of this chapter discussed how robots might suffer consequences for "misbehavior" and in that sense be held at least partially "responsible" but surely violations of the laws of war require more.

Two possible sets of candidates for accountability for crimes committed by LAWS are the designer/programmer and the commander/superior officer. Naturally, designers and programmers are held liable for flaws in robots that don't work as they are intended but, apart from that, the concept of product liability has been extended, in the case of cigarettes, to products that work exactly as they are expected to but have deleterious consequences. In 2014, a Florida jury awarded the widow of a former smoker $23 million, later reduced to $17 million in a wrongful death lawsuit against tobacco manufacturer R. J. Reynolds.[94] Despite federal laws that shield gun manufacturers from liability for the use to which their weapons have been put, the parents of children murdered at the Sandy Hook elementary school in Newtown, Connecticut, in 2012 are pursuing a case against gun manufacturers based on marketing claims that appealed to those capable of violent criminal behavior.[95] It is not inconceivable that someday designers and programmers of killer robots might be held to bear some degree of accountability for the violations their products commit.[96]

A more likely locus of responsibility, however, is commanders of killer robots and their superiors. Human Rights Watch argues that, because commanders can't be expected to anticipate all future actions of an autonomous robot—after all, that is the meaning of autonomy—there can be no command responsibility.[97] But commanders can't be expected to anticipate all future actions of their human subordinates either (human beings are also autonomous agents), just as dog owners can't anticipate every wayward snarl or bite of their dogs, and yet we apportion responsibility to both commanders and dog owners depending upon the degree of caution and control they have exerted over their charges. Did the commander or dog owner have good reason to believe that their killer robot or dog would not act inappropriately? If they did, we might reduce the degree of accountability they bear but not eliminate it altogether; the fact that robots and dogs may be somewhat unpredictable or can make "mistakes" does not alleviate their commanders and owners from liability.

Although legal standards of accountability may need to be elaborated in the face of LAWS beyond their current mainstream interpretations, it seems likely, in the face of these options, that liability may be obtained in the case of killer robots, just as it will need to be in the case of driverless cars, one of which killed its first pedestrian in 2018.[98] Just as self-driving car owners will be required to obtain no-fault insurance, so employers of killer robots will be expected to bear the consequences of their devices' errors.

All these objections to LAWS, some of which, as previously discussed, have more merit than others, are important to consider. But perhaps at the heart of the skepticism and fear is the fact that killer robots violate human dignity and, hence, by the authors' definition, should not be employed by a good society. This last claim needs to be examined with some care.

*LAWS violate human dignity.* The renowned philosopher of war Michael Walzer has said, "You can't kill unless you are prepared to be killed."[99] If this is true, killer robots, which presumably cannot be killed (though they can certainly be disabled), would be illegitimate instruments of war. But of course so would drone pilots who sit in the comfort and security of their command headquarters in the United States while directing lethal attacks by drones far, far away. Indeed, if war strategists could devise a way to carry on combat with no risk whatsoever to their warriors, would that be dishonorable or would it be to exercise the highest ethical duty to preserve as much life as possible, especially the lives of those in one's care? If police don full body armor, thus inoculating themselves from the possibility of being killed, before addressing a dangerous situation, have they done something unethical?

Perhaps what Walzer means is what other observers have said about LAWS: that their mechanical nature makes the death they inflict more dehumanizing than death at the hands of a fellow human. U.N. Special Rapporteur Christof Heyns puts this objection nicely:

> It has been argued that to have the decision whether you live or die—or be maimed—taken by machines is the ultimate indignity. . . . Death by algorithm means that people are treated simply as targets and not as complete and unique human beings who may, by virtue of this status, deserve to meet a

> different fate. A machine, which is bloodless and without morality or mortality, cannot do justice to the decision whether to use force in a particular case, even if it may be more accurate than humans.[100]

The philosopher Peter Asaro, in arguing that a human must always be "in the loop" when it comes to robotic weaponry, adds, "For the killing of a human to be meaningful, it must be intentional"—a capability Asaro assumes robots lack. "In the absence of an intentional and meaningful decision to use violence," he goes on, "the resulting deaths are meaningless and arbitrary and the dignity of those killed is significantly reduced."[101]

These contentions carry great emotional appeal but are they valid? In the first place, some human always makes the decision to deploy LAWS—to decide intentionally that some adversary will die, not live—even if the killer robot selects the specific targets. Secondly, except in the case of drones instructed to carry out individual assassinations, most warfare is not conducted in a fashion that allows for consideration of the "complete and unique human beings" who are its victims. Conventional missiles and the officers who authorize their launch don't distinguish between men and women, tall people or short, generals or grunts. They are all "treated simply as targets." And if a machine was "more accurate than humans" in its targeting, wouldn't that be a huge advance in the cause of ethical warfare?

Even more telling than these objections is simply this: does a dignified death turn on the intentional decision of a human being? Was Robert Williams's death at that Ford Motor Company casting plant in 1979 automatically rendered undignified or meaningless because it came at the hands of a machine that lacked intentionality? What about deaths by auto accident? By accidental self-electrocution? Those are unintentional but are they thereby meaningless deaths? And how about capital punishment or first-degree murder? Both are certainly intentional killing but does that make them dignified ways to die? Political scientist Michael Horowitz summarizes the matter this way: "Why is being shot ... and instantly killed by a machine necessarily worse than being bludgeoned by a person, lit on fire or killed by a cruise missile strike? The dignity argument has emotional resonance but it may romanticize warfare."[102]

THESE FOUR OBJECTIONS TO LAWS, then, carry different degrees of resonance but, on balance, the objections to using killer robots outweigh the potential advantages ... at the moment. To the extent that killer robots are unpredictable and subject to glitches, they are dangerous weapons that should be outlawed. That they cannot yet be programmed to abide by IHL or police best practices and to make the kind of subtle ethical judgments a human can are strong strikes against them even if we can determine loci of accountability for their actions and even if the argument that they violate human dignity is flawed.[103] For these reasons the safest course is to insist that a human with meaningful control always remain in—or at least on—the loop when robotic weapons are deployed.

Some have suggested that, if LAWS are to be deployed, they only be allowed to carry nonlethal weapons, such as acoustical devices that emit sound waves at such frequencies that they incapacitate people but don't kill them.[104] In addition, policies could be established that LAWS will only be used to target property or other LAWS.

In the long run, however, these may be but temporary solutions and a ban on LAWS may be rendered obsolete. It is not solely that the full development, much less the use, of LAWS by one party would probably trigger their adoption by another and that, if the history of weaponry is any guide, that development is more likely than not. It is that Moore's Law, which holds that the overall processing power of computers will double every two years, may well be conservative.[105] Who knows whether LAWS will be able to meet the most salient objections to it at some point in the future? It would be unwise to assume blithely that it won't and, if it does, we will need to think very carefully about what such a development means for the maintenance of a good society.

IF THE NOTION THAT ANIMALS and even, conceivably, robots may be awarded rights has left readers unsettled, our next topic may stir the waters into a maelstrom. Animals certainly have consciousness and the need to flourish; deep-learning robots act as if they are conscious and display moral agency. Treating them both as creatures with rights, as honored members of the good society, redounds to our own dignity at least, if not to theirs. But what about the natural world? Does a weed have dignity? Is a river conscious? Does a rock have rights?![106] Or have we all gone . . . haywire? The discussion turns now to the rights of Nature.

# 8

# Should Rocks Have Rights?
## The Nature of Nature

How narrow we selfish, conceited creatures are in
our sympathies!
How blind to the rights of all the rest of creation!

—John Muir, 1867

FROM BILL'S STUDY IN HIS HOME on the coast of Massachusetts,
he can look out on a 180-degree panoramic view of the Atlantic
Ocean. To the right of his four-story condominium is an enormous
glacial erratic, a huge granite boulder that was deposited during the
last Ice Age. With lichen, plants, and flowers growing out of its rocky
seams, it's about half the height of the house. Occasionally a coyote,
fox, or even a snowy owl can be spied lurking in its crevices.

Between the house and the ocean stretch wide wetlands pierced
with rivulets and teeming with nutrients that feed fish and help
maintain climate control.[1] When the tide is high and the moon is
right, the wetlands fill almost to the brim with water, forming an inland lake. As the lake recedes, the egrets and blue herons return to
their perches and peer out to sea. Oh, and yes, because a city is

nearby, a road runs through the wetlands, meaning that humans are part of the picture too. Once, when he was walking on the beach, Bill even saw a child playing with BB-8, a Star Wars robot for kids.

Even though she lived in urban settings in India, Sushma's windows nevertheless revealed a host of animal life: stray dogs roaming the street, the occasional elephant or camel resplendent with a bejeweled seat, a white horse bedecked in finery for a wedding, monkeys jumping from tree to tree looking down on unsuspecting passersby, brightly colored parrots, mynahs, glossy black crows, and so on. The birds nestled in mango and peepal trees, the dogs rested under the shade of sweeping banyan trees, and even the smallest bush could be seen housing a variety of small birds and insects.

Bill's and Sushma's windows frame a whole community of rights claimants, starting with the humans but including animals, and maybe even (more advanced versions) of the robot. But what about the ocean, wetlands, trees, bushes and the plant-bearing boulder? Or perhaps the ecosystem of which they and the animals are all a part? Is there any sense in which these entities could be considered rights holders? Humans and animals are conscious, animate creatures that can experience pain. Deep-learning neural networks have a kind of consciousness and can engage in acts that have moral consequences. But do oceans, wetlands, and rocks share these characteristics?

Of course such an idea would not sound so outlandish if we were adherents of Japanese Shinto who believe that land, mountains, and even the wind are manifestations of *kami,* which is usually translated as "spirit," a kind of energy that is not inherently different from that found in human beings.[2] In the Hawaiian tradition humans are considered the offspring of the sacred taro plant.[3] Many indigenous tribes in the Americas believe that earth, rocks, water, and wind are not inanimate entities, as the prevailing Western view would have it, but, in the words of the American Sioux Indian John Fire Lame Deer, "very much alive."[4] Similar views held by native peoples in Latin America and New Zealand have had a profound impact, as discussed later, on the evolving understanding of Nature's rights. Indeed, those rights, informed as they are in part by views of the natural world at odds with the traditional Western canon, put to the test the common criticism that rights are a phenomenon derived solely from Western culture and imposed upon the rest of the world through imperialist legerdemain. To make the case that it is legitimate to invest flora, bodies of water, and ecosystems with rights will require us to think of those things in ways the industrialized world rarely does—not in terms of property and ownership but in terms of common bonds and mutual dependence. ("We laughed when [white people] told us they wanted to buy land," recalled Chief Oren Lyons of the Onondaga tribe. "You might as well buy air.")[5]

This chapter is premised upon the assumption that climate change is real and our ecosystems in peril. The authors are not willing to argue this point; those who dispute this should stop reading right here. Under current conditions of global warming, sea level is likely to rise up to forty-eight inches by the end of the century, devastating major coastal areas and wiping out some low-lying countries.[6] By mid-century as many as fifty percent of species may become extinct.[7] Entomologists have detected a vast decline in insect populations.[8] Bolivia alone has lost the equivalent acreage of the state of Rhode Island every year since 2011 from deforestation.[9] And eight million tons of plastic make their way into the oceans every year.[10] The statistics are telling and the stories are poignant. Caribou in eastern Greenland, to recite but one, migrate inland each spring from the coastal regions to give birth to their calves. Both mother and calf are dependent upon abundant Arctic plants that, as Greenland has warmed, are now sprouting twenty-six days earlier than they did a decade ago. This means that the caribou are missing the peak greening season and their calves are dying of hunger in greater numbers.[11] What makes this chapter especially compelling is the fact that near worldwide consensus holds that significant environmental degradation threatens life on earth as we know it.

Where that consensus breaks down is not only in terms of what to do about the threat but, more specifically, how to regard the relationship between the human community and the natural world. This chapter will consider the question from the standpoint of rights, including but not limited to the human right to a healthy environment. That right is a relatively uncontroversial assertion. Where the matter becomes complicated is if we want to contend that elements of Nature, such as plants or trees or rivers or mountains, are themselves rights bearers or that all of Nature ought to be extended the protection of rights.

The fact that animal rights activists are sometimes at odds with environmental advocates has already been mentioned. The pioneering American ecologist Aldo Leopold, whom readers will meet again, articulated the environmentalists' perspective neatly: "A thing is right," Leopold wrote in his most famous work, *A Sand County Almanac,* "when it tends to preserve the integrity, stability and beauty of the biotic community. It is wrong when it tends otherwise."[12] What are we to do, then, when animals threaten that system's stability through such actions as overgrazing?

Conflicts between rights bearers are not unusual but the notion that the "biotic community"—a system, as opposed to an individual or even a group—might legitimately claim rights . . . well, that seems very strange. Trees and canyons, much less biotic communities, are not self-conscious beings; they can't be expected to take responsibility for their acts. Is there any way we can speak intelligently about pond scum having "dignity"? And since both humans and animals need to eat in order to live, there is no way we could affirm *flora's* unqualified "right to life" without condemning all humans and animals to death.

These are just some of the quandaries this chapter explores. Those quandaries are real and complex but the authors hope to show that the concepts of "dignity" and "flourishing" apply to Nature as well and, hence, that a good society will take very seriously the idea that

Nature does indeed have rights. The next section starts by trying to get a little clearer about what this thing we call "Nature" actually is.

"NATURE" IS A BIG WORD. It is sometimes used to refer to Everything That Is, all of Creation, the whole of space, the plenum. But that can't be exactly right because there are a lot of things, like cardboard boxes, among Everything That Is that aren't considered "natural" or parts of Nature. Furthermore, although the planets, galaxies, our universe, and beyond may technically be part of "Nature," we usually reserve the word for earthbound things. To begin, then, the authors are referring here to the nonmanufactured elements of the planet Earth. "Nonmanufactured" is important because, while many products can be created out of natural substances, genetically modified food being one of the most contentious examples, there is a customary distinction made between such products and their original component parts appearing in their "natural state."

Another common use of the word "Nature" juxtaposes it to "human." Dictionary.com describes "Nature," a bit tautologically, as "the natural world as it exists without human beings or civilization."[13] But humans and animals are very much a part of Nature— in fact, many observers, such as the ecohistorian Thomas Berry, believe that ecological disaster has resulted from the fact that human beings have understood themselves to be divided from Nature, superior to it and separate from it. Instead, Berry says, "[Humans] come into being in and through the Earth. . . . The earth is our origin, our nourishment, our educator, our healer, our fulfillment. . . . The human and the Earth are totally implicated, each in the other."[14] What this means from the point of view of rights is that whatever rights we may attribute to Nature will have to take into account human and animal rights as well or they will be at odds with themselves.

But does it make sense to attribute rights to something as vast as all of Nature as opposed to attributing them to elements within

Nature? "Human rights" refers to the rights of individual human be-ings or sometimes groups of human beings, such as persons with disabilities, migrants, and women. If we should use the phrase "rights of Humanity," we are simply employing a convenient heuristic de-vice to refer collectively to all those rights that individual humans or groups of humans could claim, not the rights of some abstract idea called "Humanity"?[15]

So what are the elements of Nature that, either individually or in groups, might be rights claimants, other than humans and animals? Well, one set of obvious candidates are plants and trees because they are living things. Within the last few years a provocative literature has sprung up describing the remarkable capabilities of flora.

One of the most controversial books, Stefano Mancuso and Ales-sandra Viola's *Brilliant Green: The Surprising History and Science of Plant Intelligence,* takes the human parallels approach and argues that, despite not having brains, plants, which make up 99.7 percent of the earth's biomass and upon which human and animal life de-pends, display distinct signs of intelligence, defined as "problem-solving ability." They have at least twenty senses (far more than our human five); they can communicate with animals and other plants, including warning one another of predators and summoning the as-sistance of allies to attack those predators; they can recognize kin; they retain memory; and their root tips can explore soils, anticipate danger, and seek favorable nutrients and living conditions.[16]

Mancuso and Viola contend that these traits are sufficient to es-tablish that plants are not passive and inert but should be regarded as intelligent and even "conscious" in the sense not of inward aware-ness but of being awake to their environment.[17] They cite a 2008 Swiss law that requires that plants be treated with dignity and see this as a "first step toward legitimizing their rights."[18] In *The Hidden Life of Trees: What They Feel, How They Communicate,* the German for-ester Peter Wohlleben documents many traits in trees similar to those Mancuso and Viola find in plants, stressing, among other things, the way trees communicate with another through soil fungi—what ecologist Suzanne Simard has called the "wood wide web."[19]

Needless to say, many botanists dispute the characterization of plants and trees as displaying "intelligence," being "conscious," or having "feelings" but what no one disputes is that, despite being sessile (remaining stationary) rather than mobile (moving around as humans and animals do), flora are living beings that can either flourish or flounder depending upon how they and their environments are treated. As discussed in the chapter on animals, even if plants display some characteristics similar to those of humans, that does not guarantee that they should be awarded rights similar to human rights. But the fact that plants, like animals, have interests in flourishing makes them at least arguable candidates for the attribution of rights.

But what about other elements of Nature, such as soil, bodies of water, rocks and mountains, or even air? Setting aside the different cultural perceptions cited earlier, it would be difficult to find scientific evidence to assert that these entities are "intelligent," "conscious," or alive. And yet, at least in the case of some rivers, they have been assigned legal rights as, recall, have corporations and ships. How can that be? Well, soil, water, and air could certainly be construed as having "interests," that is, their welfare can be affected by their relationships with others in their environments. They could be considered flourishing or not. They might even, metaphorically, be invested with dignity. For example, it does not seem silly to refer to a heavily polluted river as having suffered a blow to its dignity.

There is at least one significant difference between these natural bodies and humans or animals, however. The latter can clearly be delineated as individuals or groups of individuals. But how could we really separate out the interests of one piece of soil from another or of the soil along a riverbank from the river itself or of the air fed by evaporation from the water that feeds it? They are all part of a holistic system, along with the flora and fauna (and, indeed, humans) that make up the biotic community. In fact, that web of relationships is what is generally understood to be the meaning of the word "ecology": an interdependent, nonhierarchical conglomeration of mutual interests.

The word "Nature," then, is shorthand for this immense web of nonmanufactured entities that rely upon one another for their flourishing. The Australian scientist Ian Lowe gives a marvelous example:

> Because both truffles and [eucalyptus] trees extract water and minerals from the soil, trees with truffles in their roots obtain more water and minerals and grow better than trees without. The truffles are a favorite food of the long-footed poteroo, a marsupial . . . which then excretes the . . . truffles and thereby enhances the health of the forest. Poteroo, truffle, eucalyptus . . . are all bound together in a remarkable web of interdependence.[20]

Now we can see a crucial difference between "Nature" and "Humanity." "Nature," unlike the word "Humanity," is not just a convenient heuristic device for calling to mind a set of individual units; it is a descriptor of a holistic system the healthy maintenance of which implicates the health of its units. It is reasonable to call this system the "biotic community" even though some of its members, like rivers and soil, are not "alive" in the traditional sense.

When Martin Luther King Jr. famously declared that "Injustice anywhere is a threat to justice everywhere," he was issuing a stirring moral proclamation but not stating a fact that was literally true. The truth is that genocide in Rwanda or Sudan does not literally threaten the lives of people in Los Angeles or Jakarta even if it pricks their consciences or makes them worry about the evil humans do. Violations of the rights of Humanity have direct implications for only certain subsets of Humanity.

But violations of the rights of Nature, whatever those turn out to be, have implications for virtually everyone and everything—human beings, animals, trees, plants, soil, rivers, air. Given that plants constitute 99.7 percent of the earth's biomass, their massive destruction will have dire consequences for every living thing; climate change anywhere will literally be a harbinger of climate change everywhere.[21] It makes sense, then, to attribute rights to Nature as a whole—to the system upon which the Earth itself depends even if not every element of that system independently deserves the status of rights holder.[22]

Plenty of mountains have been destroyed through mountain top coal mining, for example. We can argue as to whether those mountains should themselves have rights but no one could deny that their removal had an impact on the larger ecosystem of which they were a part—the plants and animals for whom, like the boulder outside Bill's study window, they provided a habitat. Even if we don't want to say that rocks per se have rights, they may be part of a larger community that should. (Some deep-sea microbes, for example, breathe hydrogen released when rocks meet water.[23]) Consider an artificial heart valve. No one would argue that that valve by itself deserves rights. But, once it is inserted in a person's chest, it is a vital component of a larger human system—a person's body—that does have rights, a system that without the valve would collapse.

So the "rights of Nature" can refer to the rights of some elements of Nature—like plants and trees and maybe some bodies of water—but they refer as well to the larger whole that sustains those elements. A critical question, though, is whether those rights are determined by what is good for human beings—what is called in the chapter on animals "anthropocentrism"—or by what is good for Nature itself. It is to that fundamental question that the next section turns.

BILL LED AN AMNESTY INTERNATIONAL delegation in 2004 to Darfur, Sudan, in the middle of the genocide taking place there. The conflict had its roots in a variety of causes but a significant one was that, thanks to climate change, previously refulgent pastures were rapidly being encroached upon by desert, resulting in soil erosion. The settled farmers, who were generally members of so-called African tribes, had tended that land and grown their crops upon it for generations. The nomadic herders, who for the most part were members of so-called Arab tribes, had traditionally grazed their livestock over those same lands without incident. But as the pastureland became less verdant and productive, the farmers sought to restrict access to their lands, thereby threatening the livelihood of the herders.[24] With the encouragement of the central government of Sudan, the herders formed themselves into militia called *janjaweed* ("riflemen on horseback") and began to systematically attack and decimate farming villages. It was not that African and Arab tribalists had any inherent antagonism toward one another—both in appearance and culture they were so similar that, when Bill attended a dance festival at which various tribes were performing and asked the local police chief which was which, the chief had no idea how to distinguish them—it was that the political leaders of the country had leveraged the impetus of environmental degradation to set one set of people against another.

Ecological damage can have a profoundly negative impact upon the protection of human rights. This, along with the existential fact that human survival depends upon a livable environment, accounts for the fact that a majority of nations in the world (though not the United States) have recognized a right to a healthy environment at the national or regional level.[25] The High Court in Ireland ruled in 2017 that "a right to an environment . . . consistent with the human dignity and wellbeing of citizens . . . is an essential condition for the fulfillment of all human rights."[26] That same year a U.S. federal judge declared the right to a sustainable environment a constitutional right.[27] And in 2018 the Inter-American Court of Human Rights recognized a fundamental right to a healthy environment and that governments must address the impact of environmental disasters beyond their own territories since "the obligations to protect human rights don't stop at a country's borders."[28]

It is therefore surprising that such a right has not yet been adopted at the global level though many well-established rights, such as those to life and health, have been "greened" so that they are understood to apply to environmental issues.[29] Even the International Criminal Court has now broadened its remit to include crimes that result in environmental destruction.[30] But the lack of a free-standing globally recognized right to a healthy environment is particularly egregious in light of the general principle that if respect for one set of rights requires respect for another, then the latter set ought to be recognized too. If "everyone has the right to work, to free choice of employment," as Article 23 of the Universal Declaration of Human Rights asserts, for example, and that right can only be realized by accessing education, then it follows ipso facto that there must be a "right to education," as indeed there is (Article 26). If the human rights to life, food, and health turn on living in a healthy habitat, then humans must also have a right to such a habitat. The authors guess that such a right will eventually be incorporated into the international human rights regimen. That would be a very good thing but to frame the issue solely in terms of human interests is to remain shackled to the traditional Western understanding of Nature as important largely to the extent that its condition serves or fails to serve humans.

From God's injunction in Genesis 1:28 that humans should "be fruitful and multiply and fill the earth and subdue it, and have dominion over the fish of the sea and over the birds of the heavens and over every living thing that moves on the earth" to the common law understanding of people's relationship to the earth as primarily one of property ownership—what the famous British jurist Sir William Blackstone called "sole and despotic dominion . . . over the external things of the world"—the relationship of humans to the natural world has largely been an instrumental one or, in the words of one observer, the elements of Nature have been seen as "objects to be used" rather than "subjects to be communed with."[31]

The problem with this approach when it comes to rights is that the interests of the natural world in flourishing—the "dignity," if you will, of the flower or tree or river or soil—are only good and will only be worthy of protection to the extent that those interests coincide with human interests. Yes, it is true that Nature's interests, dignity, and rights can only be enforced if some human cares about them— Nature, like infants, cognitively disabled people, animals, and, thus far, robots, are, in philosophical terms, "moral patients" who require agents to speak on their behalf. But what gets spoken about, which violations of rights matter, may be very different from the point of view of a human acting to protect his or her own welfare than it is from that of an element of Nature in need of protection of its flourishing or an ecosystem in need of protection of its balance. If a person seeks to maintain a lake's purity or a meadow's fecundity only when and because she wants to swim in the lake or enjoy the beauty of the meadow's wildflowers, what happens to all those lakes and meadows that don't at the moment implicate a human person's perceived needs? Such a strategy leaves Nature at the mercy of people's often short-term and myopic calculations. Would it not be better to try to discern what Nature needs or at least also take that into account when deciding questions of interests and, hence, of rights?

Is this really such a strange point of view? If we see children carving deep ruts into the trunk of a tree simply to leave their marks, do we find that regrettable solely because it somehow hurts human beings or because we know it will make the tree's struggle for life more arduous? If we knew that chemical toxins had been deposited in a river so remote that its corrupted waters would have no impact on any humans, would we then judge the dumping acceptable? When we see the top of a mountain sheared off through mountaintop mining, do we react with revulsion solely because it disrupts our aesthetic sense or because it seems like some kind of insult to the mountain? And when we see those remarkable pictures of the earth from outer space, do we feel affection for our planet and want to protect it just because there are humans on it or also because it appears to be this fragile green upsurge floating precariously through a vast sea of darkness?

Whether or not we credit the idea that Nature is "alive," as some religious and indigenous traditions do, the idea that Nature has interests, worth, and "dignity" independent of its utility to humans (or at least in addition to that utility) is hardly a new one, even in Western thought. It is worth taking a few moments to look at the intellectual history of that notion.

SAINT FRANCIS OF ASSISI (1182–1226) apparently didn't get the Genesis 1:28 memo. Far from seeking to "subdue" the natural world or have dominion over "every living thing," he revered every creature from worms to wombats to women and men as equally valuable manifestations of God. Even more radically, he applied his spiritual egalitarianism in the "Canticle of the Sun" to the sun, wind, and fire, whom he called his "brothers," and the moon, stars, and water, whom he labeled his "sisters." The earth itself was "Mother Earth."[32]

Francis's view was certainly a minority one in early Christian history but it was not unrepresented among Western philosophers, where it often went by the name "pantheism" and was advocated by thinkers from the pre-Socratic Greek Thales of Miletus (624–526 BC), who substituted water for God as the original source and common element in all things, to, most notably, Baruch Spinoza (1632–1677), who saw every natural being or object as part and parcel of God, nothing higher or lower than another, all part of a divine organic whole. Charles Darwin (1809–1882), in turn, though not a pantheist, embedded humans in the natural community so inexorably that even a century and a half of antievolutionary fervor has failed to extricate them.

One of the earliest appearances in an American context of the notion that Nature might carry value apart from its utility to humans came with the work of the naturalist John Muir (1838–1914). The story of his epiphany is legendary. Unwilling to be drafted to serve in the Civil War, Muir hightailed it into the Canadian wilderness to escape conscription. One day he came upon a cluster of rare wild orchids, "sat down beside them and wept for joy." The environmental historian Roderick Nash describes the scene:

> Muir realized his emotion sprang from the fact that the wilderness orchids did not have the slightest relevance to human beings. Were it not for Muir's chance encounter, they would have lived, bloomed and died unseen. Nature . . . must exist first and foremost for itself and for its creator. Everything had value.[33]

Later Muir made the point even more concretely: "What good are rattlesnakes for?" he asked. "Good for themselves," he answered, "and we need not begrudge them their share of life."[34]

This attitude stood in sharp contrast to what would become known at the turn of the twentieth century as the "conservation" movement, a term coined in 1907 by Gifford Pinchot (1865–1946), first chief of the U.S. Forest Service, appointed to that post by the great outdoorsman President Teddy Roosevelt. In the Progressive Era "conservation" meant preserving and protecting Nature in order that it serve as a natural resource for humans.

That utilitarian approach to Nature prevailed for much of the twentieth century. It evolved into recognition of the damage environmental degradation was doing to humankind, thanks in good measure to the pioneering work of the author Rachel Carson (1907–1964) and her 1962 blockbuster *Silent Spring* exposing the dangers of pesticides.[35] It morphed into a proposed amendment to the U.S. Constitution offered in 1970 by Senator Gaylord Nelson of

Wisconsin (1916–2005), creator of Earth Day, to recognize a "right to a decent environment."[36] And it grounded the first major U.N. statement on the environment, the World Charter for Nature, adopted in 1982 by a vote of 111 to 1 with only the United States opposing it. Articulating human obligations to Nature, the charter was predicated on such premises as

> Mankind is a part of nature and life depends on the uninterrupted functioning of natural systems which ensure the supply of energy and nutrients. . . . Lasting benefits from nature depend upon . . . essential ecological processes. . . . The degradation of natural systems . . . leads to the breakdown of the economic, social and political framework of civilization . . . [and] competition for scarce resources creates conflict.[37]

One small paragraph did, however, signal a different posture toward the natural world: "Every form of life is unique," it read, "warranting respect regardless of its worth to man." That was a sentiment that had been formulated years before in philosophical terms by the environmentalist Aldo Leopold (1887–1948) and in legal ones by the law professor Christopher Stone.

Leopold, a renowned American forester often called the "father of ecology," did not live to see his great masterpiece, *A Sand County Almanac,* published. He died of a heart attack while fighting a grass-fire on his neighbor's farm one week before the book was issued in 1949 by Oxford University Press. But even without its author available to promote it, the book became one of the most groundbreaking and influential in American studies. Focused around what Leopold called the "Land Ethic," a phrase intended to include all that this chapter has described as Nature, *A Sand County Almanac,* hearkening back to John Muir, affirmed a "biotic right" guaranteeing a right to continued existence not just for humans or animals but also for plants, soil, and water. They were all a part of an indivisible organism called the Earth. "We abuse land [Nature]," Leopold wrote, "because we regard it as a commodity belonging to us. When we see land as a community to which we belong, we may begin to use it with love and respect."[38] As the word "use" indicates, Leopold acknowledged that humans could not live without some appropriation of natural resources as food to eat or water to drink or lumber with which to build shelter. What was important was that those uses be carried out with respect for the "integrity, stability and beauty of the biotic community itself," with respect, in other words, for the interests and dignity of the natural world and its ecosystems.

In one of his most searching essays, called "Thinking like a Mountain," Leopold gave a telling example of what happens when humans fail to respect that balance and stability. He had just participated in the shooting of a wolf—"I was young then and full of trigger-itch," he says—but when he reached the wounded wolf, he was struck by the "fierce green fire dying in her eyes." He knew that wolves were the predator of deer and at first he had assumed that the more deer, the better, but "after seeing the green fire die, I sensed that neither the wolf nor the mountain agreed with such a view. Since then I have lived to see state after state extirpate its wolves," he explained.

> I have watched the face of many a newly wolfless mountain and seen the south-facing slopes wrinkle with a maze of new deer trails. I have seen every edible bush and seedling browsed ... to death. I have seen every edible tree defoliated to the height of a saddlehorn. Such a mountain looks as if someone had given God a new pruning shears, and forbidden Him all other exercise.... I now suspect that just as a deer herd lives in mortal fear of its wolves, so does a mountain live in mortal fear of its deer.[39]

Of course a mountain does not literally think, but we humans can think "like a mountain." We can think about its interests and its dignity and come to recognize that wolves are not inherently bad or sheep good but that it is the integrity, stability, balance, and beauty of the system itself that count in the end.

What good is this shift in perspective, however, if it remains mere words, if it has no practical consequences? It was an American law professor named Christopher Stone who proposed a radical remedy in an article in a 1972 issue of the *Southern California Law Review* entitled "Should Trees Have Standing? Toward Legal Rights for Natural Objects."[40] The Walt Disney Company had proposed to build a huge ski resort in a wild portion of the Sierra Nevada mountains at the headwaters of the Kaweah River. The Sierra Club, a major environmental organization, had filed a lawsuit to stop Disney but had been judged not to have standing, that is, not to be sufficiently connected to the case or personally harmed by the regrettable action as to be eligible to sue. That judgment had been appealed to the Supreme Court and Stone's article was designed to introduce to the court the then-unprecedented notion that, even if the Sierra Club did not have legal standing, "forests, oceans, rivers and other so-called 'natural objects' in the environment—indeed ... the natural environment as a whole" should be granted legal standing, just as "corporations ... states, estates, infants, incompetents, municipalities or universities" have been. Each of them is spoken for by someone other than themselves and Nature could similarly be represented by a "guardian."

Stone made clear he was not saying "anything as silly as that no one should be allowed to cut down a tree" any more than children should be allowed to vote. But he went on to argue that natural elements certainly could suffer injuries and those injuries could be communicated to their guardians—"I am sure I can judge ... whether my lawn wants (needs) watering ... by a certain dryness of the blades and soil," he wrote. Furthermore, Nature could be the beneficiary of redress, which Stone proposed be in the form of trust funds for their repair. Given these characteristics, Nature and its constituents should be permitted standing in their own right, quite apart from human interests.[41]

A majority of the court did not agree, but Justice William O. Douglas, the foremost environmentalist on the court, issued a dissent in which he advocated extending standing to "valleys, alpine meadows, rivers, lakes, estuaries, beaches, ridges, groves of trees, swampland or even air that feels the destructive pressures of modern technology and modern life." He concluded with the stirring words, "The voice of the inanimate object should not be stilled."[42]

Over the last four or five decades that voice has been heard in a wide variety of contexts. The first issue of the *Whole Earth Catalog* appeared in 1968 with a photo of the earth from outer space, the first time the whole of the earth had actually been seen, not just pondered. The Norwegian philosopher Arne Naess founded the "deep ecology" movement in 1973, distinguishing it from an ecology that still put humans at the center of concern and insisting that the value of Nature is "independent of the usefulness of the nonhuman world for human purposes."[43] The chemist James Lovelock proposed a controversial theory called the "Gaia Hypothesis" that posits that organic and inorganic materials have evolved together to form a single, self-regulating living superorganism.[44] Thomas Berry articulated three fundamental rights that all Earth's components could claim "the right to be, the right to habitat, and the right to fulfill one's role in the ever-renewing process of the earth community."[45] Environmental lawyer Cormac Cullinan founded the "Wild Law" movement, which advocates jurisprudence that privileges the earth community as a whole over the sole interests of any one species, including humans.[46]

More consequential than all this theoretical work, however, has been the movement to codify Nature's rights in legal instruments. Thanks in no small measure to an NGO called the Community Environmental Legal Defense Fund (CELDF), which provides intellectual and legal assistance to those seeking to protect elements of Nature, the rights of Nature have been written into law everywhere from a small township in eastern Pennsylvania to the Whanganui River in New Zealand.

The first appearance of those rights in legal form was in a community ordinance adopted in 2006 by Tamaqua Borough, a village of seven thousand in eastern Pennsylvania that was confronting a proposal to dump sewage sludge in an area mining pit. Drafted with CELDF's help, the ordinance affirmed the human right to a healthy environment but it also declared "natural communities and ecosystems . . . to be 'persons' for purposes of the enforcement of [their] civil rights" and authorized any Borough resident to have standing to sue for violations of those rights.[47] Since then several dozen other towns and cities, including Santa Monica, California, and Pittsburgh, Pennsylvania, have adopted laws recognizing the rights of Nature.

The first national recognition of those rights to date came with the ratification of a new constitution in Ecuador in 2008. Ecuador is one of the most biologically diverse countries on earth. One tree in its Yasuni National Park may be home to as many as ninety-six species of orchids and bromeliads and forty-five species of ants.[48] But the country's mineral wealth also makes it attractive to the extractive industries. With robust communities of indigenous people who often find their interests in conflict with large oil, gas, mining and logging companies, Ecuador was an ideal location for environmental activists to introduce the first constitutional codification of the rights of Nature anywhere in the world.

Grounded in the indigenous concept of *sumac kawsay*, translatable as "good living" or "harmonious coexistence," Article 71 of the Constitution of the Republic of Ecuador declares that "Nature or *Pachamama* [Mother Earth] . . . has the right to integral respect for its existence and the maintenance and regeneration of its lifecycles, structures, functions and evolutionary processes."[49] Note the similarity between *sumac kawsay* and our guiding notion of the "good society." Though enforcement has been uneven, the provisions of the Constitution related to the rights of Nature have been success-fully invoked in defense of the Vilcabamba River in a criminal case against illegal shark fishing and in the establishment of a new protected area for the conservation of biodiversity.[50]

Two years after the adoption of the Ecuadoran Constitution, Bolivia passed the Law on the Rights of Mother Earth, similarly based on *sumac kawsay* but delineating *Pachamama's* rights in far more de-tail. Under the law, Mother Earth, defined as a living system, has the rights to maintain the integrity of that system; to preserve the variety of beings within it without genetic modification that threatens their existence; to maintain access to quality water and air; to sustain the equilibrium of the system; to restore it to balance if it is negatively af-fected by human activity; and to preserve pollution-free living.[51]

These are the two most far-reaching examples of Nature as a whole being invested by law with rights of its own but there have been additional instances in which elements within Nature have been assigned rights. In 2013 the New Zealand government, re-sponding to the Maori worldview that all things are related and in-fused with spirit, agreed that Te Urewera, the traditional homeland of the Tuhoe tribe and previously a national park, would be freed from human ownership and recognized as owning itself with a set of corresponding rights.[52] Four years later the Whanganui River was designated a legal person with the "rights, duties and liabilities" of such a person.[53] The river owned its own riverbed. That same year the High Court of Uttarakhand in India ruled that the Ganges and Yamuna rivers are "living entities," though that judgment was later overruled by India's Supreme Court.[54]

Unlike in the case of robots, where exact rights claims have yet to be delineated in much detail, the rights attributable to Mother Earth have been articulated with considerable specificity in the "Universal Declaration of Rights of Mother Earth," among other places. Adopted in 2010 by the World People's Congress on Climate Change and the Rights of Mother Earth, a conference of some thirty thousand people representing governments and civil society organizations from more than one hundred countries, the declaration adds to those rights codified in the Bolivian law "the right to regenerate [Mother Earth's] bio-capacity" and "the right ... to live free from torture or cruel treatment by human beings."[55] Such specificity does not mean, however, that the concept of the rights of Nature is without its complexities.

SHORTLY AFTER THE BOLIVIAN LAW was passed, Canadian political commentator Rex Murphy expressed his dismay: "What does the new ... law mean?" he asked rhetorically. "It means that ticks that suck the blood, the choking sulphur pits of volcanic vents, the indestructible cockroach, the arid desert wastes, and the bleak frigid spaces of the planet's poles ... are to have rights."[56] Wesley Smith of the Discovery Institute was even more wrought up: "The potential harm to human welfare seems virtually unlimited," he opined. "Take, for example, a farmer who wishes to drain a swamp to create more tillable land to better support his family. Now the swamp has equal rights with the farmer, as do the mosquitoes, snakes, pond scum, rats, spiders, trees and fish that reside therein."[57]

On the one hand, these objections are easily refuted. As discussed in the chapters on animals and robots, we need not accord rights to all elements in Nature nor equal rights to every element nor the same rights to elements of Nature that we do to humans. Ticks may be regarded as unworthy of rights altogether or their rights may be far less robust than those of a forest and, in any case, all the rights of nonhuman entities need at least to be balanced with those of humans. Moreover, the fact that natural elements do us damage ("the choking sulphur pits of volcanic vents") and can hardly be held responsible for their actions is no argument against them having rights. Consider that even a guilty murderer retains the right to a fair trial. Nor does accidentally setting a house on fire deprive a small child of its right not to be imprisoned.

Moreover, the rights of Nature refer not solely to individual units, like ticks or sulphur pits, but to the biotic community, the interdependent system as a whole. This puts Smith's objections in a whole different light. The "harm to human welfare" would be infinitely greater if Nature itself collapsed than if an individual farmer was denied the right to drain a swamp.

And yet, whether they intended to or not, Murphy and Smith have pointed to several quandaries that the rights of Nature evoke. Here's one of them: the natural world is the setting for a series of conflicts that simply "come with the territory." When the natural flow of a river carves canyons out of mountains, thereby reshaping the mountains and altering their original majesty, whose rights do we protect, the river's or the mountains'? The same might be asked of invasive plant species, the seeds of which were introduced through the wind or bird droppings but which threaten indigenous species. Do we protect the rights of indigenous species, the invasive plants, the birds, or the wind? When fire burns down a forest, do we affirm the fire's right to burn or the forest's right to be? Species have been going extinct of their own accord for millions of years, without any help from humans. Does it make sense to expend resources to save every species currently on earth or shall we allow some to perish in respect for the natural rhythms of the biotic community? Thomas Berry's rights to be and to have a habitat may sometimes contradict a pasture's right to flourish (to be) or a cow's right to chew (to enjoy its habitat). We must remain content with the fact that elements of Nature don't have claims against one another any more than the tiger's prey has a rights claim against the tiger. It is maintenance of the balance of the system itself that must prevail.

This leads, however, to another quandary. It is easy enough to say that humans should respect that balance by not interfering in Nature's natural rhythms—by not forcing the river to change course, not blasting the top off the mountain, not introducing invasive species for human benefit—but humans and animals are also part of Nature. In order for their right to food, for example, to be realized, the right to life of some elements of Nature, like plants, will need to be sacrificed. The elements of Nature surely have no nonderogable right to life, like humans do, or else humans would be obliged to allow our cultivated food gardens to return to their natural state, our water purification systems to let animal dung go untreated, and our homes to be built from nothing but synthetics.

Whatever the rights of Nature may be, they must take into account and complement the rights of other creatures in the system. Again, this is why it is the system itself that deserves the protection of rights more than the elements within it. But deciding these matters is hardly easy. If by altering plant genes, for example, we could increase food supply by 40–50 percent, as some scientists claim, ought we to ignore Mother Earth's right to "not have its genetic structure modified or disrupted" in order to ensure that humans not go hungry?[58] As with other conflicts between rights claims, adjudicatory rights bodies will need to sort out the answers.

A guiding principle may be whether human interference in natural processes threatens to undermine the entire system, as the unfettered release of greenhouse gases does, or whether limitations on Nature's rights, undertaken to serve some fundamental human right, such as the right to food, compromise the interests of only a small segment of the biotic community. And that human right does need to be fundamental. Though the smallpox virus is certainly an element in Nature, it would be legitimate to eliminate such viruses altogether (except perhaps for a controlled portion retained for research purposes) in the interests of advancing the human right to health. On the other hand, Albert Schweitzer insisted that humans should "break off no flower" and the late philosopher Paul W. Taylor contended that, absent extenuating circumstances, "the killing of a wildflower ... is just as much a wrong ... as the killing of a human."[59] Taylor's view is obviously an extreme one but, while the authors enjoy cut flowers as much as the next person, there is no fundamental human right to access beauty. In any case, flowers can be enjoyed readily in the wild so their wanton destruction purely for human pleasure must at least give us pause.[60]

And yet who gets to decide what those flowers or the ecological system of which they are a part really need? The question is not just whether trees have standing. The question is who has standing to speak on behalf of trees. Why environmental organizations instead of extractive companies? How do we know that flowers don't enjoy being picked or mountains leveled?

At first this would seem to be an insurmountable objection to the idea that Nature has rights that can be enforced with the aid of a guardian. Animals and robots, at least until the latter become fully autonomous, are subject to the same types of queries. But then so are children, the cognitively disabled, and the comatose, and yet we don't hesitate to allow human guardians to make decisions on their behalf about the exercise of their rights. Those decisions are based upon commonly accepted perceptions of what human capabilities remain to them without which they would not be able to live lives of dignity and the obstruction of which would compromise our sense of what constitutes a good society. Similarly, as shown in the case of animals, humans make judgments, based upon animal behavior, about what appears to promote or retard their flourishing.

It is hardly a leap to apply a similar concept of flourishing—or, metaphorically, dignity—to both elements in Nature and the system itself. Can a river flourish if it is polluted with toxins? Can a mountain flourish if it is no longer a mountain? Can the whole ecological system flourish if its balance is thrown into jeopardy? Those who speak on behalf of such flourishing are the ones who have standing to be Nature's guardians.

WHETHER WE SEEK TO PROTECT the environment based on a human right to a livable world or the conviction that Nature and its elements ought to be awarded rights of their own may turn out to be in good measure a strategic decision. Certainly the former approach is more politically palatable than the latter; it is a lot easier to convince courts and constituencies—at least Western ones—that human interests and the full realization of our dignity and capabilities require a healthy ecosystem than that rivers and trees and mountains ought to be able to sue to defend their rights to flourish.

The whole argument of this book, however, has been that rights are transactional, that they are dependent upon humans' relationship to other entities, especially the less powerful to the powerful, and that the assignment of rights to those entities turns on what dignity and flourishing requires if we humans are to be able to say with confidence that we live in a good society.

It would make no sense to assign rights to our erstwhile cardboard box (as opposed to the trees from which the box was made). There is no sense in which humans can be said to have meaningful relations, powerful or otherwise, with cardboard boxes; no sense in which a cardboard box has "interests" or dignity; no sense in which to break down or burn a cardboard box could be said to violate its flourishing; no sense in which a society that banned cardboard boxes could be considered a bad society. There are any number of entities in the world for whom the claim that they bear rights is nonsensical.

But human beings certainly do have a profound relationship to Nature and its elements, especially its living ones; we do attempt to assert our power over Nature (though often without success—see hurricanes, tornadoes, drought, etcetera). Nature can be said to flourish or flounder, and it is hardly unreasonable to think that respect for its holistic and organic "integrity, stability, and beauty" might well be a mark of the good society. All these are reasons that the label "rights holder" may legitimately be applied to Nature.

It is not because Nature is exactly like human beings that it may be understood to be a legitimate assignee of rights, any more than that is the case with animals or robots. It is because human beings have a relationship with Nature that requires the kind of attention and care that rights signal—indeed, a relationship that becomes more and more urgent as our climate changes and our homes and habitats are threatened. If human beings were to disappear from the earth altogether, the concept of rights would disappear too—it is a human construct—while the earth in all its glory would remain. As long as we are here, however, it is wise to treat the earth with the respect that a good society requires and that our relationship to the earth demands.

# Conclusion

THE TOPICS COVERED IN THIS BOOK in no way exhaust the areas in which rights need or may be expected to change in the coming years. Here are just a few additional arenas in which rights may be in flux.

"Women and children are always the first victims," said Nadia Murad, a young Yazidi woman and trafficking survivor Sushma met at the Carr Center for Human Rights Policy at Harvard University in 2016. Nadia never dreamed she would ever leave her village in Sinjar Province, Iraq, but, as she put it, "Life takes people wherever it wants." Where it took her on August 15, 2014, was into the hands of fighters with the Islamic State (ISIS). Her "simple dreams and simple hopes" were shattered; she had become their slave. "My soul, my body, and my emotions [were] occupied and . . . used by people who look like humans, but they are not humans," she said. Many of Nadia's immediate and extended family members were killed while many young girls like her were repeatedly raped.

The Yazidis are a small and persecuted religious minority, largely located in Sinjar Province, Iraq, with syncretic beliefs that draw from Christianity, Islam, and Zoroastrianism. Denounced as infidels and devil worshippers by extremist groups, thousands of Yazidi men have been slaughtered; Yazidi women and children have been kidnapped, raped, and held in captivity. After managing to escape, Nadia became a refugee in Germany, where she is one of more than sixty-five million people around the world who are forced to migrate due to war, conflict, repression, violence, and other forms of upheaval.

Nadia is the type of person for whom the 1951 Refugee Convention was written—someone who has been forced to flee his or her country because of war or violence or a "well-founded fear of persecution" for reasons of race, religion, nationality, political opinion, or membership in a particular social group. Under the convention, refugees must be given protection and may not be forcibly returned to their home country where their life or basic security would be under threat. It's called *nonrefoulement* and, while many "host" countries, including the United States, often refuse to respect the principle, it's a well-established feature of international law.[1] Nadia is one of 22.5 million refugees around the world, over half of whom are under the age of eighteen.

There's another group of people, however, who find themselves in increasingly dire straits but for whom the Refugee Convention, as currently conceived, offers no hope at all.

The low-lying Pacific island nation of Kiribati is one of the most vulnerable countries in the world when it comes to climate change. In May 2014, thirty-seven-year-old resident Ioane Teitiota tried to become the first climate change refugee by seeking refugee status in New Zealand under the convention. The New Zealand Court of Appeal dashed his hopes when it ruled that his application was "fundamentally misconceived" and "an attempt to stand the [U.N. Refugee] convention on its head." Were his argument to be accepted, the court said, "at a stroke millions of people who are facing medium-term economic deprivation or the immediate consequences of natural disasters . . . would be entitled to protection under the Refugee Convention."[2]

Three months later a family from the country of Tuvalu, ten square miles of reef islands and atolls in the Pacific Ocean between Hawaii and Australia that is also threatened by rising sea levels, was granted legal residency in New Zealand. Their attorneys argued that "climate change and overpopulation has made life untenable on their native island" but, because the 1951 Convention Related to the Status of Refugees, often referred to as just the Refugee Convention, does not recognize climate change as a valid reason for granting protection, they also relied on more traditional arguments, such as family ties in New Zealand.[3]

As the impacts of climate change become ever more evident to residents of vulnerable lands, the unreasonable limitations of the Refugee Convention will become more obvious too. Slow-onset, climate-induced crises such as droughts as well as sudden-onset disasters such as earthquakes and tsunamis are displacing millions of people around the world, from Vanuatu to the Philippines, Somalia to Haiti. Despite so much affluence, the world today is facing at least four famines: in South Sudan, Yemen, northern Nigeria, and Somalia. The United Nations estimates that more than twenty-one million people have been displaced by climate-related disasters each year in the past decade and up to a billion will be in the coming four decades.[4] Moreover, as discussed with regard to Darfur, Sudan, climate change can be a "threat multiplier" in many of the world's conflicts, exacerbating a range of other challenges.[5]

Developed at a time after World War II when millions of people were displaced due to conflict between countries and were fleeing war and fear of persecution, the definition of a "refugee" in the 1951 Convention will simply be outdated in a future world in which climate change will displace more people than wars. President Barack Obama recognized this fact implicitly when, in his opening remarks at the Paris climate talks in 2015, he referred to "Submerged countries. Abandoned cities. Fields that no longer grow. Political disruptions that trigger new conflict, and even more floods of desperate peoples seeking the sanctuary of nations not their own."[6] Eventually the reasons for refugee status will need to evolve beyond traditional persecution of individuals like Nadia by powerful human forces to include the devastation to whole communities wrought by the "natural" forces of unchecked climate change. Given the contribution humans are making to that environmental disaster, it seems only just that nations would include its victims among those eligible for protection.

GODELIEVA DE TROYER was a sixty-three-year-old Belgian woman who had suffered most of her life from severe depression. After more than forty years of what she regarded as unsuccessful psychotherapeutic treatments, she found herself having broken up with a gentleman friend, alienated from her two children, without access to her grandchildren, and bereft of *levensperspectief*, a Dutch word meaning "something to live for."

The "right to die," that is, the right to government-sanctioned aid in dying, is legal for those with terminal physical illnesses in at least seven countries.[7] In Belgium the permissible reasons for such assistance extend to "severe and incurable distress, including psychosocial disorders" and it was under that rubric that Godelieva convinced the required number of doctors that her emotional anguish could never be remedied. Without contacting her children, physicians provided the medication that she used to end her life on April 20, 2012.[8]

Many mental health professionals argue that with proper treatment, including pharmacological strategies, depression like Godelieva's can be alleviated. What is certainly true is that physical deterioration is far more measurable and predictable than emotional. That is no doubt why most jurisdictions that permit medically assisted aid in dying limit its availability to those facing impending death. But the Netherlands and Switzerland go beyond even Belgium's liberal rationales. They have extended the right to die not just to people like the 104-year-old Australian scientist David Goodall, who, though not facing impending death, had seen a marked deterioration in his physical health and told an Australian broadcaster simply that "I greatly regret having reached [this] age.... I want to die. It's not sad particularly. What is sad is if one is prevented [from taking one's own life]."[9] No, this applies not just to the David Goodalls but to anyone, even the healthy, who feels he or she has led a full life and is ready to depart. Such decisions have been dubbed "rational suicide" and, though it is highly controversial, it is a topic that respected institutions like the Hastings Center, a bioethical research institution, and respected journals like the *Journal of the American Geriatrics Society* are addressing.[10]

Were laws and policies permitting rational suicide more widely adopted and, indeed, a human right to euthanasia or aid in dying established, then human rights, which traditionally have been designed to protect and extend life, would become indelibly associated with the ending of it—a true revolution. On the other hand, if one believes that asserting sovereignty over one's life choices, especially those that concern one's own body alone, is one of the hallmarks of dignity, then it is hard to see how such a right could be denied.

IN THE YEARS FOLLOWING THE U.S. CIVIL WAR, when paid work was hard to come by in both the North and South, unemployed men would take to the road in search of a paying job or charitable handouts. The residents of some small towns in New England who tired of what came to be called "tramps" knocking on their doors or, when worse came to worse, stealing from their gardens, prevailed upon town authorities to erect "tramp houses" where itinerants were housed before being escorted out of town. The tramp houses, some of which still exist today as museums, were little different from jail cells; the unemployed were considered by many to be incipient criminals, if not outright thieves. With improved economic opportunity and the increased availability of public assistance, tramp houses gradually disappeared by the turn of the twentieth century but the ethos that had inspired them—the notion that the poor and homeless had only themselves to blame and represented a potentially dangerous underclass that needed to be controlled—has been a part of American culture for centuries.

In 1969 Republican President Richard Nixon, of all people, seriously considered introducing legislation that, had it been in place after the Civil War, would have made tramp houses superfluous. Why not provide every citizen, he wondered, a basic guaranteed income, regardless of their condition or state of employment?[11] Though Nixon was eventually dissuaded, the idea of a basic universal income guarantee has become increasingly popular around the world, including in the United States where in 2018 the idea was supported by 48 percent of those surveyed.[12] Countries as diverse as Canada, Kenya, India, and Finland are considering the idea. Cash transfers through such programs as GiveDirectly—transfers that provide stipends to individuals in developing nations to use as they choose—appear to hold promise as a means of reducing extreme poverty.[13] It is not inconceivable that at some point in the future the general right to what the Universal Declaration of Human Rights calls "a standard of living adequate for . . . health and well-being" (Article 25) will be supplemented by the far more concrete right to a basic guaranteed minimal income.

THESE ARE BUT THREE EXAMPLES of additional areas beyond those covered in more detail in this book in which rights may very well change, either through evolution or revolution, in the coming decades. Almost every week brings a new decision by a national court or the emergence of a grassroots movement or a proposal from a legislator or advocacy group for a reinterpretation, restriction, or expansion of a current right or for the introduction of a new one.

Some of these have received widespread publicity and often reflect conflicts in rights claims, like the decisions by five countries in

Europe to ban the wearing of face veils in public, ostensibly to protect the public's right to security from terrorism, but which, since they apply almost exclusively to Muslim women, have been called by Amnesty International a violation of freedom of expression and religion.[14] Some Muslim women's groups oppose the wearing of the veil but "All women," said Amnesty, "should be free to dress as they please and to wear clothing that expresses their identity or beliefs."[15]

Another burgeoning rights issue is exemplified by the proposals in Denmark, Iceland, and elsewhere to ban circumcision of boys, a practice which some argue violates the rights to bodily integrity or the right not to be tortured. In any case, they say, this ban would be an extension of the right to health.[16] Religious groups that practice circumcision see such a ban, not surprisingly, as a violation of the right to religious freedom.[17]

Another current issue is the ongoing battle to establish fetal rights and the legal "personhood" of the fetus, reflected in the United States, for example, in the Unborn Victims of Violence Act of 2004, which makes the injury or killing of a fetus in utero in the course of the commission of any one of some sixty federal crimes of violence a crime in its own right. Supporters regard the act and similar efforts as an expansion of civil rights to a new group—which would be, in the authors' terms, a revolution. Though abortion is excluded from the list of crimes that trigger the act, abortion rights advocates naturally see the extension of legal personhood to a fetus as infringing on a woman's right to health.[18]

Additionally, consider the decriminalization of sex work, which is already in effect in at least fifteen countries and which Amnesty International called for in 2016, citing a host of rights, from non-discrimination to freedom of expression to health, which making prostitution a crime violates.[19] Many women's rights organizations and antislavery and trafficking groups oppose decriminalization, however, asserting, among other things, that sex work is not an autonomous choice but a forced decision.[20] Yin Q., a Chinese American sex worker, disputed that: "Bodily autonomy and freedom to earn a living is the American way," she said. "Feminists: stop shaming me. Liberals: stop saving me. Gay pride: stop ignoring me."[21]

Other proposals or court decisions have yet to receive significant traction, though—who knows?—they may in the future. Here are some examples:

- In 2016 the Supreme Court of Cassation in Italy, the highest court in that country, ruled that stealing small amounts of food may not be a crime if a thief is homeless and hungry, or, in other words, that the right to food trumps the right to property.[22]
- India's Supreme Court ruled in 2017 that candidates for political office may not appeal to voters on the basis of religion, caste, community, or language. This effort to protect the right to free elections by outlawing "identity politics" appears to some to tread dangerously upon the right to freedom of expression.[23]
- The right to education is contained in Article 26 of the Universal Declaration of Human Rights but ought there to be a right to an *adequate* education? A group of students in the Detroit, Michigan, public schools sued the state, citing the fact that many graduates of the school system were functionally illiterate. A court dismissed the case even though a right to an adequate education would appear to bear the same relationship to the right to education as free access to a polling place bears to the right to vote. Without the former, the latter is essentially meaningless.[24]
- The French government has extended labor rights by affirming a "right to disconnect"; that is, the right of workers to ignore work-related texts and emails outside of office hours.[25]

- One local official in Sweden, on the other hand, has proposed a right to "connect," that is, a right of municipal workers to take an hour-long paid leave each week to go home and have sex.[26] That right has not yet been adopted but a Swedish labor court did rule in 2018 that a Muslim woman had the right on religious grounds to not shake hands with a prospective employer without suffering employment discrimination.[27]

Strange as it may seem at first blush, even the dead are awarded some rights in most cultures—rights such as respect for the wishes of the deceased as to the disposal of assets or the Japanese practice of providing food to those who have died years after they have passed away—though those have not yet been codified in any human rights treaty.[28] Nor, since we are contemplating future rights-bearing entities in this book, ought we to assume that alien creatures from one or more of the roughly twenty percent of all stars that have habitable planets may not be candidates for rights. Or perhaps, since outreach to alien civilizations may be to risk human extinction should those civilizations prove hostile, there should be a human right for all earth's inhabitants to participate in the decision as to whether to engage in such outreach at all![29]

BEFORE READERS FLOAT TOO FAR off into space, however, this section returns to one of the basic questions with which this book began: at a time when even some of the most well-established human rights—from free speech to freedom from racial discrimination to immigrants' rights to democratic values themselves—are under threat from demagogues and nationalists, the alt-right and neo-Nazis, does it make sense to spend energy contemplating additional rights, much less rights for nonhuman entities like animals, robots, or Nature? Even more basically, is the whole rights enterprise at risk as a result of its own limitations and failures?

The policy analyst David Rieff, a frequent critic of the human rights movement, has questioned the assumption underlying the legal regimen upon which human rights are constructed; namely, that once you build it, the villains of the world will come ... to see the error or at least the disadvantages of their human rights–defying ways. This assumption about the inevitability of history, Rieff says, is what "a sympathizer with the human rights movement would call its moral serenity and a skeptic would call its hubris." Instead, he argues, "If the human rights movement is to have a future, it should consist of defending ... [basic] moral concern[s], not pretending that—for now at least—[they] can be expanded."[30]

In his book *Not Enough: Human Rights in an Unequal World,* Samuel Moyn, a distinguished professor of legal history, commends human rights ideals, but insists that "global justice"—a popular human rights watchword—will never be achieved without a robust assault on economic inequality and that, if not exactly a tool of capitalist neo-liberalism, "human rights law lacked the norms, and the human rights movement the will, to advocate for a serious redistributive politics." The result, he says, is that the law and movement "both failed to attack the victory of the rich and struggled to cope with the poverty of the rest ... which paved the way to populism and further rights abuses."[31] The obvious implication is that advocacy of the fundamental right to economic equality should come first before the human rights movement takes on any additional causes.

These are both serious criticisms that deserve serious reflection and a serious response. The authors do not pretend that the human rights movement is perfect. Neither Rieff nor Moyn will get an argument from them that some rights are more important than others, more central to dignity, more crucial to the fashioning of a good society, and that, therefore, as rights advocates make decisions about where to put their time and energy, those rights take precedence. Which rights those are is not always easy to decide but they are certainly rights like economic equality, upon which the realization of many other rights depend. The authors note Rieff's qualifier that rights not be expanded "for now at least" and it generates some sympathy.

One problem with Rieff's and Moyn's arguments, however, is that even many of those "most important" rights may depend upon the recognition of new or amended rights. Some economic rights, like the right to social security, have already been codified but the one mentioned above—the right to a basic annual income—has not and it may be crucial to what Moyn calls "redistributive politics."[32] Are we content to believe that we already recognize every element or permutation of even our most fundamental rights? And what good will rights to free speech, a fair trial, or even economic equality be if the use of CRISPR succeeds in radically reshaping future generations in damaging ways or autonomous weapons make war as easy as child's play or environmental disaster wipes out significant populations on the planet either because humans have failed to honor the rights of Nature or refused to expand the definition of refugees? Many rights, old and new, are entangled with one another as surely as yeast in bread.

Then, too, it is worth contemplating what a world would be like in which there were no rights norms whatsoever, human or otherwise, or those norms were significantly circumscribed. It is easy for University of Chicago law professor Eric Posner to observe from his position of economic and educational privilege that "there is little evidence that human rights treaties have improved the well-being of people. . . . Human rights law has failed to accomplish its utopian aspirations, and it ought to be abandoned."[33] But shall we tell that to the young man in a Sudanese prison who is only alive today because U.N. human rights observers checked on him regularly and warned his guards that Posner's despised human rights treaties require that he not be tortured? Or to the young women in the Nepalese marketplace who have only just established their small businesses upon discovering that there are such things as women's rights that support their securing economic self-sufficiency independent of their husbands?

Exactly the same challenge presents itself when it comes to "new" rights. What would it be like to live in a world in which rights did not evolve or change? Do we really want David Rieff or any other individual to be the one to decide which rights are not important enough to be a new "moral concern?" Shall we tell the transgender teenager considering suicide that the right to transition is not a sufficient moral concern to be a priority for becoming a newly recognized right? Shall we tell a family whose child has died because a corrupt government has siphoned off medical supplies for private gain that their despair does not warrant our energy to establish a new right to live in a corruption-free society?

The liberal enterprise upon which the whole notion of rights is based is not predicated upon Posner's "utopian aspirations" but upon the conviction that we can gradually chip away at cruelty, know though we do that the newly hewn rock will still have its defects. "The result," says the essayist Adam Gopnik, "will be ... merely another society ... that is flawed, like our own, but less cruel as time goes on."[34] What we cannot do is pretend that history has stopped; that all basic moral concerns have been identified already; or that the secret of the good society can be obtained in any one universal imperative, even as honorable an imperative as full economic equality.

Samuel Sewall, a judge at the Salem witchcraft trials, learned that the hard way when a mere five years after the trials he stood in the well of the South Church in Boston while his minister read his confession of "grave error" in presuming to judge others guilty of sorcery. Having begged God and the congregation to forgive his sin and remembering perhaps that three people of color had been included among those condemned in Salem, Sewall wrote *The Selling of Joseph*, the first antislavery tract in New England, in 1700.[35] History had not stopped for Sewall nor had moral concern (what today we would call his understanding of rights) come to a standstill. After being certain he had helped shape the "good society" at Salem, he soon saw the error of his ways and in the process discovered a new feature—the abjuration of slavery—incumbent upon any society that would call itself "good."

The premise of this book has been that, in the words of C. K. Douzinas, "Rights are not what belong to a person; they are what create the person," and, the authors would add, create "the good society."[36] Because neither people nor societies are inert, what is created will invariably change and hence many of the rights associated with the creation will too. Some rights may always stay the same; others will shift shape; and still others will be born anew. Not all will be of equal salience or worth but often we will not know which is which until we test them in the crucible of time. The only thing we may not do is to allow a small coterie of smug savants to choose our rights for us or tell us which ones really matter. That is to guarantee the perpetuation of the notion that rights are the property of a Western elite rather than a global humanity.

Law professor Patricia Williams offers us a far better way. In responding to those who would limit rights or even, à la Posner, abandon them, she says:

> In discarding rights altogether, one discards a symbol too deeply enmeshed in the psyche of the oppressed to lose without trauma and much resistance. Instead, society must give them away. Unlock them from reification by giving them to slaves. Give them to trees. Give them to cows. Give them to history. Give them to rivers and rocks. Give to all of society's objects and untouchables the rights of privacy, integrity, and self- assertion; give them distance and respect. Flood them with the animating spirit that rights mythology

fires in this country's most oppressed psyches, and wash away the shrouds of inanimate-object status, so that we may say not that we own gold but that a luminous golden spirit owns us.[37]

This book has been an attempt to unlock that golden spirit. It is now up to you to decide if you want to own gold or invite the golden spirit to own you.

NOTES

ACKNOWLEDGMENTS

INDEX

# Notes

## Introduction

1. David Brooks, "Bannon vs. Trump," *New York Times,* January 10, 2017.
2. In advocating for a further extension of rights to nonhuman creatures, the renowned biologists Paul and Anne Ehrlich described the progression of human caring "from an original concern only with the family or the immediate group . . . toward enlarging the circle toward which ethical behavior is expected. First the entire tribe was included, then the city-state, and more recently the nation. In [the twentieth] century concern has been extended . . . to encompass all of humanity." Quoted in J. Baird Callicott, *In Defense of the Land Ethic: Essays in Environmental Philosophy* (Albany, NY: SUNY Press, 1989), 150.
3. Kathryn Sikkink, *Evidence for Hope: Making Human Rights Work in the 21st Century* (Princeton, NJ: Princeton University Press, 2017).
4. Christopher Stone, "Should Trees Have Standing? Toward Legal Rights for Natural Objects," *Southern California Law Review* 45 (1972): 453.
5. "Investigation into April 2011 Friendly-Fire Incident," Internet Archive, uploaded October 24, 2013, https://archive.org/stream /295339-new-redacted-roi/295339-new-redacted-roi_djvu.txt.
6. Scott Shane, "Drone Strikes Reveal Uncomfortable Truth: U.S. Is Often Unsure about Who Will Die," *New York Times,* April 23, 2015;

"Summary of Information Regarding U.S. Counter-Terrorism Strikes Outside Areas of Active Hostilities," Office of the Director of National Intelligence, July 1, 2016, https://www.dni.gov/files/documents/News room/Press%20Releases/DNI+Release+on+CT+Strikes+Outside+Ar eas+of+Active+Hostilities.PDF; Micah Zenko, "Do Not Believe the U.S. Government's Official Numbers on Drone Strike Civilian Casualties," *Foreign Policy,* July 5, 2016, http://foreignpolicy.com/2016 /07/05/do-not-believe-the-u-s-governments-official-numbers-on -drone-strike-civilian-casualties/.

7. Matthew Rosenberg and John Markoff, "At Heart of U.S. Strategy, Weapons That Can Think," *New York Times,* October 26, 2016.

8. Allison Washington, "Girl, Disrupted: How My Body Betrayed Me," *Medium,* January 21, 2017, https://medium.com/athena-talks/ii-girl -disrupted-how-my-body-betrayed-me-73e65c3ec766.

9. Allison Washington, "Cured," *Medium,* January 18, 2017, https:// medium.com/athena-talks/cured-c49713f39c7e.

10. James C. McKinley, "Arguing in Court Whether 2 Chimps Have the Right to 'Bodily Liberty,'" *New York Times,* May 27, 2015.

11. Aristotle, *Politics,* Book VI, Chapter 16.

12. See, e.g., Susan Quinn, *Eleanor and Hick: The Love Affair That Shaped a First Lady* (New York: Penguin Press, 2016), just one of many accounts that addresses the matter.

13. This is not to say by any means that formal same-sex unions were unknown in human history. Far from it, as is made clear in such volumes as John Boswell, *The Marriage of Likeness: Same-Sex Unions in Premodern Europe* (New York: Vintage Books, 1994) and James Neill, *The Origins and Role of Same-Sex Relations in Human Societies* (Jefferson, NC: McFarland, 2009). But same-sex marriage was outlawed by the Christian emperors Constantius II and Constans in 342 CE: "When a male gives himself in marriage to a 'woman' [sc., effeminate man], and what he wants is that the 'woman' play the male role, where sex has lost its place, where the crime is such that it is better not to know it, where Venus is changed into a different shape, where love is sought but not found, we order laws to arise, justice to be armed with an avenging sword, so that the disgraced persons who are or in future shall be guilty may be subjected to exquisite penalties" (Theodosian Code 9. 7. 3). And it was rarely, if ever, recognized by church or state authorities, at least in the West, for millennia afterward.

14. "#7: First Gay Rights Group in the U.S. (1924)," Blue Sky Originals, *Chicago Tribune,* November 19, 2013, http://www.chicagotribune.com /bluesky/originals/chi-top-20-countdown-innovation-07-bsi -htmlstory.html.

15. Will Roscoe, "Mattachine: Radical Roots of the Gay Movement," FoundSF, accessed April 2019, http://www.foundsf.org/index.php ?title=Mattachine:_Radical_Roots_of_the_Gay_Movement.

16. One, Inc. v. Olesen, 355 U.S. 371 (1958).

17. Obergefell v. Hodges, 135 S. Ct. 2584 (2015).

18. Carla Denly, "LGBT Rights and Protections Are Scarce in Constitutions around the World, UCLA Study Finds," *UCLA Newsroom,* June 27, 2016, http://newsroom.ucla.edu/releases/lgbt-rights-and -protections-are-scarce-in-constitutions-around-the-world-ucla -study-finds.

19. The only participant in the conversation who agreed with Bill was Syracuse law professor David Crane, who had served as chief prosecutor at the international war crimes tribunal in Sierra Leone and who had therefore seen firsthand what enforcement of human rights law can accomplish.

20. "Freedom in the World 2018: Democracy in Crisis," Freedom House, accessed December 4, 2019. https://freedomhouse.org/report /freedom-world/freedom-world-2018.

21. Notably and perhaps most controversially, Harvard professor of psychology Steven Pinker in *The Better Angels of Our Nature: Why Violence Has Declined* (New York: Viking, 2011).

22. Stephen Hopgood, *The Endtimes of Human Rights* (Ithaca, NY: Cornell University Press, 2013); Eric Posner, *The Twilight of Human Rights Law* (New York: Oxford University Press, 2014).

23. Marina Lostal, "The ICC Convicts Al Mahdi for the Destruction of Cultural Heritage in Mali," Global Policy Forum, October 19, 2016, https://www.globalpolicy.org/home/52882-the-icc-convicts-al-mahdi -for-the-destruction-of-cultural-heritage-in-mali-.html.

24. John Vidal and Owen Bowcott, "ICC Widens Remit to Include Environmental Destruction Cases," *Guardian,* September 15, 2016, https://www.theguardian.com/global/2016/sep/15/hague-court -widens-remit-to-include-environmental-destruction-cases.

25. Office of the High Commissioner for Human Rights, "Core Human Rights in the Two Covenants," Global Alliance of National Human

Rights Institutes, September 2013, http://nhri.ohchr.org/EN/IHRS
/TreatyBodies/Page%20Documents/Core%20Human%20Rights.pdf.

26. "Britain's Strong, New £5 Note Isn't Completely Meat-Free," *New York Times,* December 1, 2016.

27. "Nebraska," Dumb Laws (website), 2019, http://www.dumblaws.com
/random-laws.

28. "The Core International Human Rights Instruments and Their
Monitoring Bodies," Office of the High Commissioner for Human
Rights, 2019, http://www.ohchr.org/EN/ProfessionalInterest/Pages
/CoreInstruments.aspx. The core instruments, in addition to the
so-called International Bill of Rights, which consists of the UDHR,
the International Covenant on Civil and Political Rights, and the
International Covenant on Economic, Social and Cultural Rights,
relate to racial discrimination; women's rights; torture and cruel,
inhuman, and degrading treatment; children's rights; protection of
migrant workers; forced disappearances; and the rights of people
with disabilities.

29. It's not clear as of this writing how Brexit may affect the United
Kingdom's relationship with the European Court of Human Rights.

30. Atkins v. Virginia, 536 U.S. 304 (2002); Roper v. Simmons, 543 U.S. 551
(2005).

31. For a description of how transnational activist networks influence
human rights change, see Margaret Keck and Kathryn Sikkink,
*Activists beyond Borders* (Ithaca, NY: Cornell University Press, 1998).

32. "Where Do Human Rights Begin?," Facing History and Ourselves,
2019, https://www.facinghistory.org/universal-declaration-human
-rights/where-do-human-rights-begin.

33. Public Facilities Privacy and Security Act, H.B. 2, General Assembly
of North Carolina 2016 Extra Session 2, http://www.ncleg.net
/sessions/2015e2/bills/house/pdf/h2v4.pdf.

34. Mark Scott, "Google Fined in France over 'Right to Be Forgotten,'"
*New York Times,* March 25, 2016.

35. Margaret Talbot, "Taking Trolls to Court," *New Yorker,* December 5,
2016.

36. Nick Wingfield, Mike Isaac, and Katie Benner, "Google and Facebook
Take Aim at Fake News Sites," *New York Times,* November 14, 2016.

37. Mike Isaac, "For Facebook, Censorship Tool Could Reopen a Door to
China," *New York Times,* November 23, 2016.

38. Maud Newton, "America's Ancestry Craze," *Harper's Magazine,* June 2014, 33.
39. Diana Brazzell, "Who Owns Your Genes?," *HuffPost,* October 27, 2015, http://www.huffingtonpost.com/footnote/who-owns-your-genes_b _8392556.html.
40. Michael Ignatieff, "Revolutionary Dreams," *New York Times Book Review,* May 22, 2016, 24.

## 1. Why Rights Change

1. Aristotle, *Rhetoric,* Book 1, Chapter 15.
2. Page DuBois, *Torture and Truth* (London: Routledge, 1991).
3. Jacques Maritain, *Introduction to Human Rights: Comments and Interpretations* (New York: Allan Wingate, 1949), 9.
4. Genesis 1:26.
5. Matthew 25:35–40.
6. Surah 15:28–29.
7. "Major Religions of the World Ranked by Number of Adherents," Adherents.com, last updated 2014, http://www.adherents.com /Religions_By_Adherents.html.
8. Tom Heneghan, "'No Religion' Third World Group after Christians, Muslims," *Reuters,* December 18, 2012, https://www.reuters.com /article/us-religion-world/no-religion-third-world-group-after -christians-muslims-idUSBRE8BH0KG20121218.
9. Richard Rorty, "Human Rights, Rationality, and Sentimentality," in *On Human Rights,* ed. Stephen Shute and Susan Hurley (New York: Basic Books, 1993), 115.
10. Hugo Grotius, Prolegomena to *On Laws of War and Peace,* in *The Human Rights Reader,* ed. Micheline R. Ishay (New York: Routledge, 1997), 73.
11. Thomas Hobbes, *The Leviathan,* in *The Human Rights Reader,* 84.
12. Popularized, for example, in Richard Dawkins's best-selling book *The Selfish Gene* (Oxford: Oxford University Press, 1976).
13. Herbert Gintis, "Human Rights: An Evolutionary Perspective," in *Understanding Social Action, Promoting Human Rights,* ed. Ryan Goodman, Derek Jinks, and Andrew K. Woods (Oxford: Oxford University Press, 2012).

14. Francis Fukuyama, "Natural Rights and Human History," *The National Interest,* Summer 2001.
15. Thomas Jefferson, *Notes on the State of Virginia* (Philadelphia: Prichard and Hall, 1788), Query XIV, https://docsouth.unc.edu /southlit/jefferson/jefferson.html.
16. David Boucher, *The Limits of Ethics in International Relations: Natural Law, Natural Rights and Human Rights in Transition* (Oxford: Oxford University Press, 2009), 333.
17. Fukuyama, "Natural Rights and Human History." It is ironic that if anything would seem to be a natural law, it would be the need for food, water, and shelter, but such economic rights are exactly what those that conservatives like Fukuyama are most prone to dismiss.
18. Catherine A. MacKinnon, "Crimes of War, Crimes of Peace," in *On Human Rights,* 97.
19. Robin Fox, "Human Nature and Human Rights," *National Interest,* Winter 2000–2001.
20. Fukuyama, "Natural Rights and Human History."
21. Carlo Rovelli, *Seven Brief Lessons on Physics* (New York: Riverhead Books, 2016), 67.
22. John Rawls, *The Law of Peoples* (Cambridge, MA: Harvard University Press, 1999), 50.
23. Martha Nussbaum, *Creating Capabilities: The Human Development Approach* (Cambridge, MA: Harvard University Press, 2011), 31.
24. Richard Rorty, "Solidarity," in *Contingency, Irony and Solidarity* (New York: Cambridge University Press, 1989).
25. Charles Murray and Richard J. Herrnstein, *The Bell Curve: Intelligence and Class Structure in American Life* (New York: The Free Press, 1994).
26. Nussbaum, *Creating Capabilities,* 32.
27. Kathryn Sikkink, conversation with authors, December 2, 2016.
28. That civilian immunity is more and more frequently breached is demonstrated by the fact that in World War I, 15 percent of casualties were civilian, whereas in the Korean War it was 84 percent, in the Vietnam War 90 percent, and in the Rwandan genocide well over that ("Impact of Armed Conflict on Children," UNICEF, accessed March 19, 2019, https://www.unicef.org/graca/patterns.htm).
29. Michael Walzer, *Just and Unjust Wars* (New York: Basic Books, 1977), 131.
30. Walzer, *Just and Unjust Wars,* 195.

31. "Translated Excerpts from the Taliban Code of Conduct," *CNN*, July 30, 2009, http://edition.cnn.com/2009/WORLD/asiapcf/07/30/taliban.code.excerpt/index.html?iref=24hours.

32. Colm McKeogh, *Innocent Civilians: The Morality of Killing in War* (New York: Palgrave Macmillan, 2002), 23–24.

33. Celtic tribes had spared bards and poets in their enemy's camp in order that there be someone left alive to tell the story of their victory!

34. Richard Shelly Hartigan, *Civilian Victims in War: A Political History* (New Brunswick, NJ: Transaction Publishers, 2010), 112.

35. There is considerable scholarly disagreement about the reason women have frequently been listed as exempt from being targeted in war. James T. Johnson holds to the traditional view that, while women have sometimes engaged in military operations, they have usually been regarded as too weak to bear arms and hence restricted to "women's work" (James T. Johnson, "The Meaning of Non-combatant Immunity in the Just War / Limited War Tradition," *Journal of the American Academy of Religion* 39, no. 2 [June 1971]: 151–170). Helen Kinsella argues that children and the elderly, though also thought in medieval times not strong enough to bear arms, were regarded as potential adversaries, either because of their cunning in the first instance or their wise counsel in the second, and that women were excluded simply because of stereotypical assumptions based on gender (Helen Kinsella, *The Image before the Weapon: A Critical History of the Distinction between Combatant and Civilian* [Ithaca, NY: Cornell University Press, 2011]).

36. James Turner Johnson, *Just War Tradition and the Restraint of War* (Princeton, NJ: Princeton University Press, 1981), 121–171. See also Frederick H. Russell, *The Just War in the Middle Ages* (Cambridge, MA: Cambridge University Press, 1975), 16–27.

37. Colm McKeogh, "Civilian Immunity in War: From Augustine to Vattel," in *Civilian Immunity in War,* ed. Igor Primoratz (Oxford: Oxford University Press, 2007), 68–72.

38. McKeogh, *Innocent Civilians,* 116.

39. Johnson, "The Meaning of Non-combatant Immunity," 153.

40. Hartigan, *Civilian Victims in War,* 111.

41. Francis Lieber, *Instructions for the Government of Armies of the United States in the Field,* originally issued as "General Orders No. 100" (1863; repr., Washington, DC: Government Printing Office, 1898), Article 37, http://avalon.law.yale.edu/19th_century/lieber.asp.

42. The Hague, "Convention (II) with Respect to the Laws and Customs of War on Land," July 29, 1899, 32 Stat.1803, Treaty Series 403, Article 46, http://avalon.law.yale.edu/19th_century/hague02.asp.

43. International Committee of the Red Cross, "The Geneva Conventions of 1949 and Their Additional Protocols," October 29, 2010, https://www.icrc.org/eng/war-and-law/treaties-customary-law /geneva-conventions/overview-geneva-conventions.htm.

44. American Red Cross, "Summary of the Geneva Conventions of 1949 and Their Additional Protocols," April 2011, https://www.redcross .org/images/MEDIA_CustomProductCatalog/m3640104_IHL _SummaryGenevaConv.pdf.

45. Zhu Li-Sun, "Traditional Asian Approaches—The Chinese View," *Australian Year Book of International Law* 40 (1980).

46. "10 Islamic Rules of War," 100 Good Deeds, November 20, 2012, http://1000gooddeeds.com/2012/11/20/10-islamic-rules-of-war/.

47. International Committee of the Red Cross, *Protocols Additional to the Geneva Conventions of 12 August 1949* (Geneva: International Committee of the Red Cross, 2010), https://www.icrc.org/eng/assets/files /other/icrc_002_0321.pdf.

48. "St. Maximilian," Catholic Online, 2019, http://www.catholic.org /saints/saint.php?saint_id=5018.

49. McKeogh, *Innocent Civilians,* 19–22.

50. Hartigan, *Civilian Victims in War,* 55–77.

51. Rick Beard, "The Lieber Codes," *New York Times Opinionator* (blog), April 24, 2013, https://opinionator.blogs.nytimes.com/2013/04/24/the -lieber-codes/; McKeogh, *Innocent Civilians,* 124; The Hague, Convention (IV) Respecting the Laws and Customs of War on Land, October 18, 1907, 36 Stat. 2277, Treaty Series 539, Article 23, http://avalon.law.yale.edu/20th _century/hague04.asp; Walzer, *Just and Unjust Wars,* 253–254. After the German raid on Coventry in 1940, British bombers were instructed to "aim at the center of a [German] city," not restricting themselves to military or industrial targets, in order to terrorize the civilian population and destroy its morale. Working-class residences were to be the prime target with a goal of rendering one-third of the people homeless.

52. International Campaign to Ban Landmines, "The Treaty," 2019, http://www.icbl.org/en-gb/the-treaty.aspx.

53. International Committee of the Red Cross, Geneva Convention (IV) Relative to the Protection of Civilian Persons in Time of War,

August 12, 1949, Article 27, International Committee of the Red Cross Treaties, State Parties, and Commentaries database, https://ihl -databases.icrc.org/applic/ihl/ihl.nsf/Article.xsp?action =openDocument&documentId=FFCB180D4E99CB26C12563CD0051BB D9; Lindsey Crider, "Rape as a War Crime and Crime against Humanity: The Effect of Rape in Bosnia-Herzegovina and Rwanda on International Law," prepared for the Alabama Political Science Association Conference, Auburn University, Auburn, Alabama, March 30–31, 2012, p. 2, http://www.cla.auburn.edu/alapsa/assets/file/4ccrider.pdf.

54. Beverly Allen, *Rape Warfare: The Hidden Genocide in Bosnia-Herzegovina and Croatia* (Minneapolis: University of Minnesota Press, 1996), 457.

55. Caroline Kennedy-Pipe and Penny Stanley, "Rape in War: Lessons of the Balkan Conflicts in the 1990s," in *The Kosovo Tragedy,* ed. Ken Booth (Portland, OR: Frank Cass, 2000), 67–83.

56. Human Rights Watch, *Shattered Lives: Sexual Violence during the Rwandan Genocide and Its Aftermath* (Washington, DC: Human Rights Watch, 1996), https://www.hrw.org/reports/1996/Rwanda.htm.

57. David Russell, "Statistics," Survivors Fund, October 19, 2009, http://survivors-fund.org.uk/resources/rwandan-history/statistics/.

58. Johnson, *Just War Tradition,* 150.

59. National Association of the Deaf v. Netflix, Inc., 869 F. Supp. 2d 196 (D. Mass., 2012).

60. Sankalan Baidya, "Viśpálā—The Legendary Warrior Queen from Rig Veda," Facts Legend, June 20, 2015, http://factslegend.org/vispala-the -legendary-warrior-queen-from-rig-veda/.

61. Edwin Black, "The Horrifying American Roots of Nazi Eugenics," History News Network, September 2003, http://historynewsnetwork .org/article/1796.

62. Carol Poore, *Disability in Twentieth-Century German Culture* (Ann Arbor: University of Michigan Press, 2007), 277.

63. Richard K. Scotch, "Politics and Policy in the History of the Disability Rights Movement," *Milbank Quarterly* 67, no. 2 (1989): 380–400.

64. For a comprehensive history of the disability movement in the United States, see Doris Zames Fleischcher and Freida Zames, *The Disability Rights Movement: From Charity to Confrontation* (Philadelphia: Temple University Press, 2001) and Jacqueline Vaughn Switzer, *Disabled Rights: American Policy and the Fight for Equality* (Washington, DC: Georgetown University Press, 2003).

65. Swantje Köbsell, "Toward Self-Determination and Equalization: A Short History of the German Disability Rights Movement," *Disability Studies Quarterly* 26, no. 2 (2006), http://dsq-sds.org/article/view/692 /869; "Union of the Physically Impaired against Segregation," Encyclopaedia Britannica, accessed March 19, 2019, https://www .britannica.com/topic/Union-of-the-Physically-Impaired-Against -Segregation.

66. Martand Jha, "The History of India's Disability Rights Movement," *The Diplomat,* December 21, 2016, http://thediplomat.com/2016/12/the -history-of-indias-disability-rights-movement/.

67. Melissa Denchak, "Flint Water Crisis: Everything You Need to Know," Natural Resources Defense Council, November 8, 2018, https://www .nrdc.org/stories/flint-water-crisis-everything-you-need-know.

## 2. Beyond Pink and Blue

1. Will Oremus, "Here Are All the Different Genders You Can Be on Facebook," *Slate,* February 13, 2014, http://www.slate.com/blogs /future_tense/2014/02/13/facebook_custom_gender_options_here _are_all_56_custom_options.html.

2. Maya Salam, "Mattel, Maker of Barbie, Debuts Gender-Neutral Dolls," *New York Times*, September 25, 2019, https://www.nytimes.com/2019 /09/25/arts/mattel-gender-neutral-dolls.html.

3. Martha Nussbaum, *Creating Capabilities: The Human Development Approach* (Cambridge, MA: Harvard University Press, 2011), 31.

4. This chapter does not, for example, address conversion therapy in which "therapists" or spiritual counselors attempt to change one's sexual orientation, mostly because it has been so widely discredited. It does not delve into the treatment of LGBTI prisoners, either with regard to body searches, housing, or medical treatment, even though the U.N. Standard Minimum Rules for the Treatment of Prisoners does not explicitly mention them (text of the Standard Minimum Rules available at https://www.penalreform.org/resource/standard -minimum-rules-treatment-prisoners-smr/). It does not reference the controversies over intersex athletes (see, e.g., Jeré Longman, "Understanding the Controversy over Caster Semenya," *New York Times,* August 18, 2016) and will not touch at all upon the question of

whether there is or ought to be a right to sexuality, which might entail addressing such matters as polyamory (for a groundbreaking look at prospective rights to "sexual citizenship," see International Council on Human Rights Policy, *Sexuality and Human Rights: Discussion Paper* [Versoix, Switzerland: International Council on Human Rights Policy, 2009], http://www.ichrp.org/files/reports/47/137_web.pdf).

5. International Lesbian, Gay, Bisexual, Trans and Intersex Association, "IGLA Releases Global Research of Attitudes toward LGBTI People," May 17, 2016, http://ilga.org/global-survey-attitudes-lgbti-riwi-logo/.

6. "Sexual preference" is different from "sexual orientation" and refers to the particular types of sexual gratification one prefers.

7. A "Q" referring to "queer" is often added to the acronym "LGBTI"; Sam Killermann describes "queer" as "an umbrella term to describe individuals who don't identify as straight . . . who have a non-normative gender identity, or as a political affiliation." See "Comprehensive List of LGBTQ+ Vocabulary Definitions," accessed March 20, 2019, http://itspronouncedmetrosexual.com/2013/01/a-comprehensive-list-of-lgbtq-term-definitions/#sthash.7R3WWsVF.dpbs.

8. Katy Steinmetz, *Time*, March 27, 2017. Kate Bornstein's 1994 coming-of-age story *Gender Outlaw: On Men, Women and the Rest of Us* (New York: Vintage Books), reissued in 2016, has been credited by Jennifer Finney Boylan with "populariz[ing] the idea that gender isn't a binary" ("The Best Draft of the Self," *New York Times Book Review*, June 18, 2017). There have been many more such memoirs of trans and gender fluid individuals since then, including, notably, Finney Boylan's own *She's Not There: A Life in Two Genders* (New York: Broadway Books, 2003).

9. Anne Fausto-Sterling, *Sex/Gender: Biology in a Social World* (Abingdon, U.K.: Routledge, 2012), 13.

10. Ian Buruma, "The 'Indescribable Fragrance' of Youths," *New York Review of Books*, May 11, 2017. Such gender-bending identities have been common throughout history from the *hijiras* in India, mentioned earlier, to Native American "two spirit" people who can see the world through both male and female eyes and often dress accordingly, to the twentieth-century Czech artist Toyen, born Marie

Cerminova, who purposely cast aside femininity in order to succeed in the male-dominated art world (see Karla Tonine Huebner, "Eroticism, Identity, and Cultural Context: Toyen and the Prague Avant-Garde" [PhD diss, University of Pittsburgh, 2009], http://d-scholarship.pitt.edu/10323/).

11. Raillan Brooks, "'He,' 'She,' 'They' and Us," *New York Times,* April 5, 2017.

12. Article 16 reads "Men and women . . . have the right to marry and found a family. They are entitled to equal rights." It is true that the UDHR guarantees all rights "without distinction of any kind, such as . . . sex . . . or other status" and activists have often claimed that "sex" and / or "other status" includes all gender identities and sexual orientations, though that is unlikely the interpretation the declaration's authors had in mind.

13. *Convention on the Elimination of All Forms of Discrimination against Women,* Article 2C, New York, 18 December 1979, *United Nations Treaty Series,* vol. 1249, p. 13, available at https://treaties.un.org/doc/Treaties/1981/09/19810903%2005-18%20AM/Ch_IV_8p.pdf.

14. Council of Europe, "France: Judges Reject Same-Sex Marriage Human Rights Complaint," June 10, 2016, http://www.humanrightseurope.org/2016/06/france-judges-reject-same-sex-marriage-human-rights-complaint/.

15. "Who Can Adopt?," RainbowKids Adoption and Child Welfare Advocacy, last updated 2014, http://www.rainbowkids.com/adoption/who-can-adopt.

16. "What Is Gender-Based Violence?," European Institute for Gender Equality, 2019, http://eige.europa.eu/gender-based-violence/what-is-gender-based-violence. In addition, Lara Stemple of the University of California, Los Angeles School of Law, former executive director of Just Detention International, has argued that "gender-based violence" is rarely considered to include violence against males despite the fact that "3% of men worldwide have been raped in their lifetime," often in detention or wartime circumstances ("Male Rape and Human Rights," *Hastings Law Journal* 60, no. 605 [2009]).

17. See, for example, U.N. Office of the High Commissioner of Human Rights, "Born Free and Equal: Sexual Orientation and Gender Identity in International Human Rights Law" (New York and Geneva: United Nations, 2012).

18. Siobhan Fenton, "LGBT Relationships Are Illegal in 74 Countries, Research Finds," *The Independent,* May 17, 2016, http://www.independent .co.uk/news/world/gay-lesbian-bisexual-relationships-illegal-in-74 -countries-a7033666.html.

19. Ekaterina Sokirianskaia, "Chechnya's Anti-gay Pogrom," *New York Times,* May 3, 2017.

20. Omar G. Encarnacion, "The Global Backlash against Gay Rights," *Foreign Affairs,* May 2, 2017.

21. United Nations Development Programme, "Discussion Paper on Transgender Health and Human Rights" (New York: 2013), 9, http://www.undp.org/content/undp/en/home/librarypage/hiv-aids /discussion-paper-on-transgender-health—human-rights.html.

22. Human Rights Campaign, "Violence against the Transgender Community in 2016," accessed March 20, 2019, http://www.hrc.org /resources/violence-against-the-transgender-community-in-2016; and see Jamai Lewis, "The Thrill and Fear of 'Hey, Beautiful,'" *New York Times,* July 1, 2017. Some U.S. states, such as West Virginia, still do not include attacks based on sexual orientation in their hate crimes law ("Anti-gay Attacks Not Covered by West Virginia Hate Crime Law, Court Rues," *New York Times,* May 13, 2017).

23. United Nations OHCHR, "Born Free and Equal."

24. Pew Research Center, "Support for Same-Sex Marriage Grows, Even among Groups That Had Been Skeptical," June 26, 2017, http://www .people-press.org/2017/06/26/support-for-same-sex-marriage-grows -even-among-groups-that-had-been-skeptical/.

25. Julie Ray, "Reflections on the 'Trouble in Little Rock,' Part II," *Gallup,* March 4, 2003, http://news.gallup.com/poll/7900/reflections-trouble -little-rock-part.aspx.

26. Martin Luther King Jr., "Letter from a Birmingham Jail," April 16, 1963, https://www.africa.upenn.edu/Articles_Gen/Letter_Birmingham .html.

27. Theresa Papademetriou, "European Court of Human Rights: Decision on Gay Marriage in Italy," Global Legal Monitor, Library of Congress, September 4, 2015, http://www.loc.gov/law/foreign -news/article/european-court-of-human-rights-decision-on-gay -marriage-in-italy/.

28. Claire Poppelwell-Scevak, "The European Court of Human Rights and Same-Sex Marriage: The Consensus Approach" (master's thesis,

University of Oslo, 2016), http://www.jus.uio.no/pluricourts/english
/publications/2016/2016-09-23-poppelwell-thesis.html.

29. Pew Research Center, "Same Sex-Marriage around the World,"
    October 28, 2019, https://www.pewforum.org/fact-sheet/gay
    -marriage-around-the-world/.

30. Pew Research Center, "Gay Marriage around the World," last
    updated June 30, 2017, http://www.pewforum.org/2017/06/30/gay
    -marriage-around-the-world-2013/.

31. "Russia's Putin Signs Anti-U.S. Adoption Bill," *CNN*, December 28,
    2012, http://www.cnn.com/2012/12/28/world/europe/russia-us
    -adoptions/index.html.

32. "Surveillance," International Federation of Fertility Societies,
    accessed March 20, 2019, http://www.iffs-reproduction.org/?page
    =Surveillance.

33. To say nothing of couples in which one or both partners is trans or
    intersex—or of single people of every gender or sexual orientation.

34. Mollie Reilly, "Same-Sex Couples Can Now Adopt Children in All 50
    States," *HuffPost*, March 31, 2016, http://www.huffingtonpost.com/entry
    /mississippi-same-sex-adoption_us_56fdb1a3e4b083f5c607567f. Some
    states still allow adoption agencies with religious objections to be
    exempt from that ban and second-parent adoptions are not always easy
    (Elizabeth A. Harris, "Same-Sex Parents Still Face Legal Complications,"
    *New York Times,* June 20, 2017). By the estimate of the Williams Institute
    of the University of California, Los Angeles School of Law, which
    specializes in gender issues, as of 2015 some 210,000 children were
    being raised by same-sex married couples in the United States. Of these,
    58,000 were adopted or foster children ("700,000 Americans Are Married
    to a Same-Sex Spouse, Married Same-Sex Couples More Likely to Raise
    Adopted, Foster Children and Are More Economically Secure, New
    Reports Show," Williams Institute, March 5, 2015, https://williamsinstitute
    .law.ucla.edu/press/press-releases/married-same-sex-couples-more
    -likely-to-raise-adopted-foster-children-and-have-more-economic
    -resources-new-reports-show/).

35. "LGBT Adoption," Wikipedia, last updated April 24, 2019, https://en
    .wikipedia.org/wiki/LGBT_adoption.

36. "Countries That Allow for International Adoptions by LGBT
    Prospective Parents," Next Family, August 18, 2016, http://

thenextfamily.com/2016/08/countries-that-allow-for-international
-adoptions-by-lgbt-prospective-parents/.

37. Ananyo Bhattacharya, "Human-Rights Court Orders World's Last
    IVF Ban to Be Lifted," *Nature News Blog*, December 28, 2012, http://
    blogs.nature.com/news/2012/12/human-rights-court-orders-worlds
    -last-ivf-ban-to-be-lifted.html.

38. International Federation of Fertility Societies, "IFFS Surveillance
    2016," *Global Reproductive Health* 1, no. 1 (September 2016): 1–143.

39. National LGBT Health Education Center, "Pathways to Parenthood
    for LGBT People" (Boston: Fenway Institute, 2016), https://www
    .lgbthealtheducation.org/wp-content/uploads/Pathways-to
    -Parenthood-for-LGBT-People.pdf; Dov Fox and I. Glenn Cohen, "It's
    Time for the U.S. to Cover IVF (for Gays and Lesbians Too)," *HuffPost*,
    March 18, 2013, http://www.huffingtonpost.com/dov-fox/it-is-time
    -for-the-us-to-_b_2900323.html.

40. Frank Browning, *The Fate of Gender: Nature, Nurture and the Human
    Future* (New York: Bloomsbury USA, 2016), 152–153.

41. Liz Bishop and Bebe Loff, "Making Surrogacy Legal Would Violate
    Children's Rights," The Conversation, August 20, 2014, http://
    theconversation.com/making-surrogacy-legal-would-violate
    -childrens-rights-30716.

42. Ronli Sifris, "Commercial Surrogacy and the Human Right to
    Autonomy," *Journal of Law and Medicine* 23, no. 2 (2015): 365–377.

43. See Caitlyn Jenner, *The Secrets of My Life* (New York: Grand Central
    Publishing, 2017) and Matthew Shaer, "Becoming Chelsea Manning,"
    *New York Times Magazine*, June 18, 2017. Before them came such
    figures as musician Chaz Bono, tennis star Renee Richards, travel
    writer Jan Morris, and Christine Jorgenson, the first person widely
    known in the United States to have had sex reassignment surgery, a
    procedure carried out in Denmark in 1951.

44. Amanda Michelle Steiner, "Tony Award Winners 2014—Full List,"
    Hollywood Life, June 8, 2014, http://hollywoodlife.com/2014/06/08
    /tony-award-winners-2014-tonys-winner-list/.

45. "The Transgender Tipping Point," *Time*, June 9, 2014.

46. "The Gender Revolution," *National Geographic*, January 2017.

47. Alyson Krueger, "Transgender Models Find a Home," *New York Times*,
    March 4, 2017.

48. Motoko Rich, "Japanese Transgender Politician Is Showing 'I Exist Here,'" *New York Times,* May 19, 2017.
49. Carol Lynn Martin and Diane N. Ruble, "Patterns of Gender Development," *Annual Review of Psychology* 61 (2010): 353–381.
50. "Varied Views of Gender," *New York Times,* January 24, 2017.
51. Interestingly enough, the policy of the Girl Scouts of the USA is that "if the child is recognized by the family and school/community as a girl and lives culturally as a girl, then Girl Scouts is an organization that can serve her in a setting that is both emotionally and physically safe" (Daniel Victor, "Transgender Boy Is Told to Leave the Cub Scouts," *New York Times,* December 30, 2016).
52. Sophie Lewis, "World Health Organization Removes 'Gender Identity Disorder' from List of Mental Illnesses," *CBS News,* May 29, 2019, https://www.cbsnews.com/news/world-health-organization-removes-gender-dysphoria-from-list-of-mental-illnesses/.
53. "Varied Views."
54. Degner and Nomanni, "Pathologization."
55. Jack Turban, "How Doctors Help Transgender Kids Thrive," *New York Times,* April 8, 2017.
56. Ann P. Haas, Philip L. Rodgers, and Jody L. Herman, *Suicide Attempts among Transgender and Gender Non-conforming Adults: Findings of the National Transgender Discrimination Survey* (Los Angeles: Williams Institute, 2014), https://williamsinstitute.law.ucla.edu/wp-content/uploads/AFSP-Williams-Suicide-Report-Final.pdf.
57. Ross Toro, "How Gender Reassignment Surgery Works (Infographic)," *Live Science,* August 26, 2013, https://www.livescience.com/39170-how-gender-reassignment-surgery-works-infographic.html.
58. Neela Ghoshal and Kyle Knight, "Rights in Transition: Making Legal Recognition for Transgender People a Global Priority," in *World Report 2016* (New York: Human Rights Watch, 2016), https://www.hrw.org/world-report/2016/rights-in-transition.
59. M. Dru Levasseur, "Gender Identity Defines Sex: Updating the Law to Reflect Modern Medical Science Is Key to Transgender Rights," *Vermont Law Review* 39, no. 4 (2015): 943–1004.
60. Holly Young, "Trans Rights: Meet the Face of Nepal's Progressive 'Third Gender' Movement," *Guardian,* February 12, 2016, https://www.theguardian.com/global-development-professionals

-network/2016/feb/12/trans-rights-meet-the-face-of-nepals
-progressive-third-gender-movement.

61. S. J. Langer, "Our Body Project: From Mourning to Creating the Transgender Body," *International Journal of Transgenderism* 15, no. 2 (2014): 66–75.

62. Young, "Trans Rights."

63. Andy Newman, "Male? Female? Or 'X'? Drive for a Third Choice on Government Forms," *New York Times,* September 27, 2018.

64. Kristian Foden-Vencil, "The Medical Pros and Cons of Suppressing Puberty in Transgender Teens," *Oregon Public Broadcasting,* March 26, 2015, http://www.opb.org/news/article/the-medical-pros
-and-cons-of-suppressing-puberty-in-transgender-teens/.

65. "Varied Views."

66. Riemer's story is told in John Colapinto, *As Nature Made Him: The Boy Who Was Raised as a Girl* (New York: Harper's, 2000).

67. Leonard Sax, "How Common Is Intersex? A Response to Anne Fausto-Sterling," *Journal of Sex Research* 39, no. 3 (2002): 174–178. It has recently been discovered that Casimir Pulaski, often called the "father of the American cavalry" was probably intersex (see Sarah Mervosh, "Casimir Pulaski, Polish Hero of the Revolutionary War, Was Most Likely Intersex, Researchers Say," *New York Times,* April 7, 2019).

68. Anne Tamar-Mattis, "Exceptions to the Rule: Curing the Law's Failure to Protect Intersex Infants," *Berkeley Journal of Gender, Law & Justice* 21 (2006): 59–110.

69. Sylvan Fraser, "Constructing the Female Body: Using Female Genital Mutilation Law to Address Genital-Normalizing Surgery on Intersex Children in the United States," *International Journal of Human Rights in Healthcare* 9, no. 1 (2016): 66–72.

70. Council of Europe Commissioner for Human Rights, *Human Rights and Intersex People: Issue Paper* (Strasbourg, France: Council of Europe, 2015), https://book.coe.int/eur/en/commissioner-for-human
-rights/6683-pdf-human-rights-and-intersex-people.html.

71. Council of Europe, *Human Rights and Intersex People,* 37; Melissa Eddy, "Not Male or Female? Germans Can Now Choose 'Diverse,'" *New York Times,* December 14, 2018.

72. Morgan Carpenter, "UN Special Rapporteur on Torture Calls for an End to Coerced and Involuntary Genital-Normalising Surgeries,"

Intersex Human Rights Australia, February 7, 2013, https://oii.org.au/21687/coerced-normalizing-treatment-torture/.

73. Author Schulz conversation with Kyle Knight of Human Rights Watch, May 22, 2017; Council of Europe, *Human Rights and Intersex People.*

74. Charlotte Greenfield, "Should We 'Fix' Intersex Children?," *Atlantic Monthly,* July 8, 2014.

75. Author Schulz conversation with Justus Eisfeld, June 28, 2017; Meka Beresford, "Sweden to Offer $26,000 Compensation to Trans People Who Were Legally Forced into Sterilisation," *PinkNews,* March 26, 2017, http://www.pinknews.co.uk/2017/03/26/sweden-to-offer-26000-compensation-to-trans-people-who-were-legally-forced-into-sterilisation/.

76. Heath Fogg Davis, *Beyond Trans: Does Gender Matter?* (New York: New York University Press, 2017).

77. Spencer Kornhaber, "RuPaul Gets Political," *The Atlantic,* June 2017.

78. Quoted in Leopoldine Core, "Risk and Reward," *New York Times Book Review,* May 7, 2017.

79. Anna Merlan, "Trans-Excluding Michigan Womyn's Music Festival to End This Year," *Jezebel,* April 22, 2015, http://jezebel.com/trans-excluding-michigan-womyns-music-festival-to-end-t-1699412910.

80. Susan Cox, "Coming Out as 'Non-binary' Throws Other Women under the Bus," *Feminist Current* (blog), August 10, 2016, http://www.feministcurrent.com/2016/08/10/coming-non-binary-throws-women-bus/.

81. Cathy Perifimos, "The Changing Faces of Women's Colleges: Striking a Balance between Transgender Rights and Women's Colleges' Right to Exclude," *Cardozo Journal of Law & Gender* 15 (2008): 141–721.

82. Author Schulz conversations with Kathy Kaufmann, Wellesley trustee (April 3, 2017), and professors Charlene Galarneau (May 8, 2017) and Catia Confortini (May 10, 2017).

83. "Mission and Gender Policy," Wellesley College, accessed March 20, 2019, http://www.wellesley.edu/news/gender-policy#fyK2UkOZeHffUR7b.97.

84. *Convention on the Rights of the Child*, Article 7, New York, 20 November 1989, *United Nations Treaty Series*, vol. 1577, p. 3, available at https://treaties.un.org/doc/Treaties/1990/09/19900902%2003-14%20AM/Ch_IV_11p.pdf.

85. "Victims of Sexual Violence: Statistics," Rape, Abuse and Incest National Network, 2019, https://www.rainn.org/statistics/victims -sexual-violence.

86. Toonen v. Australia, Communication No. 488 / 1992, U.N. Doc CCPR / C / 50 / D/488/1992 (1994), http://hrlibrary.umn.edu/undocs /html/vws488.htm.

87. As long ago as 1991, a proposal was circulated in the newsletter of the International Foundation for Gender Education for the creation of a "Gender Bill of Rights." Five years later the International Conference on Transgender Law and Employment Policy adopted an "International Bill of Gender Rights" that articulated the rights of all people, among other things, to define their own gender identity "regardless of chromosomal sex, genitalia, assigned birth sex or initial gender role"; enter into marital contracts; conceive, bear, and adopt children; and "change [one's body] cosmetically, chemically or surgically, so as to express a self-defined gender identity." Because the conference was a private gathering of largely American lawyers, educators, and activists, its impact was limited (see "History of the International Bill of Gender Rights," International Bill of Gender Rights, Transgender Legal, last updated January 21, 2001, http://www.transgenderlegal.com/ibgr .htm).

88. That action and others were prompted by the adoption of the first comprehensive statement of rights related to gender minorities at the global level. Called the Yogyakarta Principles after the Indonesian city where a consultation of human rights experts from twenty-five countries took place, the statement addressed many issues of discrimination but did not call for a right to same-sex marriage or consider explicitly most of the issues described in this chapter ("Principle 24: The Right to Found a Family," ARC International, http://www.yogyakartaprinciples.org/principle-24).

89. "Argentina Gender Identity Law," Country Information, Transgender Europe, September 12, 2013, http://tgeu.org/argentina-gender -identity-law/.

90. "Human Rights Victory! European Court of Human Rights Ends Forced Sterilisation," Transgender Europe, April 6, 2017, http://tgeu .org/echr_end-sterilisation/.

91. It was even controversial when then-U.N. Secretary General Ban Ki-moon extended health benefits to the spouses of gay and lesbian

United Nations employees (see Reid Standish, "U.N. Extends Marriage Benefits to Gay Employees," *Foreign Policy,* July 8, 2014, http://foreignpolicy.com/2014/07/08/u-n-extends-marriage-benefits-to-gay-employees/).

92. United Nations OHCHR, "Born Free and Equal," 10.
93. Annette Gorden-Reed, "Sally Hemings, Thomas Jefferson and the Ways We Talk about Our Past," *New York Times Book Review,* September 24, 2017.
94. Ben Hubbard, "Saudi Arabia Agrees to Let Women Drive," *New York Times,* September 26, 2017.
95. Quoted in Jonathan Mirsky, "The True Story of Izzy," *New York Review of Books,* September 24, 2009.

### 3. Here's Looking at You

1. American Civil Liberties Union, "Surveillance under the Patriot Act," accessed April 2, 2019, https://www.aclu.org/issues/national-security/privacy-and-surveillance/surveillance-under-patriot-act.
2. Natasha Singer, "Mapping, and Sharing, the Consumer Genome," *New York Times,* June 16, 2012.
3. Singer, "Consumer Genome."
4. "What We Do," Acxiom, accessed April 2, 2019, https://www.acxiom.com/what-we-do/consumer-segmentation-personicx/.
5. Samuel D. Warren and Louis D. Brandeis, "The Right to Privacy," *Harvard Law Review* 4, no. 5 (1890): 193–220.
6. Nina Totenberg, "Supreme Court Hears Case on Cell Phone Location Information," *National Public Radio,* November 29, 2017, https://www.npr.org/2017/11/29/567313569/supreme-court-hears-case-on-cell-phone-location-information.
7. Adam Liptak, "In Ruling on Cellphone Location Data, Supreme Court Makes Statement on Digital Privacy," *New York Times*, June 22, 2018, https://www.nytimes.com/2018/06/22/us/politics/supreme-court-warrants-cell-phone-privacy.html.
8. Carpenter v. United States, 585 U.S., No. 16-402 (June 22, 2018).
9. Alana Semuels, "Tracking Workers' Every Move Can Boost Productivity—and Stress," *LA Times,* April 8, 2013.

10. American Association for the Advancement of Science, "What Are Geospatial Technologies," accessed April 2, 2019, https://www.aaas.org/content/what-are-geospatial-technologies.

11. Monte Reel, "Secret Cameras Record Baltimore's Every Move from Above," *Bloomberg Businessweek,* August 23, 2016.

12. Reel, "Secret Cameras."

13. Jefferson Graham and Laura Schulte, "Wisconsin Workers Embedded with Microchips," *USA Today,* August 1, 2017.

14. "FDA Approves Pill with Digital Tracking Device You Swallow," *CNN,* November 15, 2017.

15. Alessandro Acquisiti, "Why Privacy Matters," filmed June 2013 at TEDGlobal, https://www.ted.com/talks/alessandro_acquisti_why_privacy_matters.

16. Alvaro Bedoya, "Who Owns Your Face?," *USA Today,* March 24, 2017.

17. Shweta Banerjee, "Aadhaar: Digital Inclusion and Public Services in India," *World Development Report 2016,* World Bank, 2, http://pubdocs.worldbank.org/en/655801461250682317/WDR16-BP-Aadhaar-Paper-Banerjee.pdf.

18. Banerjee, "Aadhaar," 4.

19. The Constitution of India, Art. 21, 26 January 1950, available at: https://www.india.gov.in/my-government/constitution-india/constitution-india-full-text; Julie McCarthy, "Indian Supreme Court Declares Privacy a Fundamental Right," *National Public Radio,* August 24, 2017, https://www.npr.org/sections/thetwo-way/2017/08/24/545963181/indian-supreme-court-declares-privacy-a-fundamental-right.

20. Manveena Suri, "Aadhaar: India Supreme Court Upholds Controversial Biometric Database," *CNN,* September 26, 2018, https://www.cnn.com/2018/09/26/asia/india-aadhaar-ruling-intl/index.html.

21. Vidhi Doshi, "India's Top Court Upholds World's Largest Biometric ID Program, within Limits," *Washington Post,* September 26, 2018.

22. "Aadhaar Not Mandatory for Opening Bank Account," *Business Insider India,* June 13, 2019.

23. Michelle FlorCruz, "China to Use Big Data to Rate Citizens in New Social Credit System," *Business Insider,* April 28, 2015, http://www.businessinsider.com/china-to-use-big-data-to-rate-citizens-in-new-social-credit-system-2015–4.

24. Rogier Creemers, "Planning Outline for the Construction of a Social Credit System," *China Copyright and Media* (blog), April 25, 2015,

https://chinacopyrightandmedia.wordpress.com/2014/06/14
/planning-outline-for-the-construction-of-a-social-credit-system
-2014–2020/.

25. "China to Bar People with Bad Social Credit from Planes, Trains,"
   *Reuters,* March 16, 2018, https://www.reuters.com/article/us-china
   -credit/china-to-bar-people-with-bad-social-credit-from-planes
   -trains-idUSKCN1GS10S.

26. Jack Karsten and Darrel M. West, "China's Social Credit System
   Spreads to More Daily Transactions," *TechTank* (blog), Brookings,
   June 18, 2018, https://www.brookings.edu/blog/techtank/2018/06/18
   /chinas-social-credit-system-spreads-to-more-daily-transactions/.

27. "The New Way Police Are Surveilling You: Calculating Your Threat
   Score," *Washington Post,* January 10, 2016.

28. Keith Kirkpatrick, "Battling Algorithmic Bias," *Communications of the
   ACM* 59, no. 10 (October 2016): 16–17.

29. Kirkpatrick, "Battling Algorithmic Bias."

30. Clare Garvie and Jonathan Frankle, "Facial Recognition Software
   Might Have a Racial Bias Problem," *The Atlantic,* April 7, 2016.

31. Center for Constitutional Rights, "Hassan v. City of New York," last
   modified April 5, 2018, https://ccrjustice.org/home/what-we-do/our
   -cases/hassan-v-city-new-york.

32. Kirk Semple, "Missing Mexican Students Suffered a Night of 'Terror,'
   Investigators Say," *New York Times,* April 24, 2016.

33. John Scott-Railton et al., "Reckless Redux: Senior Mexican Legislators
   and Politicians Targeted with NSO Spyware," Citizen Lab, June 29,
   2017, https://citizenlab.ca/2017/06/more-mexican-nso-targets/.

34. Ryan Devereaux, "Three Years after 43 Students Disappeared in
   Mexico, a New Visualization Reveals the Cracks in the Government's
   Story," *Intercept,* September 7, 2017, https://theintercept.com/2017/09
   /07/three-years-after-43-students-disappeared-in-mexico-a-new
   -visualization-reveals-the-cracks-in-the-governments-story/.

35. Scott-Railton et al., "Reckless Redux."

36. Ryan Gallagher and Nicky Hager, "Private Eyes," *Intercept,* October 23, 2016, https://theintercept.com/2016/10/23/endace-mass
   -surveillance-gchq-governments/.

37. Gallagher and Hager, "Private Eyes."

38. Darren Schreiber et al., "Red Brain, Blue Brain: Evaluative Processes
   Differ in Democrats and Republicans," *PLoS ONE* 8, no. 2 (2013): E52970.

39. Adam L. Penenberg, "NeuroFocus Uses Neuromarketing to Hack Your Brain," *Fast Company,* August 8, 2011, https://www.fastcompany.com/1769238/neurofocus-uses-neuromarketing-hack-your-brain.

40. Marcello Ienca and Roberto Andorno, "Towards New Human Rights in the Age of Neuroscience and Neurotechnology," *Life Sciences, Society and Policy* 13, no. 1 (2017): 1–27.

41. "'Right to Be Forgotten' Online Could Spread," *New York Times,* August 5, 2015.

42. "Right to Be Forgotten."

43. "Privacy Expert Argues 'Algorithmic Transparency' Is Crucial for Online Freedoms at UNESCO Knowledge Café," UNESCO, December 4, 2015, https://en.unesco.org/news/privacy-expert-argues-algorithmic-transparency-crucial-online-freedoms-unesco-knowledge-cafe.

44. These capabilities are drawn from Martha C. Nussbaum, "Capabilities and Human Rights," *Fordham Law Review* 66, no 2 (1997): 288.

45. Nussbaum, "Capabilities and Human Rights," 287.

## 4. Adam and Eve, CRISPR and SHEEF

1. "The Discovery of DNA," yourgenome, Public Engagement and Wellcome Genome Campus, updated February 26, 2018, https://www.yourgenome.org/stories/the-discovery-of-dna.

2. Heidi Chial, "DNA Sequencing Technologies Key to the Human Genome Project," *Nature Education* 1, no. 1 (2008): 219.

3. More information on DNA can be found at "Genetics Home Reference," U.S. National Library of Medicine, last updated November 26, 2019, https://ghr.nlm.nih.gov/ and John Archibald, *Genomics: A Very Short Introduction* (Oxford: Oxford University Press, 2018).

4. Michelle McNamara, *I'll Be Gone in the Dark: One Woman's Obsessive Search for the Golden State Killer* (New York: Harper Collins, 2018), 141.

5. Avi Selk, "The Most Disturbing Parts of the 171-Page Warrant for the Golden State Killer Suspect," *Washington Post,* June 2, 2018.

6. GEDmatch, accessed March 25, 2019, https://www.gedmatch.com.

7. Jamie Ducharme, "Investigators Collected the Suspected Golden State Killer's DNA While He Shopped at Hobby Lobby," *Time,* June 2, 2018.

8. Ian Cobain, "Killer Breakthrough—The Day DNA Evidence First Nailed a Murderer," *Guardian,* June 7, 2016, https://www.theguardian.com/uk-news/2016/jun/07/killer-dna-evidence-genetic-profiling-criminal-investigation.

9. Tracey Maclin, "Government Analysis of Shed DNA Is a Search under the Fourth Amendment," *Texas Tech Law Review* 48 (2015): 287–505.

10. Maureen S. Dorney, "Moore v. the Regents of the University of California: Balancing the Need for Biotechnology Innovation against the Right of Informed Consent," *Berkeley Technology Law Journal* 5, no. 2 (1990): 333–369.

11. Francisco Goldman, "Children of the Dirty War," *New Yorker,* March 19, 2012.

12. Erin Blakemore, "Argentinian Mothers Are Using DNA to Track Down Stolen Children," *Smart News,* Smithsonian, September 3, 2015, https://www.smithsonianmag.com/smart-news/argentinian-grandmothers-are-using-dna-track-down-stolen-children-180956486/.

13. Noa Vaisman, "Relational Human Rights: Shed-DNA and the Identification of the Living Disappeared in Argentina," *Journal of Law and Society* 41, no. 3 (2014): 391.

14. *Maryland v. King,* 569 U.S. 435 (2013).

15. The Innocence Project, accessed November 18, 2019, https://www.innocenceproject.org/. It is important to note that although DNA profiling can help to solve criminal cases, DNA is not always conclusive evidence, and its use in forensic analysis has led to wrongful convictions in some cases. See, for example, Nicola Davis, "DNA in the Dock: How Flawed Techniques Send Innocent People to Prison," *Guardian,* October 2, 2017, https://www.theguardian.com/science/2017/oct/02/dna-in-the-dock-how-flawed-techniques-send-innocent-people-to-prison; Sense About Science, *Making Sense of Forensic Genetics* (London: Sense About Science, 2017), https://senseaboutscience.org/wp-content/uploads/2017/01/making-sense-of-forensic-genetics.pdf.

16. Forensic Genetics Policy Initiative, "Establishing Best Practices for Forensic DNA Databases," September 2017, http://dnapolicyinitiative.org/wp-content/uploads/2017/08/BestPractice-Report-plus-cover-final.pdf.

17. Kristine Barlow-Stewartand and Leslie Burnett, "Ethical Consider-ations in the Use of DNA for the Diagnosis of Diseases," *Clinical Biochemist Reviews* 27, no. 1 (2006): 53–61.
18. "Kuwait: Court Strikes Down Draconian DNA Law," Human Rights Watch, October 15, 2017, https://www.hrw.org/news/2017/10/17/kuwait-court-strikes-down-draconian-dna-law.
19. Federal DNA Collection, Electronic Frontier Foundation, accessed March 25, 2019, https://www.eff.org/cases/federal-dna-collection.
20. Michael Specter, "The Gene Hackers," *New Yorker,* November 16, 2015.
21. "Brave New World Quotes," Goodreads, accessed March 25, 2019, https://www.goodreads.com/work/quotes/3204877-brave-new-world.
22. Antonio Regalado, "China's CRISPR Twins May Have Had Their Brains Inadvertently Enhanced," *MIT Technology Review,* February 21, 2019, https://www.technologyreview.com/s/612997/the-crispr-twins-had-their-brains-altered/.
23. Ian Sample, "Genetically Modified Babies Given the Go Ahead by UK Ethics Body," *Guardian,* July 17, 2018, https://www.theguardian.com/science/2018/jul/17/genetically-modified-babies-given-go-ahead-by-uk-ethics-body.
24. Daniel Fernandez, "Can the Northern White Rhino Be Brought Back from the Brink of Extinction?," *Smithsonian Magazine,* June 2018, https://www.smithsonianmag.com/science-nature/northern-white-rhino-brought-back-brink-extinction-180969000/.
25. Ciara Nugent, "What It Was Like to Grow Up as the World's First Test-Tube Baby," *Time,* July 25, 2018.
26. Tamar Lewin, "Babies from Skin Cells? Prospect Is Unsettling to Some Experts," *New York Times,* May 16, 2017.
27. Carl Zimmer, "A New Form of Stem-Cell Engineering Raises Ethical Questions," *New York Times,* March 21, 2017.
28. John Aach et al., "Addressing the Ethical Issues Raised by Synthetic Human Entities with Embryo-Like Features," *eLife* 6 (2017): e20674.
29. Aach et al., "Addressing the Ethical Issues."
30. Sharon Begley, "In a Lab Pushing the Boundaries of Biology, an Embedded Ethicist Keeps Scientists in Check," *Stat,* February 23, 2017,

https://www.statnews.com/2017/02/23/bioethics-harvard-george
-church/.

31. Aach et al., "Addressing the Ethical Issues."

32. Antonio Regalado, "Artificial Human Embryos Are Coming, and No
One Knows How to Handle Them," *MIT Technology Review,* September 19, 2017, https://www.technologyreview.com/s/608173
/artificial-human-embryos-are-coming-and-no-one-knows-how-to
-handle-them/.

33. *Merriam-Webster,* s.v. "chimera (*n.*)," accessed March 25, 2019,
https://www.merriam-webster.com/dictionary/chimera.

34. Kara Rogers, "Chimera: Genetics," Encyclopedia Britannica, accessed
March 25, 2019, https://www.britannica.com/science/chimera
-genetics.

35. David Robson, "The Birth of Half-Human, Half-Animal Chimeras,"
*BBC Earth,* January 5, 2017, http://www.bbc.com/earth/story
/20170104-the-birth-of-the-human-animal-chimeras.

36. International Covenant on Economic, Social and Cultural Rights,
opened for signature December 16, 1966, United Nations Office of
the High Commissioner for Human Rights, accessed March 25,
2019, https://www.ohchr.org/en/professionalinterest/pages/
cescr.aspx.

37. Francesco Francioni, "Genetic Resources, Biotechnology and Human
Rights: The International Legal Framework," in Francesco Francioni,
*Biotechnologies and International Human Rights* (Portland, OR: Hart
Publishing, 2007), 7.

38. "WHO Expert Advisory Committee on Developing Global Standards
for Governance and Oversight of Human Gene Editing," World
Health Organization, accessed June 18, 2019, https://www.who.int
/ethics/topics/gene-editing/call-for-members/en/.

39. "WHO Expert Advisory Committee."

40. Sheila Jasanoff and Benjamin Hurlbut, "A Global Observatory for
Gene Editing," *Nature* 555 (2018): 435–437.

41. Jasanoff and Hurlburt, "A Global Observatory."

42. Office of the High Commissioner for Human Rights and World
Health Organization, "The Right to Health," June 2008, https://
www.who.int/gender-equity-rights/knowledge/right-to-health
-factsheet/en/.

### 5. From Petty to Panama

1. "What Is Corruption?," Transparency International, accessed May 21, 2019, https://www.transparency.org/what-is-corruption.
2. International Council on Human Rights Policy and Transparency International, *Corruption and Human Rights: Making the Connection* (Versoix, Switzerland: International Council on Human Rights Policy, 2009), http://www.ichrp.org/files/reports/40/131_web.pdf; Ray Fisman and Miriam Golden, *Corruption: What Everyone Needs to Know* (New York: Oxford University Press, 2017), 242.
3. "What Is Grand Corruption and How Can We Stop It?," Transparency International, September 21, 2016, https://www.transparency.org /news/feature/what_is_grand_corruption_and_how_can_we _stop_it.
4. Karen Dawisha, *Putin's Kleptocracy: Who Owns Russia?* (New York: Doubleday, 2014).
5. "What Is Corruption?"
6. Fisman and Golden, *Corruption,* 135.
7. "Combatting Corruption," World Bank, last updated October 4, 2018, http://www.worldbank.org/en/topic/governance/brief/anti-corruption.
8. Jake Bernstein, *Secrecy World: Inside the Panama Papers Investigation of Illicit Money Networks and the Global Elite* (New York, Henry Holt, 2017), 3–4.
9. "Corruption Perceptions Index 2016," Transparency International, January 25, 2017, https://www.transparency.org/news/feature /corruption_perceptions_index_2016.
10. Brook Larmer, "Corrupt Leaders Are Falling around the World. Will It Boost Economies?," *New York Times,* May 2, 2018.
11. Fisman and Golden, *Corruption,* 3.
.12. Michael T. Rock, "Corruption and Democracy," *Journal of Development Studies* 45, no. 1 (2009): 55–75.
13. Shaul Salvi, "Behavioral Economics: Corruption Corrupts," *Nature* 531, no. 7595 (March 24, 2016): 456–457.
14. Dan Ariely, "Experiment 1: The Price of a Bribe," Dan Ariely (website), 2019, http://danariely.com/research/learn/the-price-of-a -bribe/.
15. "The Water Crisis," Water.org, 2019, https://water.org/our-impact /water-crisis/.

16. Kenneth Odiwour, "In Africa, Corruption Dirties the Water," *IRIN,* March 14, 2013, http://www.thenewhumanitarian.org/analysis/2013 /03/14/africa-corruption-dirties-water.

17. "Water," United Nations, accessed May 21, 2019, http://www.un.org /en/sections/issues-depth/water/.

18. Finn Heinrich, "Corruption and Inequality: How Populists Mislead People," Transparency International, January 25, 2017, https://www .transparency.org/news/feature/corruption_and_inequality_how _populists_mislead_people.

19. Facundo Alvaredo et al., *World Inequality Report 2018* (Paris: World Inequality Lab, 2018), 11, 14.

20. Siddharth Kara, *Modern Slavery: A Global Perspective* (New York: Columbia University Press, 2017).

21. Meirion Jones and Caroline Hawley, "UK Government Promoted Useless 'Bomb Detectors,'" *BBC Newsnight,* January 27, 2011, http:// news.bbc.co.uk/2/hi/programmes/newsnight/9377875.stm.

22. Fisman and Golden, *Corruption,* 4.

23. Josh Cohen, "Why Is Ukraine Attacking Anti-corruption Activists?," *Newsweek,* October 14, 2017, http://www.newsweek.com/why -ukraine-attacking-anti-corruption-activists-684602.

24. "Honduras Arrests 'Mastermind' behind Berta Caceres' Murder," *Al Jazeera,* March 3, 2018, https://www.aljazeera.com/news/2018/03 /honduras-arrests-mastermind-berta-caceres-murder -180303085808456.html.

25. Global Witness, *Honduras: The Deadliest Place to Defend the Planet* (London: Global Witness, January 2017), 5, https://www .globalwitness.org/ru/campaigns/environmental-activists /honduras-deadliest-country-world-environmental-activism/.

26. Alexei Navalny, "Секретная дача Дмитрия Медведева [Dmitry Medvedev's secret cottage]," video footage published September 15, 2016, https://www.youtube.com/watch?time_continue=118&v =nMVJxTcU8Kg.

27. I Paid a Bribe (website), accessed May 21, 2019, https://ipaidabribe.com.

28. "Loss to Pakistan Economy Due to Corruption," I Paid a Bribe (website), http://www.ipaidbribe.pk/home/graph., accessed December 11, 2019.

29. Alberto Alesina and George-Marios Angeletos, "Corruption, Inequality and Fairness," (Working Paper 11399, National Bureau of

Economic Research, Cambridge, MA, June 2005), http://www.nber
.org/papers/w11399.pdf.

30. "Ebola Victims Sue Sierra Leone Government over Mismanaged
Funds," *Reuters,* December 15, 2017, https://www.reuters.com/article
/us-health-ebola-leone/ebola-victims-sue-sierra-leone-government
-over-mismanaged-funds-idUSKBN1E92NE.

31. "Ebola: Mapping the Outbreak," *BBC News,* January 14, 2016.

32. Ruth Maclean, "Red Cross 'Outraged' over Pilfering of Ebola Aid,"
*Guardian,* November 3, 2017, https://www.theguardian.com/global
-development/2017/nov/03/red-cross-outraged-over-pilfering-of
-ebola-aid-millions-by-its-own-staff.

33. "IFRC Statement on Fraud in Ebola Operations," International
Federation of Red Cross and Red Crescent Societies, October 20, 2017,
http://media.ifrc.org/ifrc/ifrc-statement-fraud-ebola-operations/.

34. Joshua Berlinger, "Duterte Tells Rights Investigators 'Don't F*** with
Me' in Speech," *CNN,* March 2, 2018, https://www.cnn.com/2018/03
/02/asia/duterte-philippines-un-probe-intl/index.html.

35. "Russia: Government versus Rights Groups," Human Rights Watch,
March 6, 2018, https://www.hrw.org/russia-government-against
-rights-groups-battle-chronicle.

36. "What Is Corruption?"

37. United Nations General Assembly, *Universal Declaration of Human
Rights,* 217 A (III) (Paris, 1948), Article 25.

38. "Exposed: Child Labour behind Smart Phone and Electric Car
Batteries," Amnesty International, January 19, 2016, https://www
.amnesty.org/en/latest/news/2016/01/child-labour-behind-smart
-phone-and-electric-car-batteries/.

39. Chrysantus Ayangafac and James Wakiaga, "Governance of Natural
Resources in Africa: Why Some Countries Fail to Negotiate Fair
Contracts" (working paper, United Nations Development Program,
Ethiopia, January 2014).

40. "Nigeria Facts and Figures," Organization of Petroleum Exporting
Countries, 2018, http://www.opec.org/opec_web/en/about_us/167
.htm.

41. "Haiti Earthquake Fast Facts," *CNN,* December 20, 2017, https://www
.cnn.com/2013/12/12/world/haiti-earthquake-fast-facts/index.html.

42. Nicholas Ambraseys and Roger Bilham, "Corruption Kills," *Nature*
469, no. 7329 (2011): 153–155.

43. "Extent of Corruption around the World Tied to Earthquake Fatalities," *CU Boulder Today,* University of Colorado, Boulder, January 12, 2011, https://www.colorado.edu/today/2011/01/12/extent-corruption -countries-around-world-tied-earthquake-fatalities.

44. Stephanie Chen, "Pennsylvania Rocked by 'Jailing Kids for Cash' Scandal," *CNN,* February 24, 2009, https://www.cnn.com/2009 /CRIME/02/23/pennsylvania.corrupt.judges/.

45. "'American Dream Is Rapidly Becoming American Illusion,' Warns UN Rights Expert on Poverty," U.N. Office of the High Commissioner for Human Rights, December 15, 2017, https://www.ohchr.org /EN/NewsEvents/Pages/DisplayNews.aspx?NewsID=22546& LangID=E.

46. Matthew Murray and Andrew Spalding, *Freedom from Official Corruption as a Human Right* (Washington, DC: Brookings Institution, 2015).

## 6. "Ask Now the Beasts and They Shall Teach Thee"

1. Joyce Tischler, founder of the Animal Legal Defense Fund, conversation with coauthor Schulz, August 23, 2017.

2. Human Rights Watch, *Blood, Sweat, and Fear: Workers' Rights in U.S. Meat and Poultry Plants* (New York: Human Rights Watch, 2004), https://www.hrw.org/report/2005/01/24/blood-sweat-and-fear /workers-rights-us-meat-and-poultry-plants.

3. Quoted in Sue Donaldson and Will Kymlicka, *Zoopolis: A Political Theory of Animal Rights* (Oxford: Oxford University Press, 2011), 21.

4. Cynthia Hodges, "The Link: Cruelty to Animals and Violence towards People," Michigan State University College of Law, Animal Legal & Historical Center, 2008, https://www.animallaw.info/article /link-cruelty-animals-and-violence-towards-people.

5. C. M. Clark, "Deep in the Volcano," *New York Review of Books,* April 7, 2016, 60.

6. John Lanchester, "How Civilization Started," *New Yorker,* September 18, 2017, 26.

7. 1 Corinthians 9–10.

8. Aristotle, *Politics,* Book I, Chapter 8.

9. Rene Descartes, Letter to the Marquess of Newcastle, November 23, 1646, in *The Philosophical Writings of Descartes: Volume III, The Correspondence*, trans. John Cottingham, Robert Stoothoff, Dugald Murdoch, Anthony Kenny (Cambridge: Cambridge University Press, 1984), 302.

10. Immanuel Kant, *Lecture on Ethics* (New York: Harper and Row, 1963), 239.

11. Frans de Waal, *Are We Smart Enough to Know How Smart Animals Are?* (New York: W. W. Norton, 2016), 268.

12. Roger Panaman, "Jeremy Bentham and Animal Rights," chap. 7 in *How to Do Animal Rights* (e-book, first published 2008), http://www.animalethics.org.uk/bentham.html.

13. Saf Shaikh, "Japanese Symbolic Animals and Their Meanings," *The Japanese Shop* (blog), August 14, 2018, https://www.thejapaneseshop.co.uk/blog/japanese-symbolic-animals-meanings/.

14. Roderick Nash, *The Rights of Nature: A History of Environmental Ethics* (Madison: University of Wisconsin Press, 1989), 18.

15. The philosopher Mary Midgley says that the first antivivisection society in Europe was founded by the wife and daughters of the French physiologist Claude Bernard when they came home to find that Bernard had vivisected the family dog! (Mary Midgley, *Animals and Why They Matter* [New York: Penguin Books, 1983], 28). Michigan State University law professor David Favre has drafted an "International Treaty for Animal Welfare," though he also recognizes all the obstacles to its adoption (Favre, "An International Treaty for Animal Welfare," *Animal Law* 18 no. 2 [2012]: 237–280).

16. "Inhumane Practices on Factory Farms," Animal Welfare Institute, 2018, https://awionline.org/content/inhumane-practices-factory-farms.

17. William Cummings, "Airlines Ban Hunters' Big-Game 'Trophies' after Uproar over Cecil the Lion," *USA Today*, August 3, 2015, https://www.usatoday.com/story/travel/flights/todayinthesky/2015/08/03/american-airlines-animal-trophy-ban/31090331/.

18. Christopher Mele, "Ringling Bros. and Barnum & Bailey Circus to End Its 146-Year Run," *New York Times*, January 14, 2017. The success of Cirque de Soleil, which uses no animals in its performances, would seem to argue that audiences will support acrobatic and other acts with solely human performers.

19. Megan Specia and Gaia Pianigiani, "Italian Gets Paid Leave for Sick Dog," *New York Times,* October 13, 2017.

20. American Pet Products Association, *2017–2018 National Pet Owners Survey* (Greenwich, CT, 2018).

21. Gary Francione, *Animals as Persons* (New York: Columbia University Press, 2008), 26.

22. "Vegetarianism in America," *Vegetarian Times,* May 10, 2017, https://www.vegetariantimes.com/uncategorized/vegetarianism-in -america.

23. Most courts, regarding pets or service animals as property, will only pay out, in cases of compensation-qualifying death, the cost to purchase a replacement but will not include emotional damages in their judgments despite the profound emotional bond between many domestic animals and their guardians.

24. James Gorman, "Do Bees Know Nothing?," *New York Times,* June 7, 2018.

25. Rebecca Rifkin, "In U.S., More Say Animals Should Have Same Rights as People," Gallup, May 18, 2015, http://news.gallup.com/poll /183275/say-animals-rights-people.aspx.

26. "Client, Kiko (Chimpanzee)," Nonhuman Rights Project, accessed May 4, 2019, https://www.nonhumanrights.org/client-kiko/. The owners claim to run a nonprofit corporation called The Primate Sanctuary, currently operated out of their home.

27. One sympathetic judge did note that "Efforts to extend legal rights to chimpanzees are . . . understandable; some day they may even succeed. Courts, however, are slow to embrace change." The judge then quoted U.S. Supreme Court Justice Anthony Kennedy, who wrote in *Lawrence v. Texas,* which struck down sodomy laws, "Times can blind us to certain truths and later generations can see that laws once thought necessary and proper in fact serve only to oppress." A better statement of the thesis of this book would be hard to find! ("Clients, Hercules and Leo [Chimpanzees]," Nonhuman Rights Project, accessed May 4, 2019, https://www.nonhumanrights.org /hercules-leo/); Stephen Wise, conversation with coauthor Schulz, September 2, 2017.

28. Gabriel Samuels, "Chimpanzees Have Rights, Says Argentine Judge as She Orders Cecilia Be Released from Zoo," *Independent,* No-

vember 7, 2016, http://www.independent.co.uk/news/world
/americas/argentina-judge-says-chimpanzee-poor-conditions-has
-rights-and-should-be-freed-from-zoo-a7402606.html. In 2017 another
court in Argentina declared Sandra, an orangutan, a nonhuman
person and ordered her released from a Buenos Aires zoo to a
sanctuary.

29. "Chucho, el oso de anteojos que triunfó en la Corte Suprema de
Justicia," *Semana,* July 27, 2017, http://www.semana.com/nacion
/articulo/chucho-el-oso-que-gano-un-habeas-corpus-en-la-corte
-suprema-de-justicia/534034.

30. Burwell v. Hobby Lobby Stores, Inc., 134 S. Ct. 2751 (2014).

31. Carl Safina, *Beyond Words: What Animals Think and Feel* (New York:
Henry Holt, 2015), 21; anthropologist Barbara Smuts quoted in
Donaldson and Kymlicka, *Zoopolis,* 25.

32. Paola Cavalieri, *The Animal Question: Why Nonhuman Animals Deserve
Human Rights* (New York: Oxford University Press, 2001), 78.

33. Peter Godfrey-Smith, *Other Minds: The Octopus, the Sea, and the Deep
Origin of Consciousness* (New York: Farrar, Straus and Giroux,
2016), 94.

34. Jonathan Balcombe, *What a Fish Knows: The Inner Lives of Our Under-
water Cousins* (New York: Farrar, Straus and Giroux, 2016), 81–82. Fish
are also known to experience depression. See "Can Fish Get De-
pressed? Seriously," *New York Times,* October 24, 2017.

35. Balcombe, *What a Fish Knows,* 83.

36. "Apes vs. Toddlers," *Science Update,* American Association for the
Advancement of Science, podcast transcript, October 5, 2007,
http://sciencenetlinks.com/science-news/science-updates/apes-vs
-toddlers/. One way to measure intelligence is by the size of the brain
relative to the size of the body. This is called the encephalization
quotient. For humans it is 7.0, for dolphins 4.2, and for chimps 2.3
(Balcombe, *What a Fish Knows,* 173).

37. Godfrey-Smith, *Other Minds,* 64.

38. Godfrey-Smith, *Other Minds,* 55–64.

39. Kenneth Oakley, *Man the Tool-Maker* (London: British Museum,
1972).

40. Diana Reiss, *The Dolphin in the Mirror: Exploring Dolphin Minds and
Saving Dolphin Lives* (Boston: Houghton Mifflin Harcourt, 2011), 192–194.

41. Cited in Jon Mooallem, "Wildly Intelligent," *New York Times Book Review,* May 1, 2016, quoting from Jennifer Ackerman, *The Genius of Birds* (New York: Penguin, 2016).

42. Safina, *Beyond Words,* 67–68.

43. Reiss, *The Dolphin,* 204.

44. Sam Roberts, "William J. L. Sladen, 96, Expert on Penguin Libidos," *New York Times,* June 19, 2017.

45. Carl Zimmer, "Death Lessons over Dinner," *New York Times,* October 6, 2015.

46. Megan Cross, "Mother Cow Proves Animals Love, Think and Act," Global Animal, April 13, 2012, https://www.globalanimal.org/2012/04 /13/cow-proves-animals-love-think-and-act/.

47. Emily Underwood, "Rats Forsake Chocolate to Save a Drowning Companion," *Science,* May 12, 2015, http://www.sciencemag.org/news /2015/05/rats-forsake-chocolate-save-drowning-companion.

48. Philip Low, "The Cambridge Declaration on Consciousness," June 7, 2012, http://fcmconference.org/img/CambridgeDeclarationOnConsci ousness.pdf. "The absence of a neocortex," the declaration said, "does not appear to preclude an organism from experiencing affective states. Convergent evidence indicates that non-human animals have the neuroanatomical, neurochemical and neurophysiological substrates of conscious states along with the capacity to exhibit intentional behaviors." Interestingly enough, the declaration singled out the African gray parrot as having "near human-like levels of consciousness."

49. Noam Chomsky, "On the Myth of Ape Language," interview by Matt Aames Cucchiaro, 2007–2008, transcript of email correspondence, accessed May 5, 2019, https://chomsky.info/2007____/.

50. Ferris Jabbr, "Can Prairie Dogs Talk?," *New York Times Magazine,* May 12, 2017.

51. "The Sounds of Language," The Why Files (website), ed. Terry Devitt, University of Wisconsin-Madison, https://whyfiles.org/058language /ape_talk.html. As one animal activist says, "Animals are not voiceless. We may not understand them but that doesn't mean they are voiceless" (Rebecca Angle, conversation with coauthor Schulz, September 12, 2017).

52. Peter Singer, *Animal Liberation* (New York: Harper Collins, 2009).

53. Singer, *Animal Liberation,* 63.

54. Singer, *Animal Liberation,* 103.
55. However, recent research seems to show that honeybees are conscious and can "feel" (James Gorman, "Do Honeybees Feel? Scientists Are Entertaining the Idea," *New York Times,* April 19, 2016).
56. Actually, as a utilitarian, Singer prefers not to speak in terms of rights at all.
57. Tom Regan, *The Case for Animal Rights* (Berkeley: University of California Press, 1983), 243. Because he bases his theory on natural law, Regan is forced to acknowledge that "to view certain individuals . . . as having equal inherent value is a *postulate*—that is, a theoretical assumption" (p. 247), as opposed to something that can be proven.
58. Donaldson and Kymlicka, *Zoopolis.* For a shorter explanation of the theory, see Adriano Mannino, "Will Kymlicka on Animal Denizens and Foreigners in the Wilderness—Interview Part 2," GBS Switzerland, December 11, 2014, http://gbs-switzerland.org/blog/will-kymlicka-on -animal-denizens-and-foreigners-in-the-wilderness-interview-part-2-2/.
59. Emanuella Grinberg, "In Gorilla's Death, Critics Blame Mother, Cincinnati Zoo," *CNN,* May 30, 2016, http://www.cnn.com/2016/05/29 /us/cincinnati-zoo-gorilla-shot/index.html. See also "After Frenzied Criticism, No Charges for Mother of Boy Who Slipped into Gorilla Pen," *New York Times,* June 7, 2016.
60. Even the most attentive parents sometimes lose track of children, for instance, and the zoo said that a tranquilizer gun would not have worked quickly enough.
61. Sonali K. Doke and Shashikant C. Dhawale, "Alternatives to Animal Testing," *Saudi Pharmaceutical Journal* 23, no. 3 (2015): 223–229.
62. A *New Yorker* cartoon depicts a bear housewife holding a dust pan and broom while her lazy bear husband sits in a recliner, beer in hand, cigar in mouth, looking at the television. "I'd like to hear less talk about animal rights," says the bear wife, "and more talk about animal responsibilities" (*New Yorker,* July 16, 1990, 34).
63. However, Carol Adams points out that only 6–20 percent of animals are predators (Carol Adams, conversation with coauthor Schulz, September 7, 2017).
64. Francione, *Animals as Persons,* 65–66.
65. Martha C. Nussbaum, "Beyond 'Compassion and Humanity': Justice for Nonhuman Animals," in *Animal Rights: Current Debates and New*

*Directions,* ed. Cass Sunstein and Martha Nussbaum (Oxford: Oxford University Press, 2012), 299–320.

66. David J. Wolfson and Mariann Sullivan, "Foxes in the Hen House: Animals, Agribusiness, and the Law: A Modern American Fable," in Sunstein and Nussbaum, *Animal Rights,* 207.

67. Wolfson and Sullivan, "Foxes in the Hen House," 209.

68. "All research labs that use animals in the United States are required to appoint an internal review board known as an IACUC (Institutional Animal Care and Use Committee) to oversee all experimentation" (Kathy Rudy, *Loving Animals: Toward a New Animal Advocacy* [Minneapolis: University of Minnesota Press, 2011], 154). The World Congress on Alternatives to the Use of Animals in the Life Sciences urges adoption of the Three Rs approach to animal experimentation: (1) *replacement* of animals with other mechanisms, wherever possible; (2) *reduction* of the number of animals used; and (3) *refinement* to minimize pain and damage to animals ("The Three R's," accessed May 5, 2019, https://norecopa.no/alternatives/the-three-rs).

69. See, for example, Josephine Donovan, "Attention to Suffering: Sympathy as a Basis for Ethical Treatment of Animals," in *The Feminist Care Tradition in Animal Ethics: A Reader,* ed. Josephine Donovan and Carol J. Adams (New York: Columbia University Press, 2007), 174–197.

70. Tony Milligan, *Animal Ethics* (London: Routledge, 2015), 126.

71. Edward Group, "9 Health Benefits of a Vegetarian Diet," Global Healing Center, September 30, 2015, https://www.globalhealingcenter.com/natural-health/9-health-benefits-of-a-vegetarian-diet/; "Meat and the Environment," People for the Ethical Treatment of Animals, accessed May 5, 2019, https://www.peta.org/issues/animals-used-for-food/meat-environment/; "Lactose Intolerance," Genetics Home Reference, U.S. National Library of Medicine, accessed May 5, 2019, https://ghr.nlm.nih.gov/condition/lactose-intolerance; "Food," Impossible Foods Inc., accessed May 5, 2019, https://www.impossiblefoods.com/burger/; Clean Meat, accessed May 5, 2019, http://cleanmeat.com; Bruce Friedrich, executive director of Good Food Institute, conversation with coauthor Schulz, August 31, 2017.

72. "Do You Believe Animals Deserve Basic Legal Rights? Stand with Us against Animal Cruelty," Animal Legal Defense Fund, accessed May 5, 2019, https://act.aldf.org/page/5515/petition/1?locale=en-US.

73. *New Yorker,* September 4, 2017, 51.

74. Margaret Gates, "Answers: What Exactly Is an 'Obligate Carnivore?," Feline Nutrition Foundation, April 23, 2019, http://feline-nutrition .org/answers/answers-what-exactly-is-an-obligate-carnivore.

75. Donaldson and Kymlicka, *Zoopolis,* 150–151.

76. Michael Pollan, *The Omnivore's Dilemma* (New York: Penguin, 2006), 326.

77. Miguel de Unamuno, *Tragic Sense of Life* (New York: Dover, 1954).

78. Balcombe, *What a Fish Knows,* 19.

79. Donaldson and Kymlicka, *Zoopolis,* 36.

80. Jim Robbins, "Animals Are Losing Their Vagility, or Ability to Roam Freely," *New York Times,* February 19, 2018.

81. Tischler conversation.

82. Pollan, *Omnivore's Dilemma,* 324. See also Matt Simon, "To Save an Endangered Fox, Humans Turned Its Home into a War Zone," *Wired,* August 14, 2016, https://www.wired.com/2016/08/save-endangered -fox-humans-turned-home-war-zone/.

83. Gerardo Ceballos, Paul R. Ehrlich, and Rodolfo Dirzo, "Biological Annihilation via the Ongoing Sixth Mass Extinction Signaled by Vertebrate Population Losses and Declines," *Proceedings of the National Academy of Sciences of the United States of America* 114, no. 30 (July 2017): E6089–E6096, https://www.pnas.org/content/114/30/E6089; Laura Goldman, "10 Animals That Have Gone Extinct in the Last 100 Years," Care2, September 30, 2018, https://www.care2.com/causes/10-animals -that-have-gone-extinct-in-the-last-100-years.html.

84. Tia Ghose, "Artificial Ear Grown on Rat's Back," *Live Science,* July 31, 2013, https://www.livescience.com/38577-artificial-ear-created.html.

85. Nicholas Wade, "New Prospects for Growing Human Replacement Organs in Animals," *New York Times,* January 26, 2017.

86. Gina Kolata, "N.I.H. May Fund Human-Animal Stem Cell Research," *New York Times,* August 4, 2016.

87. "ALDF Opens New Frontier for Animal Personhood as Scientists Create Human-Animal Chimeras," Animal Legal Defense Fund, May 15, 2015, http://aldf.org/blog/aldf-opens-new-frontier-for-animal -personhood-as-scientists-create-human-animal/.

88. The neurotic behavior of some animals in zoos has prompted zookeepers to administer Prozac to them in "pet-friendly flavors." See David Sharfenberg, "Did Humans Drive This Polar Bear Insane?," *Boston Globe,* July 13, 2018.

89. Ross Andersen, "Welcome to Pleistocene Park," *The Atlantic,* April 2017.

90. Adams conversation.

91. The irony of the comment was that this board member kept a dog as a house pet whom he professed to love and even admitted tearing up at a film about cruelty to animals. But then, as Carol Adams observed to Schulz in their September 2017 conversation, "Human beings are afraid to care deeply about animals because, if they did, all the pain that has been inflicted [on those animals] would bring them a grief that is unbearable."

92. "Loren Eiseley Quotes," AZ Quotes, accessed May 5, 2019, http://www.azquotes.com/quote/472521.

## 7. Robots, Weapons, and War

Wiener coined the word "cybernetics" to describe the relationship between living beings and robots. Quoted in Robert Fuller, "Ducking Death; Surviving Superannuation," *Berrett-Koehler Publishers Blog,* February 27, 2015, https://www.bkconnection.com/bkblog/robert-fuller/ducking-death-surviving-superannuation.

1. Richard Yonck, *Heart of the Machine: Our Future in a World of Artificial Emotional Intelligence* (New York: Arcade, 2017), 194–195.

2. With the added advantage that when you tire of Solana's face, you can replace it with that of another sexbot of your choice (Zeynep Yenisey, "This Ultra-realistic New Sex Robot Not Only Has a Personality, She's Also Customizable," *Maxim,* January 12, 2018, https://www.maxim.com/gear/new-customizable-sex-doll-2018–1).

3. Rob Waugh, "Male Sex Robots with Unstoppable Bionic Penises Are Coming This Year," *Metro,* January 8, 2018, http://metro.co.uk/2018/01/08/male-sex-robots-unstoppable-bionic-penises-coming-year-7213306/.

4. "Love, Android Style: Sexy and Confusing," *New York Times,* January 20, 2019.

5. Des Shoe, "Do Androids Dream of Being Featured in Portrait Competitions?," *New York Times,* September 6, 2017.

6. In 2018, for example, a Japanese man married a hologram. Emiko Jozuka, "Beyond Dimensions: The Man Who Married a Hologram," *CNN*, December 29, 2019, https://www.cnn.com/2018/12/28/health /rise-of-digisexuals-intl/index.html.

7. Joy Buolamwini, "The Hidden Dangers of Facial Analysis," *New York Times,* June 22, 2018.

8. See "The Toronto Declaration: Protecting the Rights to Equality and Non-discrimination in Machine Learning Systems," Access Now, May 16, 2018, https://www.accessnow.org/the-toronto-declaration -protecting-the-rights-to-equality-and-non-discrimination-in -machine-learning-systems/.

9. Sherif Elsayed-Ali, "Why Embracing Human Rights Will Ensure AI Works for All," World Economic Forum, April 13, 2018, https://www .weforum.org/agenda/2018/04/why-embracing-human-rights-will -ensure-AI-works-for-all/.

10. Ava Kofman, "Suspicious Minds," *Harper's Magazine,* June 2018; "Asilomar AI Principles," Future of Life Institute, 2017, https:// futureoflife.org/ai-principles/.

11. Todd Haselton, "Elon Musk: I'm About to Announce a 'Neuralink' Product That Connects Your Brain to Computers," *CNBC,* September 7, 2018, https://www.cnbc.com/2018/09/07/elon-musk -discusses-neurolink-on-joe-rogan-podcast.html.

12. Tad Friend, "How Frightened Should We Be of AI?," *New Yorker,* May 7, 2018.

13. Kate Darling, "Extending Legal Protection to Social Robots," IEEE Spectrum, September 10, 2012, https://spectrum.ieee.org/automaton /robotics/artificial-intelligence/extending-legal-protection-to-social -robots.

14. Joel Garreau, "Bots on the Ground," *Washington Post,* May 6, 2007.

15. Darling, "Extending Legal Protection."

16. And even if they don't take human form, they may be subjected to attacks: witness the assaults on driverless cars (Simon Romero, "Wielding Rocks and Knives, Arizonans Attack Self-Driving Cars," *New York Times,* December 31, 2018).

17. Norri Kageki, "An Uncanny Mind: Masahiro Mori on the Uncanny Valley and Beyond," IIEE Spectrum, June 12, 2012, https://spectrum

.ieee.org/automaton/robotics/humanoids/an-uncanny-mind
-masahiro-mori-on-the-uncanny-valley.

18. Todd Leopold, "HitchBOT, the Hitchhiking Robot, Gets Beheaded
in Philadelphia," *CNN*, August 4, 2015, https://www.cnn.com
/2015/08/03/us/hitchbot-robot-beheaded-philadelphia-feat/index
.html.

19. Eighty percent of Swedes expressed positive views of robots,
whereas 72 percent of Americans were trepidatious about a robot-
dominated future (Peter S. Goodman, "The Robots Are Coming, and
Sweden Is Fine," *New York Times*, December 27, 2017).

20. A translated version of Capek's play is available online at http://
preprints.readingroo.ms/RUR/rur.pdf, trans. Paul Selver and Nigel
Playfair.

21. Peter Apps, "The Next Super Weapon Could Be Biological," *Reuters*,
April 19, 2017, https://www.reuters.com/article/us-biological-weaons
-commentary-idUSKBN17L1SZ.

22. Kenneth Roth, "Must It Always Be Wartime?," *New York Review of
Books*, March 9, 2017.

23. Joseph Needham, *Mathematics and the Sciences of the Heavens and the
Earth* (Taipei, Taiwan: Caves Books, 1986), 2:53.

24. "Ada Lovelace Wrote the First Computer Program," Fact / Myth,
September 7, 2018, http://factmyth.com/factoids/ada-lovelace-wrote
-the-first-computer-program/.

25. P. W. Singer, *Wired for War: The Robotics Revolution and Conflict in the
Twenty-First Century* (New York: Penguin, 200), 53.

26. Goodman, "The Robots Are Coming."

27. "About Us," DeepMind, accessed June 6, 2019, https://deepmind.com
/about/.

28. "Machine Vision Algorithm Learns to Recognize Hidden Facial
Expressions," *MIT Technology Review*, November 13, 2015,
https://www.technologyreview.com/s/543501/machine-vision
-algorithm-learns-to-recognize-hidden-facial-expressions/; Chelsea
Gohd, "AI-Powered Google Clips Camera Decides When to Take a
Photo So You Don't Have To," Futurism, video, October 8, 2017,
https://futurism.com/ai-powered-google-clips-camera/.

29. Friend, "How Frightened Should We Be?"

30. Cade Metz, "Paul Allen Wants to Teach Machines Common Sense,"
*New York Times*, February 28, 2018.

31. A. M. Turing, "Computing Machinery and Intelligence," *Mind* 59, no. 236 (1950), https://www.abelard.org/turpap/turpap.php.

32. "Ray Kurzweil: Singularity Will Arrive by 2045," Futurism, September 25, 2017, https://futurism.com/videos/ray-kurzweil-singularity-will-arrive-by-2045/.

33. James Vincent, "Elon Musk Says We Need to Regulate AI before It Becomes a Danger to Humanity," *The Verge,* July 17, 2017, https://www.theverge.com/2017/7/17/15980954/elon-musk-ai-regulation-existential-threat.

34. Singer, *Wired for War,* 403.

35. Chris Field, "South Korean Robot Ethics Charter 2012," *Enlightenment of an Anchorwoman* (blog), accessed June 6, 2019, https://akikoko12um1.wordpress.com/south-korean-robot-ethics-charter-2012/.

36. Cleve R. Wootson Jr., "Saudi Arabia, Which Denies Women Equal Rights, Makes a Robot a Citizen," *Washington Post,* October 29, 2017.

37. Alex Hern, "Give Robots 'Personhood' Status, EU Committee Argues," *Guardian,* January 12, 2017, https://www.theguardian.com/technology/2017/jan/12/give-robots-personhood-status-eu-committee-argues.

38. Neil M. Richards and William D. Smart, "How Should the Law Think about Robots?," in *Robot Law,* ed. Ryan Calo, A. Michael Froomkin, and Ian Kerr (Cheltenham, U.K.: Edward Elgar, 2016), 18.

39. Joanna J. Bryson, "Robots Should Be Slaves," in *Close Engagements with Artificial Companions,* ed. Yorick Wilks (Amsterdam, Netherlands: John Benjamins, 2010), 63–74.

40. Recall Chapter 6 on animals.

41. Human beings cannot even prove for sure that other humans are sentient; only that they say they are and appear so.

42. Though someone in a persistent vegetative state who can no longer experience pain may not be able to claim an enduring right to life, they still may not be tortured or abandoned.

43. Wendell Wallach and Colin Allen, *Moral Machines: Teaching Robots Right from Wrong,* (New York: Oxford University Press, 2009), chap. 12.

44. European Parliament, *European Parliament Resolution of 16 February 2017 with Recommendation to the Commission on Civil Law Rules on Robotics,* P8_TA(2017)0051, http://www.europarl.europa.eu/sides

/getDoc.do?pubRef=-//EP//TEXT+TA+P8-TA-2017
-0051+0+DOC+XML+V0//EN.

45. Steve Lohr, "Facial Recognition Is Accurate, If You're a White Guy,"
*New York Times,* February 9, 2018. Machine learning has been
implicated in other forms of discrimination, including disproportionately identifying people of color as more likely to commit crimes
or excluding people with mental disabilities from consideration for
jobs. See Global Future Council on Human Rights 2016–2018, "How
to Prevent Discriminatory Outcomes in Machine Learning" (white
paper, World Economic Forum, March 2018), https://www.weforum
.org/whitepapers/how-to-prevent-discriminatory-outcomes-in
-machine-learning.

46. However, some 280 roboticists and ethicists have signed a letter
descrying the parliament's action as based on "science fiction":
"Open Letter to the European Commission Artificial Intelligence
and Robotics," accessed June 6, 2019, http://www.robotics
-openletter.eu/.

47. John P. Sullins, "When Is a Robot a Moral Agent?," *International
Review of Information Ethics* 6 (2006): 23–30, http://www
.realtechsupport.org/UB/WBR/texts/Sullins_RobotMoralAgent
_2006.pdf.

48. The question of how to respond to mistreatment of robots has not
been limited to a social scientist's experiment. According to Wendell
Wallach, writing in 2015, "A few years back, the manufacturer of a
speaking robot doll considered what the doll should say if treated
abusively by a child. . . . After analyzing the issues and consulting
with lawyers, they decided that the doll would say and do nothing"
(Wendell Wallach, *A Dangerous Master: How to Keep Technology from
Slipping beyond Our Control* [New York: Basic Books, 2015], 224).

49. Mark Coeckelbergh, "Robot Rights? Towards a Social-Relational
Justification of Moral Consideration," *Ethics and Information Technology* 12, no. 3 (2010): 209–221. To be clear, Coeckelbergh favors a
more relational approach to robot rights than even the term "soft
rights" implies.

50. Rachel Withers, "A Monkey Can't Hold Copyright. But What about a
Robot?," *Slate,* May 3, 2018, https://slate.com/technology/2018/05
/artificial-intelligence-may-soon-have-more-rights-than-animals-in
-the-u-s.html.

51. The futurist George Dvorsky has suggested they might include such things as the robot's right to have full and unhindered access to its own source code, the right to copy or not to copy itself, and the right to conceal its own internal mental states (George Dvorsky, "When Will Robots Deserve Human Rights?," Institute for Ethics and Emerging Technologies, July 6, 2017, https://ieet.org/index.php/IEET2/more /Dvorsky20170706).

52. Analee Newitz, "Robots Need Civil Rights, Too," *Boston Globe,* September 8, 2017.

53. In at least one instance a corporation agreed that damage to a mobile assistance device (which is not something that is physically incorporated into a human body) constituted damage to a person, not just to his property (Linda McDonald Glenn, "Case Study: Ethical and Legal Issues in Human Machine Mergers [Or the Cyborgs Cometh]," *Annals of Health Law—ASLME Special Edition* 21 [2012]: 175–180).

54. Eric Schwitzgebel and Maria Garza, "Designing AI with Rights, Consciousness, Self-Respect, and Freedom," Department of Philosophy, University of California at Riverside, February 15, 2018, http://www.faculty.ucr.edu/~eschwitz/SchwitzPapers/AIRights2 -180215.pdf.

55. David Cravets, "Jan. 25, 1979: Robot Kills Human," *Wired,* January 25, 2010, https://www.wired.com/2010/01/0125robot-kills-worker/.

56. Divya Joshi, "Exploring the Latest Drone Technology for Commercial, Industrial and Military Drone Uses," *Business Insider,* July 13, 2017, http://www.businessinsider.com/drone-technology-uses -2017-7.

57. Cade Metz, "Good News: Drone Technology Is Getting Cheaper. That's Also Bad News," *New York Times,* February 20, 2018; Andrew Ross Sorkin, "Larry Page's Flying Taxis, Now Exiting Stealth Mode," *New York Times,* March 12, 2018.

58. John Sifton, "A Brief History of Drones," *Nation,* February 7, 2012.

59. "Drone Warfare," Bureau of Investigative Journalism, accessed June 6, 2019, https://www.thebureauinvestigates.com/projects/drone-war.

60. "I can look at their faces," one CIA drone operator said, "see these guys playing with their kids and wives.... After the strike, I see bodies being carried out of the house. I see the women weeping and in positions of mourning. That's not PlayStation; that's real." Quoted

in Rosa Brooks, *How Everything Became War and the Military Became Everything: Tales from the Pentagon* (New York: Simon and Schuster, 2016), 110. See also Eyal Press, "The Wounds of the Drone War," *New York Times Magazine,* June 13, 2018.

61. Amitai Etzioni and Oren Etzioni, "Pros and Cons of Autonomous Weapons Systems," *Military Review* (May-June 2017): 72–81.

62. United States Department of Defense, "DoD Directive 300.09: Autonomy in Weapon Systems," November 21, 2012, https://www .hsdl.org/?abstract&did=726163.

63. Matthew Rosenberg and John Markoff, "At Heart of U.S. Strategy, Weapons That Can Think," *New York Times,* October 26, 2016.

64. Izumi Nakamitsu et al., *United Nations Office for Disarmament Affairs (UNODA) Occasional Papers 30, November 2017: Perspectives on Lethal Autonomous Weapon Systems* (New York: United Nations, 2017); Frank Slijper, *Where to Draw the Line: Increasing Autonomy in Weapon Systems—Technology and Trends* (Utrecht, Netherlands: PAX, 2017), https://www.paxforpeace.nl/publications/all-publications/where-to -draw-the-line.

65. Tamir Eshel, "IAI Introduces New Loitering Weapons for Anti-radiation, Precision Strike," *Defense Update,* February 15, 2016, https:// defense-update.com/20160215_loitering-weapons.html.

66. Jeffrey Lin and P. W. Singer, "China Is Making 1,000-UAV Drone Swarms Now," *Popular Science,* January 8, 2018, https://www.popsci .com/china-drone-swarms.

67. Rosenberg and Markoff, "At Heart."

68. Gordon Johnson, *Unmanned Effects (UFX): Taking the Human Out of the Loop,* Rapid Assessment Process (RAP) Report #03–10, (Norfolk, VA: United States Joint Forces Command, September 2003). https://www.hsdl.org/?abstract&did=705224.

69. Ryan Browne, "US General Warns of Out-of-Control Killer Robots," *CNN,* July 18, 2017, https://www.cnn.com/2017/07/18/politics/paul -selva-gary-peters-autonomous-weapons-killer-robots/index.html; George Lucas, "Engineering, Ethics and Industry: The Moral Challenges of Lethal Autonomy," in *Killing by Remote Control: The Ethics of an Unmanned Military,* ed. Bradley Jay Strawser (Oxford: Oxford University Press, 2013), 217.

70. According to a U.N. report, notable failures to outlaw new weapons stretch from "attempts to ban the crossbow in Europe in the twelfth

century [to] early twentieth century attempts to ban aerial attacks on cities" (Izumi Nakamitsu et al., *UNODA Occasional Papers*).

71. See Anne Jacobsen, *Phenomena: The Secret History of the US Government's Investigation into Extrasensory Perception and Psychokinesis* (New York: Little, Brown, 2017).

72. "Robotic Armed Forces of Liberation" (Wallach and Allen, *Moral Machines*).

73. "Autonomous Weapons: An Open Letter from AI and Robotics Researchers" (presented at the International Joint Conference on Artificial Intelligence, Buenos Aires, July 28, 2015), https:// futureoflife.org/open-letter-autonomous-weapons/.

74. "About Us," Campaign to Stop Killer Robots, accessed June 6, 2019, https://www.stopkillerrobots.org/about/#about; European Parliament, *Resolution of 16 February 2017*.

75. Bonnie Docherty, "We're Running Out of Time to Stop Killer Robot Weapons," *Guardian,* April 11, 2018, https://www.theguardian.com /commentisfree/2018/apr/11/killer-robot-weapons-autonomous-ai -warfare-un.

76. Mary Shelley, *Frankenstein* (1818), chap. 9, https://boutell.com /frankenstein/chapter9.html.

77. Singer, *Wired for War,* 63.

78. Gary Wills, "What Is a Just War?," *New York Review of Books,* November 18, 2004.

79. Todd Beer, "Police Killing of Blacks: Data for 2015, 2016, 2017, and First Half of 2018," *Sociology Toolbox* (Blog), Society Pages, August 24, 2018, https://thesocietypages.org/toolbox/police -killing-of-blacks/.

80. Singer, *Wired for War,* 394.

81. Strawser, *Killing by Remote Control,* 17.

82. Sherif Elsayed-Ali, "Why Embracing Human Rights."

83. Tara Siegel Bernard et al., "Equifax Says Cyberattack May Have Affected 143 Million in U.S.," *New York Times,* September 7, 2017.

84. Cade Metz, "Teaching A.I. Systems to Behave Themselves," *New York Times,* August 13, 2017.

85. Isaac Asimov, *I, Robot* (New York: Bantam Books, 1950).

86. European Parliament, *Resolution of 16 February 2017*.

87. And this is to say nothing about the danger to civilians from unexploded munitions from cluster bombs that, not unlike land

mines, may remain hazardous to unsuspecting civilians for years after combat ends.

88. "Basic Principles of IHL," Global International Humanitarian Law Centre of Diakonia, accessed May 22, 2019, https://www.diakonia.se /en/ihl/the-law/international-humanitarian-law-1/introduction-to -ihl/principles-of-international-law/.

89. Quoted in Armin Krishnan, *Killer Robots: Legality and Ethicality of Autonomous Weapons* (Burlington, VT: Ashgate, 2009), 105.

90. George Orwell, "Looking Back on the Spanish War," *New Road* (1943), http://www.george-orwell.org/Looking_Back_On_The_Spanish_War/0 .html.

91. Daisuke Wakabayashi, "Self-Driving Uber Car Kills Pedestrian in Arizona, Where Robots Roam," *New York Times,* March 19, 2018.

92. Human Rights Watch and International Human Rights Clinic, *Shaking the Foundations: Human Rights Implications of Killer Robots* (New York: Human Rights Watch, 2014), https://www.hrw.org/report/2014/05/12 /shaking-foundations/human-rights-implications-killer-robots.

93. U.N. General Assembly, *Report of the Special Rapporteur on Extrajudicial, Summary or Arbitrary Executions, Christof Heyns,* Human Rights Council, 23rd session, A/HRC/23/47 (April 9, 2013), http://www.ohchr .org/Documents/HRBodies/HRCouncil/RegularSession/Session23/A -HRC-23-47_en.pdf.

94. Kathleen Michon, "Tobacco Litigation: History and Recent Developments," Nolo, accessed May 22, 2019, https://www.nolo.com/legal -encyclopedia/tobacco-litigation-history-and-development-32202 .html.

95. Rick Rojas and Kristen Hussey, "Sandy Hook Massacre: Remington and Other Gun Companies Lose Major Ruling over Liability," *New York Times,* March 14, 2019.

96. See Nehal Bhuta and Stavro-Evdokimos Pantazopoulos, "Autonomy and Uncertainty: Increasingly Autonomous Weapons Systems and the International Legal Regulation of Risk," in *Autonomous Weapons Systems: Laws, Ethics, Policy,* ed. Nehal Bhuta et al. (Cambridge: Cambridge University Press, 2016), 154–158.

97. Human Rights Watch and International Human Rights Clinic, *Shaking the Foundations.*

98. Daisuke Wakabayashi, "Self-Driving."

99. Michael Walzer, *Arguing about War* (New Haven, CT: Yale University Press, 2004), 101.

100. Christof Heyns, "Autonomous Weapons Systems: Living a Dignified Life and Dying a Dignified Death," in *Autonomous Weapons Systems,* ed. Bhuta et. al., 10–11.

101. Peter Asaro, *"Jus nascendi,* Robotic Weapons and the Martens Clause," in *Robot Law,* ed. Ryan Calo, Michael Froomkin, and Ian Kerr (Cheltenham, U.K.: Edward Elgar, 2016): 367–386.

102. Michael C. Horowitz, "The Ethics and Morality of Robotic Warfare: Assessing the Debate over Autonomous Weapons," *Daedalus* 145, no. 4 (Fall 2016): 32.

103. The Martens Clause of the 1977 Additional Protocol II to the Geneva Convention holds that acts not specifically prohibited by law may still not be permissible if they violate "principles of humanity and the dictates of the public conscience." Many argue that to meet the dictates of the Martens Clause, meaningful human control of autonomous weapons will need to be maintained (Peter Asaro, "Chapter 14: Jus nascendi, robotic weapons, and the Martens Clause," in *Robot Law,* ed. Ryan Calo, A. Michael Froomkin, and Ian Kerr (Northampton, MA: Edward Elgar Publishing, 2016, available at http://www.peterasaro .org/writing/Asaro%20Jus%20Nascendi%20PROOF.pdf).

104. Singer, *Wired for War,* 83. The Pentagon has developed or is developing a wide array of nonlethal weapons from munitions that deliver flash-bang effects to nonblinding lasers to obscurant smoke systems to grenades that release hundreds of rubber pellets. See U.S. Department of Defense, Non-Lethal Weapons (NLW) Reference Book (Quantico, VA: Joint Non-Lethal Weapons Directorate, 2012), https://www.supremecourt.gov/opinions/URLs_Cited/OT2015/14 -10078/14-10078-3.pdf.

105. "Moore's Law," Encyclopaedia Britannica, accessed December 6, 2019, https://www.britannica.com/technology/Moores-law.

106. Like some animal rights activists, the Swedish philosopher of robot rights Nick Bostrum and the AI researcher Eliezer Yudkowsky have a hard time imagining that the natural world might have rights. "A rock has no moral status," they have written. "We may crush it, pulverize it, or subject it to any treatment we like without any concern for the rock itself" (Nick Bostrom and Eliezer Yudkowsky, "The Ethics of Artificial Intelligence," draft for *Cambridge Handbook of Artificial Intelligence,* eds. William Ramsey and Keith Frankish [Cambridge University Press, 2011], https://nickbostrom.com/ethics /artificial-intelligence.pdf).

## 8. Should Rocks Have Rights?

1. "Why Are Wetlands Important?," United States Environmental Protection Agency, last updated June 13, 2018, https://www.epa.gov/wetlands/why-are-wetlands-important.
2. "Kami," Religions, *BBC,* last updated September 4, 2009, http://www.bbc.co.uk/religion/religions/shinto/beliefs/kami_1.shtml.
3. "Taro," HawaiiHistory.org, accessed May 30, 2019, http://www.hawaiihistory.org/index.cfm?fuseaction=ig.page&PageID=533.
4. Quoted in Richard Erdoes, *Lame Deer: Seeker of Visions* (New York: Simon and Schuster, 1976), 101.
5. Barry Lopez, "The Leadership Imperative: An Interview with Oren Lyons" *Orion,* January/February 2007, https://orionmagazine.org/article/the-leadership-imperative/.
6. "Infographic: Sea Level Rise and Global Warming," Union of Concerned Scientists, 2014, https://www.ucsusa.org/global_warming/science_and_impacts/impacts/infographic-sea-level-rise-global-warming.html#.WwMVTEgvzcs.
7. "The Extinction Crisis," Center for Biological Diversity, accessed May 30, 2019, http://www.biologicaldiversity.org/programs/biodiversity/elements_of_biodiversity/extinction_crisis/.
8. Brooke Jarvis, "The Insect Apocalypse Is Here," *New York Times Magazine,* December 2, 2018.
9. Hikoro Tabuchi, Claire Rigby, and Jeremy White, "Amazon Deforestation, Once Tamed, Comes Roaring Back," *New York Times,* February 24, 2017.
10. "Getting Serious about Overfishing," *Economist,* May 27, 2017.
11. Livia Albeck-Ripka and Brad Plumer, "5 Plants and Animals Utterly Confused by Climate Change," *New York Times,* April 4, 2018.
12. Aldo Leopold, *A Sand County Almanac* (New York: Oxford University Press, 1949), 224–225.
13. Dictionary.com, s.v. "nature," accessed June 4, 2019, http://www.dictionary.com/browse/nature.
14. Thomas Berry, *The Sacred Universe* (New York: Columbia University Press, 2009), 69.
15. "Universal Human Rights Instruments," United Nations Office of the High Commissioner of Human Rights, accessed May 30, 2019,

http://www.ohchr.org/EN/ProfessionalInterest/Pages
/UniversalHumanRightsInstruments.aspx.

16. Stefano Mancuso and Alessandra Viola, *Brilliant Green: The Surprising History and Science of Plant Intelligence* (Washington, DC: Island Press, 2015).

17. Michael Pollan, "The Intelligent Plant," *New Yorker,* December 23 and 30, 2013, 101. Whether they can also meet the "definitions" of consciousness described in the chapter on animals as "the thing that feels something" or the sense that "someone is at home" is another question, but Mancuso and Viola argue that, simply because plants don't move and their processes of "consciousness" take a long time to manifest themselves and are not immediately obvious to the human eye does not mean they should be denied the appellation.

18. Mancuso and Viola, *Brilliant Green,* 158.

19. Peter Wohllenben, *The Hidden Life of Trees: What They Feel, How They Communicate* (Vancouver, Canada: Greystone Books, 2015).

20. Quoted in David Suzuki, *The Sacred Balance: Rediscovering Our Place in Nature* (Vancouver, Canada: Greystone Books, 1997), 16.

21. This is one reason the famous biologist E. O. Wilson has proposed that humans set aside 50 percent of the planet as priceless bioreserves that should be free from human exploitation ("In 'Half Earth,' E. O. Wilson Calls for a Grand Retreat," *New York Times,* March 1, 2016).

22. Recall Henry David Thoreau's famous words: "In wildness is the preservation of the world" (Henry David Thoreau, "Walking," *Atlantic Monthly,* June 1862, available at https://www.theatlantic.com /magazine/archive/1862/06/walking/304674/).

23. JoAnna Klein, "Deep Beneath Your Feet, They Live in the Octillions," *New York Times,* December 19, 2018.

24. Harald Welzer, "Darfur: The First Climate War," Audubon, July 12, 2012, https://www.audubon.org/news/darfur-first-climate-war.

25. There is even some evidence that exposure to a healthy environment helps reduce violence in children and anxiety in adults (Ming Kuo, "Aggression and Violence in the Inner City," *Environment and Behavior* 33, no. 4 [July 2001]: 543–571; James Hamblin, "The Nature Cure," *Atlantic,* October 2015).

26. Karen Savage, "Ireland Recognizes Constitutional Right to a Safe Climate and Environment," *Climate Liability News,* December 11, 2017,

https://www.climateliabilitynews.org/2017/12/11/ireland
-constitutional-right-climate-environment-fie/.

27. Randy Marse Jr., "Oregon Federal Court Issues Remarkable
Decision Finding Constitutional Right to Stable Climate," *Energy
Law Blog*, January 31, 2017, https://www.theenergylawblog.com
/2017/01/articles/environmental/oregon-federal-court-issues
-remarkable-decision-finding-constitutional-right-to-stable
-climate/.

28. Ucilia Wang, "International Court Ruling: A Safe Climate Is a Human
Right," *Climate Liability News*, February 13, 2018, https://www
.climateliabilitynews.org/2018/02/13/inter-american-climate-rights
-colombia/.

29. United Nations Office of the High Commissioner for Human Rights,
"UN Expert Calls for Global Recognition of the Right to Safe and
Healthy Environment," March 5, 2018, http://www.ohchr.org/EN
/NewsEvents/Pages/DisplayNews.aspx?NewsID=22755&LangID=E.
One of the most comprehensive examples of such "greening" is the
"Framework Principles on Human Rights and the Environment"
formulated by the U.N. special rapporteur on the issue of human
rights obligations relating to the enjoyment of a safe, clean, healthy
and sustainable environment (Office of the United Nations High
Commissioner for Human Rights, "Framework Principles on
Human Rights and the Environment (2018)," accessed May 30, 2019,
http://www.ohchr.org/EN/Issues/Environment/SREnvironment
/Pages/FrameworkPrinciplesReport.aspx).

30. John Vidal and Owen Bowcott, "ICC Widens Remit to Include
Environmental Destruction Cases," *Guardian*, September 15, 2016,
https://www.theguardian.com/global/2016/sep/15/hague-court
-widens-remit-to-include-environmental-destruction-cases.

31. Cory Doctorow, "Sole and Despotic Dominion," *Locus*, November 2,
2016, http://locusmag.com/2016/11/cory-doctorow-sole-and-despotic
-dominion/; Peter Burdon, "Wild Law: The Philosophy of Earth
Jurisprudence," *Alternative Law Journal* 35, no. 2 (2010): 62–65.

32. "Canticle of Brother Sun and Sister Moon of St. Francis of Assisi,"
Catholic Online, accessed May 30, 2019, https://www.catholic.org
/prayers/prayer.php?p=183.

33. Roderick Frazier Nash, *The Rights of Nature: A History of Environmental Ethics* (Madison: University of Wisconsin Press, 1989), 39.

34. John Muir, *Our National Parks* (Boston: Houghton Mifflin, 1901), 57–58.

35. Rachel C. Carson, *Silent Spring* (Boston: Houghton Mifflin, 1962).

36. "Nelson's Environmental Agenda," Gaylord Nelson and Earth Day (website), Nelson Institute for Environmental Studies, University of Wisconsin Madison, accessed May 30, 2019, http://www .nelsonearthday.net/collection/redefining-environmentalagenda .php.

37. Harold W. Wood Jr., "The United Nations World Charter for Nature: The Developing Nations' Initiative to Establish Protections for the Environment," *Ecology Law Quarterly* 12, no. 4 (September 1985): 977–996. The charter was supplemented in 2000 by "The Earth Charter," originally an initiative in collaboration with UNESCO but subsequently an independent effort endorsed by some six thousand governments and organizations, which lists sixteen responsibilities humans have toward the earth ("The Earth Charter," Earth Charter Initiative, March 2000, accessed May 30, 2019, http://earthcharter.org /discover/the-earth-charter/).

38. Leopold, *A Sand County Almanac,* viii.

39. Aldo Leopold, "Thinking like a Mountain," in *A Sand County Almanac and Sketches Here and There* (New York: Oxford University Press, 1987), https://nctc.fws.gov/resources/knowledge-resources/wildread /thinking-like-a-mountain.pdf.

40. Christopher Stone, "Should Trees Have Standing? Toward Legal Rights for Natural Objects," *Southern California Law Review* 45 (1972): 450–501.

41. Stone was not actually the first to advocate legal rights for Nature. That honor belongs to University of Pennsylvania law professor Clarence Lawrence in his 1964 article "The Rights and Duties of Beasts and Trees: A Law Teacher's Essay for Landscape Architects," *Journal of Legal Education* 17 (1964), but it was Stone's essay that got all the attention.

42. "William O. Douglas's Dissent in Sierra Club v. Morton (1972)," on Ken Pennington's website, accessed May 31, 2019, http:// legalhistorysources.com/Law508/DouglasDissent.htm.

43. Arne Naess and George Sessions, "The Deep Ecology Platform" (1984), Foundation for Deep Ecology, accessed May 31, 2019, http://www .deepecology.org/platform.htm.

44. "Overview," GaiaTheory.org, Entrepreneurial Earth, accessed May 31, 2019, http://www.gaiatheory.org/overview/.

45. "Thomas Berry's Ten Principles of Jurisprudence," Global Alliance for the Rights of Nature, accessed May 31, 2019, http://therightsofnature.org/thomas-berrys-ten-principles-of-jurisprudence/.

46. Cormac Cullinan, *Wild Law: A Manifesto for Earth Justice* (Devon, U.K.: Green Books, 2011), 7.

47. Mihuea Tanasescu, *Environment, Political Representation and the Challenge of Rights* (New York: Palgrave MacMillan, 2016), 108–109.

48. David R. Boyd, *The Rights of Nature: A Legal Revolution That Could Save the World* (Toronto: ECW, 2017), 165.

49. Constitution of the Republic of Ecuador (2008), Political Database of the Americas, Center for Latin American Studies, Georgetown University, last updated January 31, 2011, http://pdba.georgetown.edu/Constitutions/Ecuador/english08.html.

50. Boyd, *The Rights of Nature,* 177ff.

51. *Ley de Derechos de la Madre Tierra* [Law of the rights of Mother Earth] (December 2010), World Future Fund, accessed May 31, 2019, http://www.worldfuturefund.org/Projects/Indicators/motherearthbolivia.html.

52. "New Zealand," Earth Law Center, August 16, 2016, https://www.earthlawcenter.org/international-law/2016/8/new-zealand.

53. Eleanor Ainge Roy, "New Zealand River Granted Same Legal Rights as Human Beings," *Guardian,* March 16, 2017, https://www.theguardian.com/world/2017/mar/16/new-zealand-river-granted-same-legal-rights-as-human-being.

54. "India's Ganges and Yamuna Rivers Are 'Not Living Entities,'" *BBC News,* July 7, 2017.

55. "Universal Declaration of Rights of Mother Earth," World People's Conference on Climate Change and the Rights of Mother Earth, April 22, 2010, https://therightsofnature.org/universal-declaration/.

56. Boyd, *The Rights of Nature,* 221–222.

57. Wesley J. Smith, "Why We Call Them Human Rights," *Weekly Standard,* November 24, 2008, https://www.weeklystandard.com/wesley-j-smith/why-we-call-them-em-human-em-rights.

58. Justin Gillis, "With an Eye on Hunger, Scientists See Promise in Genetic Tinkering of Plants," *New York Times,* November 17, 2016.

59. Cited in Nash, *The Rights of Nature,* 155.

60. Albert Schweitzer, *Out of My Life and Thought: An Autobiography* (Baltimore: Johns Hopkins Press, 1933), 254. The philosopher Mary Warnock objected to Christopher Stone's attribution of rights to Nature by insisting that she would never "allow [her] garden to grow [stinging] nettles," despite their being a good habitat for butterflies and other insects and that "destroying them has an adverse effect on the environment" because nettles "are the most hateful of weeds, being not only ugly and invasive but painful" (Mary Warnock, "Should Trees Have Standing?," in *Should Trees Have Standing? 40 Years On,* ed. Anna Grear [Cheltenham, U.K.: Edward Elgar, 2012], 65). Of course were Warnock to kill the weeds in order to protect and preserve the flowers and then agree not to *pick* the flowers, which of course are themselves attractive to insects and good for the environment, she might have a defensible rationale for getting rid of those ghastly nettles!

## Conclusion

1. Office of the United Nations High Commissioner for Refugees, "The 1951 Refugee Convention," accessed December 4, 2019. http://www.unhcr.org/en-us/1951-refugee-convention.html.
2. Kathy Marks, "World's First 'Climate Change Refugee' Has Appeal Rejected as New Zealand Rules Ioane Teitiota Must Return to South Pacific Island Nation of Kiribati," *Independent,* May 12, 2014, https://www.independent.co.uk/news/world/australasia/world-s-first-climate-change-refugee-has-appeal-rejected-as-new-zealand-rules-ioane-teitiota-must-9358547.html.
3. Greg Harman, "Has the Great Climate Migration Already Begun?," *Guardian,* September 15, 2014, https://www.theguardian.com/vital-signs/2014/sep/15/climate-change-refugees-un-storms-natural-disasters-sea-levels-environment.
4. United Nations High Commissioner for Refugees (UNHCR), "Frequently Asked Questions on Climate Change and Disaster Displacement," November 6, 2016, http://www.unhcr.org/en-us/news/latest/2016/11/581f52dc4/frequently-asked-questions-climate-change-disaster-displacement.html; Cristina Cattaneo, "How Does Climate Change Affect Migration?," World Economic Forum, November 23,

2015, https://www.weforum.org/agenda/2015/11/how-does-climate
-change-affect-migration/.

5. UNHCR, "Frequently Asked Questions."

6. President Barack Obama, remarks at the First Session of COP21 (Le
Bourget, Paris, France, November 30, 2015), https://obamawhitehouse
.archives.gov/the-press-office/2015/11/30/remarks-president-obama
-first-session-cop21.

7. As of 2016, these included Belgium, Canada, Colombia, Luxembourg,
the Netherlands, Switzerland, and some states in the United
States.

8. Rachel Aviv, "The Death Treatment," *New Yorker,* June 22, 2015.

9. Yonette Joseph, "Why David Goodall, 104, Renowned Australian
Scientist, Wants to Die," *New York Times,* May 3, 2018.

10. Paula Span, "A Debate over 'Rational Suicide,'" *New York Times,*
August 31, 2018. See also Robert E. McCue and Meera Balasubrama-
niam, eds., *Rational Suicide in the Elderly: Clinical, Ethical and Sociocul-
tural Aspects* (New York: Springer, 2017).

11. Rutger Bregman, "Nixon's Basic Income Plan," *Jacobin,* May 2016,
https://www.jacobinmag.com/2016/05/richard-nixon-ubi-basic
-income-welfare/.

12. Annie Nova, "More Americans Now Support a Universal Basic
Income," *CNBC,* February 26, 2018, https://www.cnbc.com/2018/02
/26/roughly-half-of-americans-now-support-universal-basic-income
.html.

13. Charlie Wood, "Guaranteed Paycheck: Does a 'Basic Income'
Encourage Laziness?," *Christian Science Monitor,* March 1, 2017,
https://www.csmonitor.com/World/2017/0301/Guaranteed-paycheck
-Does-a-basic-income-encourage-laziness.

14. Rebecca Tan, "From France to Denmark, Bans on Full-Face Muslim
Veils Are Spreading across Europe," *Washington Post,* August 16,
2018.

15. Martin Selsoe Sorensen and Megan Specia, "Denmark's Ban on
Muslim Face Veil Is Met with Protest," *New York Times,* August 1,
2018.

16. Martin Selsoe Sorensen, "Denmark Talks (Reluctantly) about a Ban
on Circumcising Boys," *New York Times,* June 2, 2018.

17. Christina Caron, "Bill Banning Circumcision in Iceland Alarms
Religious Groups," *New York Times,* February 28, 2018.

18. Ruth Graham, "For Pregnant Women, Two Sets of Rights in One Body," *Boston Globe,* February 16, 2014.

19. Rohit Bhattacharya, "15 Countries around the World That Have Legalized Prostitution," ScoopWhoop, June 26, 2015, https://www.scoopwhoop.com/inothernews/countries-with-legal-prostitution/; Amnesty International, "Amnesty International Policy on State Obligations to Respect, Protect and Fulfil [sic] the Human Rights of Sex Workers," POL 30/4062/2016, May 26, 2016, https://www.amnesty.org/download/Documents/POL3040622016ENGLISH.PDF.

20. "The Truth about Decriminalizing Prostitution," *Week,* June 6, 2018, http://www.theweek.co.uk/fact-check/94086/the-truth-about-decriminalising-prostitution.

21. Emily Wit, "After the Closure of Backpage, Increasingly Vulnerable Sex Workers Are Demanding Their Rights," *New Yorker,* June 8, 2018.

22. Gaia Pianigiani and Sewell Chan, "Can the Homeless and Hungry Steal Food? Maybe, an Italian Court Says," *New York Times,* May 4, 2016.

23. Ellen Barry, "India's Top Court Bars Campaigns Based on Identity Politics," *New York Times,* January 2, 2017.

24. Jacey Fortin, "'Access to Literacy' Is Not a Constitutional Right, Judge in Detroit Rules," *New York Times,* July 4, 2018.

25. David Z. Morris, "New French Law Bars Work Email after Hours," *Fortune,* January 1, 2017, http://fortune.com/2017/01/01/french-right-to-disconnect-law/.

26. Dan Bilefsky and Christina Anderson, "A Paid Hour a Week for Sex? Swedish Town Considers It," *New York Times,* February 23, 2017.

27. Christina Anderson, "Muslim Job Applicant Who Refused Handshake Wins Discrimination Case in Sweden," *New York Times,* August 16, 2018.

28. Kirsten Rabe Smolensky, "Rights of the Dead," *Hofstra Law Review* 37, no. 763 (2009): 763–803. See also Pico Iyer, "The Humanity We Can't Relinquish," *New York Times,* August 11, 2018.

29. Steven Johnson, "Greetings, E.T. (Please Don't Murder Us)," *New York Times Magazine,* June 28, 2017.

30. David Rieff, "The End of Human Rights?," *Foreign Policy,* April 9, 2018.

31. Samuel Moyn, "Human Rights Are Not Enough," *Nation,* March 16, 2018, https://www.thenation.com/article/human-rights-are-not-enough/.

32. Alex May, "Basic Income: A Human Rights Approach," openDemocracy, November 7, 2017, https://neweconomics.opendemocracy.net /basic-income-human-rights-approach/.

33. Eric A. Posner, "Against Human Rights," *Harper's,* October 2014.

34. Adam Gopnik, "What Can We Learn from Utopians of the Past?," *New Yorker,* July 23, 2018.

35. Wendy Warren, *New England Bound: Slavery and Colonization in Early America* (New York: Liveright, 2016), 8.

36. C. K. Douzinas, *The End of Human Rights: Critical Legal Theory at the Turn of the Century* (Oxford: Hart Publishing, 2000), 152.

37. Patricia Williams, *The Alchemy of Race and Rights* (Cambridge, MA: Harvard University Press, 1992), 165.

# Acknowledgments

We would like to thank the Carr Center for Human Rights Policy, Harvard Kennedy School, where we were able to work on this book together, Bill as a senior fellow and Sushma as the executive director. We had terrific colleagues among its faculty, fellows, and students, as well as many others across the university and elsewhere, who provided expert input and feedback, read early drafts of chapters, and gave us moral and intellectual support. We have also drawn upon our knowledge and networks from prior positions, including at Amnesty International, the Unitarian Universalist Service Committee, the Robert F. Kennedy Center for Justice and Human Rights, the Ford Foundation, and the Open Society Foundation, as well as grassroots partners around the world. We are grateful to be part of such a vibrant and active global human rights community.

In particular, we thank Mathias Risse and Kathryn Sikkink on the Kennedy School faculty; Carr Center Senior Fellows Eric Blumenson, Steven Livingston, and Hon. Alberto Mora, who provided suggestions and feedback; members of the Harvard Human Rights Colloquium; and the Carr Center study group we convened over two years to workshop the draft chapters.

Many individuals shared their expertise and insights with us and for that we are much indebted. They include Carol Adams, Rebecca Angle, Luís Roberto Barroso, Jacqueline Bhabha, Catia Confortini, Manisha Dhakal, Justus Eisfeld, Ron Engel, Stephanie Farrior, David Favre, Bill Frelick,

Adrienne Frick, Bruce Friedrich, Charlene Galarneau, Chris Green, David Gunkel, Sarah Gunther, Michael Heflin, Kathy Hessler, Deborah Hughes Hallett, Patricia Illingworth, Doug Johnson, Sara Katsanis, Zachary Kaufman, Kathy Kaufmann, Kyle Knight, Vivek Krishnamurthy, Matthew Liebman, Jeantine Lunshof, Tim McCarthy, Amber Moulton, Barbara Newell, Serena Parekh, Phuong Pham, Sarah Pickering, Marc Rotenberg, Renato Sabbadini, John Shattuck, Salil Shetty, Leonardo Soares da Cunha de Castilho, Kim Stallwood, Joyce Tischler, Patrick Vinck, Steven Wise, and Mark Wolf.

We are grateful to have had the opportunity to work with stellar research assistants over the past three years, including Matt Keating, Tom O'Bryan, Jillian Rafferty, and Amanda Watson. Amanda played a crucial role in cross-checking citations and getting the manuscript ready for submission. Carr Center staff members Jana Brown, Gillian Daniels, Karen McCabe, and Nimesha Perera helped organize and support our study groups over the course of the past two years. Thoko Moyo and her communications team at the Kennedy School and Valerie Weis of Library and Research Services helped with research and communications resources.

Our editors at the Press, Thomas LeBien and later James Brandt, made significant suggestions to improve the book. We are particularly grateful to Thomas for understanding the vision of the book from its very inception. Three anonymous reviewers provided thoughtful and substantive comments to strengthen our work and we incorporated many of their suggestions. Needless to say, despite all this support and assistance, our thesis is a controversial one and the book is surely far from perfect. For both of those realities, we take full responsibility.

For their patience and good humor during the research, writing, and editing process, Sushma thanks her husband, Troy, and children, Laila and Alaan, and Bill thanks his wife, Beth. Finally, Sushma is grateful to her sisters and both Sushma and Bill are grateful to their parents for shaping their formative years and commitment to lifelong learning.

# Index